THE HAUNTING OF THE IMMORTAL KILLER

THE FIRES OF QAF: BOOK THREE

KYRO DEAN & LAYA V SMITH

EIGHT MOONS PUBLISHING

This book is dedicated to Janelle Youngstrom.

Publicist, friend, superhero.

We could never do it without you.

The Royal House of Shihala

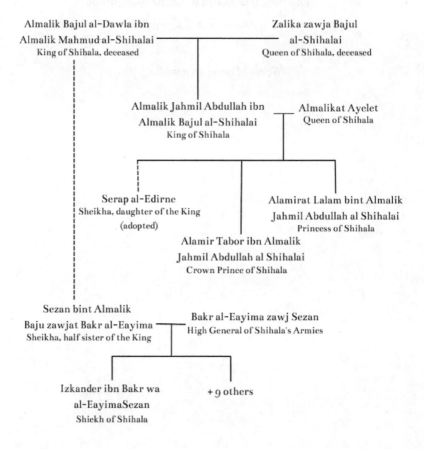

Almalik Bajul al-Dawla ibn
Almalik Mahmud al-Shihalai
King of Shihala, deceased

Zalika zawja Bajul
al-Shihalai
Queen of Shihala, deceased

Almalik Jahmil Abdullah ibn
Almalik Bajul al-Shihalai
King of Shihala

Almalikat Ayelet
Queen of Shihala

Serap al-Edirne
Sheikha, daughter of the King
(adopted)

Alamirat Lalam bint Almalik
Jahmil Abdullah al Shihalai
Princess of Shihala

Alamir Tabor ibn Almalik
Jahmil Abdullah al Shihalai
Crown Prince of Shihala

Sezan bint Almalik
Baju zawjat Bakr al-Eayima
Sheikha, half sister of the King

Bakr al-Eayima zawj Sezan
High General of Shihala's Armies

Izkander ibn Bakr wa
al-EayimaSezan
Shiekh of Shihala

+9 others

CHAPTER ONE

Serap

Serap waited for a full degree before darting out into the kaleidoscope of lights strewn along the tree-lined streets of Karzusan. The blue-white glow of Qaf's fifth moon peeked over the horizon, completing the set. All the djinn would be out that night, celebrating the Festival of the Eight Moons.

All the djinn—and her.

Excitement clung to the air, the revelry in full swing by the time Serap had been able to ditch her escort and escape. Her 'abi was always worried about nothing. She was always alone in the palace. What difference did a few walls make? She'd be fine on her own.

Fire jugglers and coal walkers performed their tricks on every corner, lights dazzling and sparkling under the dusky light of the moons. She leaned back to avoid the flames, passing a bright cluster of vivid purples that rivaled the leaves of the *'arjwani* trees. Chupkin, her white wisp of rogue magic and silent companion, whipped around her coin-laced headband. She giggled as his cloudy puff zipped through her cotton scarf embroidered with flowers and into her sleeve. Safe inside her shirt, he sunk into her belly button, misty without making her skin wet.

Serap laughed. "It's just a bit of fire play, you scaredy-wisp. And frankly, they're cheating, considering every djinn carries their own fire and can't be burned by it."

Chupkin squished into a tight ball of light on her palm. She sighed in agreement. Her hands and feet itched to join them, to show off her juggling and acrobatics from her younger days on the streets of Edirne, but she was a human and *could* get burned.

She also was supposed to meet Paco, her most recent suitor, by the water fountain in two degrees.

She pushed her lips side to side, then glanced down at Chupkin and shrugged. "I might as well. What's an accidental fiery death when my life is so short, anyway?"

His dim light flickered twice.

"It is, too," she bickered with him. "I'll live a mere sixty years if I'm lucky, and all the djinn here could go to two hundred or more. And what about you? You're just light and mist. You could live forever for all I know."

He reached a wispy tendril in the direction of Eashiq Font, a famous fountain entwined with two coiled drakonte who playfully spat water at each other. Lovers—supposedly—caught up in each other and no one else.

Serap glanced in their direction. Her stomach tightened, and she shook her head. "Paco can wait, Chupkin. If he really likes me, he won't mind. Ayelet could disappear for weeks and 'Abi Jahmil would loyally await her return without question."

Of course, Ayelet would also never do such a thing—and not just because the kingdom would be in a stir if either of her royal parents disappeared. Her adopted mother and father simply loved each other far too much.

Serap waited for an in, watching the spinning orbs of smokeless flames. The jugglers caught and threw each ball of fire with a small stick so they didn't have to touch each other's fire—a strangely intimate act—or so she had heard. All she'd get from touching one of the balls was a third-degree burn.

The flames turned in a steady and reliable circle. Serap bobbed her head in time, counted to three, and sprinted forward. The orb descended. She did a one-handed back spring, smiling wide, and landed on one hopping foot next to the startled juggler. With a fluid movement, she grabbed the stick, flicking it up and over as she took command of the act. There was no applause, of course, though a few spectators shot her a glance. The juggler scowled at first, but at least he appreciated talent when he saw it. After a few minutes of her tossing and twisting, her heart full of fun, he nodded with a grin and held out his hands. She tossed the flames back to him, then bowed.

Chupkin popped his misty self out of her sleeve and flashed.

"Thank you, dear Chupkin." She smiled and nodded.

At least someone had enjoyed the show.

Sweat upon her brow and her heart pumping from the exhilaration, Serap hurried down the tent-lined street and past a group of djinn who blew and shaped their fire into a gem-encrusted turtle, each jewel burning with a different color. She looked at her hand, then rubbed it absent-mindedly on her pants. Some of her excitement cooled, slipping away in the breeze. There was a reason there had been no applause. The tricks she learned on Ard were unimpressive in a land teeming with magic, as was she.

She popped her lips together a few times, following the scent of roasted pista-chios. Nearly everyone walking by already glowed with renewed magic despite the brightness of the sky with all of Qaf's moons out—an event that only happened every one-hundred-thirty years. The swirling skies amplified the power of the Five Winds and Eight Moons. It would be the only time she ever got to see it.

Serap stopped next to the sparkling fountain at the arranged meeting spot and tried to feel the magic of the place on the night it was strongest. The united power of the moons and their pull combined with the Great Bahamut's currents rejuvenated all living things in Qaf—well, all the natural beings who belonged there. The magic kept them from aging. Made them stronger. Prettier, though Jahmil had insisted that one wasn't true. Chupkin, too, glowed more robustly than he ever had before.

Even Ayelet's strange magic kept her young in Qaf. She closed her eyes and clenched her muscles tight, trying desperately one more time to feel the call of Shihala, of Qaf, of the place she was supposed to call home.

She felt nothing.

Opening one eye, then the other, she slumped. The water sparkled in rainbow-lit spouts, forming deep rivulets around the base of the drakonte statues that beckoned her to join. Serap dipped her hand into the arched stream of water and pretended she could feel the power just the same.

A familiar woodpecker sound of laughter drifted nearby, and Serap sidestepped her way closer, wanting to surprise Paco. She peered around a tent with burnt orange and sienna stripes and smiled. He strolled with his friend, curly blonde hair tight against his scalp and periwinkle face alight with mirth. His bright plum-colored eyes creased at the corners from too much smiling. It was what she liked about him the most.

"I can't believe you're going through with it." Devan walked in long, easy strides to the right of Paco. He was one of the higher-ranking sons in the court and usually wore a bitter grin.

Paco straightened his cuff. "Then you're as near-sighted as everyone says."

"She's *human*, though."

Serap stiffened, pulling further behind the tent as they drew nearer. She knew courtiers gossiped about her behind her back, but it always stung when she caught them. She held her breath, waiting for Paco's response.

"If King Jahmil heard you say that, he'd send you and your family to an outpost in Zabriya."

Not the answer she had hoped for....

"And," Paco continued, "Sheikha Serap is a delightful companion. Kind, simple, and readily suggestible. If not a bit impulsive. That's a far cry better than most of the vapid ladies in court."

Better... in a practical way. Though impulsive was rude. She simply lived in the moment. All the time. Either way, his words were definitely *not* romantic and left her feeling like she hadn't quite stuck a landing on an aerial cartwheel.

Devan chuckled, his brows a 'V' on his forehead. "The king's spies aren't here, if you're worried about being caught. And it's only going to get worse, trying to keep your tongue all the time. How are you going to keep it a secret you despise your wife for your entire marriage? Plus, she's always covered in metal jewelry. How would you even touch her? And you know how the king feels about concubines since he married that mon—" Devan stopped himself, shooting a wide-eyed and worried glance around him.

Serap squeezed her fist. She had a mind to go stand up for herself. Though she couldn't help but smirk despite her loneliness. Her step-mother's ability to end a djinn's life with the simple curl still struck fear into those who weren't completely stupid.

Devan cleared his throat. "You know what I mean."

Paco waved a hand airily at his friend. "I never said I despised her. She's pleasant enough to be around and soft, which is something to be said for a courtesan. Who wants a woman with eyes like diamonds if they feel as sharp as one in bed?" He smirked. "I am certain she'll take off the necklaces for me. She just needs a little... convincing."

Serap blushed, certain her already pink cheeks looked downright Ghaluman.

"And it's not a life sentence." Paco waved his hand to the side. "As you said, she's human. I'm looking at fifty years, tops, and probably only thirty until she's old enough to put away."

"Unless the queen can keep her young with magic."

"If there was evidence Queen Ayelet's wisps could do that, they'd be bottling it up and shipping it out to all of Qaf. Her Highness's magic only imbues herself in that way. Nobody else. Besides, being a doting husband for even seventy years is easily worth it to me for a lifetime appointment to King Jahmil's inner circle."

Paco's logic-laced coldness soaked into Serap's bones with a painful shiver.

"If you say so." Devan shrugged. "Felicitations, chump."

"I haven't asked her to marry me yet. That's at the end of this week. I have a full procession planned. A parade. Elephants from Ard—they're supposed to be terribly magnificent. I want everything to be perfect when I ask the princess to marry me. I just need to ease her into the idea first and seal the deal with the king and queen." Paco's smile widened. "You'll be calling me Sheikh Chump soon enough."

Serap stood motionless, her mouth wide enough to catch flies. She knew Paco was a more serious suitor, but marriage already? And without a hint of love or romance. She slumped into the shadows of a tent as the two turned towards the fountain. Above, more sky flowers burst with a dozen colors of crackling djinn fire. Chupkin brushed her cheek with a tendril. The moons moved overhead. And all Serap could do was stare at nothing as she stomped back towards the palace, her dreams of romance shattered and her humanity under assault—again.

She would definitely be ditching her date with Paco tonight, and all future dates. But even as she huffed and muttered, she found her rage to be a slippery fish—one moment thrashing at Paco, the next at herself, and the next at Shihala. But it wouldn't stick.

Her shoulders slouched in a sigh. "Paco's reasons are sound, Chupkin, even if they do cut me so and are far from a sonnet."

The wisp fluttered before her, a gentle pulse of light.

"I mean, what man would want a wife who will grow wrinkly and old while they are still in their prime without a personal benefit attached? I'm a guaranteed burden."

His light grew stronger, and he jutted side to side in agitation.

"I'm not being unreasonable." She crossed her arms as she marched faster to nowhere in particular. "And it's not like I've given up on love. Not entirely. There's a small chance a man could want my position and still love me, despite the fact that I will go the way of all the earth very, very soon."

Chupkin squished into a tight ball.

"Rude. You little—" She chomped her teeth at him playfully, though syrupy loneliness still coated her heart, thick with Paco's words. "Are my expectations too high? My parents weren't even looking when true love found them. And Bakr Amca and Zan Hala burn through theirs daily and still have enough left for eternity. Without my position, without something to offer, I wouldn't have any hope of finding someone. At least it gives men the incentive to get to know me. That's the best I can hope for in the Court of Shihala, where the politics of marriage run rampant. Maybe Paco is the best offer I'll get?"

Chupkin swished his tail in two sharp whips.

"The best, and the best I'll ever get are very different things." She sniffed. "But I *will* speak to 'Abi Jahmil about that sniveling weasel, Devan." Her top lip curled just thinking of his smug grin. "We'll see if he's so haughty in the snowy mountains of Zabriya."

A voice hacked at her from between the flaps of a nearby tent. Serap lifted her eyes up to the sign. *Pasha's Fortunes and Witching.*

"Or better yet...." She grinned.

Serap slid a hand through the dirty canvas and slipped inside. A bone-carved chandelier, complete with little green pools of fire on each nub, lit the tent in an eerie light. Chupkin curled up at the base of her neck in a cool, misty puddle. He absolutely hated this place. He already shook with fear against her skin, which was how she'd found him five years ago. Huddled and quaking under a brass urn full of tinctures in this very tent.

Nothing had changed about the place since then. Heavy curtains striped in purples, blacks, and greens hung from wooden beams overhead, herding whoever came into the tent in a specific path. Fleshless skulls of ghouls and effrits sat atop dusty old chests, and peculiar feathers in bright orange and sapphire blue hung from cords along the ceiling. Thick genealogy books of lost kings and mythological kingdoms, of magic ancestry lines and strange powers stacked high in the back, always open to some page or another. A strange set of eyeballs attached to nothing glowed, flickering between a smoky gray and poison green.

Serap poked one as she passed, unable to resist seeing what would happen. The detached pupil spun around, twitching every which way, searching for the perpetrator and unable to do a thing about it.

On the ceiling, painted in deep blues and creamy yellows, were the constellations of both Qaf and Ard. Cassiopeia, Lyra, and the beautiful Ursa Major, oversized and center. Then others around the edges like Samadon, and Palaneous. The Celestials, or the eternal beings from which witches were supposed to draw their powers.

Serap rounded the final turn in the tapestry maze and grinned at the Pasha, the witch.

Her skin shone a shade of light green, and her brown hair stuck out in lightning bolts around her narrow face, each tip zinged with a hint of purple, and her tiny nose protruded like a rosebud. Her eyes matched the hue of her pink-tipped nose, only they caught the light and had a hint of yellow sweeping about in the background. The witch dressed in full harem pants cinched at the ankles, a short, white skirt draped over those, and a scarf tied atop that. Her top hung loose, covered in even more scarves, with none of the patterns matching. It was chaotic and spectacular and just what Serap had always pictured a witch would wear.

Pasha spoke in a raspy, alluring voice. "And who has braved the realms to come and talk to The Eternal Witch of Fi—Oh, it's you." Her voice cleared to the ting of a bell.

"You don't have to sound so disappointed," Serap teased.

Pasha scoffed, her gap-toothed grin taking up her face. "Disappointed? Never. Just bored. Shihalans only enter my tent when desperate or drunk. The second of which is forbidden by Allah, of course." She winked and took a sip from a nearby goblet, pinky out and a smirk on her lips.

Serap shrugged. "Festivals make djinn a bit of both, Allah and 'Abi Jahmil's laws notwithstanding. Give it an hour."

"I always do." Pasha practically floated forward, her striped pants draped so wide and full, they hid her slippers. Another one of the witch's tricks that Serap couldn't get enough of. Such simple things could delude people's minds. It reminded her of the sleight-of-hand shows she'd performed as a child back on Earth, or Ard as the djinn called it.

The thought sunk like a ship in her stomach. What if the only way she could find someone to love her was by going to Ard? Not that she needed a man—but watching 'Abi Jahmil and Ayelet made her yearn for the love they had. A person she could be herself around and who loved her unconditionally. And for children, for a legacy to outlive her, since death planned to snuff out her life far before she was ready.

"Something's bothering you," Pasha said, shaking a lime green finger in her direction.

"I was hoping you'd help me put warts on a courtier's face."

Pasha's grin sharpened as she grabbed up vials of swirling liquid and sparkling powders and started pouring them into a bowl. "Yes, please."

The witch's fingers moved with a deft dexterity that Serap could only envy.

She tried to be patient. To quell the slippery fish in her belly, but she could take it no longer. "How old are you?" She asked abruptly.

"One-hundred-twenty-five." Pasha shrugged. "Why?"

Serap groaned. "You look like you're thirty. Like a human thirty."

"I'm not exactly sure what that looks like, but thank you?"

"It was a compliment," Serap assured her. "Did you know I'll never live to be as old as you? People in Ard who die at fifty are considered ancient."

"Dreadful," Pasha gasped, her pink morganite eyes flashing with even darker hints of yellow.—the color of anadulterated disdain.

Serap groaned.

"I'm so sorry, sweetie. I knew humans were frail little things, but I didn't realize you were *that* frail."

Serap pouted and sat next to one of the skulls. The heavily-incensed air made her eyes sting with sandalwood and cinnamon and made her nose wish it had a cold.

"That's why no one bothers to get to know me here. They think, '*Why? She'll be dead soon, anyway.*' And there's not anything I can do about it."

"That doesn't sound like you at all," Pasha tutted. "If you had thought that way, we never would have become friends. But you were always trying to be so *alrataq* helpful, insisting you could accomplish anything a djinn could. I had to give in. Otherwise, you would have ended up breaking all my potions with your soft hands. I was certain you were one disaster away from screwing up one of my contracts with the Celestials. Ursa Major is not a patient being, I'll tell you that. You do *not* want to go against them. But now I'm glad I did take you in. You proved yourself well enough. You're certainly scrappy and a hard worker."

Serap looked at her smooth, princess fingers. She hadn't always been soft, but the calluses she had gained from working to the bone as a child had long since faded.

What a strange thing time was.

At least now she understood why no one in Shihala would teach her anything. The return on investment would be dismal. Even Pasha had only bothered to teach her how to be helpful, reading simple recipes and spells from the stars with no ability to complete any of them without magic.

She darted her eyes back up to Pasha. "And what am I supposed to do about dying young? Besides moving to Ard to find someone with a similar expiration date? I don't want to do that. I've been in Qaf for ten years. I'll slip up and mention the Fifth Moon or a drakonte to an Ardish man, and he'll think I'm crazy and have his family run me out of town with torches and dogs."

"Then why don't you find a way to live longer?"

Serap scoffed. "Everyone's already tried that."

"Not everyone." Pasha shrugged. "Where there's a will and a wisp—"

"There's always a way," Serap finished the saying with a sigh.

She hadn't considered finding a way to extend her life... but the idea was sounding better and better with every degree. If no one else would let her help them, maybe it was time she started helping herself.

"Do you think there *is* a way to make me live longer that 'Abi and Ayelet haven't' tried yet? One that they may have missed?"

Pasha stopped fiddling with the tray of glass jars and added in one last green hair. "I suppose that depends on just how fragile you are. There are many paths to a heart's desire, but not many meant for soft hands."

Serap pulled her shoulders straighter, not sure she liked the insinuation. "I've not always been soft, you know. I know how to work hard and be resourceful, you said that yourself. I was a street urchin once. Not always a princess."

"But you *are* human." Pasha's lips twisted to the side.

"We've been around just as long as the djinn. And with shorter lives and no magic, too. I think that shows we're actually more handy at the whole living thing."

Pasha grinned. "You mean the whole reproducing thing."

Serap blushed, but she kept her chin up. "Tell me how to live longer. If I can just prove to these djinn that I'll be around, they'll start seeing me as equal and not just a path to a title."

Pasha hemmed and hawed, swirling a glass spoon around in the mixture she had made for Serap. Little bubbles formed on top, popping with a putrid smell.

"If you're certain it won't get you killed...."

She raised a sharp, purple-tipped brow, and Serap nodded eagerly.

"Fine." Pasha smirched a few times, head bobbing back and forth. "Though I really ought not to be sharing this with you. The answer lies with a being who has been amassing power and prowess for centuries. Who challenges even the walls of Ashkult with his strength, and who has felled nations with his secrets."

"I am not afraid." Serap leaned in, her stomach twisting in knots.

"Very well." Pasha released a heavy sigh, eager keenness growing in her pink yes. "The Immortal Traitor Faris Khayin D'Jaush did it."

"And turned into a monster." Serap pressed her lips together and hefted one of the gnarly skulls with jagged teeth. She opened and closed its jaw to mimic talking. "I don't want to be a hideous creature everyone wishes were dead. It would defeat the purpose."

Pasha chuckled. "I bet he would know of something, though. Something to help you live a decent amount longer before kicking the bucket and without the whole nasty beast bit."

"And why would the Immortal Traitor tell me anything?"

"Doesn't your dear 'abi still have a question left? One the traitor must answer?"

"Yes..." Serap answered, her stomach growing queasy with each of Pasha's words. "But if I use his last question, 'Abi has to fulfill his promise to kill the traitor, which is kind of a problem with the whole him-being-immortal thing. If I asked the question, 'Abi wouldn't be able to kill him, and then he'd break his oath and die because *no one* knows how to kill Khayin."

"That's not entirely true," Pasha said, cloudiness swirling behind her light pink eyes.

Serap set down the skull with a soft *clunk*, wary of the muddled colors in Pasha's eyes. She called herself a witch for a reason. "What do you mean?"

"Good royal folk don't fraternize with my type. Not unless they want a potion for warts, that is." She popped a cork onto the glass jar and handed it to Serap with a wink. "That's why the gullible idiots are always falling victim to their circumstances, convinced there's no point in thinking about the impossible when there's really no such thing."

Serap raised a brow.

"*I* know, child. *I* know of someone on Ard who can kill the immortal. I didn't master Secrets Sorcery and earn the title of the Witch of Eternal Finding for naught. But he's a beast of a man. I don't know if you will survive it."

Serap caught the pucker trying to form on her lips and pressed it smooth. Pouting was exactly the thing someone who couldn't handle a quest for immortality would do. Instead, she took a deep breath and met Pasha's eyes.

"That is for me to decide, not you."

"Your parents wouldn't like it." Pasha tutted. "And the last thing I need is another monarchy hunting me down."

"Another monarchy?" Serap pulled her chin back and cast the witch a nervous eye.

"Oh nothing, dear. You know how things can be for the otherwise gifted. Some royal noble is always blaming us for a well drying up or a country going to war or important people disappearing. For unexpected warts that appear on a young courtier's face. All nonsense, of course." Her lips twisted over a small grin.

"You're not wrong…" Serap rubbed her tongue against the top of her mouth. "But I am royalty. Your highest-ranking sheikha, in fact. So if I command you to help me in honor of the Crown, you're just helping me reach my goals. That should be anything but treason."

Pasha tilted her head to the side so the zings of her hair quivered at the end. She shrugged. "Good enough for me."

She slapped the wooden table between them, leaning in so the shadows in the room grew deeper. Even the lights in the room seemed to grow darker, the disembodied pupils shining an eerie red in the light. Chupkin coiled tight in a shivering mess against Serap's navel.

Her voice dropped to an ominous, harsh whisper. "I know of a cruel brute who hides in the shadows and talks to strange spirits. Who could put you on your deathbed with a single look and curdle the milk in your stomach with his sneer."

She curled her fingers in front of Serap's face as if to mime said curdling.

"Both men and djinn fear him, and rumors say he knows the way of the djinni-trapping magic and is a merciless master. Many moons ago and in a time without time, he walked into the Bahamut and came out with a gift: the power to slay immortals. But that is not all he slays, and he hates all things magic and djinn."

Pasha's voice popped back up to normal with a shrug, the room brightening once more.

"All you have to do is find him and flash your innocent human eyes. With a wisp—" She smirked and nodded toward where Chupkin hid. "—that should be simple enough."

Serap wrung her hands together. Pasha's words made her sweat in her mohair-lined pants. This man did not sound pleasant to be around, much less like someone who would grant favors to young women seeking longevity.

But he did sound like the sort of man who might happily kill an immortal and disgusting traitor of Shihala.

Pasha was right. Serap did believe there was a solution to every problem, and she was going to find it.

She curled her soft hand into a tight fist and smacked it on the table. "Tell me how to find the Immortal Killer."

CHAPTER TWO

JAVIER

Javier never remained at home on the night of a new moon.

Most of the cultures he'd encountered in his wide travels believed in some way that the full moon inspired evil to new heights, but that was counterintuitive. The moon was a mirror of the sun, the ultimate enemy of darkness. So it was that when the job of illuminating the earth fell to the insufficient stars, darkness-loving monsters came out to play.

Javier was always among them.

He was a colossal man—like three ordinary men in one—with the chest and shoulders of a prize bull. If he was seen at all, even from a distance, he was always remembered.

Dressed in black, he kept to the shadows and his soft boots that made no din as they padded across cobblestone. He wore a scarf to conceal his face—hand-stitched by his sister, who had insisted on embroidering blue roses onto it—though he'd specifically requested her not to. She always thought she was doing him a favor.

Secured to the back of his left wrist was a *katar*: a punch dagger he'd picked up on the farthest eastern edge of the Safavid Empire many long years ago. He'd rigged up a rope mechanism inside his glove so if he clenched a fist, the dagger would tighten securely against the back of his hand. Otherwise, it hung loose enough to allow his wrist a full range of motion. Inside the folds of his jacket were four more daggers made of the finest Genoese steel, and in his boot a single-shot wheel-lock pistol.

Javier pressed his back against the stone outer wall of the abbey and took a moment to rummage through his pack: a coil of rope, a skeleton key, a lock pick, oil of vitriol, healing potions, smoke bombs, Vesparian fire-starters, and a hatchet.

He cursed the clutter, then smiled when his fingers found half a loaf of *barra de pan* stuffed with *jamon*, Manchego cheese, roasted *piquillo* peppers, and fresh olives he'd picked from his tree only that morning. Infiltrating the strongholds of the horrifying and indestructible was hungry work. Too many times he'd gone out with nothing but weapons and malice, only to find himself trapped somewhere for hours and forced to listen to his stomach growl.

Going on a job without bringing a picnic was as ridiculous as leaving behind his magic armor, which cushioned him from all manner of lethal blows and substances.

Javier took a bite and chewed quietly. The sandwich needed garlic and onion, but the creature he was hunting was known to have a keen sense of smell. All he needed was to be given away by a whiff of sulfur. Again.

The Abbey of Xeres lay before him. The great church at the center had once been a Moorish castle before the Reconquista. The ruins of a forgotten city peppered the surrounding fields, blunted stones twisting out from the church like coils of smoke on an aspergillum.

Guessing by the size of the fields, a few hundred monks called these grounds home, under the care of *Abad Urbano San Pedro*. The abbot had a reputation across Christendom as a powerful exorcist—a man destined for sainthood—who regularly suffered demon possession himself. They said the Devil knew how strong he was and was desperate to tempt him from the righteous path.

It was a good story, Javier had to admit. Creative and elaborate enough that pilgrims traveled from the farthest reaches of Christendom to stand in this abbey. They wept for the privilege to hear Abad Urbano preach and fell over themselves to pay him tithing. But all the fascinating talk of demons did a far more important job for the abbot. It covered up his eccentricities, offering a ready explanation to anyone who happened to notice he never seemed quite human.

Nothing about Abad Urbano was human.

Javier wrinkled his nose at the church. The creature was in there somewhere. Perhaps lying on a bed of silk and sleeping off a gluttonous meal of naïve oblates and powerless orphans.

Abad Urbano's commission had come to Javier from Señora Suma Sacerdotisa Aldonza la Indomable, High Priestess of the Coven of Ninety-Nine.

Whatever that meant.

Javier didn't care for titles, including his own, Don DeMario. He'd taken the commission because Señora Aldonza had made a good case, confirmed by reliable sources, and she paid an acceptable honorarium. And because, like himself, Aldonza was a professional monster hunter. He had to make allowances for a certain degree of professional courtesy.

Standard everyday, risen-from-the dead-ghouls—while powerful, hideous, and utterly relentless—were not immortal in the strictest sense of the term. Sure, they'd keep moving if you cut their heads off, but if you threw them into a pot of molten lead they were done for. Javier didn't usually lower himself to deal with them for this very reason.

But there were exceptions. The *al'Abi wal'umu alghul*—father and mother ghouls—who had the unique power to create more of their own kind by raising the dead or infecting the living. These creatures were not only immortal, but also intelligent, pretty enough to pass as human, and often quite difficult to detect. Some of them ruled kingdoms of ruins or hid at the centers of festering swamps. Others quietly joined society and feasted on the lowest echelon.

Señora Aldonza said her people had only found Urbano because the ghoul had remained in one place for so long. Seven years now, Abad Urbano San Pedro—better known on the underground as Alab Alghul Silrok—had been farming the local population. Not only to feed itself but also its growing family who dwelled in the catacombs that ran under the abbey.

Once the abbot was dead, Señora Aldonza and her soldiers would come to clear the place out. Javier had one job, and he was the only man in two worlds who could do it.

He scanned the map Señora Aldonza had provided of the abbey, memorizing the twists of halls that led to a door on the top floor where rested the unholy.

It did not strike Javier as odd that such a creature was posturing as a priest. The Church of Rome was corrupted and the Kingdom of Spain was even worse. Both had proven time and again that no atrocity was beyond them. Why wouldn't an opportunistic ghoul search for a way to benefit from the chaos and cruelty that held Javier's homeland in an iron grip?

He finished his sandwich, wiped the crumbs on his pants, and refocused himself on the task ahead.

Javier didn't scale walls or pull silly stunts if he didn't have to, as such things always drew more attention than they averted. Instead, he waited outside a side door in the shadow of a poplar until the small, keyhole-shaped partition was thrown open and an old monk with a lumpy torso came out to dump a large chamber pot. As he waddled towards a nearby stream, Javier slipped through the door unnoticed and closed it behind him. The latch fell into place exactly as it might have had a gust taken hold.

The monk pounding on the door trying to get back in would keep the other brothers distracted, at least for a little while.

Javier walked through the kitchen, his eyes scanning a cut of pork laid out on a butcher's block smeared with pink slime that looked warm and smelled salty. He wrinkled his nose at the *haram* meat before noticing a small jar of saffron on the shelf above it with some fifty strings still inside.

Javier didn't hesitate to take it. It was expensive, he was almost out, and he was fairly certain the abbot wasn't going to be needing it.

Pausing at each corner to listen for the sound of scratching quills, soft footfalls, or gentle prayers, Javier made his way to the top floor without incident.

He checked his map once again to see if he was in the right place, then grasped the handle. His rough hand eclipsed the iron.

Pressing an ear against the door, he waited.

Silence.

Gently, he slipped inside. Darkness greeted him, cut only by the pale shimmer of stars through thin curtains and the lazy cackle of embers in the fireplace. A canopy bed stood beside it, velvet bed curtains drawn.

Smells assaulted his senses as the darkness stole away his vision. Blood, flesh, and hair—the components of death, which were the life source for Alab Alghul Silrok.

All ghouls eat bones and only bones. Of the dead. Of the living. They don't mind either way. They crunch them with their razor teeth, slurp the marrow with their long tongues, and crush them with their piercing claws. If pressed, a starving ghoul might eat animal bones, but human and djinn bones are the only kind that even momentarily satisfy the devastating, immortal hunger that categorizes their infernal condition.

They don't eat blood, flesh, or hair. When they rip flesh from the bones, they spit it out like seeds. When they accidentally drink too much blood, they vomit it out like cats. Javier knew that was what he was smelling.

Somewhere in the room was a pile of everything that remained of a human after the bones were violently extracted.

Javier padded across the red Persian carpet and twitched his fingers, trying to loosen them without clicking any heavy knuckles. Tightening his katar to his fist, Javier readied himself to strike the killing blow and pulled back the curtain.

The father of ghouls looked peaceful, with twitching eyelids and a small smile on his lips. Silrok's head was bald and, like all *al'Abi* and *umma* ghouls, had skin that grew over where its eyes were supposed to be. The creatures didn't need eyes to see; they had other senses of which the human imagination could hardly conceive. Hairless, gaunt, and corded in muscle, its grotesque and not-quite-human-looking body was mostly naked.

The smell of the creature was unmistakable, no matter how it tried to hide with perfume and rose oil. Silrok emanated the putrid stink of congealed blood. It was all coming from inside the bed, and there on the corner of the monster's lips, Javier saw three dots of red.

Holding his breath, Javier moved to puncture the throat when a soft gasp stole his attention.

He whirled around. A girl stood at the edge of the room, slack-jawed and wide-eyed, her chemise billowing around her thin legs in a soft wind. Scraggly brown hair hung in large brown eyes that shimmered in the gleam of firelight.

A survivor. Ghouls rarely left those.

The contents of his stomach curdled. What had those fire-lit eyes witnessed this night?

He lifted a finger to his lips. "Shh."

"Please." She wrapped skeletal arms over her sunken chest. "Please, help me."

He nodded slowly but pressed his finger to his lips again. The fact that ghouls had yet to be awakened by this racket was a small miracle given how keen their hearing was.

The girl's back was to an enormous fireplace with an iron grate in front of it. As Javier moved closer, he realized she was chained to it by her ankle. He wanted to set her free right then. He didn't want her to have to witness what he was about to do, though there was no doubt in his mind she had seen worse.

Hot, popping embers bit at her calves and thighs. She was already as far away from the fire as her chained ankle would allow. He could only imagine how hot the metal cuff must have felt on her skin.

Slowly, he began to turn back to the bed, lifting his blade.

An inhuman scream greeted him. With such speed it cannot be seen by the human eye, Silrok leapt from its bed and slammed into Javier's chest.

Together they tumbled into the fire. Javier found the presence of mind to snatch the girl in one hand to try to uphold her from the hot grate, instead taking it with his chest. If he hadn't been wearing his enchanted leather armor, the hot grate would have left black lines on his flesh. The girl screamed her ankle strained.

Javier kicked up and threw the monster across the room so it slammed into its own bed and smashed the frame.

The creature's thin veneer of humanity had peeled away, revealing the ghoulish interior: a mouth of razors and skin that shined like wet organ meat.

Javier grabbed the chain holding the girl's leg. Yanking hard with both hands, he pried open one of the thick metal coils. She was almost free.

Silrok hailed its approach with another ear-splitting shriek. It slashed its claws, catching Javier's chest armor over and over. Javier wasn't fast. Not compared to a quick human and certainly not compared to a ghoul. He weathered the assault waiting for an opening and when he saw it, punched his katar into the monster's neck.

Black blood oozed down Javier's arm and spackled the scarf that covered his mouth and nose. The smell was worse than raw sewage. Javier choked on a dry heave and ripped away the soiled fabric.

He kicked the beast off his knife, sending it flying backward with such force that the body left a dent in the wall where it struck. Then it slumped to the ground.

Javier scrambled and was about to jump on the monster to finish the job when he heard the girl crying and choking behind him. She clawed at the coil he'd started to open.

He ran back to her, snatched the chain from her hands, and yanked open the coil.

The girl screamed and pointed, scrambling back. Before he could react, claws sank into his back, so deep they yearned for his very bones. Javier was dropped to his knees, blinded by the pain.

His armor protected him so there would be no blood. But he could feel it. Like a hay rake falling on him from three stories up, he felt it.

The girl scurried to her feet, but as she turned to run away, the ghoul backhanded her. She fell over the slanted iron grate and into the fire.

Javier ripped a dagger from its holster and swung back, cutting the fingers from the hand so they were left clinging to his flesh. He lunged for the girl. She shrieked and thrashed, embers flashing into flames when they touched her dress and hair.

The monster screamed like a blade scraping across a whetstone and cradled its mutilated hand. Javier flipped over his dagger, catching it by the blade, and chucked it at the beast. It flew end over end and slammed into the ghoul's chest, burrowing down to the hilt.

The creature slipped to its knees, then fell hard on its face.

Javier rushed to the girl, submerged his arms in the fire, and yanked her free. She swatted wildly and slashed his eyes with her nails. Javier yanked off his wool cloak and smothered the fire.

Hisses and scrapes rushed up the hall towards them. Shrieks of fury and pain. Alba Silrok's children had experienced the death of their father, feeling it in the depths of their hive mind. They were coming for vengeance—their final purpose before they expired without their leader. It was the only time ghouls were ever motivated by something other than hunger.

Hundreds of them were rushing from the catacombs by the sound of it. Monks screamed as the monsters overcame them.

Javier looked back at the burned girl. Her legs and arms were red and dotted with blisters, her face unrecognizable. The fire had not finished her off, but the ensuing humoural imbalance would.

He rushed to the window, kicked open the wooden shutter, and looked down. Three stories and no trellis or friendly lumps of jutting stone to scurry down. Across a narrow alley from the building lay a haystack. Perhaps large enough, but perhaps too far off. He could make it on his own, but the shock of the landing would hurt the girl. In her delicate state, it might even kill her.

The door burst open and dozens of ghouls rushed inside—pulsing, vascular muscle and pale, papery skin. Black claws and wild, foaming mouths stuffed with needle-like teeth. Some crawled along the ceiling like bats, others pounced like lions.

Señora Aldonza and her troops would be here soon if they weren't already rushing the abbey walls. If it weren't for the dying girl in his arms, Javier could have held them off.

She was convulsing now, her body seizing and preparing for death, even if her mind hadn't caught up. She wouldn't be given the chance to die a slow, painful death from ill-balanced humous. The shock of what had happened to her was already about to stop her heart.

He hadn't brought cobalt potion with him that night because he didn't usually need it, and it glowed in his pack which had the possibility of giving him away.

Javier lifted the girl into his arms. Her broken body twitched, eyes quivering.

"*La muerte es todo lo que es seguro en la vida,*" he said and jumped out the window.

CHAPTER THREE

SERAP

Serap hurried down the marble hallways of Karzusan palace. Ayelet and Jahmil had called for her first thing that morning, and she suspected it had to do with her abandoning an about-to-propose Paco at the festival. That, and she had been avoiding them and everyone else the entire week since.

Rumors of elephants in the courtyard only tightened her chest more.

It wasn't that she had written Paco off completely, though the angry part of her still wanted to. She had found a better use of her time than dealing with an unromantic man-child who only sort of wanted to marry her. And who she less than sort of wanted to marry in return. At least she hadn't been swept up by him, ogling him every second like Zan Hala did Bakr Amca even though they bickered more than half the time. Serap would know who she should marry when she got that feeling. The feeling of being ripped from her shoes and thrown into love.

And now that she had a renewed hope for love and longer life, she need not settle for the likes of Paco.

Of course, her adoptive parents would never force her into anything she did not want to do, especially a marriage. But that didn't mean a long lecture on etiquette didn't wait on 'Abi Jahmil's tongue. Or that Ayelet wouldn't purse her lips with worry, a hoard of wisps at the ready to avenge any perceived injustice.

Serap stopped at doors that rose two stories high, inlaid with rubies. She patted down her clothes to smooth any wrinkles in the silk. Her pants and vest were the same as she wore at the festival—formal Turkish clothes required for the week-long celebrations of the Eight Moons and the original giving of the Royal Gifts of Elm. As a sheikha, she acted as a diplomat for Ard, though no one paid her much mind. Most djinn hadn't even seen a human outside of Shihala.

Certain she looked decent, she stood up straight with a tired groan.

Chupkin wriggled down her white muslin shirt and nestled into her belly button. She smiled as he scrunched in deeper, his cool mist far too big and spilling over the edges in tickling tendrils. Three pats stilled him, and she put a hand on the door. She needed an excuse for where she had been. They would not appreciate that she had spent all her spare time (and some that wasn't so spare) with Pasha as the moons passed to sleep every day this past week. Or her being with Pasha anytime, for that matter. Their rule had been very clear, in fact. *No Pasha. Ever.* And though Serap was twenty now, it meant very little to overprotective parental types who would to their two-hundreds.

Serap had yet to think of an excuse when the door slid open. She tumbled into the room with a yelp. A wide-eyed servant dodged from her path and scuttled out in a hurry. She offered a sheepish smile and straightened.

Jahmil and Ayelet reposed formally at the head of the emptied banquet hall with—she choked—Paco sitting to their right. None of them looked happy. Though none of them looked quite unhappy, either. Moderate indifference was never a good sign. It meant they were waiting for someone else to decide something. Someone like her.

Serap walked up like a tamer to a wild colt, hands open and out to the sides.

"Serap." Ayelet waved her over with that habitual smile she always had tucked into place. "Come. We wish to speak with you."

"Where are Lalam and Tabor?" Serap asked, grasping at straws so she wouldn't have to find out the purpose for whatever this meeting held. "We usually eat breakfast all together when we're in the dining room."

"The little *waliu aleahd* and *amira* have already eaten their breakfast and gone to their lessons," Jahmil said, his words as formal as his kingly attire. Crisp and suave and always chosen with great care. "I will send for your morning refreshment, *saghirati*."

She shook her head. "I'm not hungry."

It wasn't true but would be if whatever they needed to say made her as queasy as she anticipated.

"Serap," Paco said with a nod of his head.

"*Sheikha* Serap," Jahmil corrected.

A hint of irritation twitched on Paco's warm smile, and a shard of pink uncertainty clung to the center of his calm, dark eyes.

He bowed his head. "Sheikha Serap."

She nodded back, embarrassed over Jahmil's cordiality, and pressed her lips flat. "So, what's going on? Not even Zalika Jida's funeral was this grim."

"Not grim." Ayelet chuckled. "Just unexpected."

"What is?"

Jahmil's lips slumped in a cool grin. "Paco's proposal."

"Wha?" She couldn't even finish the word, which 'Abi Jahmil always hated. But sometimes it couldn't be helped.

"Tighten your tongue, child." There was no sting in 'Abi Jahmil's voice. He lifted one eyebrow, then cleared his throat. "Paco arranged this meeting before the festival. Though he said he would have a conversation with you, first. I take it that never came to fruition along with you attending the festival with an escort to begin with."

She glanced at Paco who had that same fixed smile and hint of pink in his eye. She waited a breath longer, hoping he would intercede on her behalf, but he would not. *Payback*, she thought. Then, *Fair*.

Chupkin squished tighter into her stomach.

"Weird about the escort. My lady-in-waiting was there one moment and then gone the next."

Jahmil's eye twitched. "Your protection is not a joke. Heirs go missing. Even the King of Elm couldn't protect his from disappearing in the middle of broad daylight."

Chupkin flickered against her skin, and she pressed a hand to quell him, equally irritated.

"Just because one disappears doesn't mean I will. And as for Paco, I... had something come up," she said, showing teeth, unsure if it was a smile or a grimace. "I'm sorry I missed our meeting." She nodded to Paco. "May I ask what the proposal concerns?"

"It's not just some proposal." Ayelet's facial features shifted between perplexed and bemused. "It's *a* proposal. There's a full procession waiting behind the gates, ready to announce your betrothal to the city."

Serap's teeth-showing widened, and she refused to budge, to acknowledge for one moment what they were saying even though she'd had a week to prepare. A small part of her never thought it would come to fruition. That he'd actually ask.

"For *what?*" she repeated.

"For your hand," Paco blurted out, "in marriage," Paco finished, then cast his eyes to the floor.

A romantic display, that, she thought dryly, lowering her hand to rub at her eye. Even always-smiling Yousef would have winced. And Zan Hala would have kicked him out right then, with Bakr Amca laughing all the way. Not for the first time, she wished her uncle and aunt lived in Shihala instead of Eayima with their ten kids. Of course, she'd normally say all that aloud, but that would be rude. So she settled for silence and a little bit of gob-smacking.

"Saeed Paco has extended a formal request for your hand and offered an adequate bride price." Jahmil's diamond eyes sparked in a strange mixture of black fear and pale-blue hope. He lifted his chin. "What is your answer?"

"I don't know." Serap rolled her shoulders in sloppy fashion.

Paco went straight as a cedar tree. Jahmil's upper lip curled, though she couldn't tell if he was pleased or disappointed.

"Not to be rude, but we kind of rushed the courtship thing." She turned to Paco. "I mean, we haven't even kissed, yet. You could have weird lips, or a sharp tongue, or taste funny. Or I could, for that matter."

Paco's shade of periwinkle deepened along his cheekbones and across his neck.

"Paco, dear, why don't you step out and take a walk around the courtyards?" Ayelet said in her motherly tone. "We will summon you once we conclude our discussions."

He readily obliged, storming out on stiff legs, his face still afire and the laughter in his plum eyes buried in the awful orange of embarrassment. Serap tilted her head, too many feelings pushing back against Chupkin as she watched him go.

Jahmil rested two fingers on his temple with a sigh. "Explain yourself."

Resigned was better than upset. She had only seen him mad at her once, and that was when she let the herd of sea dragons in Eard Almuhit out during Shihala's Festival of the Seven Waters. They had looked so much like large sea horses she had assumed...

The important thing was no one died. And only a few people lost their hearing from the dreadful screeches.

"He's kind of stuffy, don't you think?" Serap sighed, not wanting to tell them her shame. "Or is it just stuffy in here? Have the servants been lighting too many fires again? They always struggle to find the right balance as the cold of night gives way to the less cold of day night." She let out a nervous laugh. "Though I suppose I can't blame them. Even though I've been in Qaf for ten years, I still have trouble sorting out the days and nights. On Ard, it is so easy to tell."

"I don't know," Ayelet said in her easy way. "Dear Paco's an easy laugher. That's a trait that's hard to find."

Jahmil's eye twitched.

"I'm just not interested." Serap scanned the room like she had just walked into it for the first time. "Not today."

"Am I to understand that to mean you were interested yesterday, or perhaps you will be tomorrow?" Jahmil coaxed. "If you were to have asked me five days ago what your answer would have been when Paco inevitably asked for your hand, it certainly would not have been *he might have weird lips*. What has changed?"

"Do I need a reason?"

"No." Ayelet jumped in.

Jahmil turned to his wife, a gentle smile playing on the corner of his lips.

She chuckled. "But we are worried. It is not like you to stand someone up, especially someone whom you have been spending a lot of time with. We know..." Her brows knitted with worry. "...that friends can be hard to come by here. You can't even seem to keep a lady-in-waiting you like for longer than a few weeks. Are you sure there is nothing you want to tell us?"

Serap waffled. She could put the matter to rest easily enough, but a realization had bubbled up inside. "Now that you mention it..." She paused and waited—as all good performers do—for them to lean in. "I have been missing Ard's sun. I think some time to sort everything out away from Qaf would do me well."

"Splendid idea." Ayelet jumped up. "We shall go today."

"Not *we*." Serap forced her eyes to stay on her parents. Their startled and hurt faces made her want to run away. But she was no longer a child and not so easily persuaded by their heart-rending looks. "I want to sojourn on my own for a while."

"You wish to travel to Ard unaccompanied?" Jahmil narrowed his eyes and stood silent, then shook his head. "Out of the question."

"Hear her out," Ayelet prodded gently, touching his arm.

Serap smiled nervously, thankful for Ayelet's intercession. "First, you don't have to worry about me on Ard. I can call Bakr Amca if I get into any trouble. He's a lilu, right? He can hear me in both worlds and the space in between."

Jahmil grumbled. "Half a lilu who only responds half the time."

"Better than nothing," she mumbled, then bolstered her fortitude. "And I'm technically never alone. I have Chupkin." Her little wisp poked his head out of her collar and nuzzled her chin.

Ayelet shook her head. "I still have no clue what you did to that thing."

"Why? The wisps cling to you."

"Yes, but that is because they're responding to my emotional needs. Yours acts more like a dog." She tilted her head, her gray eyes curious and careful. "I cannot comprehend what made that bit of magic go rogue for so long."

Chupkin flashed with indignation, and Serap pressed her lips together to keep from laughing.

"Though that does remind me..." Ayelet perked up, a mischievous look in her storm-gray eyes. "I have something for you from your jida's collection. Something that might make this whole Paco debacle a little lighter."

"Debacle may be an understatement," Serap sighed, wishing to get the conversation over with but a slave to her insatiable curiosity. She leaned in.

"I have been working on something for you." Ayelet rifled through her dress and its infinite number of deep pockets.

"Are you sure she is ready?" Jahmil's shoulders stiffened, a wary look in his eyes.

His words plucked at a wound in her heart. He was worse than Pasha. He didn't think her capable of doing anything on her own.

"Of course, she is." Ayelet didn't look up, rummaging through her blue silk skirt. "*Oba*! Here it is."

Her thin fingers pulled free a square, copper amulet laced onto a chain so fine it glimmered from across the room. A little sliver of metal that would burn a djinn, but was far more delicate than the coin necklaces she wore from Bakr Amca.

Serap took the amulet in her hand. It filled the center of her palm and had seven-by-seven rows etched into its surface, each box filled with a symbol, some ancient-looking Arabic, some Qafian symbols she had seen on tombs but couldn't understand, and some she didn't know at all.

"To keep away evil spirits," Ayelet said. "And to let us know you are okay whenever you are away. I know it's hard not to be able to travel between worlds through the void like djinn can. It is one of the few forms of magic my wisps don't allow for, and that leaves even me feeling..." She paused, tapping her chin. "Forsaken. But this should help. I found it in your Zalika Jida's *khazina* of magical artifacts and have been tinkering with it. One swipe across—"

Serap stepped closer, and Ayelet pointed to the top row.

"—then down the third row will send a wisp to let me know you are well whenever you are away. Two across and down the third will tell us you miss us and will be home soon." She smiled softly, her eyes round with crinkles on the edges. "And three across, third down will tell us you need help and have a wisp take us to you. Understand?"

Serap nodded, marveling over the rosy metal. "And which one tells you I'm hiding from Paco and his elephants and need reinforcements?"

"Elephants." Jahmil clenched his teeth and shook his head. "Those infernal creatures are making a mess in the courtyard."

Ayelet laughed. "I would not try any other combinations. There is a lot of other magic in that amulet, and I don't actually know what it is capable of."

"That is a bit of an understatement, don't you think, oh *huba hayati*?" Jahmil lifted his eyes to Ayelet. "Last week harpies terrorized our bedroom because you couldn't stop poking at that thing."

Serap's eyes widened, the metal of the amulet warm in her hand despite the cool temperature of the marble room. "Is that how that happened? Everyone was certain a path to Jahannam had opened up below the palace."

"I would not discount it completely. *La samah Allah*." 'Abi Jahmil smiled.

Ayelet shrugged with a blush. "Now you know what not to do. It is powerful, so please be careful. I only give it to you because I know I—*we*—can trust you." She glanced at Jahmil. "And because I know how it is to feel helpless on Ard."

"You've never been helpless a day in your life." Serap grinned.

Jahmil's persistent frown softened. "True enough."

Serap took heart, encouraged by Jahmil's break in solemnity. She looked between the two of them, nervous to press her luck. "With this amulet, I can be on my own and have a way to reach you without any djinn fire. Does that mean you'll let me go to Ard now?"

Jahmil let out a throaty groan. "I stand by my judgment. You can't go to Ard alone. And if you won't go with Ayelet, you must select a suitable chaperone or postpone your trip to a later date. You have nowhere to stay. Yousef and Khalida are on a cross-world business trip with Jericho and the girls. They'll be in Ghaluma for the next month."

"So?" Serap shrugged.

She had no plans to spend time with her more upstanding cousin and his family, anyway. She'd get absolutely nowhere on her quest for the Immortal Killer if she did. Yousef was far too cheery and helpful to leave her on her own long enough to sneeze without handing her a tissue.

"If I *have* to have someone to accompany me—" The words never tasted so bitter. "—I'd prefer to stay with cousins Balian and Iesha, anyway."

"Out of the question." Jahmil scoffed. "The only thing worse than Balian is his cat-eyed Ahmaran hitwoman. You can argue that he is just harmless riff-raff, but she attempted to murder both Ayelet and myself, and came pretty close if I must remind you."

Serap sighed, used to 'Abi's complaints about the Ardish side of her family. She was still convinced that whole thing had been a hilarious misunderstanding. She turned her big eyes to Ayelet, but her hopes fell when she bit her lip and looked away. If even Ayelet wasn't on her side, she'd have to stand on her own.

The skin on her neck grew clammy. She'd never talked back to 'Abi Jahmil before. Not like this. But it would be okay. They would be. Once she was immortal, she'd have all the time in the world to make things right between them.

Serap cleared her throat. "I like Iesha. And I've seen you cat-eyed, too. It's how we first met."

"That is not what I meant."

"Besides, Balian has never been so good since she came around. I think they could help me with... with growing old."

"Growing old?" Jahmil's eyebrow shot up.

Serap flashed a tight smile. "I meant growing up."

"That depends on what you intend to grow up to be." Jahmil ran his thumb and forefinger over his trim black beard. "If you intend to be a mobster and a drunk, then by all means. You are certainly impulsive enough to make such a foolish choice. But if not, I strongly suggest you stay clear."

Serap's shoulders sank, but Chupkin nudged her gently. She took another breath. "And what if that is what I intend to be? It's my choice, isn't it? What if I don't want to be a sheikha all the time? To always have to think over what I do a thousand times before I do it? It's exhausting. And frankly, it hasn't done much for me, anyway."

"Hasn't done much for you?" Jahmil's upper lip twitched before settling back in place.

That wasn't good. That was a sea dragons sort of lip twitch.

"Shihala has only fed your belly, given you a place to sleep and beautiful clothes to wear, and provided you an education like nothing you could have dreamed of."

With a cold chuckle, 'Abi Jahmil waved his hand. "You're upset about your situation with Paco. I understand. But that is no reason to behave like a petulant child."

"This has nothing to with Paco," Serap snipped, an unexpected sourness rising in her stomach. "And everything to do with the fact that I'm not a child at all, let alone a petulant one. I'm grown up, 'Abi. I can make decisions for myself without you hovering over my shoulder, telling me I'm making mistakes all the time. I need to *tighten my tongue*. I need to study more. I need to give silly little boys answers to questions they shouldn't be asking. I want to go to Ard. Today."

"The only reason there are silly boys demanding answers to questions they shouldn't be asking is because you insisted on the freedom to make your own marriage arrangements. Which I granted. Though given the elephants, I dare say you are seriously mishandling your affairs." His teeth tightened, upper lip beginning to furl. "And I think you've forgotten what a dangerous place Ard can be. I'm not about to allow my *saghirati* to travel there, or anywhere unaccompanied. We are done discussing this topic."

A shot of pain quivered through Serap's heart. Anxiety, hurt, anger. It didn't matter. She clenched her teeth together.

"No."

"I beg your pardon?"

"I'm not frail and breakable. I'm strong. I lived a life far harder than anything you ever did before you dropped into our lives. Isn't that right, Ayelet?"

She looked to her for comfort and found soft eyes but sealed lips. Her chest tightened.

"Or do you think I'm weak, too? If I am, it is this palace that's made me this way. And I won't stay here any longer, wasting away until I die." Serap turned on her heels and marched toward the door.

"*Fatat ghayr muhtarama*," Jahmil muttered before barking, "Stop right this moment."

Serap's body betrayed her, freezing out of habit. She glanced warily over her shoulder. His normally royal-blue cheeks had taken on a distinct shade of purple. This was far worse than the sea dragons.

"Jahmil." Ayelet reached once more to squeeze his hand.

He gritted his teeth and rolled his shoulders back. "You have forgotten not only how fortunate you are but also your manners. I suggest you stay in chambers until you remember."

"Are you sending me to my room like I'm Tabor or Lalam?" She turned, a fire in her eyes that felt wholly new, strangely empowering, and altogether terrifying. "Like I'm a little kid who wipes their nose on their sleeve?"

A sheen of disdainful yellow flashed through his diamond eyes before hardening into crystal. "You are being ridiculous."

"You can't just turn into a kitty cat and slip through the bars of a prison to save me from my problems anymore, 'Abi. I'm grown up and don't need your help. I insist you let me go to Ard."

"Not alone. And not into the care of Balian and his unhinged butcher of a wife." Every muscle in Jahmil's face and hands tightened. "I've explained myself thoroughly, and I will not do so again."

"The only thing you've thoroughly done is push me away." Serap bristled, then appealed one last time to the woman who had always been there for her. "Ayelet, you know I'll be fine. That I'm scrappy and Edirnian, just like you. Born of tougher stuff than Qaf."

Ayelet's unflappable smile faltered. She touched a hand to Jahmil's shoulder. The two exchanged glances, an entire conversation unfolding without a single word. It left Serap feeling all the more hollow. Alone.

"You are seen, Serap," Ayelet finally spoke, her voice gentle. "And you are, indeed, tough and smart and capable. But Iesha runs in dark circles I don't understand. Circles of magic and murder. It's one thing to be an acrobatic nomad, another entirely to be an assassin."

Serap's stomach twisted, and Chupkin curled up under her chin like he always did when he could feel her agitation. She was on her own, and she would not wait for another no.

"I will not stay here," she declared, chin tilted higher as she forced herself to meet 'Abi's flashing eyes. "My life is short enough. And I'm certainly not going to spend it confined under your rule, *remembering my manners*."

Jahmil began to speak, but she raced toward the ruby-clad doors and slammed them shut behind her. Then she pelted down the hallway, slipping the magical amulet around her neck. She signed against the Evil Eye, worried she was trying the patience of both her 'abi and Allah.

When she reached her chambers, she slid inside and locked the doors behind her.

"Surprise!" Pasha cackled.

Serap clapped a hand over her heart. "You're not supposed to be here," she chided, a tightness gripping her throat.

'Abi would never let her attitude sit in the banquet hall like that, which meant he was on his way. With Pasha here, things could only get worse.

"How did you even get in, anyway? Apparation into the palace by non-royals is forbidden. There are firewalls thick as the current in Jasraib around this place."

Pasha grinned her gap-toothed smile. "A little bit of this and a little bit of that. I am known for my ability to find things, it's sort of my whole job description. Are you ready?"

"Not as ready as I need to be. I may have—"

A knock thudded on the door. She froze, shoulders tight. Pasha slinked into the shadows behind the armoire near her bed.

"Serap?" Jahmil's voice came muddied through the door. "Please open the door. I would like to speak with you."

Her eyes widened. Pasha turned her palms up with a questioning glance. Serap shrugged. Back and forth they did this dance of gestures.

Pasha spoke up, her voice twisted into a terrible impression. "Oh... N-no thanks. Now is not a good time."

Serap scowled. Pasha grinned.

"Please, *saghirati*," Jahmil continued through the door. "We both have spoken harsh words. Let us find peace again."

"I don't want to," Pasha interceded again, adding in a completely uncharacteristic *harrumph*.

Serap pushed back the ache in her stomach and stomped her foot at Pasha. She mimed locking her mouth shut, then stormed over to where Pasha pressed herself against the wall. "What are you thinking?" she whispered.

"He needs to go."

"He's my father, and you—I—er, you as me can't treat him like that. He's sensitive, and I don't want to hurt his feelings. We just had a huge fight, and I don't know what he'll do. I said terrible things and... and he's only ever been kind to me."

"First off..." Pasha frowned and flicked a finger at her. "He's not *really* your father."

"I don't see it that way. When he married Ayelet, he took me in. No questions asked. Just scooped up a dirty kid and let her live in his palace." The words stuck in her throat as she remembered what she had yelled at him not two degrees ago. She clenched her teeth before she lost her resolve. "It doesn't matter, just don't treat him like that."

"*You're* the one sneaking around behind his back. So if anyone is going to break your old man's heart, it's you." Pasha poked her in the chest.

Serap groaned. "Just quit it."

"Serap?" Jahmil's voice carried through with a softness that made her heart ache. "Please come out. I apologize for losing my temper." She heard what was probably his head thunk gently against the door. " You know that I would do anything to protect you."

She wrung her hands together. She wanted to throw open the doors, bury her head in his shoulder, and tell him everything. But then her plans would be over. He wasn't even willing to let her go to Ard to stay with her own family. He would never support her idea to run off and make deals with immortal killers and traitors for immortality. And she wasn't ready to give up on her newfound dream. Not when it would allow her so much more time to make things right.

"What a whiny man." Pasha curled her fingers and looked at her nails. "Though they tend to all be like that. He's going to break down that door if you don't do something. Unless you want me to keep talking to him for you."

"No, thank you," Serap snapped through her clenched teeth. "I'd prefer not to sound like a hundred and twenty-five-year-old woman pretending to be twenty while being rude to my father."

"I thought you said I was a spry thirty in human years."

"I never said spry." Serap shook her head.

"Serap?" Jahmil rapped on the door, this time more urgently. "Please. I'm worried for you. I understand you're upset, but I can't abide you not talking to me."

She glanced at the door, heart stammering. She needed to leave. To be anywhere but the palace so she could do something for herself for once. If he caught Pasha in her room after their fight, he'd never trust her again, not that he even did. This was her last chance. Ayelet's amulet hung heavy on her neck, the hard metal a reminder of his wary judgment against her.

You are certainly impulsive enough to make such a foolish choice.

He always thought he was right, so why not prove him so?

"We need to get out before he comes in." Serap looked at Pasha's light pink eyes. "And we certainly can't use the door. Can you do anything?"

"Anything for Shihala's highest-ranking sheikha." Pasha grinned. "Do you have Chupkin with you?"

Chupkin's cool mist retreated from her collarbone to her back, giving Serap a degree of pause. "Why?"

Jahmil knocked on the door even harder. "Serap, what's going on? Do you have someone else in there with you?"

"A will and a wisp, dear. You still need the second ingredient, unless you've lost the first already?" Pasha lifted her brows and cupped her hands.

"Of course, I haven't," Serap stammered, clenching her stomach muscles.

Chupkin shivered and dove into Serap's shirt, but Pasha's hand darted out and snatched him. The witch took out a vial and let three drops of fuchsia liquid fall into his mists. He twisted and swirled, shrinking and expanding at an alarming speed, his light flickering like a candle that had worn the wick down all the way to the wax. Then he vanished.

"Chupkin!" Serap cried, a wholly new form of panic stabbing her gut.

"Serap?" Jahmil's voice carried the crisp urgency of a protector. The door handle shook as he rattled it from the other side. "Answer me, child." Then the ebony handle began to glow white hot.

"Wait, no, 'Abi Jahmil, I'm—"

"We gotta go, girl," Pasha said in her deadpan way.

She grabbed Serap's arm and smirked. They disappeared in a flash of acrid, lime-tinted smoke just as the door burst open in a spray of splinters. Jahmil's fierce, blackened eyes and blazing fists were the last thing Serap saw.

CHAPTER FOUR

JAVIER

The sun rose lazily in the eastern sky, backlighting Javier's three-story villa with purple and orange. The building was ancient and overgrown, flanked on all sides by crowded evergreens and vines twisting up into the crumbling facade. Ivory plaster had peeled away in several places, exposing bright red, crumbly brick. When first erected, the villa had been the very mecca of fashionable architecture—high rounded gables, dozens of keyhole windows. Now, it looked abandoned.

Javier liked it that way.

He sat in the driver's seat of a worn, wooden wagon, a sturdy donkey hitched to the breaching. The reins hung loose in his grasp, shoulders hunched, his cowl low over his eyes to keep his ears warm. Strapped up in the wagon alongside his delicate, unexpected cargo were a few barrels of milled cereals, a bolt of black wool, spices, lamp oil, and nineteen new books—everything he would need for the coming month. He often combined his monthly trip to the market with his new moon escapades, desiring not to venture out any more than was absolutely necessary.

People were excessively draining—human, djinn, ghost. All of them. He felt depleted, and not only by the unexpected complications of the excursion. Being away from home on its own was exhausting. All he wanted to do was go inside, bar every window, lock all the doors, cook himself dinner, sit in his favorite chair, and read. Sappho would be waiting by the door, he was sure, wondering why he had been gone so long. She was probably going to scold him, but that was alright. It let him know that she cared.

Unfortunately, the events of the night were bleeding into daytime, invading his personal sphere. He hated that. He'd only slated three days of recovery for this job and then he had two tremendous pains in the neck to contend with. Given how much his shoulder hurt, he figured he may even have to move things back another day. He was only human, after all. And while he had access to the finest magical potions and tinctures that Allah's two worlds could offer, magic could only do so much for a man's mental state after enduring such punishment. He'd learned that lesson the hard way when he'd first returned to Spain from his extensive sojourns and nearly worked himself to death trying to single-handedly rid the world of all the ills which he alone had the power to combat.

His work was important, yes. One might even call it paramount. But his books were important, too. So were the crops growing in the farmland around his villa. And so was his aching back. Life was a series of moments, each as fleetingly precious as the last. Each a gift from God meant to be enjoyed. His existence was one of loneliness and endless servitude, but even he had found ways to bring in simple pleasures. He was but mortal, so no matter how much he devoted himself to his work it would never really be done. He had to strive for balance.

As Javier drew the wagon up to the front door, he noticed the shadow of a nightkeeper waiting for him. The djinn's skin was as black as pitch and he was dressed very finely—thick orange robes, a strange brownish fur tied over his shoulders against the autumn chill, and lousy with jewels. Pale white fire licked over his knuckles, and his eyes flashed with bright pinks and grays. The basics of djinn color left the Qafian beings easily read by anyone who knew the rules, and when their eyes flashed pink, it meant they were experiencing anxiety. Gray, on the other hand, represented awe.

Based on the djinn's appearance it was easy to surmise he'd come from Izrak, a little volcanic kingdom on the far *shama'al* corner of the lower continent of Qaf. Javier had been there a handful of times, never staying longer than a few hours. But he was constantly being solicited by its monarch, Mapenuk, the infamous Bloody Queen. She never had any shortage of *effrits* she needed vanquished. And she never ceased to ask for Javier's help with the matter, though he'd told her fifty times that he wasn't going to help her commit genocide on the native fire spirits simply because she disliked that they were more powerful than her.

As the wagon approached, the djinn flinched and took a step back, his eyes sparking with twists of black fear. Javier watched him through his peripheral vision as he hopped down from the carriage and went about unhitching the donkey. Humans in general could not see djinn in Ard unless the djinn chose to be seen. But after so much time spent in Qaf and having so many spells placed on him over the years, Javier could spot a djinn from a parasang away as easily as a beacon burning on a mountaintop. Most djinn expected it of him. He was the Immortal Killer, after all.

If this one was silly enough to think he couldn't see him, then let him go on thinking so, at least until he could size him up.

The Izraki djinn held a scroll in his hand, which he'd decided to deliver personally because apparently, he was too stupid to notice the box out front with the words *"deposit proposals" here* written on it in seven different languages, including three dialects of Qafian Arabic.

"Idiota."

Javier set the donkey loose in the front garden, then turned his attention to unloading the wagon. One blanketed piece of cargo twitched as he opened the gate.

He had already given the girl both of the healing potions he'd had on him, but they only had the effect of slowing her breathing and sending her off to sleep. He hoped it had also staved off the blinding pain. Then he had wrapped her in a satin sheet he had stolen from the abbey and loaded her up.

She was so young, younger even than he had first realized. His tired body and logical mind cursed his own delicate heart and its unflinching adherence to a strict and frequently inconvenient moral code. It caused so much trouble, so much pain. How beautiful life must be for the shallow, the vapid, and the amoral. How he envied their ignorance and callousness, even as he despised them for it.

The poor child was covered in burns. When he looked at them, Javier swore he could feel them on his own skin. Half of her hair had been singed off, and one side of her face was crinkly, black, red, and coated in fresh pus. He hadn't seen the rest of her body, but with the way she had rolled around in the embers...

The Izraki djinn took a deep breath and slammed a fist into his thigh. Perhaps he had found his courage.

Javier grunted, glancing askance at the djinn. "Didn't you see the box for mail out front?"

The djinn flinched and rubbed his hands together, his shimmering eyes darting from side to side. His lips twitched, tongue nervous behind bright wide teeth. Javier opened his eyes very wide at him, in case he was wondering whether or not he could, in fact, see him. Still, the fidgeting djinn said nothing.

Javier lifted his brows. "Silence is a profound melody."

"A-are you Don DeMario?" The djinn's deep voice tripped over every consonant. "The one who...?"

"You tread a dangerous line." Javier tightened his fist and lifted the steel katar so the djinn could see the glint of the blade. "If you cannot be bothered to find out precisely who I am and how I do business, then I don't see why I should waste any of my precious time listening to you. In fact, if you do not cease your stuttering, I may be forced to add your blood to the colors that already make a mural on my threshold." He swept his other hand to indicate the stones on his stoop, covered in brown and rust-colored stains. They had been made by blood. Mostly from chickens and geese, but the djinn didn't need to know that.

"You will not hear my request?"

"I only accept written proposals, no more than a single page in length, with three attached references, and accompanied by a proper honorarium." Javier's lips twitched in irritation. "This, however, does not guarantee my services, only that I will read the proposal in full and make a sound determination of eligibility based on my own criteria. Then you go in the hat—"

"Forgive me, O Amaranthine One." The djinn swept into a low and dramatic bow, holding out the scroll to him. "I have brought your honorarium and references."

Javier did not reach for it, his brows pulled together in frustration. It had been some weeks since he had been forced to deal with one so thick. "The box is out front."

The djinn looked up and smiled. His mouth opened, and Javier could all but see the tremendously long and complicated anecdote coiled on his tongue. Insufferable.

"I offer you the chance to give audience to the wisdom of the ancients." Javier cleared his throat. "Happiness and freedom begin with a clear understanding of one principle. As aptly stated by the immortal Epictetus: *some things are within your control and some things are not.*"

Thick eyebrows drew together on the jet-black face. "I don't understand."

"It is within your control to leave this place." Javier reached into his jacket and drew out one long dagger. "You have the power, and I pray the motive, to flee these grounds and never return. I pray you find happiness in exercising your control swiftly and decisively. For there is another thing over which you have no control. That, of course, being what I will do to you should you choose to remain."

The djinn's dark eyes clouded over with a dull mist of fear as they darted from side to side. "You said that you would—"

"Your repeated breaches in protocol have made my decision for me." He waved a hand flippantly. "I will not consider your proposal."

"Please. You must listen." His eyes sparkled with desperate pink, and he stepped nearer on unsteady feet. "Our kingdom has been invaded by a horrific immortal beast."

"So what else is new?"

The djinn's gaze flashed between Javier's eyes and the dagger in his hand. "The creature has slaughtered entire villages. A thousand men, women, and children have fallen to its appetite."

"That is unfortunate. But that kind of thing is *always* happening somewhere. I can't help everyone. Difficult decisions must be made." Javier pushed out his bottom lip and stroked his long, bushy beard. "Perhaps next time you will have a care and not condemn your people to further suffering because you are too stupid to use a *clearly labeled* mailbox." Javier flipped the dagger in the air so the steel shimmered and danced in the sunlight. He caught it by the blade and tipped it back over one shoulder.

"The Queen of Izrak has authorized me to pay you seven thousand *qafiz* worth of precious gems for your services. Please!"

"I do not accept payment for my services. I humbly request a reasonable honorarium to consider proposals because my time is precious." He tightened the muscles in his arms and shoulder, making a good show that he was about to throw the dagger. "Couple that with a simple respect for my established protocol and you would not be in this situation."

The djinn fell to his knees. "O, Generous Slayer of Beasts! Have mercy on me!"

"Tell your queen to send someone less stupid next time." The dagger ignited in blue fire. The Izraki djinn screamed and rose to run but tripped over his ostentatious robe after only a few paces and fell to the earth. Javier growled, puffed himself up, and stalked after him. The djinn scrambled to his feet, lifting his robes to reveal knobby knees covered in coarse white hairs. Javier aimed carefully and threw his knife so it would brush the djinn's thigh as he raced away.

In a panic, the djinn lifted his arms into the air and transformed. A flash of brilliant white light, and suddenly a little fox scampered forth, clothes abandoned in the high grass. Javier took out another knife and chucked it at the earth right in front of the fox's twitching nose. The blade burrowed in, and the creature tumbled over itself to change direction, then darted between the donkey's legs, disappearing through the crude triangle formed by the earth and two of its legs.

Javier sighed and rolled his shoulders. He walked across the field and grunted like an old man as he bent to retrieve his knives. Once the blades were safely back in the holsters inside his jacket, he returned to the wagon.

With nervous fingers he lifted the girl into his arms and carried her into the stable, a small building of mostly rotted wood that leaned so far to one side, the doors would not even close anymore. His animals never used it except in the dead of winter, so the hay on the ground was fresh and dry.

He used his teeth to unhook his cloak then threw it down on the hay and used his foot to straighten it before laying down the girl's body. Kneeling at her side, he pulled aside the satin sheet and looked at her face. The sickly-sweet smell of pus assaulted his senses. Bright red bubbles covered one entire side of her face. His eyes swept quickly down her frame and frigid darkness pulled at his heart. Most of the skin on the left half of her body had melted in the fire.

Leaving her laying in the hay, Javier went into his kitchen and pawed through the overstuffed cabinets until he found the potion he needed: bright blue and sparkling like starlight in the glass vial. Qafian cobalt.

He returned to the girl and knelt at her side. Propping her head back, he used his fingers to part her lips, then poured the sparkling potion down her throat. He held her nose to make her swallow, then sat back on his knees. He supposed he ought to find some soap and bandages, maybe boil some water, but tending to her wounds the old-fashioned way was not going to save her. That was why he had had no choice but to bring her home. If she was too far gone that even cobalt could not bring her back, then nothing could.

Guilt was doing terrible things to his mind. He needed to find a way around it, to think clearly. The logical part of his brain screamed that he never should have brought her here. But the other half of him—the half that felt a stabbing sensation in his guts when he looked at her charred flesh—was screaming much louder.

The potion would work, and then he could let her go in the local village. Alive and in no worse circumstances than she had been when he found her. And then he could forget this feeling, this hideous feeling.

He hated feeling things, every emotion experienced like indigestion or a bad headache. A waste of time and energy.

Javier stood and brushed clinging hay from his knees. Sappho's cry cut into his thoughts—a high-pitched mewl that demanded attention—and she rubbed her body against his boots, doing circles around his legs. Smiling, he bent to pick her up. The black and white speckled cat hissed and moaned, pushing her face hard into the twists of his long brown beard. He ran his hand over her soft fur, his eyes still fixed on the girl. Waiting for something, anything to start happening.

"I don't know what's wrong with me," he told the cat, rubbing her stiff ear with one finger. "I should not have brought her here."

The grouchy old cat made a low growl and kneaded his arm with her two front paws.

The girl began to shiver as the potion snaked through her blood. Her veins showed slightly blue in her neck, and a pathetic whimper fell from her lips.

"I'll set up a bed in here for her. She can have the mohair blanket and sleep it off. I'll make porridge. No, a tortilla. No, she needs meat. I'll make *pollo asado y verduras con crema de azafrán*. Yes, that is best."

He reached into his pocket and took out the small jar of saffron he'd stolen from Silrok. He tossed it up in the air, caught it, and popped out the cork. Then took a deep inhale of the subtle, intoxicating aroma.

"Pure Iranian rubies, no less." Javier sighed and shook his head. "I'll leave the door open, not that I have a choice." He grimaced at the tilted door frame. "I'll feed her, then when she has regained her strength, she can make her way to the village on her own. It shouldn't be too cold tonight." He took a step towards the door, narrowing his eyes at the sky. Bruising gray clouds lumbered lazily in a slow, biting breeze. "It's not going to rain, is it?"

Sappho crawled up onto his shoulder and rubbed her face into his beard. He scratched her head absently.

"I'll leave her a few coins, too." He reached into his pocket and took out a handful of silver, which he piled on the ground next to the girl. "There."

Javier sighed and set a hand over his eyes. "Oh, it's all so superficial. But what else can I do? She cannot come into the house. Rain, ghouls, and bandits notwithstanding, she'll be safer out here. I cannot have her in my house."

He narrowed his eyes at the sky as the first of many fat raindrops plunked to earth with petulant thuds.

"Not in *my* house."

CHAPTER FIVE

SERAP

She landed in Ard with a *thud* that rivaled the drop of her heart. 'Abi Jahmil was devastated. Betrayed. And so, so angry.

Serap ripped her arm from Pasha and glared as instant regret filled her up. "I'm going to be in so much trouble! 'Abi Jahmil and Ayelet will be worried sick looking for me." She lifted her amulet from off her neck and looked down at the strange symbols. "I have to let them know where I am."

"Nope." Pasha snatched the copper amulet and swiped her finger down a row before letting it drop.

Her eyes widened. "What did you do?"

"Told mommy and baba you are fine." Pasha smiled a wicked grin.

"How did you even know the combination?"

"Witch." Pasha rolled her eyes, then turned from Serap and pulled a branch down to survey the clearing just beyond the treeline.

Serap's attempt at composure evaporated. Now her parents would think she ran away and then glibly sent a message saying she was fine without them. Would Jahmil look for her with all of Shihala's army now, or write her off as an impulsive child who deserved what she got?

She shivered and shifted her feet in the muck, decidedly sick over how things were going. She could send a wisp to call for help, but then she'd have done all this for naught.

There are many paths to our heart's desire, but not many meant for soft hands, Pasha had said. And she was right. Eternal life didn't come through waiting, it came from doing the right things. And she didn't need her parents' help, not when she had...

An electric zip coursed through her. "Where's Chupkin?"

They had appeared in an evergreen thicket where the smell of pine was even thicker than the blanket of trees surrounding them. A small opening in the branches revealed a dismal, run-down town cowering under gray skies. The soft earth held moisture from recent rain, and Serap's leather boots squelched in puddles of mud. A few villagers whose skin was a shade browner than her own peachy color yelled in the distance. Their harried calls were in a language she didn't recognize but a tone she knew well from her days in Edirne.

They were scared. Hungry. Alarmed. Something bad was coming. It sent her heart and mind racing, an urgency to find her only companion pounding in her temples.

A shot of relief coursed through her as her eyes alighted on a breath of white tucked under a nearby tree.

"Chupkin!" She knelt where quivered in the pine needles, clearly shaken by what Pasha had just shoved him through.

"What did you do to him?" Serap hissed, scooping him up with tender fingers.

Thank Allah he looked fine now, nothing but a disappearing tint of pink left in his white. He would be moody about this for days.

"Meh." Pasha waved her off. "Your wisp is fine. I just mixed his magic with a bit of locator potion made from the blood of a dead immortal."

Serap grimaced at the thought of something so dirty being inside her Chupkin. "Where did you bring me, anyway?"

"To where the spell dictated."

"And where is that?"

"The most direct path to meeting the Immortal Killer, the one who will slay the traitor."

A shrill cry broke through the branches behind them. Serap's heart seized. "Take me back," she whispered, regretting her decision to come to this place already.

"You'll be fine, remember? You're tough and human and all that. Something about reproducing well? Or was it living?" She let out a quick laugh, then kissed Serap's forehead. "Anyway, I've got to go, sheikha. It's not safe for djinn here. I'll see you soon."

"But—"

In another green flash, Pasha vanished through a triangular cross of branches between nearby trees. Serap crouched in the dried pine needles alone, regret tainting each sniffle as her guard dog trembled inside her coat.

She would be fine. She would be fine. Impulsive children threw fits, according to 'Abi Jahmil, and she was definitely not that. This was what she wanted. To live longer and prove her worth, not to cower in the woods. And that's exactly what she would do.

As soon as the ominous sounds faded and she didn't feel so sick.

Serap stayed crouched in the woods until her knees burned and her calves went numb. So when Chupkin finally braved the moist air and ventured out of her jacket, she followed. He wound through the spice-scented trees and onto the path toward the small village. To her relief, whatever had frightened them in the night must have vanished with the light, leaving a village full of tired eyes staring with vehemence at the strange new woman who strolled into town.

She ambled along the path, some of it cobbled with thick, uneven stones of mottled brown and tan, and some of it not. Her shoulders tightened with every step. She did not recognize this place; the trees that grew in simple shades of green without the bright splashes of color found in Qaf, the simple and sturdy dress of the people, or the sharp kick in her nose when she walked past homes, doors open and smelling of breakfast.

Chupkin twirled to and fro, blowing past the simple white apron of a woman tending to a small garden. The woman clamped a hand down over it to keep it on, oblivious to the source of the unexpected breeze. Just like most things Qaf, humans overlooked the breath of magic when it passed them by. It was her time in the land of djinn that had made her so sensitive.

"I see what you mean," Serap whispered to him upon his return. "I think I am overdressed."

She looked down at her Turkish mohair pants and embroidered scarf, the metal coins that hung from her necklace, and the gold and silver embroidery on her black vest. It was the dress of Turkey, her first home, and something she refused to change even in the courts of Qaf. But in this place of hardship and hunger, some of her pride slipped into self-consciousness. Maybe she *had* become too soft and spoiled to make it on her own.

"I am the only one wearing pants. Or necklaces. Or shiny anything. Even my headscarf sticks out here. I should have changed before I left. I should have planned better. I shouldn't..." *Have lost my temper.* The last bit tasted as blunt as the strange spice wafting in the air. "And Pasha should not have left me that way. I don't even know where I am. And how does she expect to find me upon return? It's not like she's an Ahmaran princess or something and can teleport to whomever instead of wherever she pleases. Who tells someone about a monster of a man who ruthlessly kills immortals, and then dumps them in the woods in *the most direct path* of such a person without any instruction or help, anyway?" She scowled and shook her head. "It was simply rude."

She groaned. Complaining would do nothing for her. At least, not at this time. She would save her remonstrances for later. For now, she needed answers, or more specifically, directions.

Serap tried waving at the first few gaunt faces she passed with a tepid smile and had doors shut in her shadow and ragged curtains drawn in haste. Next, she saw a group of youthful villagers, their clothes anything but clean or fancy. Simply cotton shift shirts and dirty trousers caked in mud. If she couldn't impress the upper-class djinn of Shihala, maybe she could impress these simple humans. She grabbed a few rocks for a juggling trick and finished the routine with a smiling flourish. They cast her wary glances and scuttled away.

She scrunched her face into a pout. It can't have been her execution that drew such a cold response. Her performance had been flawless. Which meant it was *her*.

A coldness sat in her belly that she worked to ignore. She had thought a man from Ard might not marry her because her ideas and knowing were strange and different, not because she simply appeared so. But in this part of Ard, she wasn't welcome, either.

She jutted her chin higher to compensate for her slouching shoulders and tried avoiding the villagers' gazes altogether. Perhaps, if she ambled aimlessly with an air of hopelessness, some friendly local would offer her assistance.

She was met with the same response. And the same fire that had lit in her yesterday returned and solidified her resolve. If the cowardly villagers were going to spook no matter what she did, why not be direct? She was a sheikha, after all, even if they didn't know it.

She spied a tanned man whose ancient face dripped with wrinkles and said in Turkish, "*Affedersiniz?*"

"*Lárgate!*" He shoved his hands at her.

She took a step back, not needing to know the word to understand the spit that flew from his mouth. *Unwelcome*, and that was being polite.

Serap hurried to the next foot-beaten street where brittle houses put up a front against the wind swooping in over the forests and into the scant clearing. The sun had bleached the south-facing wood to a dull gray, and the green of moss and black of mold crept up from the soggy earth and into the bottom planks of each home.

"Everything here is going to be damp," she said to Chupkin with a sigh. She turned her face up toward the sky and soaked in the warm rays of glistening light. "The sun is nice after so many months under Qaf's moons, though. I have missed it so."

An elderly woman sat in a clunky wooden chair, her gnarled and swollen knuckles working away at a rough bit of weaving.

Serap puckered her lips, twitching them to and fro. Turkish hadn't worked and the only other language she knew was Arabic. She would try that this time. "*Sabah alkhayr, Jida,*" she said with a small bow.

The woman looked up with wide eyes, one milky, one blue.

"*Hal tafham?*" Serap pressed, encouraged by a response other than disdain.

The woman shook her head and pointed down the road.

Serap bowed again and rubbed her headband against her scalp before turning away. "It's better than the nothing I've gotten so far."

Chupkin flicked the end of his white tail, unconvinced.

Around the corner, her heart lightened. A small, quaint building sat at the end of the road, vines eating at the plaster and rain at the thatched pieces of roof. Otherwise, the rounded stone walls and small minarets that poked at the sky looked as they should; strong, resolute, and welcoming. A mosque.

She hurried forward, grateful for the shared language between Qaf and this small haven in a foreign countryside. Allah may have two worlds, one for djinn and one for humans, but he loved all creatures equally.

There was no door on the keyhole-shaped entrance, but the red tile that lined the floor was free of dust and dirt, and the washbasin beside the door had clean, placid water that reflected the gray skies above. She slipped off her boots and made sure her flower-embroidered scarf covered all her hair. Then she dipped her hands in the cool water for ablution before stepping inside. The mihrab glistened on the wall to her right, pristine despite the tarnish spots unavoidable with age. Worn red and gold columns climbed to the high ceilings around a large, gilded dome in the center.

"*As-salam Alaikum*," said the Imam in a kind, dry voice as he emerged from a back room. He touched his hand to his heart and inclined his head with a smile.

"*Wa 'alaikum-as-salam*," she replied, mirroring the gesture.

"It is not often we get such visitors to our little mosque," he continued in Arabic, his accent narrower on the tongue than a Shihalan's. "Not since the Reconquista."

She tilted her head a bit further. "Reconquista?" She raised a brow, at once grateful that the Imam couldn't see Chupkin zooming about the dome in a whirlwind.

The Imam's kind eyes softened further. "Where are you from, child? And how did you find yourself here?"

"I am looking for an answer," she said, though why everyone had taken to calling her child... but that was neither here nor there. "Well, really for a man who can help me get the answer I seek."

She inhaled and held her breath, unsure what humans on Ard would think of such things. Especially wherever it was that she now stood. In Edirne, the mythical were well-known, oft-blamed, and otherwise generally ignored. But the frightened villagers of this place lingered on her mind. The imam, however, was supposed to be a wise who sees what others cannot.

"I'm looking for a man known... for his ability to slay deathless beings." She winced.

The Imam's gentle smile tightened along with the skin around his eyes. "Are you sure what you seek is not a monster?"

"No," she said, straightening. "Monsters do not scare me."

"The wholesome seek eternal life, not the way to end it."

She couldn't help a smile. "I agree. But in this case, they are one and the same."

"Why?" The Imam prodded, a gentle curve to his brow.

His face was so patient, like 'Abi Jahmil's was whenever he caught Tabor stealing candied almonds. Of course, little Tabor always denied he did it, even with his palms sweating on the treats. Jahmil always won through unwavering eye contact and the weight of silent expectation.

Her chest ached deep beneath her sternum. He had sounded so sad on the other side of the door, and she had vanished as he ran to her aid. What must he think of her? Her hand itched toward the copper amulet, but after the wisp Pasha sent, continuing to tell them she was fine without them felt wrong.

She pulled herself back to the Imam's waiting eyes, realizing she hadn't quite heard what he said. Not listening to her 'abi was one thing, not listening to Allah's earthly guide in his place of worship was far more egregious.

"I'm sorry, Imam. I do not mean to be ungrateful for my blessings, but I simply must know all the answers to immortality."

"Immortality and eternal life are not necessarily the same. One is empty and hollow, without purpose, and the other divine and complete. The answers to the second, you can find here." He raised a shaking, wrinkled hand toward the dome. "Or anywhere. But it would be a much safer and far more edifying journey for a lost child like yourself."

There was the child remark again. She pressed a hand to her heart once more with a little nod. "I am sure that is true. But, while I praise Allah's greatness and seek his mercy daily, this part of my journey is about how to end eternal life, not enjoy it."

"Very well." The Imam's face fell, deepening the creases in his skin. "Heaven whispers to me that you are one of his wandering children, meant to find peace through a trial. If you are so determined on your path, you can find the man you seek down the same road you arrived on, past the graveyard, and up the south slope into the dark woods."

Why did his words sound as ominous as they did helpful?

"*Shukraan jazilaan lak*," she said gratefully, then turned to leave.

"*Sayida*," he called to her.

She twisted to look once more upon the wise man.

"The monster you seek has no god. No morals. He is filled with hate and revenge. He sees only blood. Blood spilled by hate and blood spilled by his own hands in retaliation."

She forced her weakening smile to stay in place. But the Imam was not done.

"He fears neither djinn, nor beast, and keeps evil spirits chained within his home. Screams come from his hill. Death follows his footsteps. And yet even death is beholden to him."

She shifted from foot to foot, the tile a biting cold against her skin. She nodded once more and hastened out of the mosque.

"*Sayida*," he called again, stopping her in her tracks. "The time has come for prayer."

She stopped mid-step and dipped into a bow to hide the fear in her eyes, grateful for once she was not djinn. "Of course, Imam."

And so, she found a spot on the floor facing Mecca, kneeled, and bowed her head to her hands in prayer. But really, all she thought of was a beast of a man cloaked in shadows and laughing evilly with eyes that dripped with blood. Not that she wasn't grateful to Allah; she was, she just had no intention of joining him in Heaven any time soon.

She knelt for what felt like an eternity and rose to her feet determined to one day find out just how long that was.

When at last the prayer finished, Serap sprinted from the mosque, worried she'd be stopped once more and worried she would stop herself.

No man could be as terrible as Pasha and the Imam had said. He was a human, after all. And so was she. They shared the fragility of humanity. A common fear of death. That was something she could appeal to when she begged her case. She had not come all this way to be defeated by rumors. And that's possibly all they were. Nasty things people said behind this Immortal Killer's back. She knew how that felt. The ones said about her often weren't true, either. He could simply be different from everyone else.

He would have to be after surviving the Bahamut, the eternal fish whose flicking tail churned Qaf's skies and seas. Living through an ordeal like that was sure to come with some baggage, vapid rumors, and a general sense of misunderstanding. But that didn't make him a beast. And even if he was, she hadn't lied to an Imam in Allah's holy place.

She was not afraid of monsters.

Serap headed south through town and toward the graveyard the Imam had mentioned. The cemetery was even older than the mosque and filled with tombstones crumbling with decay. The carved names on each had long worn away, leaving only a forlorn sense of despondency. It was not a cemetery quite like the ones in Qaf, with their white sarcophaguses that sparkled in time with the stars overhead, but the crosses that were etched into the gray stones gave a similar austerity.

It was a sacred place. A quiet one. The graves lay a stone's throw from the road but felt as if they were upon her. Shadows stretched long. The sun seemed to dim. She quickened her pace, then heard a scream. A snarl. And the grating of stone that froze her in her tracks.

"*¡Ayúdame!*" cried the voice of a girl.

Chupkin shot like a star straight up and over in an arc, disappearing behind a tombstone on the far end. Serap hesitated a moment, but if even Chupkin felt it a worthy cause, she could not argue. Human suffering was human suffering, regardless of what snarled like a sea dragon out of her sight. She could not let an innocent die. Not ever. Not if she could help it.

She grasped the copper amulet Ayelet gave her in one hand and hurled herself toward the graveyard.

Serap squished and slid through a patch of mud before making a sharp turn. A girl lay on the ground, a faint blue glow to the veins in her neck and a flesh-slicked ghoul raking her nightdress as she screamed.

Serap stumbled back. The ghoul flashed its hollow eyes. Green-tinted saliva dripped from its cracked, yellow teeth. It was the size of a man, hunched like a beast, with shreds of soiled cloth draped around its shoulders, hips, and loins. The white bones of its rib cage hung freely in jagged crags. The exact image Ayelet had painted from when she had fought the *eimlaq*, only so much worse.

The ghoul turned its face back to the helpless child who could be no more than twelve, and Serap felt a fierceness rise in her chest. She had once been that girl when Jahmil braved the iron of a slaver's prison to get her out. When Ayelet coaxed the poison of magic from her blood and pulled her from the grasp of Köle. She would not leave the girl. Not ever.

"*¡Ayúdame!*" The little girl screamed again.

Serap hastened through the brush and spied a termite-infested branch longer and thicker than her arm laying against a stone nearby. She whipped it into her grasp, barely able to hold its weight. With a battle cry, she ran toward the ghoul who looked up too late.

The branch shattered a rib and stabbed through to the other side of the ghoul as it screeched. Its jaws sputtered putrid phlegm. Fangs longer than her hands clacked in agitation.

The ghoul left the screaming child and lunged. Pulling. Clawing. Scraping its way up her stick to reach her.

Serap slipped once more in the muck and fell back, hitting her side against a tombstone. She jumped over it and ran toward the road, but the ghoul caught her pants. Its dagger-long nails shredded the hem of the fine fabric and nicked her flesh underneath.

A shot of pain spidered across her skin underneath its claws. A cry of pain tore from her throat, and she fell to her knees, crawling forward as fast as she could manage as dirt smeared her palms.

"Bakr Amca!" she cried, praying this was one of the times her fearless uncle would hear the magical call of his own name. "Bakr!"

The ghoul screeched. Warm blood bloomed. She clawed her way forward, escaping the monster's grasp, but no sword-strapped lilu appeared. She had lost the coin toss this time.

Splintered nails slashed once more, catching skin and muscle. She screamed again and twisted around as the skeletal monster jumped on top of her. Serap grabbed her amulet and swiped her thumb up and down across its etched surface in a frantic mess, desperate for something, anything to happen other than her face getting torn clean off.

The copper flashed hot beneath her fingers. A waft of salty waves and drying seaweed hit her first. Then, with the sound of a gasping breath, a torrent of freezing salt water poured out from the small rectangle as if from a spring in the ground. The force pushed her back in the mud, the gush like a weight slamming into her chest. Serap sucked in a heavy draught of air and puffed her cheeks full. The icy water consumed her.

The ghoul hissed, its spit burning and popping in the frigid swell of ocean. Then another wail pierced the air, ethereal and cacophonous, deeply low and shrill at the same time. A long, seal-skinned hand slithered out from her amulet, red shell nails and twitching, worm-like fingers reaching for anything it could find. Its slimy, gray arm filled the entirety of the metal and stretched and bent it to fit through, temporarily cutting off the swirling tide.

Serap shuddered and half-crawled, half-swam back on her hands, trying to escape before it reached backward and found her. But it was no use, not when the amulet sat around her neck.

Then the blood-red nails found purchase around one of the gnarled teeth of the snarling ghoul. The monster whined and squealed, but the silvery, slick hand refused to give way. In one hard yank, it dragged the ghoul forward and into the amulet like a leaf down a whirlpool. In an instant, the pour of water ceased, and the sun shone brightly once more on her salt-streaked skin.

Serap lay in the drenched grass for what felt like the closest thing to eternity she had experienced before finally lifting her head. Chupkin huddled next to her in a tiny ball, avoiding the droplets of water like humans did djinn.

"What was *that*?" she asked, still breathless as she thought about the hand of death and its vast ocean that had poured from her amulet as easily as sugar from a jar.

Then she heard snuffling. The child stumbled out of the graveyard, dry at least. The faint glow that had tinted the girl's skin had faded, making Serap wonder if she had seen it at all. Serap pulled herself to her feet, shook off what water she could—the mohair would take a full day to dry on its own—and approached the poor thing.

"Are you okay?" she asked, speaking in Turkish.

But the girl shook her head, spewing out whatever language she spoke in rapid, painful bursts, eyes full of fear. She pointed up the hill to where the Imam said the monster lived, tears streaming down her face and her voice pitched with terror. Up close and without the nuisance of a flesh-eating ghoul, the girl's state was more readily apparent. Half her hair had been singed off, her nightgown burned in several patches that flaked like paper. Worst of all, a bubbling scar marred a large portion of her face, the flesh still a tender purple and pink. Had the immortal killer done this to her?

Serap shivered.

The girl pawed Serap's coat and wept for several excruciating degrees, which left Serap feeling helpless and awkward. Then, the girl found her feet and the courage to run. Serap let her. What else could she do?

She eyed the wooded hill, knowing the chill in her blood was not from the ocean that appeared out of nowhere.

She touched the amulet around her neck once more. She would have to use that more judiciously. Calling something that would just as easily kill her as anyone else was of little use to her. Though in emergencies, it certainly offered the element of surprise.

She pushed the frayed ends of her nerves out in a strained chuckle. She had not remembered Ard being so dangerous.

"What do you think, Chupkin?" she asked, setting him on her shoulder. "Whatever's in that house couldn't possibly be worse than what we just went through, right?"

Chupkin scrunched in tight, his white mist quivering.

"You're a yellow-livered ninny, you know that?"

He twisted and slipped down her back, giving her goose pimples. She headed up the hill toward the thicket of hunter-green trees that smelled of wet cedar. Near the top, she slipped behind the treeline on the side of the road so she could approach unseen. Just in case. At the top sat the house the Imam said belonged to the blood-thirsty man. The one Pasha had said belonged to the merciless master and trapper of djinn. The one she had to find to live with Jahmil and Ayelet longer, to find a husband who loved her and not her title, to have a family of her own. To not be forgotten.

The craggy structure looked more like a ruin than a place to live; its weathered facade dripped with vines, grayish-white plaster peeled to a red brick, and curved windows completely devoid of curtains or cleaning dotted the three stories. Three peculiar boxes lay at the base of the road in direct line of sight from the house. She frowned. It made sense that a monster would be a terrible housekeeper. She pinched her skin hard at the thought. All of those warnings were just rumors. All rumors. Except for the fear in the child's eyes. She slapped her cheeks a few times to forget all about it and signed against the Evil Eye.

She would follow her plan. Find the immortal killer. Use her *human eyes*, as Pasha said, and appeal to his humanity. What person could dismiss someone who so desperately wants to live so she can love?

Now or never.

She took a step toward the front door, then turned and ran around the side. Only an idiot would walk right up to the front door of a killer. No, she would go around back and maybe through a kitchen. Her stomach rumbled pathetically at the idea, and she hurried her feet, ignoring the thought that tumbled through her mind.

Only an idiot would try to find a killer at all.

CHAPTER SIX

JAVIER

Finely julienned zucchini, red peppers, aubergine, yellow carrots, and white onion glistened in a bath of extra virgin olive oil over a low fire to his back. Javier used a small brush to baste the perfectly crispy skin of a roasted chicken in salted butter. Using a cloth to shield himself from the burning hot pan, he lifted the bird to eye level and mimed kissing it on both breasts.

"*Que linda, pollo.*" He set a sprig of fresh rosemary on top. "Forgive me for staring, my sweet little chicken. The passion that burns in my blood when I look upon you threatens to devour my very soul. You are too beautiful not to be adored, savored, worshipped by all men."

One hand reached back and tossed the veggies in the pan without looking. "But no, my crispy, juicy darling. I refuse to share you. I will consume you to keep you faithful to me." He kicked his foot back and flipped a dagger from the counter into the air, then snatched it in his hand. "Your skin is so sensual, it will sear my tender lips." He growled huskily. "But I cannot resist you any longer!"

He cut a wing from the hot bird and quickly sucked the flesh from the bone, moaning in pleasure as the juices filled his mouth. "*Dios mio.* You are even more delicious than you are beautiful."

He flicked a cloth from the top of a bowl where, inside, the silky dough had finished doubling in size. He punched it down, then sprinkled the wooden counter with flour and turned it out. Dinner was practically ready. This bread would be for breakfast tomorrow, served with eggs, roasted peppers, and the fresh butter he intended to churn before going to bed.

"*De colores, de colores se visten los campos en la primavera*," he sang, as he punched and slapped and massaged the dough. His hips swung lightly to his own music as he shaped four long ropes, then plaited them together and tucked under their ends. He brushed the loaf with some olive oil and covered it with the cloth for a second rise.

He cut the chicken into pieces and set half a breast and one leg on a lacquered wooden plate, then carefully arranged the roasted vegetables next to it. He cut a few slices of bread from an oat and wheat loaf he had made yesterday and drizzled everything delicately with saffron cream. Then he poured a small glass of grape juice, mixed with water and honey. He covered the plate with a cloche, tossed a cloth over one arm, and headed out to feed his guest.

When he had left the girl, she had stopped twitching and was looking considerably better. She may always have some scarring from her ordeal, but the potion had stopped the damage in its tracks and forced it into retreat. Javier paused in his spare bedroom and picked up the mohair blanket, the warmest he owned, and draped it over his shoulder. Perhaps if he went through his things, he would be able to find some fresh clothes for the girl. Her own were looking quite haggard. He could not in good conscience send her off to the village in such rags. He vaguely remembered a trunk stuffed with silks and linens in his basement—clothes for his sisters whenever they came for one of their impromptu visits.

"*Y por eso los grandes amores, de muchos colores me gustan a mí,*" he sang under his breath as he strode out the backdoor and through the tall grass over to the stable. He paused just outside the hanging door and took a deep breath, hoping against hope that she would still be asleep. Even though she likely would not recognize his face (his face had been shrouded when she saw him earlier), it still would be simple for her to deduce who he was from his height and the breadth of his shoulders. And who knew what damage she might cause to herself trying to get away? Besides, he was tired. He didn't have it in him to force another conversation today.

With a resigned nod, Javier turned the corner into the stable. His eyes swept the fresh hay and empty stalls.

The girl was gone.

He sighed, his shoulders slumping. He had hoped to at least feed her and let her get a little rest before she ran off. She hadn't even given him an opportunity to tell her which way to go, to avoid the ghoul-infested graveyard to the south and stick to the open path leading north towards Pozoblanco.

Señora Aldonza was supposed to come in a clear the graveyard sometime in the next week or so. It had been part of their deal over Silrok, a professional courtesy. Javier was concerned there might be a *al'Abi 'aw al'umu* ghoul hidden somewhere in the graveyard. If Señora Aldonza found one, he'd agreed to come and kill it. Theirs was a symbiotic relationship based on mutual goals. And the stern, one-eyed, rapier-wielding woman was the closest thing to a friend he had. Other than his cat, of course.

It briefly crossed his mind to go after her, but he dismissed the thought. She was well enough to run away, and so she had. His moral responsibility had been fulfilled and that was all that mattered.

Making his way back towards the kitchen door, which he had left hanging ajar, he noticed the barest hint of a shadow slip inside. Nothing so unusual in his house, yet his skin tightened. Perhaps the girl had not run off. Would she have been brave or curious enough to try to infiltrate his home? A sinking sense of panic wrapped around his heart. She could not go into the house.

He jogged lightly across the grass, careful not to spill the water or upset the plate of food. Inside the kitchen, everything looked as it had been. The table was set with his own food, a bottle of water, and two candlesticks with eternal flames burning. His copper pots and pans hung on the far wall beside the cauldron. A cannonball stove for baking bread in the corner. On another wall, a shelf stuffed with books, scrolls, and his own handwritten recipes. Nothing out of place, the red lace tablecloth as stained and askew as ever.

Javier set the plate he had made for the girl on the table across from his own and pulled out his wooden chair, which screeched on the smoke-stained stones beneath. He sat down and looked across the table at the empty space. It was always empty and usually, he paid no mind. But seeing it with a plate of food set and no one to eat it punctuated the reality of his circumstances and drew a low sigh from his throat.

He opened the cloche on his dinner, steam billowing out. Sappho hopped up on his lap, meowing for her share of the spoils. He picked her up and set her down in the chair before the plate he had made for the girl.

"A feast tonight, my ferocious feline friend."

She bit daintily into the chicken.

One last time his eyes swept the room before he shrugged, reached into his coat pocket, and took out his book—*La Celestina* by Fernando de Rojas.

He piled some chicken and vegetables onto the bread, smeared it with creme, and stuffed it all in his cheek. Then, he read aloud through the food, "*O world, world when I was younger, I thought there was some order governing you and your deeds. But now you seem to be a labyrinth of errors, a frightful desert, a den of wild beasts, a game in which men move in circles...*"

A shifting in the kitchen snatched Javier's attention. He paused and looked up, his mouth still puffed with food. A rat, perhaps? There was no shortage of those. Or perhaps something more sinister. There was no shortage of those either.

He swallowed and washed his mouth with water. "I warn you, djinn," he said, his deep voice echoing through the tiny chamber, "disturbing my dinner is not the way to win my favor."

He waited, but there came no response. Javier settled deeper into his chair and took another bite. Perhaps the sound had been the girl, stashed away somewhere. The thought made him feel hopeful, even as it pumped him with dread. Paralyzed by the memory of her screams in the fire, he did not want to get up and look for her any more than he wanted her wandering alone through his house of anomalies.

"*A stony field,*" he read aloud, "*a meadow full of serpents, a flowering but barren orchard, a spring of cares, a river of tears, a sea of suffering, a vain hope...*"

And then he saw it. The plaited loaf was uncovered, and somebody had deflated a spot as large as a fingernail with their unwelcome poke. Javier's eyes widened painfully. He closed his book and stood.

"*Bien,*" he said loudly. "Come out, girl. I've had enough of this."

No sound, no movement. His eyes swept the kitchen, lingering on every possible hiding spot.

Sappho shook her head back and forth, trying to tear through a bit of tendon. The chicken leg was thrown from the table. She hopped down after it, playing with it. Then she rushed at the cupboard. She pawed at the door, her high raspy meow crackling like a campfire.

Javier wiped his mouth with his palm and walked to the pantry door. He grasped the handle and yanked it open expecting to see the tiny, frightened, burned girl gazing back up at him with her wide brown eyes. But that was not what he found hiding in the barely tenable empty space of his overstuffed cupboard.

Brown eyes, yes. Soft and dark, staring at him as if he were a bull about to gore. He was used to that. What was alarming were the parted lips, cheeks so red you'd think somebody had rubbed them with sand. And her strange clothes—puffy pants, a white veil, an embroidered vest, the girl was lousy with silver and brass coins. They were sewn into her headdress and hung like a waterfall around her neck. A protection against djinn, perhaps?

Or, perhaps nothing so deliberate. Turkish clothes, that's what they were. Javier almost smiled when he realized it. He hadn't seen anyone who looked remotely like her in many years. And he certainly had not expected to find someone like her—a small, delicate-featured, young Turkish woman, soaked to the bone and covered in mud and grass—hiding in his kitchen.

Had she missed the mailbox too? Did he need another sign?

"*¿Por qué estás en mi casa?*" he growled, then watched as he face contorted with palpable confusion.

Based on her clothes, Javier switched to Turkish. He hadn't conversed in the language in many years. Not since he lost the person who had meant more to him than any other, the one who had taught him how to speak.

He lifted her up by her shoulders. "What are you doing in my house?"

"I'm sorry I poked your bread." She squirmed, face even more flush. "I was just hungry, and it looked so good rising there. You wouldn't kill me over bread, right?"

He held her up so he could look square at her face, her feet dangling. "This is an unforgivable breach in protocol."

Her eyes grew as wide as the dinner plates, then shrunk under furrowed brows. "Let me go, and I won't call for help. And trust me, you don't want to see what comes when I call."

His eyes narrowed at the threat. "What are you doing in my house?"

He shook her and her headdress fell back. Then she snapped her head straight, lips puckered angrily and blood creasing a corner where she must have bitten one. "Nothing. Er, bread. I said bread. I'm just hungry. And there was this ghoul and this girl, but not a girl ghoul, well it could have been. I don't know. Put me down!"

His eyes began to cross listening to her babble. Javier carried her outside and dropped her in the dirt. "Go away." He turned back towards the house.

"Wait," she cried, scrambling to her feet. Then, she made her eyes large and shiny. "Bread?"

He threw his arms out to the sides. "Does this look like a bakery to you?"

"It looks like a hoarder's den. But that doesn't mean you don't have food to share. Who gives a whole plate of food to their cat? That's just excessive. Don't you know there are people starving around here?"

"I'll feed my cat whatever I damn well please," he growled, then he shook his head hard. "I'm going to give you three seconds to get off my property."

Her face soured, and she folded her arms, not budging.

"One." He reached into his jacket and pulled out a dagger. She eyed it warily, some of the pink draining from her cheeks.

"Two." He flipped it over in his hand and caught it by the blade. Her eyes narrowed, and her feet danced back and forth. He cocked an eyebrow, drawing out the moment, waiting for her to move. She raised her eyebrows and pursed her lips flat, eyes still trained on his blade.

"Three."

"I'm going, I'm going," she cried and danced away toward the dirt road. "Where does your property end? How would I know? Am I off it yet?"

"I can still skewer you from here."

"You know," she said, still scrambling up the hill. "Your reputation as a brutal killer would be a lot more believable if you threatened traitors like Khayin instead of noble young women. It's despicable."

"Khayin?" The name fell on his shoulders like a cloak of fresh snow. A cold shiver raced down his spine as heat built in his forehead. He twirled the knife and gripped the handle tight, leather squeaking under his fist, and snapped his eyes up to meet hers. "Why don't you come back over here, senorita?" He lifted a hand to beckon her. "I think I do have some bread to spare, after all."

Her face drained of color and her wide eyes barely fit on her face. She stopped dancing around, spun, and pelted off toward the forest.

Javier cracked his neck and ran after her.

CHAPTER SEVEN

SERAP

Serap skidded down the side of the hill, slipping in more infernal mud as she made a wild dash for the trees. Why did she talk so much when she was scared? And why hadn't he shared his bread? And why did saying Khayin's name put a murderous look in his eye? And isn't that what she had been hoping for?

Most of all, if he wanted Khayin dead as she did, why was he trying to kill her?

All questions that would be impossible to ask with a slit throat. She jumped over a hollowed-out log rife with fungi. Glanced back. Tripped on climbing ivy and fell into a sickly-sweet bush of honeysuckles.

Iron-soaked blood coated her lip where she had bitten it earlier. She scrambled up and ran helter-skelter through the overgrown brush, checking behind her over and over again so she could watch the murderer gain ground. He was tall, wide, like a bear only so much more menacing. A drakonte. Yes, that's what he was, a drakonte of a man. His dark hair, nearly black eyes, and curly beard made him look all the more terrifying. He didn't need to run to keep up. Just to take huge, fast steps on his massive legs.

Chupkin slithered out of her shirt and whisked away the sweat building on her neck.

She turned to check the shadows for the monster. Giant hands reached for her. She screamed.

"I'm off your property, I'm off your property," she managed to squeak out as his fingers wrapped around her forearm hard enough to bruise.

He yanked her up by the arm so her feet were off the ground, then threw her over his shoulder.

"Too late for that."

She punched his back, a bee sting to a bear, then kicked her legs as hard as she could.

"Are you going to cut me up for dinner? Baste me like you did that bird? With some saffron? Rosemary? And you haven't even fattened me up first. You're an infidel who's going to pay for laying your hands so brutally upon a sheikha of the Shihalan court!"

He thumped her with his shoulder. Her body bounced up, then smacked back down, knocking the breath out of her.

Serap seethed. She screamed and yelled and called for help until her throat ran dry, the thick and empty woods absorbing her pleas. She was tempted to rub her copper amulet right then and there but feared he would pull a seal-skinned monster or harpy out of the amulet before one could pull him in. He wound his way deftly through the forest and back toward his stuffy house, where the heat of her anger was swept away in chills.

Would he really kill her?

His broad shoulder pressed against her queasy stomach like a giant stone, his heart just as hard.

They arrived back at the house. He carried her through the front door, kicking it shut as he stomped in. The iron chain on the lock swung up and slid itself shut, the invisible fingers of magic at play. He was no ordinary human, either.

Serap yelped and pinched his skin through his shirt, flailing as much as possible. It made no difference, for as they entered the house, her screams dimmed as if they had been caught in a barrel of cider. Muffled and sloshy. Then she realized why.

Books.

On the walls. The stairs. The tables. Stacks on the floor, and climbing all the way up to the very corners of the ceiling.

"Murderers don't read," she said, shocked numb at her capture. "At least, I hadn't thought so."

The Immortal Killer said nothing as he tramped up the stairs, which too were lined with stacks of books. His huge, muscular body weaved through them nimbly without knocking any over. It made her terribly mad, the fact that he could so easily navigate a literary disaster while carrying her over his shoulder. How many times had he done this before? Hundreds of answers slipped through her mind and stole her next breath. If attacking the man had no effect, then she'd try attacking something else.

Serap shoved the next stack of books they passed and watched with glee as it tumbled over. If he was going to kill her, she'd take as many books as she could with her.

"Why you..." he growled and repositioned higher on her shoulder.

The scraggly, dappled cat from the kitchen hopped out from behind a stack and followed them up the stairs, complaining loudly all the while.

Chupkin flinched and dove from his hiding place on the nape of her neck and into her pocket.

"It's just a cat, Chupkin," she groaned. "So much for a guard dog."

She grabbed at another pile of books near the top of the stairs and shoved it down the steps, spines cracked and pages bent.

He growled and squeezed her hard. Pain wove between her ribs, coming out in a cough. They reached the top of the stairs and turned down a long, dark hallway, this too crowded with stacks of scrolls and leather-bound codices. He kicked the door at the end open, stomped inside, and threw her down.

Dust puffed up around her, but whatever she landed on was soft. The room was pitch-dark, musty, and cold. She jumped up and made a beeline for the door, trying to dodge around his tree-like legs. He caught her with one hand and threw her back on the mattress. Iron coated her tongue once more, and she wiped the blood from her mouth with the back of her sleeve.

A stab of fear shot like ice through her veins. She had heard stories of terrible men who did terrible things to women in dark rooms on beds made of hay. She scrambled to the back corner and slapped a hand over her chest. The coins Bakr Amca gave her would be useless against this hulk of a human, but maybe the hard edges of her rings would bite into his skin. She would not let herself be taken this way; on a dusty bed by an awful man without a hint of romance or even human decency. And especially not before she had had her first proper kiss with anyone in general.

"Don't you touch me," she said, a tremble wiping out any confidence in her voice.

She clutched her amulet. She would use it to defend her honor, seal claw or not. He snatched her hand in his, bending back her fingers until she couldn't keep her hold on the amulet any longer. Each tug sent pain splintering through her joints. The delicate gold chain around her neck snapped.

"No!" Serap grabbed at his hands. Rough, calloused hands. Hands that were so much more capable than hers.

He pushed her back so her shoulder hit the wall. A web of pain shot across her spine. He lifted the amulet to his eyes and sneered, then stuffed it in his pocket.

Serap sunk into a heap, true fear bubbling up for the first time. She had no way to call home. To escape. To ever be free again. In one cruel yank, he had taken her future from her. She had never stood a chance.

She covered her face with her hands. "So you're just going to lock me up in your stupid tower? That's the most cliche thing I've ever heard of. The oldest trick in the book, which you should know because you own a million of them."

She wanted to say more, to rant and rage and threaten to burn his precious library to the ground, but it wouldn't make a difference.

His fingers went to his temples. "Do not fret, señorita," he said, his voice so deep it shook the coins on her necklace.

He walked to the window and slapped closed a few iron latches, which locked into place on their own. Walking back to the door, he grabbed the handle and opened it a crack. Light streamed inside, illuminating one-half of his face so she could see his cruel grin. "The creativity is all in what I do to you while you're here."

A chill ran up her spine and pooled with the hunger gnawing at her stomach. She couldn't help but pull her knees to her chest.

"You should start by feeding me," she said in a bitter whisper. "Unless you're a complete barbarian."

He cocked his head to one side and narrowed his eyes at her. Then he stomped out of the room, slamming and locking the door behind him. His footsteps faded down those creaky, old stairs. When she could hear them no longer, she jumped up and pounded her fists on the splintery wood.

"Bread!" she yelled one last time, then pressed her back against the door. Her stomach rumbled with hunger and fear clung to her clammy skin. "Oh, Chupkin." She sighed. "If I had just refrained from poking that stupid loaf of shiny dough, I would still be hiding in the kitchen, eating preserves and filling my belly."

Chupkin poked out from where he had been hiding in her clothes, his light weak and timid. Then she groaned and banged her head softly against the door, straightening her headband he had so coarsely knocked free.

The Killer was indecent. Disrespectful. He didn't honor her religion any more than her age, her gender, her station, or her growling stomach. Chupkin curled around her finger, pulsing gently to comfort her.

"He's a brute, indeed, Chupkin. And also a thief. And to think I had given him the benefit of the doubt. Ungrateful."

Serap stumbled in the dark toward the window, knocking over books and hitting the edge of the bed so her knee smarted. She tried the iron latches. When they didn't move, she scowled. She couldn't get them to budge with her weak, little muscles. And that fanned the flames in her blood further. If she were a djinn, she could just pop out of this stupid prison. But her humanity—which she now believed The Immortal Killer had none of—once again made her useless.

She couldn't just sit around and do nothing. If she was going to die early, at least she would do so trying to change fate. He hadn't killed her. Not yet. For a man with such a terrible reputation, that had to mean something.

Serap tried pacing the floor, but there were stacks of books everywhere and no light to see by. When she could stand it no longer, she set to work shoving half of them over. That only made a worse mess of the floor. She sighed and started plucking them up one at a time, throwing each against the wall on the other side of the room with a loud *thud*. Chupkin clung to the cuff of her jacket, illuminating the cover of each book before she hurled it. *Cantar de Mio Cid*? Boo. *The Canterbury Tales*? Gug. *The Odyssey*? What were these titles anyway?

She picked up a book of poems by someone named Sulaymon ibn Gabirol and hesitated. Her one literary soft spot was poetry. She just couldn't deny the romance of it, collecting and memorizing her favorites so she had them if ever the occasion arose.

It hadn't.

A bone-chilling rattle shook the floor behind the bed.

The hair on the back of Serap's neck rose, sending chills down her spine. She dropped the book and eased closer, one foot at a time. The Imam had mentioned haunted beings living in the house. How haunted was he talking? Curiosity raised its tandem head. She swallowed but kept going. Things really couldn't get any worse.

The scratching scrapes continued like a brass lock being forced open. A hint of red glimmered through a knot in the wood. She flinched and chewed her top lip. Did the monster of a man really keep evil spirits locked up in his house?

Serap dropped to her knees and crawled the last few inches toward the red glow, tempted to put her eye flush with the floor and get a better look but terrified the glow belonged to some nefarious creature. One that would burn her flesh or steal her soul or any number of horrid things she simply couldn't imagine. Wherever on Ard she had landed had to be the armpit of the world; dank, dark, wretched, and hidden.

But finding something out would be better than waiting for that cruel cretin to come barging in so he could throw her around and bruise her arm and steal more of her things. She should have listened to the Imam. Allah have mercy on her soul. In the meantime...

She coaxed out Chupkin with a curl of her finger.

"Go see what it is," she said and pointed at the hole.

Chupkin recoiled.

"Come on, you let a murderer seize me and throw me into a dusty, lumpy prison. The least you can do is go see what's making the creepy sound."

He crunched in even tighter.

She sighed and lifted him in front of her eyes. "Please? I don't know what else to do. I'm not getting out by myself. I'm too... human. I can't do it. The imam mentioned screams coming from the house. If there are things lurking in the house that hate him just as much as we do, maybe they can help."

Chupkin flickered before extending a tiny tendril and slipping from her hand like a child testing the waters at the beach. He flicked white in her direction.

"Good boy," she said with an exhale. "Thank you."

His wispy glow circled the knot three times before falling inside like he had been sucked through. She waited. And waited. And counted to ten, ten times. When he still didn't return, panic rose in her throat.

"Chupkin?"

Silence.

She clawed at the board and raked her fingers against the wood, splinters stabbing under her nails.

"Chupkin!"

She stumbled around the shadowy room, searching the pressing dark for something to pry the wood up. A drop of moonlight illuminated a large book of maps in the corner, its cover sturdy and hard. She grabbed it from the pile, sneezing from the dust. Her heart raced. Sweat coated her palms. What was happening to Chupkin? What had she done?

Serap threw the atlas open on the ground, then placed one foot on the crinkly pages painted in delicate reds and blues and golds. She grabbed the cover with her hands and *rrrrripped* it from its spine, then tossed the book carcass to the side. Fingers trembling, she shoved the corner of the cover in the gap between the two planks. With a great deal of shimmying and pushing, she pushed the cover through to the other side. Then she leaned against it like a lever, raising the board until she could get her fingers underneath it.

Once she had a firm hold, she yanked, using her body weight to help break free the nails that held it into place. In a shattering *pop*, the board splintered and broke free. She fell back with a *thump*.

"Chupkin?" She trembled, voice a whisper.

Serap crawled toward the dark abyss. She took an oversized breath for courage and leaned over the hole. Dark. Dark. Dark. Then a flash of red. Her heart both stopped and raced in a painful cacophony. She flinched, hands flying to her face.

Nothing.

She moved her fingers to peek.

The light swirled in mid-air, like an iris gone mad, looping around and around in an unseen eye. Equal parts horrified and painfully curious, she reached a finger toward it, pulled back, then reached again.

Chupkin burst out in a flash of white from an unseen corner, whipping and wrapping himself around her face. She tumbled backward.

"Chupkin," she gasped, swatting him away. "You startled me, you wretched little thing."

He settled at last, his light throbbing like the gentle pulse of the third moon. Serap peered again into the dark, but the red eye had gone. Even with all the magic she had seen and experienced in Qaf and with the magically diabolical Köle on Ard, the glowing eye made her heart twitch like a flea-bitten Elmaran two-headed goat.

Then an unpleasant trickle of desperation dripped as sweat from her neck and down her clavicles. She sank onto her knees, shoulders slouching in defeat. "I've been foolish, coming to Ard by myself. Haven't I, Chupkin?."

His sweet, white light pulsed gently and brushed against the corner of her eyes, wiping away the wet beginnings of desperation. His tenderness struck something deep inside her. She had come all this way so she could be with the people she loved forever. She couldn't give up yet. She wouldn't. But what did she have to work with?

Serap settled back, tugging on her headscarf. "Khayin obviously means something to the Immortal Killer. That had to be a connection we can exploit, don't you think, Chupkin? If I can't appeal to his humanity, maybe I can appeal to the murderer in him. It is why we've come in the first place, isn't it? To get the evil killer to kill something evil?"

Chupkin twirled into a corkscrew, releasing like a rag recently rung out.

She pursed her lips. "I think it could work. I just need to find a way to reason with him. Even if he is rude. And rough. And gruff. And owns a very many weapons that he throws about without getting hurt. So what if he's also cruel, and unkind, and alarmingly good at hunting girls down in the woods?"

Her stomach tightened into a ball smaller than Chupkin as her run through the woods, sweat dripping and heart pounding, resurfaced in her mind.

"His eyes had looked like a lion's, Chuppy." She shivered. "Glittering in the moonlight. I was certain I was done for, so how I sit here with you now is a mystery to me. The only thing not evil about him is that his food smells so good."

Her stomach pained with insatiably greedy hunger, and she pressed a hand to it to keep the rumble from bursting.

"Oh. He also owns a cat."

Chupkin stretched in a wavy line, his shape much like a curved eyebrow.

She shrugged with a tiny grin. "I don't know why that's on the not-evil list, but it feels right, so I'm going to leave it there. I certainly won't be including his ungodly amount of books. Allah, he's a hoarder. How have I managed to track down the world's most boring killer?"

Serap plucked up the nearest book—a delicate number with carefully inked calligraphy that included pictures of trolls hiding within each vowel. She leafed through each page, rubbing the tiny faces with her thumb in Chupkin's dim, white light.

"Not that I hate books. In fact, I'd call my relationship with them decidedly neutral. I might even like them more if 'Abi hadn't forced me to study a very great deal of them about Ard and Arabic and the history of Shihala."

She frowned and set the book down. Thinking of Jahmil scratched at her heart. He had done so much for her, but he also refused to let her grow and be.

"Too much of anything is a bad thing, don't you think, Chupkin? Like honey. Too much will make you sick. Or parental oversight. It'll drown even the most obedient fish." She nudged and wiggled her legs between two piles of scrolls. "Books are another prime example. And the killer crossed the line of too many two stories down."

She pouted and eyed the dark hole again, then tilted her head to the side, breathing in the dank scent of stale air. Convinced the red eye was wholly absent, she reached her hand in the gap in the floorboards and felt around. Sticky spider webs. The tickle of an actual spider that she flung off with a shudder. Dust. And room. Enough room that, with a good many more planks removed, she could form a small crawl space between. A space she could shimmy through. Maybe once inside, she could remove more planks and find a way to the next floor down.

Then... what?

She could steal a chance to roam the killer's house and find out his secrets. Secrets she could use to leverage him into doing what she wanted.

Serap stared into the inky crevice for a while longer, then grabbed the cover from the map book and set to work.

All she needed was her will and her wisp. She wasn't just a weak human. She was a sheikha. A Shihalan. An Edirnian. A Turk. A Muslim. And a woman.

If the last one alone couldn't solve everything, then she'd never eat again.

CHAPTER EIGHT

JAVIER

Javier slammed his office door behind him and flung himself into his favorite chair.

All he had wanted all day was to sit in this chair with its worn armrests and familiar stains, but after everything he had endured, he couldn't enjoy it.

An eternal candle burned on his desk, one of many honorariums he'd received through the years. It never went out nor consumed any wax, and its flame grew and faded counter to the sun so the space was always efficiently lit. He had dozens of them.

Papers and scrolls were piled by every wall, the bookshelves and files overflowing. A large tree grew from a small pot on one wall. It had but one branch that twisted in on itself like the shell of a nautilus. An enchanted calendar that kept time with Ard's only moon as it grew and shed from month to month. The curled branch was sectioned like the scales of a snake, each representing one day. Javier's imprecise writing covered the blank bits of wood—several colors of ink and different symbols to keep his hectic schedule clear.

Sappho leapt up onto his shoulders and dug her claws into him affectionately, kneading through his muscles and down to the bone as if that would make her perch softer. He winced as her nails nicked his skin. It was past time he gave them a trim.

He reached up and grabbed her, cradling her with one arm and rubbing her ears. He searched for calm in the moment, but the girl he'd just captured was still screaming in terror in his mind.

"That was not good. Why did you let me do that?"

She purred and pressed her face into his palm.

"You're supposed to help me control my temper. That's why I let you stay when I found you scrounging in the barn all those years ago. But all you do is complain that I don't feed you enough."

She peered through him with her cold, yellow eyes. He grunted and gave her another pet. "I don't even know what's in that room. What I've put in there, or what might have crept in while I wasn't looking."

A chill rushed up his spine. He dropped the cat and stood, pacing in a tiny circle in front of his chair.

"I have to get her out."

Sappho looked up at him and cocked her head to one side.

"But she knows Khayin. And he is the most conniving, unpredictable, evil son of a snake to never die." Javier clenched his aching fingers into fists. "She's either here to steal something or to try to force my hand in some way."

Javier looked down at Sappho again, desperate for any kind of input.

A cold, distant voice scraped up his spine like jagged fingernails. "I'll kill her for you."

Javier crushed his eyes shut. This was all he needed.

The specter loomed at the edge of the room—tall and lean. Light passed through him as dust before a window. He waved in and out of existence with every flicker of candlelight.

A ghost, or so Javier had thought when he first saw it, but that was not the case. This was not the ghost of anyone who had died.

The djinn's skin was jewel green, his eyes a fiery purple. He wore no shirt, just an array of lacy black tattoos that swirled up his arms and over his chest. It looked something like Arabic calligraphy, except that Javier could not read it. His ears grew long out to the sides. Four massive horns protruded from his skull, curling to the front like a ram, but more delicate and certainly more sophisticated, inlaid with large, smooth black stones.

No djinn had horns anymore, though legend stated they all had once. Long, long ago before the Nine Kingdoms formed. When djinn had the power to wander freely wherever they pleased, beings forged of pure fire. They were free beings that could move and go wherever they pleased, even into heaven to listen to angels speak of the future.

That was before the djinn of Qaf intermarried with humans and lost their purity. The King of Elm and Iblis himself were said to be the last of the pure race. A race of immortals.

This King of Kings who had been alive since before Adam was born didn't look more than twenty. His face was also the most famous in all of Qaf, instantly recognizable for his twisty black horns. His seal, which looked like a stylized approximation of his own face, secured the value of the paper dinar used as currency in seven of the Nine Kingdoms, as well as notarizing virtually every contract.

More than a thousand years had passed since anyone had seen him in person, even in his own court. The specter that stood before Javier was the most anyone ever saw. Incorporeal, yet able to wield all the king's unfathomable magic and interact with the physical world however he pleased. He was untouchable. Invincible. Not even Javier could end his infernal life, which he would have if he could. Because no sinner in the history of souls had ever sinned like the King of Eastern Elm.

The djinn king crossed one leg over the other as he settled into Javier's favorite chair. "We both know you lack the stomach to kill that girl."

Javier growled and clenched his fists. "Get out of my chair."

The king smiled and dipped his head, then stood. "I could make this whole mess go away. All of it. If you're prepared to make a deal."

Javier chuckled, his shoulders shaking. "That has to be your least appetizing proposal yet. You really are scraping the bottom of the proverbial barrel."

"My dear Don DeMario." The king always insisted on referring to Javier by his proper title, which precisely nobody ever did. He was the Immortal Killer. *El Asesino Inmortal. Alqatil Alkhalid.* To his face, most people just called him some version of the word *Sir.*

Don DeMario, that was his father.

"We have been having this same conversation for years now," the king sighed. "If you truly tire of it, as you ceaselessly protest, then there is one option open to you that will solve absolutely everything."

Javier rolled his eyes and drummed his fingers on the desk. "Don't you have a kingdom to squeeze the life out of, you litigious vampire?"

The king smiled indulgently, as he always did. For years the bright green bastard had been barging into Javier's home uninvited, sometimes as often as twice a week, and never once had Javier succeeded in getting under his skin.

"Barbaric societies respect the rule of force. Civilizations respect the rule of law. Without law, there is nothing."

"The just do not need laws to force them to act justly." Javier scarcely had the mind for yet another socio-political debate with the eternal lawyer. And yet he could never seem to stop himself. "And sinners will always find a way to sin."

"Not in Qaf. Not with my Seal guiding every contract and keeping the dishonesty of mortals in check."

"Ha!" Javier spat, then flopped down in his chair. At just that moment a thump came from above, drawing his attention back to problems that lay much closer to home.

"Khayin sent her," he said, even though he knew the king would offer no assistance without demanding quid pro quo, and there was only ever one thing he wanted. "A noble of Shihala? But she's human. I don't understand."

"I know who she is. And I know why she's here." The king rolled up his long delicate fingers as he leaned his hip on Javier's desk. "I'd be happy to let you in on my information. If..."

"No."

"Don DeMario, be reasonable."

"No." His fingers gripped his armrests until they squeaked. "How many times do I have to tell you no before you leave me in peace? En Español, *no*. In Arabic, *raqm*. In Turkish, *hayır*. In Greek, όχι. In Latin, *minime*."

"I still feel as if you are not fully comprehending the paucity of my position in my current circumstances. For if you did, surely the moral code of which you are so proud would compel you to come to my aid, even if you continue to dislike me personally."

"Oh, I will always dislike you personally."

"You must appreciate, Don DeMario, that you are the only being in both of Allah's worlds with your unique abilities. You have a responsibility..."

"You dare condescend to me about my own gift?" Javier tongued one of his canines in irritation. "My unique abilities are precious and in high demand. Only the most deserving *and* the luckiest will be chosen. Never the most persistent."

"Allow me to recap my situation one more time." The king showed the most condescending smile Javier had ever seen. It practically dripped with bitter candy. "The Queen of Western Elm..."

"Your ex-wife disliking you is not a good enough reason to kill her."

He clenched his fingers slowly into a fist. Though at times the specter of the king may have looked like a mirage, his physical form was anything but. He could fight and use magic. He could also summon the largest, most expensive army in two worlds with a snap of his fingers. But what would be the point? It was part of the Bahamut's blessing that Javier's gift could only be used of his own free will. Incapacitating him, tying a sword to his head, and using him as a battering ram would not get the job done.

Or at least, Javier had gone to great lengths to spread the rumor that such was the case. The truth was, his power would leave him once his short human life came to an end. All the more reason for djinn from all five winds to harass him relentlessly. His entire lifespan was a drop in the bucket to those fire-wielding, rainbow-colored freaks.

Javier looked up at the king and hardened his face. "Get out of my house."

A loud crash sounded, shaking the ceiling and sending tiny puffs of dust into the air. Javier lifted his eyes. It sounded like somebody was moving around the furniture and tearing apart the walls.

"¡*Qué mierda*!"

The king laughed and leaned deeper into his hand. "You've invited a giant termite into your home. Are you sure you wouldn't like me to exterminate it for you?"

"*Madre.*" Javier rushed up the stairs back toward the room where he'd locked up the woman. Unhooking the chain, he slapped open the door to see the girl standing in a small hole where she had ripped up several floorboards. She'd also knocked over a stack of his books and was using the cover of one to pry up the wooden slabs. Was that his Atas of Cathay?

"*¿Qué estás haciendo?*"

Her eyes snapped up. He glared before he remembered that he'd been speaking to her in Turkish earlier.

It was his mother's language. He'd spoken it growing up at least as much as Spanish, but tonight was the first time he had uttered a single word in five years. Not since he lost the one who named him.

The full reality of that hit him all at once, and his eyes unfocused. The language had tasted like sugar on his tongue—a whisper of childhood and home, a time when things were simpler. Better. Or at least they had felt that way because his mother was there with him, sitting across from him in the candlelight. Reading in silence together, laughing together, discussing everything under the sun. Most of the time, he didn't think about it much, but looking at the girl in her Turkish clothes, and earlier, listening to her little voice so lightly speaking the language of his youth—it brought everything crashing over him.

He felt sick. Hot lumps compacted in his guts, sensations of loss, misery, and white-hot fury. He wanted to run away and vomit out everything he had eaten, then curl into a little ball on his bed and spend the night remembering when somebody had loved him.

Clenching his teeth, he forced it all down. He had more urgent problems.

But his *anne*'s eyes were in his mind now. Dark brown, oversized. Shining with mischief and unanswered questions. And the girl's eyes partially hidden under her veil were the same color. The same size. They caught the light the same way.

He looked away and tried to forget. But now that he'd seen it, he could not unsee it.

"*Onu yere koy,*" he finally managed to say. "Put that down."

She glanced between him and the hole she stood in, then dove, wriggling and twitching to slip away from him and into the floor. He snatched the back of her shirt and tugged, but she didn't come up smoothly, like she was either stuck or holding onto something. She kicked against his grasp, her heel landing a strike on his chin.

Tasting blood, his head snapped back, but he grabbed her ankle and tugged.

"There is nowhere to go, *señorita*."

Her voice was muffled under the floorboards. "I plan to determine that for myself."

Javier sighed and shook his head, feeling utterly ridiculous and not liking it one bit. He held her one foot high in the air, her head dipped under the floorboards. Heaven only knew what kind of mess was down there—spider webs and rat droppings at the very least. He tugged lightly on her ankle, checking to see if she would come up freely. She still held tight. He could rip her out with sheer force, but that might damage the floor further, not to mention her bones.

He tugged. "Let go."

"No."

"Let go now before I yank you out and break both your arms in the process."

Her muscles tensed then released, body going slack in his hand. He pulled her up from under the floorboards and lifted her in the air by one leg like a trapped rabbit.

She watched him, eyes round and full of fear. Then she covered her face with her hands. A tremor wracked her chest. The tiny, submissive, frightened gesture tore at his senses, but he pushed that back and focused his eyes forward. He marched through the door and carried her down the stairs, holding her far away from his body and high up so she wouldn't smack her head or knock over any more of his books.

Eventually, she stole a peek between her fingers, her gaze sliding up and down his frame. She wriggled her foot in his hand. When she spoke, it was quieter than the turn of a page. "You're hurting me."

Javier's heart twisted. With a sigh that hurt his intestines, he flipped her around in his arms and threw her over his shoulder, a position that would be altogether more comfortable for both of them. Then he continued towards the door that led to the basement.

"Why are you doing this?" she asked between pinched breaths. "You didn't want me here. You told me to leave. So why? Why..."

That was a good question. His jaw twitched as he considered whether he should answer. He didn't want her here. He wanted her gone. And there was a part of him that wished she had just left when he told her to. But now he knew she had been by Khayin, he needed to know why.

Arguably more importantly, he wanted to understand *how*. How was Khayin able to project his power beyond the walls of Ashkult—the infamous prison where magic cannot enter—through the veil, across worlds, and into his house? How had Khayin even hired this young Turkish woman with eyes that sparkled just so?

Had she been sent to seduce him? Surely the rubbery-skinned immortal djinn knew him better than that. The girl herself was ostensibly perfect from the color of her eyes to the language on her tongue. But Javier was fundamentally un-seducible. It was one of his superpowers, or so his cousin and other shipmates had said when their vessel washed up on the island of the *jazirat aljamila*. Javier was the only one who had stayed aboard and never run the risk of having his voice box or testicles eaten by a siren. He'd had to save all of those lovesick idiots that day. They had praised him for his iron will.

He alone among men was un-seducible.

But the truth was, he'd simply never had any interest in women. He'd never had a seducible interest in anything, except food.

Was Khayin desperate enough to waste his money hiring a seductress from the Weave so she could come into his house and... what? Poke his bread?

Why else send a young woman who was so easy on the eyes?

He needed more time to think. He needed to convince her to stop running so he could get answers out of her.

He came to the iron-plated door and had to fumble in his pocket for a key before drawing it open.

A small line of stone stairs led down into musty darkness. He carried her down, past rows of chests and barrels filled with old honorariums and gifts from his clients, to a tiny cell he kept empty for such occasions. He'd only ever used it once before and had been hoping not to have to use it again. But he could not tolerate her tearing up his floor and ripping the cover off his two-hundred-year-old atlases.

When he paused before the iron bars, she gasped at the sight. Then he drew the door open and shoved her into the tiny cell.

The second she hit the floor, she scurried to the back corner and scrunched into a tight ball, whispering something into her shirt. Her wide eyes watched him over her knees, catching a hint of light that filtered through the open door at the top of the stairs.

"How long? How long until you..." She turned away, resting her cheek on her clenched shoulder.

He didn't answer.

She looked so fragile and small, innocent and unassuming. But looks can be deceiving. Some of the most dangerous things come equipped with long eyelashes and tiny voices. And if she was a seductress, she knew exactly what she was doing looking at him like that.

Javier locked the cell door, then turned and jogged up the stairs.

"I'm hungry." Her tiny, muffled voice chased him. "Please."

His eyes slid over his shoulder, wanting to look down at her. But that was exactly what she wanted him to do. He shook his head and stomped upstairs, slamming the door behind him.

The braided loaf he had made earlier still rested on the counter, the little dimple staring at him like a curse. If he didn't bake it soon, it would be over-proofed and ruin the texture.

Sighing, he sat down beside the oven and stoked the embers to life.

She was hungry. That could be useful.

CHAPTER NINE

SERAP

Serap sat still, arms wrapped painfully tight around her legs, her knuckles aching from the force. Chupkin pooled by one of her ears, petting her head gently in wispy strokes. Memories of the slavers' prison she had spent several days in when she was a child crept into her periphery, and she chomped her teeth together to get them back. She didn't want to think about how scared she was then, how terrified she was now. So instead, she hummed, starting with the first song cousin Balian had taught her and through all the others she could remember.

For twenty-three songs, she stayed like that, her limbs frozen in fear and her heart burning with anger. Anger at Pasha for ditching her in Ard. Anger at herself for lying to Jahmil and Ayelet. And anger at the murderer for turning out to be exactly what everyone said he would be. The rumors about her were untrue, but this blood-thirsty barbarian deserved every disdainful and hate-filled exclamation he got.

Shivering on the cold stone floor, she began to drift into a fitful, exhausted sleep when a glimmer of red once more caught her eye. She started, crushing her back against the wall as each bone in her spine crunched from the force. Chupkin vanished into her headdress. The red pupil hovered on the other side of the bars, eye level if she had been standing. It focused its crimson light on her for but a breath, then twisted side-to-side in a fit of seeming paranoia. It blinked into darkness.

"Don't go," she cried, then clapped a hand over her mouth. She did not want that thing to stay. It reeked of evil magic; the kind of spell even Pasha would be hesitant to take on. "Pasha," she growled under her breath.

"Yes?"

Serap flinched, darting her gaze into every corner. Nothing. But she swore she heard the voice clear as the black of fear in djinn eyes.

"Pasha?" she whispered once more.

"Serap? Is that you?" Pasha's voice sounded like a call upon a wind-swept bluff, her face nowhere in sight. "Where are you? Are you okay?"

Serap wet her tongue to reply when Pasha's voice faded like a coin down a well.

"Pasha?"

Silence.

"Chupkin?"

His dim, beautiful light wriggled out from under one of her arms, and she released some of the tension that had been aching in her back. He would not leave her.

"I'm not going mad, am I? You heard her, too?"

Chupkin blinked a few times, and she released a sigh.

"What kind of person lives in a haunted house?"

Chupkin spiraled tight then puffed out wide, casting a soft light on the dirty floor and the rough bars of the cell. The air smelled of wet hay and tasted of dust.

"Do you think the spirits in this place are all the immortals he's killed? Maybe he can't actually kill them. Maybe he just cuts them up into tiny little pieces and scatters them about, keeping the best parts in his home as trophies?" The damp cold of the dungeon turned to dagger-sharp icicles prickling the back of her neck. Did he keep trophies of his other victims? Would he of her? Her eye, maybe? Or the ankle he had nearly twisted tossing her about with as much regard as a wolf does a carcass?

A chuckle sounded to her right, and she tripped over herself jumping away. Then a voice smooth as apricot cider and just as sickly sweet said, "*Silly child, silly child, hunting a hunter.*"

"Who are you?" she asked in a shaky voice, though she wanted to ask *what*? All she could see through the bars was a shadow of a being, which made no sense in the complete dark. Like Chupkin's light only bluer, dimmer, and with a flicker of something sharper inside.

"*Far more bears are caught with blood than they are with honey.*"

She swallowed hard, the nothing in her throat scratching down the dryness. "Go away." She clenched her hand and added, "Now."

"*What is now? What is then? If you can't live forever? The question, child, is how to bend the will of a raging monster?*"

Serap pressed her frigid hands to her cheeks and shook her head. She did not talk to evil, to be called a child by an ephemeral being, but its smooth words trickled down her throat with the illusion of water, and she wanted desperately to drink. She still had to find a way to gain the help of the man who had so savagely thrown her down here without knowing her name or why she came and not caring in the least.

"I'm listening," she said, and Chupkin slid down her spine to hide in the dip of her waist.

"*A family, a home, a land. He lost it all and now demands blood for blood in repayment.*"

"But what's that got to do with me? Or Khayin?" She was still curious why the name had sent such blackness into the Killer's already dark eyes.

"*What would it to any man?*"

She thought only a moment before raising her shoulder in a shrug.

"*Justice,*" the voice hissed.

"What am I supposed to do?"

"*Live.*"

"That's it?" she asked, voice flat.

"*You shall see, you shall see. But now you'll give a gift to me.*"

She frowned and tugged at the cuffs of her jacket. Of course, he'd want something in return. Otherwise, she wouldn't be worth his time.

"What is it?" She ducked her head and cringed, envisioning terrible deeds and acts of horror.

"*Read.*"

"Read what?"

The door at the top of the rickety stairs smacked open, illuminating the leviathan frame of her kidnapper. The hunter. The bear. The Immortal Killer.

Footsteps echoed as he plodded down into the dungeon, the light from the torch in his hand casting long shadows on the wall. His own shadow cast through the rusty bars, sweeping over her like a chill. The cold reached her bones and sent memories shivering through her of the last prison she had been in as a young girl. Slavers. Chains. Beasts and magic. And then one small kitten who could not save her this time.

She pulled into a tight ball, eyeing her captor. His body was knit with corded muscles—shoulders, chest, arms, and thighs—that showed clearly under his loose, black clothing even in the dark. His long, dark brown beard was well-kempt, his hair cut short and slicked back on the sides. The torchlight illuminated his face, revealing dark, serious eyebrows and clear, caramel-colored skin. His large brown eyes sparkled like water in sunlight. So soft they looked unnatural as if they belonged to an entirely different face.

A smell assaulted her senses, and she forgot everything else—freshly baked bread, sweet berries, coffee, even the faint hint of butter.

The killer sat down on the bottom step some five cubits away from her cell door and laid the large plate of food on the stone beside him.

She nearly fell against the bars, it smelled so good. Her stomach groaned in agony, wishing it could rip itself from her body and gorge on the food that mocked her. She flicked her eyes back and forth between the red of the berries and the brute of a man. The sheen of butter and the bearded scowl that guarded it.

"What do you want?" she asked, hoping there was something, anything she could give him for a bite of bread other than her soul. She hadn't been this hungry since she was ten, before Jahmil took her to Qaf.

Her captor reached into his jacket and took out a long, silver dagger that he then used to cut a thick slice of bread. The blade was so sharp the soft loaf didn't even bow under the weight. He smeared the bread in butter and took a bite.

"I'll ask the questions if you don't mind," he said through a full mouth.

Serap flashed her eyes in anger, wishing she had fire to go with it. She glanced at the corner, but the presence had dissipated, leaving her with only the Killer. The sting of hunger helped quell the sniveling fear in the back of her brain.

"Fine. But I want some of that bread."

"We'll see." He picked up a strawberry the size of a child's fist and sunk his teeth into its flesh. Her arid throat stung just watching the red juice dribble down into the curls of his beard. "Let's start off easy. What is your name?"

She ground her teeth, sizing him up and finding nothing she didn't know already. But a performer could neither divulge too much nor give too little. She must walk the line carefully. And with how he had sneered at her amulet and Khayin's name with the fire of hate, she knew mentioning magic would be a terrible idea. She needed his help, yes, but she also needed to live.

"Serap."

"Very good." He took the lid from a decorative porcelain container and spooned some sugar into a small coffee cup, then stirred and took a sip. "And where are you from?"

More teeth grinding. "Edirne."

"Edirne," he repeated, sounding pleased. "That is a very beautiful city, and quite far from here. However did you find your way to *España*?"

"It is a beautiful city," she sighed, wishing she had gone to see Balian and cousin Yousef instead of coming here. But she wasn't sure how to answer the next question. By boat? Did wherever España was have a coast? By caravan? Or did the local leaders ban trade with foreigners? The mosque looked neglected, though not abandoned. She bit her lip. "I did not find my way here."

"I wouldn't linger over semantics if I were you." He took another bite of bread. "It is a game for which I have little patience."

"Maybe I would think better if my stomach wasn't howling."

He watched her for a while, the torchlight sparkling orange in his eyes. Then he lifted the knife and cut another slice of bread. She couldn't help but lean in. He smeared it in a thick sheen of butter, then stood up with a low grunt and approached the bars slowly.

She tried to still the toes twitching in her boots and worked to iron out the eagerness she was sure lit her face. The beggars in Edirne who looked most desperate always got the least.

He leaned his huge shoulder against the wall and gazed into the cell, holding the bread just beyond her reach. "Why did you break into my house?"

She could hardly hear him, her blood pounded so hungrily for the silky butter and fluffy bread. "I told you... I was hungry. I still am. Please, may I have something to eat?" She nearly choked on the sugar with which she coated the words. She hadn't had to plead so pitifully... ever.

"Well, since you asked so nicely..." He moved the bread closer to the bars. She reached out to snatch it, but he pulled it back and shoved the whole thing into his mouth.

She gasped. Never before had she endured such a hideous betrayal. "You are an ogre."

He moaned with pleasure and licked the butter from his fingertips. "Still warm."

Serap turned around, unable to look at the horrific sight any longer. Her stomach squirreled about with every yeast-scented breath. "Just tell me what you want."

He walked back to the stairs to wash down his bread with a long gulp of coffee, then he turned back to her. "Now then, *Edirneli Serap*. There is really only one thing I want from you. Answer this question, without lying, and perhaps you will eat today."

Today? She hadn't even considered being here longer than that, and certainly not without food. Who could live like that? She'd wither away like the evil in the corner.

"And how will you know if I'm telling the truth?"

"You'll just have to be persuasive."

She groaned. "Fine. Ask your question."

He walked closer. "What is your connection to Faris Khayin?"

She turned slowly until she could just see the twin fires reflecting in his eyes that gazed at her from the corner of her own. Murderous. That's what she'd call the look in them. More than usual. But what harm would come of telling at least some of the truth? Perhaps if she described Khayin terribly enough, The Immortal Killer would do his job and kill him. Then her heart squeezed. If she was locked up here while Khayin died, she wouldn't get to ask her question. She would have to find a way to get Khayin killed only after she was free to ask.

She licked her lips. "He is a traitor."

He lifted one dark eyebrow. "To Shihala?"

"To Shihala. To Qaf. To anyone decent." She paused. "So maybe not to you."

"Tell me more about Shihala."

"Tell me more about España."

"Perhaps if you would look at an atlas rather than tearing it to pieces, you would know."

"The only schooling I received in Edirne was about how to survive. What good would a map do me if I can't navigate my own city?" He did not need to know about the hours of lessons in Qafian Arabic, astronomy, mathematics, and poetry she received in Karzusan.

The Killer cleared his throat. "*Reino de España* is now a Christian kingdom, which occupies about eighty-five percent of the Iberian peninsula. It is a combination of the erstwhile kingdoms of Aragon and Castile, unified by the marriage of King Ferdinand and Queen Isabella, two of the most despicable tyrants to ever walk the earth, though we will not hold that against the country as a whole. It has a diverse, though largely temperate climate, and is geographically, architecturally, and culturally storied. In the north—"

"Shihala is a kingdom," she cut him off. *Gug.* She only understood half of what he said and had faded off long before.

"Yes, I know. In Qaf."

She watched his face, worried he would turn his murderous look on her. Magic was bad in his eyes. But what else could she say? He clearly loved his stupid maps. "Yes."

He sighed and pressed two fingers against his forehead. "Are you going to make me twist your arm for every detail?"

She puckered her lips and twitched them side to side, just itching to say yes. "I don't know what you already know with your hoarder's house stuffed full of books."

"I know Shihala is one of the Nine Kingdoms of Qaf. I know it was ruled by Vespar until recently. And I'm afraid that is where my knowledge on the subject ends. I should like to know more." He leaned his shoulder against the bars and the metal creaked. "I think you'll find a good approach when teaching any subject is to assume that your student is intelligent, but doesn't know anything, and then adjust from there."

"I find a good approach to learning is making sure your teacher doesn't starve to death." She pressed a hand to her belly where Chupkin slid back and forth along her skin. Useless, once again, yet still so comforting. "I could tell you a million-and-a-half things about Shihala. Maybe you could suffice with four of your choosing."

He sliced off another piece of bread, smeared it with butter, then walked over to her cell and slid his hand through the bars.

She eyed him suspiciously, not wanting to fall for another heart-wrenching, back-stabbing dirty old trick.

"Just start talking, and when I can't take it anymore, I'll let you know." He lifted the bread a little.

Again, she switched her gaze back and forth between the man and his food. If he wanted her to talk, she could talk. Even patient 'Abi Jahmil had been known to cut her off when she really got going.

The thought of abandoning him once more panged her already gnawing stomach. She focused on the silky butter.

"As you said, Shihala is one of Nine Kingdoms in Qaf. It has a... temperate climate? Sure, that's what it has. I don't know. It's not sunny. It's moony. Lots of moons. And lakes. And giant turtles with gems on their backs. And there are seahorses, well they're sea dragons. Do *not* mistake them for horses. It will not end well for you. And as any kingdom, Shihala has a king and a queen, amirs, sheikhs, and courtiers. And then, of course, it has citizens. Lots of citizens. Some poor—"

"*Perdóneme,*" he cut her off. "Did you want this?"

"I don't know what you want me to tell you," she said, exasperated. "And obviously I do want it. I've never seen such tasty bread in all my life."

"Then will you please take it? My arm is getting tired."

She blinked. Then raised her hand as slow as she could with hunger driving her. At the last second, she snatched it and shoved a bite in her mouth, then groaned with pleasure.

He let out a relieved little grunt and stepped away from the bars to plop himself back down on the stairs. He picked up a strawberry and used the tip of his knife to dig out the stem.

Serap eyed him warily, still not sure why he gave her the bread. Had her annoying talking actually worked? Or was it poisoned? She froze, looked down at the crumbly morsels, then took another bite anyway.

"Why do you want to know about Shihala?" she asked through cheeks thick with bread.

"Is that not where Khayin is from?"

"As far as I know. But he's pretty old. Like grandfather's, grandfather's, grandfather's, *grandfather's* old."

The Killer stroked his oiled beard thoughtfully. "Can you tell me more about his betrayal? Was it against Shihala's king and queen? What did he do exactly?"

"Well, I don't know about *exactly*, but he tried to mess with Qaf's magic. It wasn't too long ago. When Jahm... I mean, King Jahmil's father was in charge. He leaked a bunch of secrets and got a ton of people killed." She stopped to chew another bite of bread. "Wives. Sons. Daughters. Slaughtered for no reason. Lands wasted. People displaced from their homes. It was a real tragedy."

He didn't say anything for a while, staring at the wall as the torchlight licked his skin and black clothes. Then he stood, walked over to the cell, and offered her the strawberry.

"Really?" she asked, still wary of another trick.

He looked up into her eyes, a strange softness to his expression. "Tell me about how he was punished?"

She took the strawberry with delicate fingers and licked around the top. "How do you punish someone who can't die?"

"I know he's in Ashkult."

"He's locked them up in a tiny box and made to feel the agonizing claws of hunger for the rest of their lives." She paused, a great wash of sympathy growing inside her for the traitor. "Terrible."

The Killer stared at the floor a hand's span before him. His eyes almost looked sympathetic too, but only for a moment before hardening again. "If I didn't know better, I might assume you had feelings for the monster."

She barked out a laugh. "I reserve my feelings for only the most suitable suitors. If there was longing in my voice, it was for this." She raised the strawberry and took a nibble of the tangy sweetness, a smile slipping on her face despite herself.

He showed a closed-lip smile, then turned away.

She watched him for a moment, his large shoulders slouching before straightening back up. No matter how hard she tried, she couldn't read him. A raging monster one second and sighing hulk the next. She had been among the djinn too long, relying on their expressive eyes, and had forgotten how to read humans. Or was it that the Immortal Killer lacked humanity?

She had come in ready to convince him to help her, assuming he would understand her desire to remedy her human frailties amongst so many magical beings. But he seemed to be a magical, unbreakable being, too. She had failed to see that. So now what was she to do? She was still certain that if she could get him access to Khayin, he would go kill him without her, and that couldn't happen.

Her best bet was to get out of the dungeon and try to find something he was willing to bargain for. Something Pasha or the evil in the corner could help her find. Or maybe Pasha could help her find something he needed. Something that meant more to him than her worthless humanity.

Taking another bite of berry, she worked up her courage. "Can I go now?"

"I shouldn't think so." He gathered up the plate and finished off his coffee. "You're still lying to me."

"Am not." She scowled. "And you have no sense of honor, accusing me like that. What could I have possibly lied about?"

"Well, for one, as good a baker as I know I am, word of my bread has not traveled as far as Edirne. And certainly not to Shihala."

"It could have."

"If you are prepared to tell me why you broke into my house, who sent you, and how, and why, perhaps I would let you go." He waited, his brows raised. When she did not answer, he grabbed the torch from its holder in the wall and started up the stairs. "*Buenos noches, señorita*. Do watch out for the rats. I don't share my bread with them either, so they're probably hungry."

She kicked the bars as he marched off. Rats seemed a paltry warning compared to the evil in the corner. Not that she wanted either. She stuffed the strawberry in her mouth so little rodent hands couldn't take it and slink into the corner.

Why did he care so much about Khayin, anyway? And even more pressing, what book hid his secrets?

Maybe whatever the being in the corner wanted her to read would give her what she needed to bargain with the Killer, to get him to do her will. After dealing with the Immortal Killer and his expectedly harsh words and strangely soft eyes, she trusted the evil in the corner more.

CHAPTER TEN

JAVIER

The next morning Javier awoke before dawn. He made himself breakfast—more of the bread from last night soaked in eggs and milk, fried in lots of butter, then drizzled with honey and dusted with cinnamon. As he sat down to eat, watching the sky shift from purple to red to dusty pink, he tried to read his book. He only got through about forty pages. His mind was so unfocused, constantly drifting back to the girl he had locked in his basement. Given the way she rambled, it was safe to assume about eighty percent of what she said was inconsequential, but he couldn't be certain which twenty percent he ought to pay attention to.

One thing had struck him: she was close to the King of Shihala. She had almost referred to him by his first name before stopping herself. And she had also let slip that she was a sheikha. But how did a human end up a princess at a djinn court, on a first-name basis with the King? The King of Shihala and Khayin the Traitor were enemies, surely.

Perhaps the king was the one who had sent her to his house. To steal something? She seemed an unlikely thief. Or maybe the king had sent her there on a mission that involved hurting Khayin. Maybe she was an assassin sent by Khayin's greatest enemy to murder Javier and make certain he could never put an end to the traitor's suffering.

Javier vacillated over these questions for a long time, then eventually moved on to trying to decide whether to feed her. There was no reason to be cruel, but it seemed food was the easiest way to get information without having to threaten her.

Even as he fried the bread, arranged berries on top, and drizzled it with honey butter, he was still debating whether to give it to her. In the end, he decided that he would feed her. But he would not give her any cinnamon, just so she knew that he was still a cruel, brutish master and that she must respect his authority.

He opened the door to the basement and slipped inside, relying on the sun that peaked through the windows in the foyer to light his way. Serap twitched but did not stand. She had curled up in the far corner, her puffy pants drawn up to her chest. She was sleeping, but fitfully, her arms wrapped around her chest.

Javier slid the plate under the bottom of the bars, careful not to touch the berries to the rusty surface. He placed a jug of water beside it, then turned to leave. But his gaze was drawn to her again and again. Her small, but curvy body. The unassuming sweetness in her soft, round face. The swell of her bottom lip where she had bit it when he shook her.

A horrible sensation swept over Javier, his skin too tight. He didn't know what it meant and he didn't like it. But he found himself hurrying up the stairs to his library to snatch a wool blanket with a red and black tartan from the back of his chair. Then he sneaked back downstairs and set it inside the bars next to her breakfast.

The tightness abating, Javier returned to his library to check his calendar. He had given himself three days to deal with Silrok and it had only taken one, so today and tomorrow were free. The day after, he was scheduled to go to Izrak on Qaf to fight an *arak hunak*, the creepily named "*I see you there*" tree. He flicked through the papers on his desk until he found the file he had composed about it. At least three thousand years old, with roots that stretched as far as a small city, and with several saplings surrounding the central tree, which was as thick as six elephants and twenty times as high.

Apparently, the people of eastern Izrak subscribed to the cult of some goddess of the wild, named Cybele, and had been sacrificing virgins to it for centuries, though what interest an immortal tree or its goddess had in the sex-lives of young djinn women seemed debatable. Either way, the Queen of Izrak was determined that the tree should finally meet its end, and Javier had agreed that this matter was more worthwhile than her other pleas. He would be the lumberjack.

He would need to sharpen his big ax.

The tree calendar shifted, the past week folding over the edge to reveal a crisp new week at the center. Javier sighed and lifted an oversized gaucho hat from under his desk and set it on the table. Inside were perhaps a hundred small strips of paper, all folded into little squares. He plunged his hand inside and felt around for a while before drawing one out at random.

No matter what sort of barriers he tried to throw up between himself and people who sought his services, there would always be more of them than there was of him. After all, he was the only person in two worlds with the ability to end the lives of immortals. And it just so happened that a large number of immortal beings were evil, flesh-eating, crop-destroying monsters.

The crushing moral responsibility of trying to decide which people were most deserving of his help had proved too much for Javier. After half a year of paralyzing indecision and even more debilitating guilt, he had given up and decided that the only fair thing to do was let fate decide for him. The randomness of his system allowed him to sleep at night. After all, he was only one man. A mortal man with a bad back who couldn't spend all his time fighting monsters. He needed rest and personal time. He was long past feeling guilty about that.

Javier shrugged. "Nobody likes the hat. Everybody wants to be in the hat."

The paper crinkled as he unfolded it and read aloud: "The flesh-eating *bunyip* of Kirsh." He rummaged through the papers in his "to-do" pile until he came across the original description he had written: *Enormous sea creature with a dog's head, a horse's tail, six flippers, tusks, horns, and a beak. Spits blinding poison and sucks the souls from those who stare into its cycloptic eye. Lurks in water at night and shrieks loud enough to burst eardrums and break glass.*

Javier wrote *bunyip* on his calendar, then tapped the quill against his chin as he read the description again. He figured he might need four days rest after such a battle, so he penned that in too.

Javier returned to his bedroom and dressed in his peasant clothes. When he removed his pants, he took the amulet he'd taken from the girl and transferred it to his new pocket. He didn't know what it was, but it was magic. Unknown magic which she might be able to use to destroy him if she ever got it back. Worse, what if she had brought it to his house for Khayin to use against him? He needed to keep it close.

He was outside before the sun finished rising. He fed the chickens, collected the eggs, fed his donkey, milked his dairy cow, and churned a new batch of butter. He harvested the ripe grapes, ten massive zucchini (they grew like weeds), and then gathered the apples that had fallen from his small tree—enough to make a tart for after dinner that night. It was mid-August, the summer heat sucking the sweat and energy from his body. He decided the time had come to plant the cool-weather vegetables—beets, spinach, lettuce, radishes, and turnips. But he'd had to slaughter his ox a few weeks ago when the old thing broke its ankle. Again.

There were only so many healing potions he could justify giving to a twenty-year-old ox.

The only beast of burden he had left was his donkey, and the heavy iron plow would surely break the poor creature's back. With a sigh, Javier hitched the plow to his own back and dragged it back and forth through the compacted soil of a field that had lain fallow since last year.

The time he spent farming was cathartic—the physical exertion, the quiet, the rewards of creating something instead of destroying it. He always did his best thinking when he was out on his land, looking after his animals and his crops. It made him feel like a different man—a simpler one. A kinder one. He didn't think about injustice, or hatred, or broiling philosophical questions, or the underhanded schemes of immortal monsters. He thought about the sun and the soil—the simple pleasure of a cool breeze on hot, sweat-soaked skin.

And today, he thought about the girl he had locked in his basement and the swell of her lip where he had caused her to bite it. The pitiful sound of her voice when he was carrying her down the stairs. "You're hurting me," she had said as if she were about to burst into tears.

The guilt of what he had done was pressing into his skin with more biting force than the pull of his plow. He was so used to fighting impossibly strong undead monsters, he had lost all awareness of his own strength. He had altogether forgotten that soft creatures existed that could be harmed by a mere shake or a little carry. It felt strange and uncomfortable, but he couldn't get it out of his head any more than he could forget the shimmer in her pretty brown eyes.

The sun passed its zenith, and he decided to break. Covered in dirt, he took off his shirt and wiped his face on the soft cotton, then turned to head back into the house. He was thinking about what he was going to have for lunch and how much of it he was going to share with his prisoner when a bone-rending scream cut into his quietude.

Slowly, he turned towards the overgrown woods. The scream was small and far-off, but he recognized it. He had heard it only the night before last when a terrified little girl had tripped over herself trying to get away from him and plunged into a fire.

Javier's breath became shallow, but the rest of his body remained still, paralyzed again by indecision. If she had been even remotely on the right road, she should halfway to Granada by now. But if she was just wandering in the woods, lost and frightened...

The scream came again, smaller and fading.

Javier never did fully make up his mind, but his feet took off without him, plunging into the woods. There was no running in here. So many fallen trees that had never been cleaned up, crisscrossed branches of prickly evergreens, and uneven terrain. He made his way through as fast as he could, snapping small branches as he went. The understory of deep thickets kept his pace slow and deliberate, so he had to lift his feet high and accept scratches on his arms and torso just to get through, which he did not appreciate.

He came upon a small stream and stomped inside, thankful for the clearing. The warble of birds and the strange clicks of animals were all around him, but a single noise cut through it all and set his hair on end: the great, echoing roar of a Cantabrian brown bear.

He hurried towards the noise, but the thick brush caught him and tried to keep him back, like fighting through the warp thread on a giant prickly loom. He saw the bear first—as long as he was tall, but probably twice his weight. It was on its hind legs at the base of a tree, clawing at the bark with its long claws, trying to get a hold. And clinging to a branch some ten cubits off the ground was a skinny girl dressed in rags and a familiar expression of utter terror in her eyes.

"*Oya!*" Javier shouted and clapped his hands. The bear turned to look at him. He lifted his arms high in the air and waved them around. "*¡Fuera de aquí ahora! ¡Vayate!*"

The bear popped its jaw and shook its head quickly, then it reared back and let out another powerful growl. It stamped the earth with its front paws several times in quick succession.

Javier clenched his fists and widened his stance, preparing for the charge. It foamed more, spittle flying from its black jaws as it roared. It lunged at him. Javier didn't buy it. He didn't move, the muscles tightening in his back. The bear pulled off to the side just before it slammed into him.

A feint.

Javier raised his arms in the air and shouted wildly at the top of his lungs, his deep voice booming. He ran at the bear. It stood its ground a moment, then turned and darted off into the woods.

Heaving a sigh of relief, Javier looked up at the girl. She was wrapped around the branch, her chin digging into a large patch of waxy sap.

"Are you alright?" he called.

She didn't answer, her amber-colored eyes glued to him. Tense eyelids, jaw dropped open and lips pulled back in a taut line—but something had changed in her expression. Her brow was furrowed and drawn together, examining him carefully.

"Please." He reached for her with one arm, hand open. "I promise, I won't hurt you."

Her eyes widened so the white was visible all around the pupil. "Look out!"

Javier didn't turn on time. The bear slammed into his back and knocked him to the ground. The first bite came to his back, like a sledgehammer with teeth. He cried out and forced all his strength into his upper body, throwing the creature back.

As he struggled to his hands and knees, the bear barked and lumbered towards him again. He whipped around and punched it in the face. It fell back, rolling onto its side. Javier got to his feet and turned on the creature. The five-hundred-pound animal reared up on its hind legs and swatted at him, its paw slamming diagonally across his chest and cutting streaks in his skin.

He rolled with the debilitating force of the blow and ducked around the thin trunk of a tall tree. The bear slammed down onto all fours and pounded after him.

He snatched a thick tree limb from the ground as big around as his thigh bone. He braced it over his shoulder like a club. When the bear came around the side of the tree, Javier swung with all his might. He caught the bear full in the face. The beast woofed and whinnied as it was thrown back, twirling on the underbrush until it came to rest on its side. It moaned in pain, the hump in its shoulders heaving with every strangled breath.

Javier threw down the branch. He snatched up a sharp, triangular stone and fell upon the bear's back. It tried to rear up, but he slung one arm around the top of its head and buried the sharp of the rock into its thick neck. Hot blood drenched his hand. The creature rolled and moaned. Javier let go of the stone, leaving it in place as he dodged away from the violent death throes. The pitiful noises it made—the terrible beast brought to its knees—cut into his heart like needles.

His arm was soaked in red, his chest and back bleeding and stinging. The pain of the force of the blows was almost worse than the broken skin. He felt like somebody had tied him to the floor and dropped rocks on his chest.

Once the bear had stopped twitching, he knelt beside it and set his hand into the thick fur on the back of its neck. Such a strong animal—beautiful and terrible. He never would have come out looking to harm it.

"*La muerte es todo lo que es seguro en la vida*," he said, closing his eyes in reverence. "Death is not the greatest of evils."

He stayed knelt for a short moment of silence, then stumbled to his feet and towards the tree. Unmoved from her perch, the girl met his eyes.

Keeping his gaze on hers, he lifted his hand again, though with rather less gusto. Then he set his arms into a cradle. He looked down at his arms, then back to her.

Her harsh pinprick pupils softened a little, but she made no move. For a long time, they stayed like that, just staring at one another as the sounds and smells of the bustling forest moved around them.

He was about to give up and lower his arms when she unwound herself from the branch and let herself drop. The impact of her meager frame was nothing compared to the bear's jaws and claws slamming into his torso. He looked down at the girl—at her wary brown eyes, her hard cleft chin, the smooth discolorations her burns had faded into. Her dress hung in tatters, her hair singed from one side of her head, hanging in limp crispy curls on the other. Her feet were bare—raw and bloody from running through the underbrush.

Her eyes studied him as well, focused on his face, moving down his beard and over his ears, then landing back on his eyes. For the first time, there was no fear on her face, only the soft angles of confusion.

"Are you okay?" he asked in his native tongue.

She shook her head quickly.

"Are you... hungry?"

She bit the corner of her lip and looked away. Then she turned her gaze back to him. "I'm starving."

"Then let's get you something to eat." It crossed his mind to set her down, but one glance at the state of her feet changed his mind. He moved her up in his arms a little so he could hold her more comfortably, then turned and carried her back to the house.

CHAPTER ELEVEN

SERAP

Serap's bones pricked with an aching cold. Her throat parched for water. A headache throbbed behind her eyes. Scratches and skitters plucked at her ears. And the sweetest smell she could have imagined—one of butter and bread, honey and warmth—wafted past her nose.

Of course, she would tend to the smell of food first.

Opening her eyes, she cast her gaze around her cell until they fell upon a simple black and red blanket and a plate of food. A gray snarl of fur darted from the corner toward her breakfast.

"No!" Serap pulled off a shoe and threw it with a hiss.

The rat gnashed its yellow teeth at her, then scurried away. She scanned the shadowy room for signs of the Immortal Killer. Not much use, as the cell was nearly as dark as the night before. But the lack of any knives, tedious questions, or utterly useless answers was enough to satisfy her that he was not there. She scrambled forward and grabbed the plate, breathing in the scent of honey and butter.

"It is a strange captor indeed who would starve his prisoner one day and then give such a sumptuous breakfast the next. Don't you think, Chupkin?"

The little wisp peeked from her cuff.

Again, the thought of poison crossed her mind. He was a killer, after all. He probably had a myriad of ways he could kill her. She held the plate beneath her nose and took another whiff. "Nothing that smelled so heavenly could kill me, right?" She paused, squinted one eye in thought, then nodded. "Right."

She lifted a bit of the fried bread and took a crispy bite. Even cold, her mouth watered, and she closed her eyes. The blend of hunger and sensational flavors rivaled that of the baklava Jahmil had given to her the first time he brought her to Shihala after rescuing her from a dungeon. She smirked. Savior and captor. How different they were from each other. But the thought turned the food in her stomach sour, so she pushed it away. When at last she had eaten every morsel and crumb and licked her plate and fingers for the last drops of honey, she sat back.

Chupkin emerged lazily from her sleeve, spreading out as if in a stretch.

"I'm glad one of us was warm last night," she said, then eyed the blanket on the floor. "When did he come in?" A chilly uneasiness sat in her chest. "I should not sleep so soundly in the future in case he decides to bring a blade, instead."

She spun the plate around on the ground, ceramic rubbing against stone in a harsh scrape. She would not be able to pry up this floor. She hopped up and tested the bars, more to say she had done so than believing they were the answer.

When she made her way to the right corner, she paused. No dim blue light hovered there. No evil whispers told her secrets. Or lies. She couldn't know.

"Perhaps I should call Bakr Amca," she groaned, looking to Chupkin. "He could definitely get me out. But this is not like the ghoul in the graveyard. We are in the house of the only man in both worlds who can kill him. If he died, I would never be able to live with myself."

Chupkin floated up in front of her, loose tendrils reaching out like sun rays.

"You're right." She pouted. "He would also probably tell 'Abi Jahmil where I am, and this would all be done."

Serap gulped. Jahmil would never let her leave the palace again. She'd grow old and shriveled on house arrest, and he'd bury her bones in the courtyard so not even her spirit could escape his heart-wounded punishment. Equally soul-crushing, she'd have to see the forced smile Ayelet used to hide her hurt and Jahmil's utterly broken face and deep-purple eyes. That face would end her, so heavy a weight did it place on her heart. And never had she done so much to deserve it by disappointing him and being so utterly selfish.

She took a breath to keep from suffocating under the thoughts. "I'm not ready to go home, yet. Not when I'd be a failure."

She pushed her bottom lip over her top and slid it back down, thinking, thinking.

"Pasha?" she called, expecting very little and hoping very much.

She waited. Sniffed and ran her sleeve across her nose. Then nearly gave up when that gusty sound she heard the day before returned.

"Serap?" Pasha's voice came through, bodiless and subdued.

"Where are you? Why can't I see you?" Serap scanned the ceiling and floor as if the witch hid in some tiny pocket of the prison she had not yet thought to check.

"I'm in Qaf, silly. Where are you?"

"Not in Qaf. Obviously. You're the one who dropped me off. I'm in a dungeon in *España*, I think he said."

"Who said?" Pasha's voice piqued with interest.

Serap sighed. "Who do you think? You sent me to find the Killer, and now I have. It's going terribly, by the way." She folded her arms and scowled, not sure whether Pasha could see her or not and wanting to look properly upset in case she could.

"He hasn't killed you yet, though. That sounds like it's going well enough."

"You left me in a strange land with nothing but a *toodeloo*, all the while thinking he might kill me?" Serap groaned in exasperation. "I thought you were trying to help me live longer, not die a gruesome death."

The sound of whipping wind cut between them. Serap's stomach tightened.

The tinny voice returned. "You told me you were strong and could handle it. And we were kind of in a time crunch since you made your baba so mad."

"You mean your terrible impression of me did."

"Not a chance, sweetie. You started the fight in the banquet hall. I just finished it up. Hang in there, sweetie. You're not a djinn. If the Immortal Killer hasn't slit your throat yet, you'll probably be fine."

Serap's throat dried with the imagery Pasha so freely provided. "Can't you at least come and get me out so I can figure things out? I feel helpless stuck in here like this."

Pasha's voice *tsked*. "Too dangerous. He'd skin me alive if he found me in his house."

"But you're talking to me through this wind tunnel or whatever, isn't that dangerous?"

"What's he going to do, knife my voice?"

Serap huffed loud enough so Pasha could hear. "Could you at least dig up some information on the Immortal Killer? More than you have? He won't listen to me about Khayin. I can tell that already. He just looks murderous and shakes me a lot. I need something I can use. Something that could motivate him."

"Hmm," the witch's voice trailed off. "I may have an idea...."

An excruciating pause filled the air. Had Pasha left? Could a disembodied voice leave?

"If the rumors are true," her voice returned, "there's an artifact stored in the Immortal Killer's house that would provide a way for you to move about without the help from me or other djinn."

Serap couldn't help but roll her eyes. "That seems a bit self-defeating, don't you think? How can I find the artifact locked in a cell?"

"Feeling saucy this morning, aren't we?" She could almost hear Pasha give one of her classic shrugs. "It's a crow's head wrapped tightly with the skin of a donkey's nose and seven-colored string."

Serap stuck out her tongue, grateful she had already eaten. "That sounds gross."

"You wanna come home, find the crow's head. It's a type of amulet made for babies to ward against the Evil Eye. Only, this one belonged to the child of a mighty wali."

Serap startled as wavy lines buttered the air where the evil presence had hovered. The blue glow gave way to a green-tinted image of a powerful Muslim wali, turban high in the air and a book in one hand, a baby in the other.

"How are you doing this?" Serap asked in wonder.

"Doing what, sweetie?"

"The pictures, the wavy air."

"I don't know what you're talking about."

"Bu—"

"Don't interrupt, child."

Serap pouted at being called a child but was soon lost in the images playing out in rivulets before her. If the green mirage came from the evil in the corner, should she watch it at all?

Pasha's voice took on an echo and filled the basement.

"The wali loved his baby second only to Allah and devoted his life to being a messenger of god and a father. But one moonstruck night, a *cadı* wandered free from Qaf and ate the baby's flesh and soul. The wali's heart broke that day, and leaving Allah's light, he set on a path of darkness, cursing the creature and its kind forevermore. He buried the baby in the opening to Qaf where the creature had come from, then used his grief and dark magic to create a magical barrier to keep the *cadı* from ever returning to Ard. He sealed the path between worlds with the damnation of his soul."

The twisted face of a hissing, vampiric wraith screeched soundlessly before fading into the green mirage, sending curdles of fear down Serap's throat. The wali's tormented face flashed with light. Shivers raced across her back. He looked far too much like 'Abi Jahmil with his anguished eyes deep with hurt and magic flaring from clenched fists. The man weeping for his lost child.

Serap covered her eyes, the image mixing with memory and feeling far too real.

Pasha continued, her voice raspy. "He kept the crow beak charm his baby had worn and blessed it with the last of his remaining life so that his weeping wife, truly alone after the loss of husband and child, could travel back and forth between worlds to visit their child's grave."

The vivid images faded with Pasha's voice, a flicker of blue all that remained in the corner. Serap blinked, pictures of the fanged face and Jahmil's sorrow imprinted on her eyelids.

"Okay..." Serap sighed, finding her right mind. "So the creepy bird head and donkey nose can teleport me to Qaf. Admittedly useful, but not when I'm still stuck in a cage."

Pasha smirched. "That sounds like a personal problem to me."

"Pasha," Serap snipped. "Help me."

"I did, sweetie. I got you to the Immortal Killer just like you asked. And now I've provided you with a way to travel where you need and get home at your leisure without help. Must I hold your hand and wipe your nose, too? Put those soft hands to work and figure it out yourself."

"Fine," Serap gritted her teeth. "I'll magic my way out of this cage without any magic, then look for the stupid crow's beak while I'm figuring out what it is Evil wants me to read. But neither of you are very helpful."

Pasha snickered. "Did you just refer to evil in familiar terms? Making new friends in Ard, are we?"

Serap opened her mouth to answer, but a gust of windless wind blew through once more, and Pasha's words cut out.

"Not helpful," she called out, knowing the connection had been lost.

A heavy door slammed overhead, shaking loose bits of dust from the cobwebbed ceiling.

Her captor was back. She sighed and looked once more at the empty plate. Maybe she had been right before, and he planned to fatten her up and eat her. She pushed her lips to the side and sighed. There were worse ways to die. She leaned against the bars near where Evil. Pasha had been right. Without realizing it, Evil had become a solid being in her mind, something more than just a presence or feeling or glass-cutting voice that spoke to her in the dark.

She tilted her head in the empty corner's direction. "Good morning, Evil. I hope you slept well."

The blue light awoke, blossoming in the corner like a lily in spring.

"I need to get out of here, could you help me?"

Boots stomped and thunked about overhead, coming closer to the door at the top of the stairs. The blue shriveled and swirled. A paper-wrapped cylinder appeared in its center.

"*A gift,*" it whispered. Then it was gone.

The object clunked onto the floor. She picked it up with two fingers. A rounded bronze tip peeked out from beneath a sheet of cream paper tied with a blue bow.

She grasped the silky threads, infernally curious. Was trusting Evil a terrible mistake?

No worse than trying to appeal to a killer's humanity.

The heavy oak door banged open and dim light burst over her, stinging her eyes so she could see only his shadow. He hurried down the stairs and turned to one side, then disappeared from sight. A heavy *thud* sounded like he had thrown open a large trunk. Objects were chucked into her line of sight. A few pots, some scrolls, a massive ladle, a fur coat...

"Misplace one of your knives?" she asked, emboldened by the food in her stomach and Evil's strange gift.

"Ah-ha!" The lid of the trunk slammed shut, and he walked back into view, a small piece of white fabric hung in the crook of one arm.

He wasn't wearing a shirt, his hair and beard disheveled and wet with mud. And blood.

Long, heavy streaks of blood all across his huge, muscular chest.

"You *are* a killer." She pointed in horror and stumbled back from the bars. *Ayahs* from the Quran tumbled from her mouth, all jumbled up in her hurry to say them.

The Killer paused and looked right at her, his brows drawn together so two deep vertical lines formed between them. He opened his mouth as if to speak, then waved a hand at her and hurried back up the stairs.

Rude.

He pushed the door closed behind him, but it didn't latch, allowing a sliver of sunlight down into her cell.

She pressed her back against the stone wall, breath heavy and mind racing. Of course, he was a killer. *The* Immortal Killer as Pasha said. But for even after he had chased her down in the woods, she had dismissed his cruelty towards her as the signs of a crazy loner, not someone who actually dug knives into people's flesh.

Her tasty breakfast sent acrid bile up her throat. She slapped her hand over her mouth and rushed forward, desperate to see anything through the crack he so foolishly left for her.

His big mass bustled past twice. Nothing but the bass of his voice muttering unintelligible words. Then a tinkling sound—the voice of a child. Serap gripped the bars, the twined paper and bronze cylinder crinkling in her hand.

He was going to kill a child.

Is that what the white cloth had been for? Burial clothes? Or did he have something far more nefarious in mind?

And all too quickly, she was the lost little girl that Jahmil had rescued. The little girl Köle had warped into a terrifying beast.

She could not let this injustice be.

Biting her lip, Serap pressed her face between the bars and yelled, "Run! Run child, as fast as you can. Get out!"

When no one responded, she grabbed her plate from off the floor and clanged it against the bars.

"If you touch her," she snarled at the murderous man, "I'll kill you myself."

Massive footsteps creaked toward the door. The Killer slammed it shut, sealing her in darkness.

Serap gritted her teeth and lay hopelessly against the bars. She clenched her fists, feeling the crinkle of paper once more. The Immortal Killer was far worse than Evil. She would trust the flicker of blue and its visions of green, instead.

With a heart full of hate for the terrible man, she pulled the string, thanked Evil, and fell through the metal bars and into white.

CHAPTER TWELVE

JAVIER

The dress drowned the girl in long sleeves and a floppy collar. And though Javier had tried to keep it clean, he'd gotten a few specks of his blood on the hem.

She tied it up in knots at the shoulders and around the middle so she could walk, making her look a bit like a sheet being wrung out after the wash. She asked for a scarf, which was much easier to find than the dress had been. When she tied the blue fabric around her face and neck in the folds of a hijab, a rock sank in his guts.

This child wasn't just any unfortunate orphan that had been carted off to a nunnery to be exploited. She wasn't even a Christian. Which meant she probably hadn't been an orphan to start with.

She looked so small sitting at his dining table, nibbling at bread, apple slices, and leftover chicken. He hovered over a washbasin, dabbing at the blood on his chest and back.

He was in so much pain it was hard to see straight.

"What was that voice?" The girl asked.

"Nothing."

Javier winced when the hot water touched the wound. He hadn't had such an injury in a long time. He was much more careful now than when he was younger. His equipment was better—the best he could get. He scheduled rest days in between every fight so he wouldn't strain his bad back. He tried to find underhanded and easy ways to attack and was more than happy to kill devilish creatures while they slept without batting an eye.

That was what he had planned to do to Abad Urbano. But the child had been there, which had changed everything.

"Is there somebody in the basement?" Her voice stung with a soft bite of fear.

"An intruder."

Javier knocked back a healing potion, then picked up a roll of muslin and struggled to wind it around his chest. The awkward angle he had to hold his arm at only made the bite mark on his shoulder blade smart more. Again, he winced, gritting his teeth against the pain.

"I'm holding her prisoner until she tells me who she has been working for."

Pain made him feel stupid, and not only because he had allowed himself to get hurt. It also made it harder to focus, damaged his memory, and dulled his reflexes.

She watched him with clever, careful eyes. "Who are you?"

"My name is Javier Don DeMario, *Alqatil Alkhalid*."

He wound the end of the muslin over his shoulder and pulled it all tight. Blood soaked through the bandage before he had even tucked it in. He grabbed a clean kitchen towel, folded it over a few times, and shoved it under the muslin to cover the wound on his back. It scraped like sandpaper.

"*Hijo de pu—*" He bit his teeth down and contented himself with grumbling incomprehensibly.

"Why did you kill Abad Urbano?"

Again, he sighed. The answer was very simple. He'd killed Urbano because Urbano was not human. It was an immortal ghoul—a father of ghouls—who had been praying on the innocents of Spain for decades. Somehow that answer was also complicated.

Her eyes remained glued to him as he sat at the table across from her and poured himself a tall glass of water.

He cleared his throat. "*Any Israelite or foreigner residing in Israel who sacrifices any of his children to Molek is to be put to death. The members of the community are to stone him. I myself will set my face against him and will cut him off from his people; for by sacrificing his children to Molek, he has defiled my sanctuary and profaned my holy name. If the members of the community close their eyes when that man sacrifices one of his children to Molek and if they fail to put him to death, I myself will set my* *face against him and his family and will cut them off from their people together with* *all who follow him in prostituting themselves to Molek."*

She squished up her nose, furrowing her brow at him. "What?"

"It's from the Bible, the Old Testament." Javier wiped his crusty lips with rough fingers and said a silent prayer to Allah that his metaphor should not be confused. "Molek is a god of blood and fire—a tyrant who demands the sacrifice of the children of his followers and their total obedience, lest he crushes their bodies and souls into paste. A cruel and intolerant master who even now seeks to control all the world and remake it in his own image. To bend its people to worship only him, abandoning their reason, their sense of moral decency, their culture, and their beliefs."

She ran her finger in a circle over the tattered tablecloth. "You mean Iblis?"

Javier smiled indulgently. He'd been living among Christians for too long. "Molek has many names. Iblis is one of them. In this age, in this part of the world, they call him Satan. Whether he is real is less important than..."

"What do you mean whether he's real?" Her words hit him like shards of rusted iron. "Of course he's real."

Javier sighed. He didn't want to get drawn into that discussion.

"There is nothing to be done about Molek. We are but mortal. It is his followers we must contend with. They are many and varied, harbingers of all that is evil. For Molek is a far jealous and suspicious god. He demands abject humiliation from all of his followers and utter destruction of all who would stand against him. To appease the disgusting, blood-covered, hissing, and pus-filled figure of Molek, his priests work to cull an entire kingdom of all the people who have ever dared to speak the name of any other god... a Muslim god, a Jewish god, and even followers of Molek himself who pronounce his name incorrectly. There is no justice under the reign of Molek, there is only terror. Terror, disease, misery, and death."

She stared at the table for a long time, her eyebrows drawn together and her lips in a long flat line. "Have you killed a lot of people..." Her tongue tripped over the word. "I mean, *monsters* like Abad Urbano?"

"Yes, I have."

The girl picked up the bread and took a big bite. "Good."

Javier smiled, watching her chew with her little chin set on her fist, elbow leaned over the table. "I think you ought to get some sleep. Come morning, I will show you the way to the nearest village."

"I'm sorry I ran away." She looked at him, her dark eyes wide and dewy like a startled deer. "Won't you please let me stay?"

Javier's face softened. "What is your name, *niña*?"

"Cova."

"*Señorita* Cova, I formally apologize for what happened and my part in it." He bowed his head slightly. "It is because I do not wish you to come to further harm that I must insist you leave my house as soon as you are able."

"But I *will* come to further harm. If you make me go into the village, I'll end up right back where you found me. I always do."

He furrowed his brow. He knew as well as anyone that the world could be a dark and unforgiving place, particularly for one so young and all alone. He could imagine what she had been through. A Muslim girl being held in an abbey had to have been a victim of the Inquisition. Perhaps she had watched her family be murdered. Or suffered in an underground prison, locked up with dozens of other sweaty, frightened, starving souls like rats in a closed sewer that was about to flood.

She had witnessed at least one atrocity that he knew for certain. For there had been blood on the abbot's lips while he slept. Evidence of his dinner. Cova had been there when he ate. Or more likely, she had been curled in a corner with her eyes clenched shut and her hands pressed over her ears as the ghoul ripped and sucked the bones from another living person.

Javier knew from experience that ghouls were slow eaters.

What if Abad Urbano's dinner had been a friend of Cova's? A relative? Or a caregiver? He didn't want to ask. He didn't want to know. Not knowing was painful enough.

The implications of her ending up where he had found her were profound and terrifying. But so was his house. The halls of his home were not made of mere bricks and wood. Because of who he was—because of his *gift*—he could only ever live alone.

He was surrounded by powerful beings who dogged his every moment and who would use any advantage they could find to get the better of him, including exploiting an innocent girl.

Javier's frown deepened. What of the young woman he had so hastily locked in his basement? Had any of the specters in his house yet thought to try to exploit her?

He looked back up at Cova and shook his head. All he seemed to make of late were mistakes. "I am sorry."

The girl slumped her shoulders and did not speak again.

She finished eating, and he led her out to the barn where he had laid her down the night before. The hay was fresh and still covered with a thick blanket. She crawled onto the makeshift bed, and he laid a second wool blanket over her.

"*Dulces sueños*," he said, then he left.

The sun was beginning to go down, purpling the clouds like fine powder. He drew a bucket of water from the well, then hurried back to the kitchen and went about washing the dishes, which he'd neglected over the last two days. He felt sore and tired, emotionally and physically, but he also didn't want to sit down. His very soul was twitching.

Sappho meowed and leapt onto the counter beside the wash basin. She hopped onto his shoulder with a rattling purr and dug her untrimmed claws into his bare skin.

"You can either knock it off or get off." He pushed her down into a seat, unable to withstand her painful kneading at the moment.

"What am I going to do, Sappho?" He took up a rag and sprinkled it with lye. "I can't keep this up. I'm already in so deep. If I let this go on any longer, I may never be able to get out."

The cat nibbled on his earlobe. He flinched away. "Stop it."

She meowed and rubbed her face against his. Then she nibbled him again and meowed.

He lifted a plate from the slippery water, twitched and fumbled, then dropped it. The soapy porcelain shattered in the basin. Groaning, he threw in the towel and turned away.

"Whatever information she may have on Khayin, this is not worth the risk. Heaven only knows what may have been happening to her, locked down there in the dark. Surrounded by the evils of this house. Even if she is a seductress Khayin hired to murder me in my bed, she doesn't deserve to be trapped in this house."

His unfocused as he remembered the terror in her voice as she called out to him earlier. She had thought he was murdering Cova, doing unspeakable things to her. And why wouldn't she? Why wouldn't anyone assume the worst about him? They always had.

Long ago he had decided to embrace it, that he would just allow the rumors that people spread about to become a part of who he was. He was a sorcerer, a devil-worshiper, a vampire, a ghoul. He was a beast concealed in the clothes of a man who fed on the essence of the innocent. Who stole children from their homes at night and made away with them. A monster, a murderer, a demon.

Javier didn't care. He didn't even know most of the things people said about him, and he felt no desire to set the record straight. It kept people away and provided him with privacy. And it was true that his house was not a safe place for anyone to live. But he could not get away from it. For it wasn't the house that was haunted, it was him. Wherever he went, the specters would follow. And that was why he would be alone forever, concealed from the world so he wouldn't cause any harm to the innocent. In the meantime, he could serve his purpose by inflicting himself upon the guilty.

Sappho meowed, louder and more insistent. Again and again, following him as he paced the kitchen.

It was appropriate for her to be there as he felt similar now to how he had when he first took the cat in. It had been a monumental decision to allow an animal into his life that he cared about and spent time with. He'd agonized over it for nearly a month, only visiting her in the barn, before he invited the hungry, little cat inside. Javier didn't regret his choice, but ever since that day, he had never been able to shake the fear that something might happen to his only friend. And it would be his fault.

The cat jumped up and meowed at his eyeball. Startles, Javier sucked in a breath to yell at her before he remembered what she always wanted.

He dropped a big pile of boned chicken meat on the empty plate Cova had left behind. The cat jumped up on the chair and waited, her little paws on the table and her eyes filled with expectation. Her swishy tail broke through his relentless thoughts, and he sighed out an exasperated smile.

Javier collapsed in the chair across from her and took out his book—*La Celestina*. Refocusing himself on the problems of the bawdy old procuress would help to relax his nerves and clear his mind, allowing him to come to a proper conclusion regarding the whole mess.

It was a raucous story, the sort Javier would have denied having read if he was ever confronted about it. The sort he read often.

A young man named Calisto is enraptured with the beautiful Melibea, but her family prevents him from going near her. So, he enlists the help of a famous procuress, the incomparable Celestina, who uses her wit and bawdy charm to convince the innocent Malibea to give Calisto the opportunity he needs to seduce her.

A blast of hot air rushed over Javier—the smell of sulfur and rotting flesh. Javier wrinkled his nose and turned, though, of course, he gazed at nothing. No visions ever accompanied that smell. That horrid stench that clawed at his bones and twisted his stomach. The blood-congealing, bile-inducing aroma. Like old meat left in the sun, slathered in curdled milk, then eaten by a cow and vomited out over and over and over.

Javier held his nose to try to keep his stomach. If only the smell were the worst of it.

"*She is murdered by Calisto's servants,*" came the voice, a scrape of rust and sand against stone.

Javier growled and clamped his hands over his ears. "Shut up!"

"*Calisto dies in an accident, and then Malibea commits suicide.*"

"Damn you." Javier hucked the book across the room and folded his arms across his chest. "Another story ruined by the immortal spoiler of joy."

He was not the loudest the specters, nor the most dangerous, nor the even most insistent. But Khayin was by far the most annoying.

"*What a fool, what a fool.*" The stench of laughter shivered through the room. "*Does it not send the great hunter into a murderous rage? What a fool, what a fool.*"

Javier gave a howl of anger and leapt from his chair. "Leave me be."

"*The power rests in your hands, as it always has. Now amplified by the needs of such sweet, young creatures. It would be a pity should anything happen to them.*"

He clenched a fist, wishing to punch the monster's allusive face. The only reason he hadn't killed Khayin yet was because the bastard wanted to be killed. And he did not deserve to get anything he wanted.

"If you do anything to either of those girls..."

"*You'll what? O master of impotency! O raging fool of utter infirmity! O great killer of immortals who lacks the fortitude even to slay a rat!*"

"Leave my rats alone!"

"*You are slipping, Don DeMario. Slipping, slipping every day into madness of your own making. The man who sailed the oceans of Qaf. Who fought the great Falzuhdub, who resisted the cadı of jazirat aljamila, survived passing through the bowels of the Eternal Bahamut. You are not that man. You are a miser, a mossback, a laughing-stock.*"

"Shut up!"

"*And there is one solution, so simple. So easy it would be. To be free of all this torment for eternity. One stroke of your blade is all it would take.*"

"I'm not listening to you." He went to the counter and took down a bowl, then poured some flour into it. "I'm just baking bread, and I'm not listening."

"*A fine wife you will make someday,*" the beast cackled.

"*Canta el gallo, canta el gallo con el quiri, quiri, quiri, quiri, qui,*" Javier sang, his voice so loud that the pots quivered on their hooks in the wall. "*La gallina, la gallina con el cara, cara, cara, cara, cara!*"

The hot air whipped around him like a tornado, nipping at his skin with malice and intent. That infernal voice was still talking, still insulting him. Like the whoosh of a rushing river, striving to ruin every tiny thing he had left to care about.

"*Los polluelos, los polluelos con el pío, pío, pío, pío, pi!*" Javier screamed the song with all the air in his lungs. "*Y por eso los grandes amores de muchos colores me gustan a mí!*"

At last, the wind dropped. The horrid smell cocooned him. He rushed to the door to throw it open, sucking in a breath of clean, night air. His chest heaved, blood peaking through the fabric wrapped around his chest, encouraged by the frantic beating of his heart.

The usual anger, disgust, and dread that came whenever Khayin showed up brewed in his heart, but there was something else, something unexpected and far more urgent.

He needed to get the girls out of his house now before it was too late.

CHAPTER THIRTEEN

SERAP

Serap floated in limbo, suspended in moisture that didn't leave her wet. The white that consumed her was much like Chupkin, only wide and vast.

Panic took hold. Was Chupkin still with her? Was this Chupkin? If she found him now, would he be consumed by the white? She reached to pat her pockets and fell out of the mist onto her back in a field of grass. The surrounding air moved in shades of green like the mirage during Pasha's story.

She stood up, dizzy and vision sparkling around the edges, and patted herself, looking for Chupkin. Movement in the field drew her attention to her immediate surroundings. Halfway through a flower-strewn and distinctly Ardish-looking pasture sat a young man with strapping shoulders, handsome dark brows, and laughter in his black eyes. The Immortal Killer and anything but.

Don DeMario, Evil's voice whispered.

Her breath caught in a little gasp. A teenaged Don DeMario laughed, his shoulders only a little less broad and his beard just starting. But his big, dark eyes looked the same, as did the meek twist of his lips. He shared a picnic of baklava and tea, of seasoned meat and pies with an older woman in Turkish clothes. Her face crinkled into a smile, and she touched his arm with such tenderness. Her eyes shone as she looked to him and laughed.

Seni seviyorum, anne. The words tickled Serap's ears through the wind-carried babble. *I love you, mother.* The woman smiled and lay her head upon his shoulders. He brushed the hair from her face. Serap's heart twinged, thinking of how close this Don DeMario must have been to his mother. And how close she had been with 'Abi Jahmil when she was young.

She ached to return to her 'abi, to say she was sorry for leaving and lay in a field with him and tell him how much he meant to her after all these years. Instead, she fumbled through the softness of the scene and the harsh reality of what Don DeMario had been the day before. A son, a child, a tender man with laughter in his eyes. A monster, a brute who threw her in a cage. She was confused, she was hurt, she missed home, she was alone. It was all too much.

The vision faded, and Serap tumbled once more through wet white and onto a pile of books. She wiped her face on her sleeve, letting tears stream until her eyes dried out.

Those are not my memories, she forced the words into her mind. *They probably aren't memories at all.*

But that was a lie. She knew such sweet kindness in such dark eyes could not be imagined. Not by her.

She sat up, tipping the pile of books as she slid off in a heap. She winced, hoping no one heard. Hoping *he* hadn't heard, because there was only one place she could be in a room piled with books and dust and oddities. DeMario's haunted house.

The Immortal Killer had packed this room so tight, the door didn't open anymore, which explained why this room held even more dust than the few she had seen before. In the corner, a globe as big as a feeder chicken rested on wooden stilts. Etched copper marked countries and places she had never heard of, and when she laid a hand on it, the ball spun around with a tiny squeak. Chupkin wriggled out through the cuff in her sleeve, the chirpy sound enough to raise his curiosity.

"There you are," she sighed, a massive weight lifting from her chest. She kissed his ethereal body three times. "I was worried you had been swept up in the white."

Chupkin corkscrewed and wrapped himself tightly around her finger, tugging her toward the door.

"Oh, don't be such a scaredy-wisp." She plucked her finger from his grasp. "Evil didn't hurt us. We're fine."

A whip of air riffled her veil, a breath of shimmering blue that matched Evil's from earlier in the corner. She turned around, still eager for answers. Along the wall, stood a shelf with marginally fewer books placed upon it than on the floor. The hardwood shelves bowed in the center. Upon the middle shelf, nestled between green leathery tomes lay a box. Silver and pink scales lined the edges, the material evoking a strange familiarity. She hiccuped and pressed a hand to her mouth, a flash in her mind of seal-skinned hands emerging from her amulet. The lock on the front shone with the red of a seashell nail. How she wished for her stolen amulet now. The brute.

Serap reached out to touch the shell when the wind snuck past her once more, tugging the ends of her hijab toward a brass pot in the far corner. She looked at Chupkin with raised brows. His light pulsed dimly before he unfurled and bobbed back and forth.

They would take a look.

She tiptoed nearer, inching forward through the tiny walkway carved in the mountain of books. When she was close enough to see inside, she closed her eyes tight, counted to three, then peeked. The room spun like a whirlpool, round and round until she lost her balance and fell into the pot. The swirling colors gobbled up her yelp and left her aimless and dizzy, grasping at everything and finding nothing.

Then a picture began to form. No whiteness this time. More grass. And the shade of night. Again, a mossy green tinted the air and everything she saw. A monastery—the church of Christians—sat atop a hill, back-lit by stars. Chupkin took one look, shivered, and hid beneath the coins around her neck with little tinks and clacks.

Where had Evil taken her this time and why?

A shadow caught her eye. Large and black and that of a man. Don DeMario. She pulled back, but the earth moved silently under her feet, like the globe in the room, twisting, twisting while she and the scene remained in the same place. And so she stayed, running in place, for she couldn't bear to stand still. Not as he crept through tiled arches and past pictures of wailing men and haughty prophets. As he sneaked through plastered hallways of white and rustic red and over orange-bricked floors, dressed all in black and with a knife at the ready.

As the Immortal Killer turned into a room.

Walked up to a sleeping man.

And slit his throat.

She screamed when his blade rose in the air. When it plummeted. When it cut through flesh and lost its shine to the stick of blood. And again, when Don DeMario moved away without a shadow of remorse, his hands red with murder.

Her screams bounded around her like they were encased in metal. Slowly, like sucking milk through a piece of straw, she was pulled back into the room with all the books. She clenched her stomach, certain she would lose the rest of her breakfast and uncertain if she would ever eat again.

Then the cooling breeze of Evil.

She groaned. "No more."

The wind pushed at her cheeks, and when she continued to ignore it, blinking between visions and reality, it nipped at Chupkin and began chasing him around the room. Her wisp whipped past her, through her clothes, tugging at her hair as a plea for help. She relented.

"What do you want me to do?" she asked, her chest tight and throat burning.

Evil's breeze left Chupkin, and she followed where it ruffled the pages of books and the tassels of markers, where it churned the dust on a shelf in the top corner of the room. She eased over, determined to find whatever it was Evil wanted. Maybe if she helped it, it would help her. Help her save the girl. Destroy the cold-blooded murderer. And maybe even find a way to kill the traitorous Khayin, too. A wicked life not worthy of immortality. She wanted to forget the memories that weren't hers to begin with and get back to her quest for longevity.

Serap tipped her head from side to side, eyeing a pathway up the shelf, then sighed. Her acrobatic skills were more than a little rusty. Still, she hadn't grown so wide on baklava that she couldn't manage it. Serap ran her eyes over the angles of the shelves, marking in her mind the places with enough room for her hands, the shelves with enough strength to hold her weight, and the estimated number of jumps to get to the top.

Then she took a breath and leapt.

The edges of the bookshelves were remarkably like the *batoude* she had used as a child to leap over other performers and their goats and dogs, and the rung of a curtain torn free from the fabric worked splendidly as a *cerceau*. And although she had always thought the names of the different stunts were silly—taught to her by a nomad from a far away Ardish kingdom called Royaume de France—the way their sounds twisted and curved on her tongue felt just right for the movements. Balancing atop the edge of the window sill on nimble toes, she spun herself in a *casse-cou* just for fun and grabbed the ledge of the shelf in the top corner. Then she pulled herself up to see inside.

In the back of the highest shelf, a familiar red eye peeked through a crack in the dark wood. She shuddered with a flinch, toes balanced precariously between the books on lower shelves.

Did Evil want her to grab that?

She looked closer, the red pupil meeting her gaze. It wasn't a crack in the wood at all. It was a keyhole.

She slid her hand into her pocket and searched for the small gift Evil had given her in the cell. The tip of metal brushed cold against her fingers. Careful to keep her hold on the shelf, she pulled it free and twisted it in the shadows, shaking off the crumpled, cream paper. The bronze cylinder had a shell on one end and what looked like shark teeth on the other. She had forgotten all about it in her fall through memories and wasn't sure how it got to her pocket, but she *was* certain what to do with it now that it tingled against her skin.

A key. A keyhole. To open a door.

She reached further into the shelf, slipped the bronze key inside the black hole, and twisted. A deep *clank* shattered the silence, and a ghostly howl swirled around the room. The wind picked up more and more, hurling into a full cyclone. It tore at the books, spun the globe, and whisked scrolls from the shelves until everything in the room flew about her in a terrible storm. She leaped to the floor and dodged twice to avoid being shivved by a quill. Just as quickly, the tumult stopped. The objects in the air clattered about her, an encyclopedia finding gravity just above her head. She scrambled out of the way so it landed with a *thwump* where she had been standing.

Serap leaned back on her hands, lungs rasping and heart pounding. "What did that do?" she asked Evil.

"*Bestowed a gift.*"

"For who?"

"A love long lost to bitter darkness."

Her sweaty fingers slipped, and she fell once more through white.

This time, she landed hard on the floor of her cell, bruising her back and knocking the wind from her lungs.

Serap rolled over, rubbing her sore spots and cursing like the street urchins she had grown up around. The street urchin she had once been.

"All that and I'm back in my cell?" She grimaced. "Thanks a lot. And you're welcome, by the way."

Heavy footsteps pounded the ceiling, powdering her headscarf with tiny streams of dust. Serap glanced up, rubbing the dirt away from her eyes.

"He's coming."

Chupkin dashed down the back of her shirt. Serap didn't blame him.

"Of course, he is," she growled with a sigh. "How long could it take to murder a child after all? He could probably do it in his sleep."

"Bakr Amca!" she called, hardly a trace of hope in her plea anymore. Whatever he was doing, wherever he was, he had decided other things were more important.

Her back tensed. For lack of anything to fight with, she clenched her fists, moving her iron and silver rings up closer to her knuckles. It was all she had left, but she wasn't going to sit around anymore. She would find a different way to kill Khayin without asking for the help of a child murderer.

The door slapped open, and torchlight rushed down the stairs into her cell. She could easily mark his silhouette in a forest of shade, so familiar had it become to her, but that only made the butter in her stomach curdle more.

"Don't come near me." She chomped her teeth down to stop her jaw from trembling.

He stomped up to the cell, unlocked the door, and let it swing open. "Go on."

She eyed him. The door. Him. Then narrowed her eyes. "I'm not coming out to be murdered. To be the next person to fall victim to your bloody hands."

"I want you out of my house."

"That's what you said the first time. And then you chased me into the woods and threw me in here."

He sighed, letting his head hang forward. "Yes, I know. I was there."

"Then you must think I'm stupid. What, do you love the thrill of the chase or something? If you're going to murder me, do it now, in cold blood in this cell. I've seen you do it before."

Another heavy sigh, thick and rusty that deflated his whole back. "I didn't kill the girl. She's fine. I'll show you."

She shook her head. "You kill people while they sleep. I'm not coming near you."

"Are you asleep? You don't look asleep."

She opened her mouth, then closed it with a smack. "What is wrong with you?"

"So many things, *señorita*. So many things."

She almost relented then, seeing his broad chest deflate and the softness he had shown to his mother return to his eyes. Was she crazy?

She would be if she gave in.

"I refuse to fall for your tricks. Your false remorse, or whatever you mean your sorry head shaking to be. If you're not a murderer, why were you drenched in blood?"

"There was a bear. What are you gonna do?" He turned his head to gaze up the stairs. Then he called out in his own language. "Cova? *Ven aquí.*"

Serap folded her arms tight across her chest. The timid girl she had seen from the graveyard stepped into the doorway. Serap breathed out a sigh of relief at the rosy color of the girl's face. The white fabric he had scooped so giddily from his trunk was to clothe a living child. Not a dead one.

Which meant he wasn't a murderer of children. Her stomach churned with indecision. If she left, she couldn't find the crow's beak or what Evil wanted her to read. She also couldn't convince or blackmail the Killer to help her. But she needed to make sure the girl was safe, just in case. She would do that first, then come back.

With one more glance at Don DeMario, Serap pressed herself against the far side of the cell and squeezed her way past him. Then, she ran up the stairs and grabbed the girl's hand.

"Come," she said, tugging her through the door and rushing her towards the kitchen where she had first come in.

The girl pulled against her, slipping her hand free as she chattered in the same silky language the Immortal Killer used.

"Please, just come with me," Serap snapped.

The girl flinched, and Serap realized she sounded just like Jahmil when he was stressed. She would have far more compassion for him the next time she heard that tone eke out of his tired throat. She glanced over the girl, desperate for a way to communicate. Then it hit her. The headscarf, just like her own.

Serap bent lower and looked into the girl's warm eyes, then spoke slowly in Arabic. "That man is a murderer. He kills people and walks around drenched in blood."

The girl lit up with understanding, washing Serap in relief.

Until she answered, "There was a bear..."

"Enough with the bear!" Serap pushed the child into the kitchen and opened the back door. "Come. I'll take you to the Imam in the mosque nearby. We will be safe there."

Don DeMario stepped into the kitchen, eyes looking anywhere but at either of them. He walked over to the table and picked up a small basket with a white cloth draped over the top. Then he held it out to Serap.

"Your bread, *señorita*."

Serap's eyes were already narrowed, but she shoved them into slits. Yeast and rosemary wafted from under the cloth, making her stomach rumble. Breakfast had already started to fade. She snatched the basket from him and grabbed the girl's hand once more.

"Come. You never know when he'll change his mind and hunt you like *you* were a bear."

The Killer stood in the far corner, his shoulders slumped.

The girl yanked against her grip again, turning her eyes back to him. "Please don't send me away. I could help you with Molek. I know stuff."

"Who is Molek? Is that the bear?" Serap asked, raking her fingers across her cheek. "What is going on?"

"Nothing." DeMario shook his head hard. "Just go. Take the girl and head north towards the village. Do not go south. There's an old graveyard there, and it's full of ghouls. The plague is in town so there are lots of them. I've arranged an undead exterminator, but I doubt she's come, yet. And don't go running off into the woods. There are bears, as we have all mentioned."

"I fear ghouls far less than you, Don DeMario," Serap declared with a confidence bestowed by righteous indignation. "For they are creatures of their own nature. You defile humanity with your blood-soaked blades."

Serap shoved the girl out the door despite her protests. In the warmth of the glorious sun, she pushed and pulled her down the road.

Don DeMario slammed the door to the kitchen behind them and drew the curtains.

"I don't want to go to the village," the little girl whined.

"And I don't want to be on Ard anymore, but here we are. Stop moping. I saved you from a ghoul earlier, the least you could do is trust me."

The girl twisted from her grasp, nearly escaping as they found their way down to the road. Three boxes lined the path with signs in Arabic requesting proposals be dropped off there. Whatever that meant. Serap sighed, blocking the way back to the house. She really was being too harsh on the poor thing. Ayelet never spoke to her like this, not as a child and not now. Allah, the girl was barely older than Tabor.

"I'm sorry," Serap sighed. "I know this must all seem overwhelming to you, but if you don't want to trust me, at least listen to the monstrous man. It's time to go. I definitely can't leave you here by yourself."

"I'll just sleep in the barn until he lets me back inside."

"Like a stray cat?" Serap asked flatly. "Don't be ridiculous. Why do you want to go inside his house of horrors, anyway?"

"He could have just left me to die, and he didn't. He saved me. Twice." She looked down at her feet and shrugged her bony shoulders. "And the food is good."

Serap puckered her lips and sighed, remembering the crispy buttered bread from that morning. "The food is good." She stood for a while on the edge of the road, Cova—that's what DeMario had called the girl, right?—staring longingly at the house. "Was there really a bear?"

"It was huge! It chased me up a tree. I thought I was going to die. It was climbing after me. He fought it for me. He saved me." Her face flattened, her dark lips pulling into a tiny pout until they were hardly visible. "I don't know why."

"I doubt even he knows why." Serap swept her gaze back to the house. "He *does* murder people, though. I've seen it with my own eyes."

"Me too." Cova nodded. "I don't know who you saw him kill, but the man I saw him kill had it coming."

Serap frowned and blinked at the girl a few times. Maybe he didn't kill the girl because he was making her an apprentice. But then why had he let her go?

"Where has he been keeping you? In the locked bedroom with the torn floor? In another cell?" She leaned in close, waiting for the answer.

Cova shook her head. "In the barn. Though he didn't really let me sleep much."

Serap held her breath, horror trickling down her spine. "Did he touch you?" She prayed the girl knew what she meant so she wouldn't have to explain and prayed even harder that she didn't.

"No." She rubbed her elbow with her hand, looking like she was about to melt into the dirt road. "He killed the creature I thought might do that."

Serap's whole body softened. "I'm so sorry," she whispered, feeling a stronger kinship for the girl than she had anyone in her life. "Why did he come save you? Are you related? Did he see you get taken?"

"He didn't know I was there. He just came to kill that man because... he just kills people... I mean, *things* like that. I asked him why he did it, but I didn't completely understand his answer. Something about Molek or Iblis and Israel. He's really smart, and kind of weird."

"He is weird..." Serap said half-mindedly.

Her thoughts were too busy sorting out what to do next. She had seen the way his sorry eyes softened when the child was near. If he didn't kill children... if Cova was right, and he *saved* them, then she had nothing to fear. Well, not nothing. But she felt fairly certain he would leave her be going forward.

Maybe her cause wasn't hopeless. He had a clear interest in Khayin, and Evil had a clear interest in him. And despite the rush of cold that came from the tiny door she unlocked in the cluttered room, an itching part of her wanted to see what *love lost to darkness* may have come out. Besides, she needed to get either her amulet back or find the crow's beak or she might never return to Qaf.

But the girl? Don DeMario may have saved the little thing's life, but so had she. That didn't mean she could go toe-to-toe with the Killer, but it had to mean her hands were not as soft as Pasha or 'Abi Jahmil seemed to think. Cova didn't want to leave this place, that much was clear. Maybe the best she could do was keep an eye on the girl with Chupkin while she hunted for answers. Twice the Killer had let them free. Maybe the third time was the charm.

Chupkin popped a tendril from her collar and stroked her cheek. She ran her finger over his misty light and nodded. This was how it had to be.

"I understand only half of what DeMario says, ever."

Serap looked once more at the girl whose eyes were still affixed to the house. She sighed. A pair of stubborn souls were they.

She shifted the basket in her arms and shrugged. "Like when he told us to leave, eh Cova? Who knows what he meant?" She took out the rosemary loaf of bread and broke it in half, handing a piece to the girl. "I'm certain he meant go have a picnic and then return for dinner. What do you think?"

Cova pushed her lips together, then looked up at Serap from under her lashes, the tiniest smile in her cheeks. "I think that sounds right."

"Excellent, young Cova. Let us find a pleasant place to dine. Then we shall return to our bear hunter."

The girl's smile grew, and she headed off to a shady spot in a field of wildflowers beneath a reaching shade tree. Serap glanced back over her shoulder at the house. Yes, going back was probably foolish and impulsive and all the things Jahmil accused her of. But she couldn't help it. Not when she had come so far.

She would once again enter the house of a killer.

CHAPTER FOURTEEN

JAVIER

"Why are they just standing there?" Javier pulled aside the ratty curtain of his living room window and watched the two young women chat on the road that led up to his house. "North, I said. Go north."

Serap turned her gaze back to the house. He dropped the fabric and stepped away. They were probably just deciding which way to go. Maybe they didn't trust him enough to tell them the way to the village. Would they go south to spite him? Maybe he should have told them to go south to give them a push in the right direction.

Maybe they didn't know which way *north* was. Maybe he should have directed them using the Five Winds as they did in Qaf. But they were both human. They should have known which way the sun moved.

He slumped down onto the chair in his kitchen. It wasn't his problem, anymore. They were gone, and he was alone once again. Alone with his relentless djinn companions. Alone with his demons, his memories, and his books. If Khayin would ever let him finish one without spoiling the ending.

All alone again. Forever.

He reached into his pocket and took out the amulet he had ripped from Serap's neck the night he met her. He'd forgotten to give it back. He clutched it in his hand and walked to the window, but when he glanced out, they were gone.

"Finally."

His eyes drifted back to the copper talisman. It was square and cut into a seven-by-seven grid, each section marked by a symbol. Some were Arabic letters and numerals, but the rest he didn't recognize. It didn't look especially valuable, at least not from a monetary standpoint. Perhaps sentimental value.

Would she come back for it? Maybe he should just set it on the stoop so she could grab it and leave. Just leave and not be forced to talk to him, or look at him, or accuse him of horrible acts ever again.

His chest was burning as if he'd just eaten an entire coil of spicy chorizo, but he tried to force down the feeling. He absently ran his fingers over the textured surface of the amulet, over the top row of symbols, and then down the last row.

The floor rumbled. Javier set a hand on the water jug on the table, his back stiffening.

When would he ever learn?

His skin tightened. Tighter and tighter until he felt like it was about to rip right from his bones. The pain knocked him to the floor. He screamed and rolled onto his back, grasping at his own contracting flesh. A white light flashed before his eyes, and the pain stopped.

All sensation fell to nothing and his senses dulled. The rumbling, which he realized now had come from his own body, was gone.

He tried to open his eyes or wiggle his fingers, but nothing happened. The white mist cleared, and he found himself looking at his own kitchen, only his vision was different. He could see in front of him, behind him, up, down, and to all sides simultaneously. The world bobbed gently up and down as if he were on a boat. He tried to rise to his feet, but nothing happened.

Sappho hopped up on the counter next to him. He tried to turn to her, but his vision just moved an inch closer. And when he opened his mouth to speak, there was no mouth to open.

The cat growled and shook her bottom, then leapt at him, claws bared. He darted out of the way, but she came after him, swatting and mewling. He tried to tell her she was bad and to stop it, but no noise came out.

He raced around the counter and caught sight of the floating, white body of a fat wisp in the shine of one of his copper pots. He turned to look at it. Even with his vision everywhere, he could not see the wisp anywhere except in the shine of the pot—a reflection.

He spun in the air trying to get his bearings, a horrible realization sinking in. He couldn't speak because he had no mouth. He could not stand because he had no feet. And the world wasn't bobbing, he was.

Serap's amulet had transformed him—clothes and all—into nothing more than a floating ball of light.

Javier jiggled up and down, his light flashing and curling in long tendrils all around him. He flew down towards the amulet and tried to rub himself against it, but nothing happened. Even if he'd had a finger to touch the talisman, he couldn't remember exactly what he had done to end up this way. Nor did he know if it would even help if he did.

He was trapped.

A low cackle resounded through the room. He anticipated the smell that always accompanied it, but he had lost that sense, too.

Khayin! He tried to shout, but no words came.

He couldn't speak any more than he could feel or smell. He could hear well enough and sort of see, if the omnidirectional assault he was experiencing could be classified as vision.

He darted back and forth across the kitchen in as close to a pace as he could manage, alternating possibilities pouring through his head. It was Serap's amulet; perhaps she would know how to change him back.

But he had sent her away. And beyond that, he had treated her so roughly, she absolutely despised him. If he went to her and asked for her help—not that he knew how to—she would probably just laugh at him. Or catch him in a jar and keep him as a lantern until, eventually, his little light went out.

Even so, she was his only hope.

He rushed towards the door. His body, if you can call it that, passed right through and out into the tepid sunshine. Maybe he didn't have to worry about being caught in a jar. A small relief, but a relief nonetheless.

He rushed over the fields, over the trenches he had dug two days before, past the grazing donkey, and beyond the cluck of chickens. He moved north along the overgrown road—the way he had told them to go—his circle of vision searching everything at once.

They weren't there.

He stopped cold and flew in the other direction towards the graveyard. Fear flashed through him as he thought of Cova and Serap wandering into that place, being assaulted by those bone-crunching monsters, and all alone.

The ghouls snapped and swatted at him as he passed in much the same way Sappho had. No screams. No fiendish feeding frenzies. Which meant Serap and Cova were not there.

Where had they gone?

If he'd had a heart, it would have been pounding. As it was, his smoky-white light shimmered with frustration as he raced back towards his house at lightning speed. Javier had never been fast, so the fleet movements of his new form were both disorienting and exhilarating. He might have laughed if he'd had a voice.

He was about to plow into the woods to continue his search, when the soft sound of female voices wafted from beyond the trees, out towards a field of wildflowers that lay to the northeast.

Javier rushed through the understory towards the sound. He almost had to back-track, so quickly did he come upon the two girls sitting together in a crushed-down circle of flowers.

He had given them a picnic, it was true. He had never expected them to sit in the grass and eat it.

Cova sat cross-legged, her eyes down as she gnawed on some *lahmacun* he had packed in the basket—a Turkish recipe of flatbread, spread with olive oil and spices and topped with feta, roasted onions, and the last of his chicken. He had been thinking about Serap when he made it—her clothes and her language. Whoever she was, and whether she was actually from Edirne, she had likely been away from home for a long time. It was a woefully insufficient apology for what he had done, but she seemed to like food, and bread in particular, so he had made it.

Serap had removed her jacket, on which she was now sitting, her ankles together and swung out to one side so her body leaned on one hand. She wore a black silk shirt with short, tied-off sleeves. Her copper necklaces sparkled in the sunlight. She had taken off her headdress, allowing her long brown hair to fall behind her in messy curls that lifted and danced in the breeze.

He felt a stirring in his...well, ball of amorphous light. But Javier felt intrusive seeing her in this state. She was a Muslim woman and if she had known that he—a man—could see her, she would have covered herself. Maybe he should alert her to his presence, but that idea drowned in a sea of anxiety before it was even fully formed. He would avert his eyes, but his vision was everywhere all at once.

Defeated, Javier allowed himself to look. The curve of her shoulder, the line of her waist and hip. Pink wildflowers danced in the wind, a perfect shade to match the permanent blush of her round cheeks and rose-petal lips. How had he not noticed any of that before?

In the gloom of his house, it was hard to see beauty in anything, even a flower in bloom.

Javier wanted to look down at his feet, but there was no way to look down and no feet to look at. Instead, he dove below the stalks of the flowers to hide. His light twitched around him—nervousness, he supposed. Perhaps a bit of shame. He hoped they would not notice the gentle flicker with all that sunlight around them.

Why were they here? And especially, why was Serap still here? She had been so desperate to get away from him. So why sit amongst the flowers and eat flatbread instead of running for the hills, back to where she came from, perhaps to return with Shihalan reinforcements to burn his house to the ground? That's what he would have done if he was on a first-name basis with a powerful djinn king.

Unless she was determined to fulfill her mission for Khayin, or the King of Shihala, or whoever else she was working for.

Whatever had brought her to him in the first place must have been the same reason she wasn't leaving. But then why had she fled his house so quickly when he told her she could leave?

"You should have seen the look on his face when I kicked over a pile of his books." Serap giggled, a sound sweeter than morning birds. "He looked like he was about to burst into a thousand tiny, little flames. And then his whole library would have gone up."

Cova smiled and shook her head. "I didn't even know there were that many books in the whole world. What does he do with them?"

"Puts them in piles to be knocked over, I suppose. Though they make excellent levers for prying up floorboards." Serap's giggles died down a bit. "Actually, I feel a little guilty about that one. But Chupkin had disappeared, and I didn't want to be alone."

Cova squished her nose up. "Who's Chupkin?"

"My wisp." Serap put a hand up to her collarbone and whispered something.

It was the same gesture he'd seen her make in his dungeon when she spoke into her shirt. He'd thought she had been talking to herself.

What in heaven's name was a *chupkin*?

"Goodness, I don't even know if you'll be able to see him or not, some people... Oh, would you just come out already? She's not going to hurt you."

A tiny tendril of white slid up and under her chin, then swirled in a sulky circle next to her face.

Serap smiled proudly. "Ta da!"

The white mist looked like a wisp—little puffs of raw magic that could sometimes be found floating at random through Allah's worlds. They were not invisible, just of such little consequence, most humans couldn't be bothered to see them.

She had been keeping that little thing a secret from him the entire time he had her locked away. Perhaps, he had underestimated the little bread-seeker from Edirne. It would not be the first time.

The last one he had seen had come in a magically imbued jar, offered to him as an honorarium. A woman with ribbons in her hair had turned up at his house with an entire cartload of glass bottles, each filled with a tiny puff of raw, white magic. She had wanted him to slay a sphinx that was causing her trouble, and, in addition to the wisps, had offered him a large sum of Turkish coins to do the job straight away.

Javier did not accept extradition fees. He took one wisp for himself simply because he was curious, and then calmly informed that woman that sphinxes are not technically immortal and therefore were not in his purview, before sending her away.

That jarred wisp was still in his house. Somewhere.

Cova moved back from the puff of magic, then slowly leaned over her legs for a closer look. "What is it?"

Serap's lips puckered. "I guess it looks a little different to everyone, though most humans are too ignorant to see them. He's a white little mist, like a piece of cloud fell from the sky." She curled him out on her finger. "Can you see him?"

Cova nodded, eyes wide.

"I thought you would." Serap smile. "Ayelet—she's the Queen of Shihala and the one who helped save me from that monster, Köle, that I told you about—she says they're pure magic. No life in them or anything. But she also says mine is broken." The wisp twisted back and forth in a rapid swirl, and Serap laughed. "Oh, don't get so upset. *I* didn't say you were broken. You're perfect."

Everything she had said—all the new information—crashed through Javier's brain like a tempest, too wild at the moment to make much sense. Köle Amir, the Queen of Shihala, wisps. Was there any Qafian pie this woman did not have her fingers in?

Cova's dark eyes sparkled, and her fingers twitched. "Can I touch it?"

Serap plucked the wisp from the air, though it moved in and out of her fingers. She brought it in front of Cova. "Go ahead."

With a nervous giggle, Cova reached a single finger forward and ran it over the back of the slinky, white mist. "*Ooo.* That's so weird."

"You should feel him in your belly button. Or whooshing through your clothes. It gives me the shivers sometimes."

The wisp floated up from Serap's hand and brushed her face. The gesture looked affectionate, but that didn't make any sense. Wisps didn't have feelings. They were just little coalitions of free magic. They were tools to use and command, but they weren't supposed to behave like that.

If that wisp had free will, perhaps he and it had something in common. Perhaps, when Serap had first pulled out her amulet, she had intended to transform him into a wisp. He had walked right into her plan.

Had she planned to make him a part of an incorporeal harem of wisp men that this woman kept stashed in her belly button?

Her daring to walk right into his house suddenly made more sense.

Cova laughed when the playful wisp brushed her chin, but the chime-like sound died out quickly. She looked down at the ground, her smile falling further and further until it was nothing.

Serap leaned forward. "What's wrong, Cova?"

The girl shrugged and turned away. "What are you going to do now? Are you going to leave? It seems like you want to go back home to... what did you call it? *Shilala*?"

"Shihala." Serap smiled softly, the sun shining in her eyes. "And yes, I should like to go back there, eventually. 'Abi Jahmil and Ayelet are my version of parents. I love Bakr Amca and his family, and cousins Balian and Yousef, too, but it's not the same. I don't know what I'd do without them."

'Abi Jahmil. The King of Shihala was Serap's father. But the brown tone of her skin and her human eyes testified she was not related to the djinn by blood. Her *version of parents* suggested the possibility of adoption. But why would a djinn king adopt a human girl?

A lump caught in Javier's throat. Maybe Serap had married into the royal family and *her version of parents* were actually in-laws.

Did King Jahmil have a son of marriageable age? He had thought him a young king, but his knowledge of the matter was spotty.

Javier tried to dismiss the uncomfortable emotions the thought of Serap's marriage brought to rise, but they lingered like a burr.

"I don't have any family left." Cova's said in a flat monotone as if she were simply conveying information.

Those simple words clawed at his heart and sent Javier's thoughts reeling in a different direction. Back in time to a ramshackle raft lost in the Far Bahamut Sea where he and his cousin had baked in the sun together, waiting to die. That is until a sphinx flew down from the heavens and snatched Alessandro in her claws, lifting him off into the infinite sky never to be seen again.

His best friend—his only friend—was lost forever that day. Javier had had no way to follow and, moments later, had found himself inside the belly of the Bahamut.

He looked back to the two girls. Serap paused, her gaze falling to her hands. "The truth is, with how things are going, I may never get back. No amulet. No crow's beak. No magic. My lilu uncle is not answering his bell."

Crow's beak? Did he have a crow's beak? Was that what she had come to his house to steal?

And what was this about a lilu uncle? Were lilu not sex-obsessed demons who delighted in torturing mortals with everything and nothing all at once? How could one be an uncle?

"How about, for now, we stick together," Serap said, "and if I find a way home, I'll take you with me. Deal?"

"Really?" Cova took a big bite of bread and spoke around it. "Is it far away?"

"It is as far away as the moon and as close as the nose upon your face. If I had my amulet—" Serap's gentle eyes hardened around the edges. "Well, anyway, if you have the right tools you can disappear and show up there in the blink of an eye."

The squirmy wisp disconcertingly called *Chupkin* gave a sudden burst of light, then twisted back and slithered through the air towards Javier.

Panic gripped him. Javier darted back through the stalks, trying to avoid being noticed, but it was too late. The tiny wisp chased him, peeking at him between the stems of the flowers. Javier tried to hiss at it, to tell it to go away and leave him alone, but that only made its light flicker.

"Chupkin?" Serap called over the flowers. She stood. "Where'd he go? He's usually too scared to run off."

Javier stayed very still. His instinct was to rush back to the house and lock himself inside, which was a queer instinct, indeed, for a brute of a man whose profession was fighting immortal monsters. But he had never in his life felt more helpless and exposed as he did now. Besides, if he ran, Serap would see him. And given her insatiable curiosity, she would chase him. Then she would go into his kitchen and see her talisman sitting on the table. She would take it and disappear back to Qaf, leaving him trapped as a wisp forever.

Yet, remaining in one spot while that skinny dab of cloud poked at him seemed like an even worse idea. He wiggled back and forth, unable to decide, as Serap stepped through the flowers.

"*Oha!* There you a—" Her brown eyes widened. "You're not Chupkin." She frowned and crouched down low, the puff of her pants billowing to each side. "Where'd you come from little... no, *biiiig* guy?"

Cova appeared next to Serap, the flowers white and yellow against her brown skin. "What's going on?"

"I found another wisp." She rubbed her nose. "He looks scared... and well-fed. Come see. Maybe he'll come out if we're sweet."

Javier's thoughts ran in loops. He could rush into the woods and circle back around to his house. But that was stupid. Hadn't he come out here to try to get her help?

Oh, it was hopeless. He couldn't talk, and if she found out it was him, she would probably stomp him into the dirt. Not that she could, him being insubstantial, but there was emotional damage inherent in being stomped that no magic could protect him from.

Javier sank down to the ground with what should have been a sigh. He missed his lungs.

Chupkin wiggled and poked him with a tendril.

"Oh, leave him be," Serap chided. "Look how sad he is. Like a pool of jam." She slid her fingers under Javier's misty form and lifted him up. Soft brown eyes brushed over him, an almost invisible rim of red around the edges of her irises.

"What shall we name him?" Serap asked.

Cova lifted her shoulders. "What do you usually call wisps? What does Chupkin mean?"

"It's a term of endearment we use in Turkey. It means a flirt. But I don't think a name like that would fit this timid, little guy. What's a good *España* name for him?"

"*En Español?*" Cova rubbed her chin. "We could call him *Gordito*. It means cute, little fatty."

I am not fat, thought Javier, then shrank remembering what he now was. *Well, I suppose I'm globular.*

"It's perfect."

Serap stroked him with two fingers, and while he couldn't actually feel it, a warmth like syrup slipped through his body. Well, not body. Shimmery sphere.

"Good little *Gordito*. Now, where did you come from? Maybe I can help you get back home. Otherwise, you'll probably have to stay with me so I can put you back in Qaf... If I ever get myself back there."

He floated up from her hand so he could see her face more clearly, examining the sunlight in her eyes. She certainly didn't seem like she worked for the malodorous traitor. What could be the connection? And what king in his right mind would let such a sweet princess come looking for... well, *him*? It didn't make sense.

And why was he worrying about that now when he didn't even have a body? Or a voice to ask questions?

The wisp swirled up next to him, poking him once more. He flinched back, irritation flaring in his guts. Well, not guts. Nebulous lump. At the same time, he had a feeling that this Chupkin—*Chupkin?*—Chupkin was not trying to antagonize him. It seemed interested in him, like a child meeting another child for the first time. Poking and prodding as if to say, *come play with me.*

Chupkin flew up to Serap's eyes, whisking by her face to try to catch her attention. Then, it waggled in the direction of the house.

Serap shrugged. "We're done eating, so we can go back. Is that where you think Gordito came from, Chupkin?"

The skinny wisp dipped once, then twice. It was answering her. This was no ordinary wisp.

Her pink lips slid into a half frown. "His house *is* full of a bunch of weird stuff, so it would kind of make sense. And if I can get him to give my amulet back, maybe I can take Gordito back to Qaf. With you, too, of course, Cova." She glanced over her shoulder with a smile.

Cova pushed her lips together and nodded. "But what about Don DeMario?"

"Do *about* Don DeMario?"

"What are we going to do about him?"

"Do *about* him? Mercy, I don't know. Can anything be done?" She walked back over to where they sat and grabbed her coat and headscarf. "I suppose we shall first have to see how happy the Immortal Killer is when he discovers we've come back. If he won't give back my amulet, we can't go anywhere. And—" She shimmied stiffly into her jacket. "—I have something I sort of need to ask him."

Javier leaned in. Well, not leaned. Floated marginally closer. Ever since he first found her hiding in his pantry, he had been desperate to know what exactly she had been hoping to find there. A question...?

Serap's sunny disposition dimmed despite the bright, cloudless sky. "I'm honestly not quite sure what I'm doing, anymore. I have a goal to reach a mountain but not a clear way up. I think I shall have to talk to Evil."

"Evil? You mean the djinn?" Cova asked.

Serap looked sideways at Cova and laughed. "I forgot how many questions you little ones ask. Ah, Lalam and Tabor would feel right at home with you. And no, djinn aren't any eviler than humans. Evil is... someone." She frowned. "Someone who gives gifts."

Javier wanted to narrow his eyes at her, instead, his light dimmed. Which of the many horrific, circuitous immortal beings that haunted his house could have been talking to her? And what hideous gifts might it have bestowed?

He never should have run after her. He should have let her go that first night.

Stupid cat.

"Come on," said Serap. "It's almost dinnertime, and you know Don DeMario will have something good cooking."

"I've never eaten so much in my entire life!" Cova smiled, biting the tip of her tongue so it poked out a little. "I think I'm going to explode."

"Me too," Serap grinned. "No wonder this wisp is so fat."

CHAPTER FIFTEEN

SERAP

Serap led Cova back to the house where they knocked on the front door. When no one answered, they knocked on the kitchen door, then a window up a trellis on the side of the house. Serap was about to try leaping onto the roof and shimmying down the chimney when Cova walked up to the front door and turned the handle.

The iron-laced door creaked open.

"The direct approach works too," Serap said with a sheepish grin as they walked inside "Maybe he's out. Though I didn't think he ever left his house with how much he hoards stuff and hates people."

"He hates people?" Cova ran her finger over the edge of a dilapidated, worn-down chair.

Serap picked up a book and fanned its pages. "Maybe not all people. He seems to like you. Me, on the other hand...." She tossed the book to the side, then felt guilty and straightened it. "Come on. Let's look around for my amulet while he's gone. Do you know where he sleeps?"

The little girl shrugged.

"Very well. Chupkin, you take Gordito and check the top floor. I'll take the second floor, and Cova, you do the first. You're looking for a copper square with seven-by-seven rows of ancient symbols. Don't rub it or touch the surface, though."

"Why not?" Cova's eyes grew round.

"Because I have no idea what will happen if you do. Magic stuff. Seal-hands, harpies, calls to home, and who knows what else." She shuddered and headed up the stairs. "In fact, you probably shouldn't touch anything else in this house for the same reason."

Chupkin and Gordito followed her upstairs, the fat one sulking in drips like gloppy butter, and Chupkin poking him all the way. She would tell Chupkin to quit, but honestly, Gordito looked like he could use all the poking he could get. Like he hadn't been poked, or touched, or loved on. Ever. The way the fat, little wisp had arched his back when she petted it had been endearing and heartbreaking. It was no wonder he didn't get any love in this cold, haunted house.

The two wisps settled onto the top step as Serap turned onto the landing of the second floor. She picked her way through stacks of scrolls. There were three doors on this floor, one on each end of the landing and one in the middle. She tried the one to the left first and found it blocked by far too many books, all on mathematics. Ich.

She pursed her lips and moved to the middle door. This one swung open on light hinges. Sunlight streamed through the opened window. Just as many tomes of literature cluttered this room as the rest, though they were pushed in tight stacks against the walls with a rectangle of walking space in the center of the room. A worn, multi-colored braided rug covered the tired wood in intricate patterns.

Serap resisted the urge to kneel down and touch the dusty pattern and walked into the empty space. The door slammed shut behind her. She jumped as high as a hissing cat and spun on her heels, surprise rippling through trembling limbs.

"Hello, child," said a strange voice, like the rustle of dry leaves.

Serap turned her head around first, body following reluctantly behind. A lithe woman stood before her, thick, jagged, and twisting horns tucked into silky gray-ish-brown strands of hair. She had a wide nose that was tipped with a hint of pink. Her ivory skin glowed in shades of slate blue wherever shadows touched: on the side of her nose, around her slender neck, and under her resolute chin. She had chrysanthemum pink lips that dipped in a heartbreaking curve and feather-brown tattoos that tapered off to the sides of her forehead like clouds of smoke slipping down the bridge of her nose. But what made Serap sweat ice were her despondently round, red eyes accented with a dark-blue blush on the corners.

Serap stumbled back a few steps toward the door. "You're Red Eye."

The woman flicked her gaze to the floor. "One of the less flattering names I've been called over the millennia."

"Sorry."

How many beings lived in this house?

Serap rubbed one foot over the other, hands clasped behind her back. "What would you like me to call you?"

The red eyes returned to hers, an ethereal sorrow clinging to the almond corners of each. "You are the one who released me from my torment, so you may call me Najima. For others less bestowed, I require the title of Queen."

Serap leaned back onto her heels, worried her brows would pop off the top of her head.

"If you're a queen, what are you doing here in this place?" She eyed the cobwebs and overwhelming clutter of books. "Where is your kingdom?"

Najima blinked, her eyelids moving down and up with the speed of a snowflake ambling its way across the sky. "I was torn from my people." Her rich, bell-like voice was weighted with sorrow. "It is an agony I've borne for the last two thousand years. But I am still their rightful queen."

Serap couldn't help a small pout. Would everyone in the two worlds live longer than she? And how could someone with so much life look so sad?

"I know from my 'abi that a ruler without her kingdom is on hard times, indeed. What happened?"

"Six millennia ago, I left my birth home in the Fyre nation—where the first drakonte was born and the fire of snakes lives in the blood of the people—to reign over a foreign country in peace and harmony with my one and only love. For four thousand years we ruled this way, but there is no such thing as love eternal, not as long as those who love also live. And when our hearts and marriage broke, so did our nation."

Serap squirmed, knowing well from Bakr Amca and Zan Hala how much heart-break could hurt the lives and kingdoms of everyone involved. Especially for royalty and diplomats. And especially when contracts were involved.

Not good.

"After a hundred years of painful warfare," Najima continued, eyes unmoving, "I was as broken as our country and our people. I begged my former love to stop and tried to make a deal. Blinded by lingering affection, I trusted he would do right by me, or at least right by our nation, our people. We spent half a decade sorting through the details, and when it was settled, I signed freely, blindly, not knowing he had betrayed his oath as an Honorable—a Binder of Seals granted power from Allah himself—and switched out the contracts. The second my ink dried on the paper, I was bound and sent into never-ending torment. That was until your merciful hands interceded on my behalf."

Serap wanted to reach out and pat Najima's shoulder, but her blue-tinged ivory skin looked icy to the touch.

"My Zan Hala knows how you feel. She always tells me never to trust a man with a silky tongue and a pen to match."

Najima tilted her head, her face as smooth and broken as ever. "Because our marriage contract required we both remain as rulers until *death* do we part, even after he tricked me and locked me away, he could not take over my right to rule. Our country split for good, my people determined to be ruled only by the one true race of pure djinn. They saw the cursed seal of the duplicitous king as a sign of subjugation and refused to take part."

Serap rolled her shoulders and tried to keep her feet from fidgeting. "Well, you're free now, thanks to me and Evil. Why don't you just go back and fix it?"

"Fix it?" Najima's head slid upright, slow and smooth, like a block of ice upon a glacier. "Reconciliation is impossible. My people have returned to their nomadic, turbulent roots while my former lover locked down his country and sought to subjugate the rest of Qaf. There can be no fixing until my former love and king pays the price for what he's done."

"You want to kill him." The thought plunked into her stomach like a worm-filled apple. "Don't you?"

"It would be the logical choice," she said, her bell voice sumptuously rich. "But even after all this time, my heart yearns for vengeance."

Serap scratched her forehead. "But not death?"

"For the King? Of course not, child." Najima's ruby-red eyes gleamed with nary a blink. "Death is a gift. An end to the toil of life and a start to whatever comes next. For immortals like myself, we must labor away in a world that never truly changes. We must see all we love pass away. It takes only a moment to kindle, a flicker in the dark, a stranger finding his way into an eternal prison and breaking the nothingness with poetry and light. But if it is true love and not fickle as the *januub* wind, those burning feelings will only wane with death, leaving you hot and empty whenever you're apart."

Her eyes flicked up to Serap's, a sudden fire in them that Serap knew came from the icy woman's heart.

Serap winced. She had ever only been told of the beginnings of love. Of sparks and flickers and the joy of fulfilling it by being together. The tragedy of love left her feeling empty. She did not want to be the reason others wept, dying away and leaving them without her.

"For degrees, for days, the burn of longing seems tolerable. A pain you can endure. Bemusing even, a sting that means hope for more. But days become months, then years, then decades and millennia, and by then, the fire is anything but hope. Unrequited love consumes you in eternal agony, all joy turning to ash so heavy, all you long for is the end of longing. Death." The light in Najima's eyes smothered in an instant. "You mortals, on the other hand, can live and love and let be, and then start all over again. Fires starting and fading with reckless abandon."

Serap shook her head, a fig-sized pain growing between her ribs. "But living forever means no one forgets you or thinks you aren't worth their time. You can love and keep loving and be loved and not miss out on family and living."

Najima's smooth face stared into hers. Serap shrank.

Then Najima's chrysanthemum lips tightened. "Do not be foolish, child. Having no end means you get only one beginning. And once it is gone, life loses its purpose. You can only watch so many hundreds of your own children die before love means nothing. You can only live so many years apart from your true love, yearning for someone you can never hold again before your heart dies inside your body but insists on still beating. Death is a blessing."

"So, you mean to punish the king by making him live forever?"

"Yes." The shadow of a smile tipped the corners of her lips for the first time, the dimmest flicker of embers shining in her eyes. "And to take away any chance he has at death, I plan to lay a trap to slay the Immortal Killer."

"You can't." Serap gasped. "Why do you want the Immortal Traitor to die?"

Najima lifted a brow, liquid eyes solemn. "To end his story and start one new. But the Immortal Killer must die."

"But I'm the one who released you from your torment," she said, fumbling for words.

Najima raised a silky, thin eyebrow.

"So you have to listen to me or something, right?" Serap crossed her arms.

"Continue," the bells said.

"No killing Don DeMario. And no killing yourself."

The embers glowed in Najima's eyes once more. "You do not know what you ask."

Serap flinched, the ring of the queen's voice loud in her ears. While she opposed killing in general, Jahmil's zeal for peace was something he made sure to instill in her. Why would anyone take life away when it was so precious? Especially their own? Only the traitorous and evil deserved death. Those who harmed innocents and wreaked havoc wherever they went.

Another zing of pain shot through her heart at the thought of Don DeMario's demise. Which was absurd. That monster killed others, so by killing him, she would be saving others, right? Though she still wasn't entirely sure who exactly the Killer had laid his hands on.

Cova's words strung through her mind like lanterns around trees during the Festival of the Eight Moons. Is the killer of monsters a monster himself? Or a hero? And what of the queen? She had been unjustly trapped in torment for two thousand years, so of course, her outlook on life was bleak. But with some time... some sunshine, she would surely realize what a gift her long life was.

A sharp uneasiness pushed against the back of Serap's eyes, and she rubbed them with her fists. "I may not fully understand, but I still ask it."

The tiny lick of flame in Najima's eyes was smothered with a gray shadow of ash. "For your service, you may have one or the other. But to ensure the King of Elm lives on forever, the Immortal Killer will be the one to go."

"Wait just a moment, now, " Serap said, injustice flaring up her chest and neck.

Najima met her eyes, then vanished.

Serap growled and kicked a stack of books so they tumbled to the earth. She winced. Why had Evil sent her to release the queen? Did he want Don DeMario dead? Or the queen? Or was there another reason to release such a beautiful, terrifying, immortal being into this already haunted house? A gift? A love released? Perhaps Najmia yearned for Evil, and he for her. But then, who was he?

And more importantly, how was all this helping her?

She ran her fingers up and down the sides of her nose. Why speculate when she could just ask?

"Evil?"

Serap listened hard, unsure if she had to be in the dungeon for the presence to hear.

A gust of breeze blew past her pants.

"Why did you have me release the red-eyed queen?"

"*Found in darkness all alone, locked up in cruel confinement. A deal I bartered long ago, enticed to see her free. Broken now from prison's sharpness, a debt of life I owe.*"

"DeMario's life?" She bit her lip hard in anticipation of the answer. She waited so long, her skin split and spilled blood on her tongue.

At last, Evil breathed the reply, "*I do not hunt the hunter.*"

Weight on her shoulders lifted as lightly as if it were Chupkin, and she patted her hand over her heart to help it calm down. The longer she stayed in the house, the more puzzled she became. Today, alone, she had been freed by a hunched and sorry man who had yesterday been a monster, found a kindred spirit in Cova, discovered an errant and chubby wisp of magic far too far from home, and freed a lost queen from eternal torment. Evil still wanted something from her, though she could not for the life of her figure out what, and her amulet and Don DeMario were conspicuously missing.

Serap scowled. The whole thing was maddening. She ran a hand across the books on the shelves and the floor, looking for her amulet. For the crow's beak. She knew Evil wanted her to read something, but there were so many books. But so far, the mystical being had guided her way, and she trusted it would be the same now.

She headed towards the door then turned abruptly and searched the room once more. No luck. Serap bustled into the landing and toward the last room when two flickers of white caught her eye. She leaned over the banister. Chupkin chased Gordito around in a violent swirl, knocking down books and reaching with his shimmering, shapeless hands as if he wished to grab a hold of the fat little wisp.

"Chupkin," she called sharply, but the two didn't stop.

What had gotten into him lately? Disappearing in the field? Lingering away from her for long periods of time? What about Gordito upset him so? Or were they friends? She frowned. She'd had Chupkin for five years now but still had trouble reading a cloud with no face or voice. How many times had she longed to talk to him? To hear him whisper secrets back? To hear the kind words of a friend or an affirmation of love. He was her best friend in both worlds, and she could not even squeeze him against her chest.

Her cheeks warmed. The only person who had ever held her so close besides her family had been DeMario. He had picked her up like a leaf in the wind out of anger or spite or malice or whatever it was that lingered in his dark, serious eyes, and yet it had still felt... nice? His hard muscles pressed against her, making her feel so delicate and small.

Gug. She slapped her cheeks a few times. The thought was utter ridiculousness. She was so desperate for what her parents and *amca* had that she was getting delusional. Or perhaps it was the magic seeping from every shelf in this house. She swore she could even feel it floating up from yet another sumptuous rug that hid beneath the stacks of books.

Why else would her mind keep wandering to DeMario and his broad shoulders? His ability to cook with adept fingers while still being able to toss her over his shoulder like she weighed nothing. His giddy joy at finding a simple, white dress. And his sunken shoulders when he finally let her go.

He had chased her down in the woods as ferociously as a wolf one day and left her warm breakfast and a blanket the next. It didn't make any sense.

She had to search for the amulet, the beak, and a way to convince the least human-like human on Ard to help her. She needed to focus. To find. Not to be distracted by *impulsive* and *childish* whims as 'Abi had said.

But that's where her thoughts lingered as she searched mindlessly in the next room, not really seeing anything. Each beat of her heart sent her whipping one way or the other. Captor. Savior. Monster. Lamb. And covering each thought like Evil's green haze, sang the word *killer*.

CHAPTER SIXTEEN

JAVIER

Javier had never felt comfortable in his own skin. When he was a child, people had always assumed he was much older than he was because he was so tall and broad. His beard started coming in when he was only twelve—the same year he joined his father's crew as a cabin boy, sailing on a merchant ship. By the time he was sixteen, he was a helmsman, and his beard was thick enough to rival any man aboard. And while he had always had confidence in his coordination and strength—in his ability to perform whatever physical labor was laid before him—he had always felt uncomfortable in his own body. There seemed to be an irreconcilable disconnect between his body and his brain.

The great Hercules that won every battle, and the insecure lump that just wanted to be left alone.

Now, all he had was the lump, and not even that. A shiny glob called Gordito. And this lump had a tiny, lightning-fast breath of cloud called Chupkin was poking and prodding him, chasing him around like a cheetah on the hunt.

What do you want? He tried to scream, but all that happened were more shimmers. *Leave me alone.*

Chupkin dove for him with even more force, a spear racing through the air trying to get at his heart. Javier dodged and rushed past a very confused-looking Serap and up the stairs into a room with a blocked door that he had abandoned to stacks of old, already-read, and not especially well-loved books. He dove behind a pile, hoping to hide, but within a moment his tormentor appeared. Chupkin slowed, floating in front of him as if gazing right through him.

Please, just leave me alone, Javier thought as hard as he could, wishing the tiny bully could just hear him.

Then—as if wrapped in the echo of a far-off canyon—the voice of a young man rang in his head: *Can you hear me? Please, please say that you can hear me.*

Javier froze, or at least the pulse of his light and infernal bobbing seemed to slow. *Yes,* he thought. *I think I can.*

Chupkin flashed with a bright yellow light and rocketed up in the air to do several loop-de-loops. *I can't believe it!* the little voice cried. *This is the best thing to ever happen! I haven't spoken to anyone in over five years!*

Who are you? What do you want?

What do I want? Chupkin dove and wrapped around him. The sensation was very much like being hugged. *What part of 'I haven't spoken to anyone in over five years' do you not understand, Mountain Man?*

The voice was brimming with so much joy. Nobody in all Javeri's life had ever been so pleased—so excited—to speak to him. It was instantly exhausting.

Don't you have any other wisps to talk to? Javier groaned.

Wisps can't talk, said Chupkin, his light laughter pulsing in Javier's mind. *They aren't even alive. They're just floating bits of magic. Like puddles or rocks. They're nothing like us.*

Us? He tried to scoff and his brain made the noise. *What are you?*

I'm a djinn. My name is Zayne, but you can totally call me Chupkin. I've gotten used to it.

Okay, Zayne, said Javier, preferring the more dignified name over the uncomfortable Turkish word for "flirtatious womanizer." *How did you end up a wisp? Did Serap turn you into one with her amulet?*

Serap doesn't know how to do that kind of stuff. She only got that amulet a few days ago. Zayne laughed and did another quick loop. He was a bolt of pure energy. *I got on the wrong side of an ugly green witch, and she turned me into this. It's not even my fault, though. She is just so...*

Moody?

I didn't even do anything to her!

I suppose that means you don't know how to turn back?

What do you think, genius? Zayne wiggled from side to side. *But at least I have you now! Somebody to talk to. Ya'ilahi! I have been dying. Serap is my* fatati, *and I would murder for her, but oha! She talks a lot. Which would be fine if I could ever, ever say anything in response. That has maybe been the worst part of being a wisp. I miss my body and my life, and eating, and drinking, and feeling anything with my skin, but I think I miss talking more than anything.*

I can imagine, said Javier, realizing he had come across yet another chatterbox.

You, by the way. I should slap you. If I had a body to slap you with, I would. Except then you'd have to have a body too, so you'd be all huge and terrifying, so I guess I probably wouldn't. But, oha! Oha! Somebody should. The wisp rushed closer and swiped his glob over Javier's as if trying to create a slap. *How could you be so mean to my girl? She is the sweetest girl in the world. How can anybody be mean to her?*

I never should have taken her prisoner. That was bad form. Javier slumped down to the ground in a little puddle. *I didn't mean to hurt her. I suppose I just forget how strong I am sometimes.*

I know. Zayne moved back a little and bobbed up and down. *But it's also kind of impossible to be afraid of you after watching you try to seduce a chicken.*

You saw that?

I did. I went on ahead. But don't worry, Serap didn't see anything. A trill of laughter filled the space. *I think you are a very silly person. Which is good. I like silly people. I'm a silly person, myself. Or at least, I used to be.*

Javier's light dimmed even further. *I wish I could apologize to her.*

It's really easy, sadiqa. You just put your lips together and say, 'I'm sorry.' Give it a try. Oh, except you don't have lips anymore. Zayne laughed, then groaned. *Sorry. It really isn't funny. Trust me, I know.*

I can't stay like this. I have important things to do. My calendar is full. Do you know what will happen to Earth and to Qaf if I just disappear?

Somebody has a high opinion of himself. Zayne scoffed. *You think I wasn't booked solid when this nonsense happened to me?*

"Chupkin? Gordito?" came Serap's voice. The door jiggled. There was no way she could get in, not with a few hundred pounds of books barring her way. "Are you two in there?"

A flicker of fear raced up Javier's globulous bulb. *We can't let her and Cova wander around in this house. There's no telling the damage they might cause. To themselves. To my things.*

Yeah, I'm starting to think you might be right about that. Your house is severely messed up.

I know, I know.

Serap just can't help herself. You know that story about that lady who's given a pretty box and the gods tell her, seriously, do not open this. All sorts of terrible stuff will fly out and mess up everything forever. But she opens it anyway, and so all sorts of terrible stuff flies out and messes up everything forever....

You mean Pandora?

I'm pretty sure that was Serap in a previous life.

Ugh, Javier groaned. *We have to get her out.*

Too late for that, Mountain Man. She's been tearing through your stuff ever since you brought us in here. I tried to stop her.... Well, I mean, not really. Because screw you for being so mean to her.

I said I was sorry.

You literally haven't. Zayne flickered with blue irritation.

"Come on out, Chupkin." Serap's fingers slipped through the tiny crack in the door. "The sad, scary lady is gone."

Sad, scary lady? Chupkin froze. Javier could all but feel terror rushing over him. *Who is the sad, scary lady?*

Search me, said Javier. *I have several sad and/or scary ladies floating around my house.*

Zayne shuddered. *Why don't you move, abu? This place is awful.*

Anywhere I lived would end up the same. It doesn't matter.

Oh, I get it. You're one of those tall, dark, handsome, and incredibly brooding types.

Did you just call me handsome? Javier couldn't help a little chuckle. *You must be as blind as you are mute and intangible.*

Well, maybe if you owned even one mirror instead of all these stupid books... Never-mind. The little wisp rushed to his side and poked him again. *Come on, let's go. She's waiting for us. Unless you want her trying to find a way to smash in that door, because I guarantee that is what she is doing right now. She's very protective of me if you haven't noticed.*

An image flashed through Javier of the torn cover of his two-hundred-year-old atlas.

Fine.

Javier followed Zayne the Chupkin into the hall. Serap was standing there with his ax in her hands—the one he needed to sharpen for his upcoming battle with the *bunyip* tomorrow. She had it lifted over one shoulder like she was about to take a swing at the door. She looked ridiculous under its weight, but when he and Zayne came floating out of the room, she dropped it with a *thunk* and broke into a smile.

"Didn't you hear me calling for you?"

Zayne rushed over to her and brushed her cheek affectionately. She giggled.

Something about that sound made Javier's light shine brighter.

A flash of green stole his attention. The distinct outline of long black horns moved through a door at the end of the hall. The litigious vampire was back.

Not now, he groaned internally.

Zayne rushed closer, flickering with tension. *What's wrong?*

It's the King of Elm.

What? Chupkin's light dashed in every direction at once before rushing back towards Serap to hide in her clothes. *Don't let him see me.*

Javier flew past them into the room where he had seen emerald skin moving in the shadows. The darkness warmed as he moved inside, and by the light of his own body, he saw the royal vulture standing in the shadows. The King's black horns gleamed, and his deep amethyst eyes flashed in a way Javier had never seen before. In his hand, was a long sword with two prongs at the tip—an ancient Elmaran battle scimitar.

The King of Elm looked directly at Javier's light and his smooth, youthful features contorted with rage. He seemed to have aged two hundred years overnight.

A flash of magic burst from the King's eyes and rushed through Javier like cold tingles.

"Don DeMario," the dark green lips hissed. "What happened to you?"

Umm... Javier tried to answer, though he had no idea if the king would be able to hear him.

He didn't owe the bastard an explanation anyway.

The king shook his head. "You let her out."

Let who out?

"No. It wasn't you. It was the termite." He heaved his massive sword over one shoulder, his eyes narrowing into cruel slits. "She dies for this."

Javier had no idea what he was talking about. But he knew one thing as well as he did his own name.

I won't let you hurt Serap.

The king threw his head back and laughed. Then he snatched Javier's glob of light with one sparkling hand. Javier struggled, but the magic grip only tightened impossibly around his light. The king cast a spell over an empty glass bottle, the sparkles from his fingers floating down to coat the glass. Then he shoved Javier inside and forced in the cork.

Javier dove for the glass, expecting to slice through it like he had the door but instead, bumped against it like a trapped fly. The King's magic held him in place.

There was no way out.

Lifting his sword and growling like a predator, the King of Elm stalked toward Serap.

CHAPTER SEVENTEEN

SERAP

The fat wisp whipped past Serap down the hallway, his blob a blurr of white. The burst of energy startled her, considering his girth and tendency to behave like cold honey.

What was with the wisps today? Chupkin kept disappearing, and this new one behaved like no wisp she had met before, all slow and gloppy.

Serap bit her lip and followed his light. "Gordito?"

She glanced between the room where she had met Najima and where Gordito had disappeared.

A growl rattled the air.

She slowed, heart picking up its march. Wisps couldn't make sounds.

Serap took a step toward the dark shadows of the far room. Two shining tips of a massive sword caught the light. Then flashed toward her. She screamed. The blade sliced through the air in front of her nose. Serap yelped and scrambled back.

A green djinn stepped into the light, his gnarly black horns twisting toward the sky in angry swirls. Rage lived in his purple eyes, and a smirk smeared his lips. He leveled his sword at her, the prominent seal of Elm evident on its hilt. Her brows pinche close. What was the King of Elm doing here? She had only ever seen his proxy bodies at royal events in Shihala. And even then, she was never allowed near, whispers of danger alive in the very air around him.

"You'll pay with your life for what you've done."

Her eyes flashed wide. They took a collective breath, eyes locked.

Then, Serap ran. As fast and hard as her feet would carry her. Down the stairs, past a ratty chair. She dove into the kitchen, looking for a knife. Why had she left the ax on the floor upstairs?

The king matched her pace, as menacing and deliberate as DeMario had been when he hunted her in the woods. Was she so slow and pathetic that all a man had to do to kill her was walk slowly behind?

Serap growled and grabbed the first weapon she could find, a dull butter knife from off the counter. She dug it into the plate of salted cream and flung the blade at the man, aiming for his eyes. A juggler, she never missed, and the glob of creamy fat hit smack between his eyelids.

He snarled and wiped the butter from his face. She dove for the door. He chucked his sword like a spear so its two prongs splintered the wood in front of her. She skidded, falling on her butt. Then twisted around. She crawled under the table, completely out of ideas.

How many murderers lived in this house? If she had known there was more than one...

She shook her head. The sound of metal being torn from wood ripped in her ear. Bare, green feet approached the table where she stood. She held her breath, knowing he saw her.

"You stupid girl." His voice was both deliciously glossy and painfully bare. "Do you know what you've done?"

Serap made ready to bolt for the door once more, when the chill of a whisper caught her ears, a hint of blue appearing above her head.

Stand up, young one. Stand up.

She glanced up at the hardwood, then grimaced.

Evil had yet to lead her astray. And who would give gifts to someone they wished dead?

Serap bit her lip and jumped up. Her head went straight through the wood and into the hole she had made in the floor of the bedroom DeMario had thrown her in.

Unwet white mist coated the space that connected the two rooms. It wrapped around her and pulled her body through. She scrambled, yanking her feet up just as a blade stabbed where she had been.

"What sorcery is this?" the king hissed.

She caught a glimpse of his murder-filled, purple irises before the hole sealed up behind her. She crawled out of the torn floorboards, her lungs burning as she caught her breath. Would she ever get used to the abrupt portal magic Evil used to thrust her to strange places?

The air shimmered, and her stomach clenched. The black of twisted horns began to materialize. She groaned and jumped to her feet, yanking open the door to run. A green hand jutted out of thin air and grabbed her wrist.

Serap screamed and pulled as hard as she could, but the grip grew like iron, cutting into her bone. She twisted and tugged, refusing to look at the cruel sneer that came so naturally to the evil man's lips.

Red light winked into existence on the bed. Serap gasped as one crimson eye and then another shimmered into existence, followed by sorrow-filled brows and soft, pink lips. Cerulean-tinted ivory skin flashed out and grabbed her other wrist, the grip like frostbite, stinging and numb at the same time.

"*Eahira.*" The king clenched his sharp white teeth. "How did you escape your prison?"

"By a human hand as you should well know," Najima's said, her tone bell-like and strangely flat. "You're the one who wrote the contract."

"You have sentenced this termite to death for your selfish deed." He pulled back his two-pronged sword and thrust.

Serap sealed her eyes shut, crumpling upon herself and waiting for the harsh bite of pain.

Nothing.

She opened one eye, then the other. She found herself standing, unharmed, on the rug in the middle room on the second floor. A blue-tinted wind died down around her, leaving her with chills.

For freeing my Queen, Evil whispered, an eagerness tickling her ears.

Chupkin swirled frantically around the ceiling, and Gordito flailed inside an empty bottle. Wood shattered and glass broke somewhere on the floor above, shaking the walls from upstairs.

Her eyes widened. "Time to go."

She grabbed Gordito's bottle and sprinted from the room. Was the King of Elm the one who had imprisoned Najima? How could she have ever loved such a terrifying beast?

Chupkin quivered just below her clavicle. She bent and grabbed the heavy ax on her way down.

"I think I may have done a bad thing," she said between the flares of tightness in her chest.

Serap pelted down the stairs and was almost out the front door when the nebulous black of horns appeared with a *pop*, blocking her way once more. She groaned, then a flash of brown caught her eye from the hallway.

Cova.

She spun around so fast her scarf whipped against her cheeks. "Run, Cova!"

"Serap!" Cova backed away, her eyes sparked with fear.

The king grabbed Serap's shoulder with one gruff hand and picked her up. A gnarled thumb dug under her shoulder blade in a stab of sharp pain. He pulled his sword back, the tips an arm's width away from Serap's side. A smile made of thin lips and cruelty flashed on the King's face. He twisted the sword just enough to catch the light, then aimed straight for her stomach. She curled up into a ball and gritted her teeth. Then turned angry eyes on the equally angry purple ones, determined to face her demise as she faced her life. Head on.

A shimmer of gray mist caught in her periphery and the smell of agarwood and fire filled the air. The King's head snapped to the side with a growl.

Then the figure of a man with bright jade eyes and sandy brown skin materialized before them.

"Bakr Amca!" Serap cried, as bewildered as she was relieved.

"Hey, Poppyseed." Her uncle flashed a white smile. "Sorry, I'm late. Zan just had triplets, and you know—"

The King's mirthless smile turned on the new arrival, fingers twitching around the hilt of his sword. "Keep out of my affairs, dirty lilu."

Bakr rolled his head toward the voice, unbothered by her precarious situation with feet off the ground. When his gaze landed on the king, his eyes bulged.

"It can't be." He laughed, setting his hand on the pommel of his steel crusader's blade. "After all these years, do I finally have the pleasure of meeting the stinking King of Eastern Elm?"

The king flashed sharp, white teeth. "There is no pleasure in meeting a dirty sack of blood like you."

Laughing so hard he had to lean forward, Bakr slowly drew his long sword. "Oh, buddy." He wiped a tear with one finger, working to control his breathing. "I am going to cut your testicles off."

Serap fought a smirk, her insides ripping about with a whirlwind of emotion. The King of Elm hissed and shook her, raising her in front of him like a shield. "All for this pathetic girl who was stupid enough to unleash a demon?"

"That's not the half of it, you filthy sack of silver. Do you know how much trouble your stupid seal has caused me? I ought to cut your limbs off on principle."

"Then there's no reason not to kill her." The King of Eastern Elm lifted his blade.

She felt a pulse of cool and looked at the bottle that contained Gordito she had forgotten was in her hand. In one heaving go, she swung the bottle.

The glass smashed against the King of Elm's head. He dropped her into a heap, bits of glass tinkling over her.

"Wretched termite." He tossed his sword straight up, re-gripping it to skewer her like a fish.

Tendrils of lilu magic wrapped around Serap and yanked her free just before the sword plunged into the floor. She could barely keep her feet under her from the dragging force, and she nearly tripped over the edge of the stairs.

The King of Elm swiped his sword up with a snarl and pointed at Bakr. Black magic streamed from his fingers to wrap around him like spider silk. He cried out in pain and struggled. The king thrust his hand to one side, throwing Bakr aside in a glittering black mass. He smashed into a massive stack of books. The shelf behind teetered, then tipped over, burying him in paper and old leather.

"Bakr Amca!" Serap yelled.

The King's flashing eyes returned to Serap. He lifted his sword above his head and marched towards her in frightening strides. Serap scurried back, hands slipping on fallen books and her heart in a tizzy. What could save her now?

Gordito popped in front of her with a flash of white. The fat wisp zoomed forward and squished himself into the King's ear canal. He screamed in pain and clapped a hand to his ear.

Serap smashed her fingers over her mouth and closed her eyes. There were horrific tales of Ayelet's abilities with the wisps: the power to suck the very life out of men, to explode their lungs and eyes, and to cave their chests in upon themselves, but she had never seen it. Is that what Gordito was doing?

The dreadful curiosity was too much. She peeked through her fingers.

The king caught her eye and lunged for her, sword poised to run her through. She screamed and fell back, covering her pounding chest with her arms.

No impact came. Just the breeze of a blade and then nothing. The king froze, the tip of the blade hovering a breath from her gut, his eyes caught in a single moment. She blinked, every muscle and tendon strained in fear. Waiting, waiting for his ugly features to twist the tip of his sword into her skin, her muscles, and her organs.

But nothing happened. He didn't even blink.

The pile of books across the room exploded, scattering pages everywhere. Bakr hopped up and raced towards her. He knocked the King of Elm back, then grabbed Serap from the floor and pulled her up in one arm, pointing his sword with the other.

The King of Elm slammed against a door, then flopped to the floor. Like a poseable doll, his limbs remained locked, the sword still held in front of him in exactly the same position.

"What's wrong with him?" Serap whispered, clinging to Bakr Amca.

"Beats me." He pulled away from her, holding out his arm to keep her behind him, and slowly crept toward the king. He held his sword at the ready until he was close enough to rest the blade against the King's throat, then poked him with his shoe. "Huh."

"Gordito went inside him," Serap said. "Did Ayelet ever tell you stories about controlling people with wisps or freezing them all creepy like that?"

Bakr's eyes rolled into the back of his head as if he were searching for memories. "She's talked about blowing people up, but I think I would remember frozen all creepy-like." Then he shook his head and refocused on her. "What is a *gor-di-to*?"

"I found another rogue wisp. A fat one. I think he's alright. Chupkin seems to like him, though if he can do something like this…"

She frowned but had no more time to think about it because Chupkin flew out from under her shirt and swirled around Bakr Amca, his light flickering brighter than the fireworks display at the Festival of the Eight Moons.

"Hey, Chuppy." Bakr laughed as the wisp nipped at his neck. He rubbed him with the tip of one finger. "How you doing, cutie pie?"

Chupkin twisted in a tight corkscrew and ruffled through Bakr's hair and down his shirt, around his torso, and out a sleeve.

"Hey, that tickles." Bakr grinned.

Serap laughed. "Not now Chupkin, you can play with Bakr Amca later. We have a bit of a problem to deal with. I don't want the King of Elm waking up and causing more trouble. If 'Abi Jahmil and Ayelet found out…" She chomped her mouth shut and looked at Bakr Amca with wide eyes. "You're not going to tell them, are you?"

"Tell them what, Poppyseed?"

He knocked the blade out of the King of Elm's grasp with his foot. It skittered across the floor, but the hands remained fixed, grasping at nothing. Bakr walked around the stiff body and picked up the sword. He lifted it to eye level and turned it in the light, then his gaze wandered around the room—to the piles of books and magical bric-à-brac that littered the hall.

He turned back to Serap. "Though I may have one or two questions."

She gave a dry, nervous chuckle. "I suppose I owe you that much. Though I had originally called you to fight a ghoul."

His lips and neck flinched. "Sorry."

She brightened. "It's okay. I ran it through with a stick and then fed it to a seal-skinned hand with red fingernails."

"Seriously?" He smiled wide, his eyes sparkling. "You took on a ghoul?"

She blushed and bit her bottom lip. "I hear about all the cool things my Amca does and had to try it for myself."

"In that case, I'm glad I didn't come when you called me." He walked to her and threw his arm around her shoulder for a little squeeze. "I'm proud of you."

Bakr Amca ran a finger over the bottom of his chin, the black onyx ring he wore glinting. A very dangerous trinket, the cursed ring could be used to drain the power from any creature that wore it. She had heard stories about it—how he and Zan Hala had used it to hide their baby's fire from a lilith. But it was Bakr Amca's wedding ring, and he wore it willingly, while his wife kept hold of its counterpart, a copper ring that could be used to steal his powers.

Just in case you start to act up, Zan Hala would always say with a smile.

"Look at this place." Bakr grinned, his bright green eyes taking in everything. "I don't have a clue in Allah's mercy what is going on, but it looks interesting."

Serap smirked. "I guess. I mean I was thrown in a prison cell for a while and starved before I made friends with Evil."

"I hear that," he groaned. "Did this greaseball imprison you?" He tipped his chin towards the frozen King of Elm.

She shook her head. "No. He was mad because I freed his ex-wife or something. I don't know where Don DeMario is, but he's the one who chased me down in the woods and locked me up in a cell in his basement. He put me on a bed first, but I tore up his floor." She touched a finger to her lips. "And threw a bunch of his books. He really didn't like that."

Bakr was careful to meet her eyes. "Are you okay?"

She knit her brows and looked away. "I don't know. I guess. He has only tried to kill me once, which is better than I expected, but..." She scraped her teeth against her top lip. "He threw me over his shoulder and shook me and slammed me against a wall. Those hurt. And when I look into his dark eyes..."

Her chest tightened. She wanted to say she saw murder there, but when he had given her and Cova the basket full of bread, that's not what she had seen at all. There had been a hint of softness. Of timidity.

Bakr Amca's face fell before settling into a pleasant neutral. "Let's get you out of here, huh? I'll come back and do something with this lump of green turd."

"I can't leave yet," she said, though the offer squeezed her heart. "I promised to take Cova home with me, but I can't do that yet because I haven't found the amulet Ayelet gave me or the crow's beak. And I haven't even done what I came here to do." She let out a deep sigh. "I'm kind of terrible at this questing thing."

"Give yourself a break, greenhorn. It takes practice."

The body of the King of Elm broke out with violent convulsions. The head slapped repeatedly against the floor, green arms and legs twitching, rolling from side to side. The eyes crossed. A long, black tongue fell out, gnashed quickly by sharp teeth. Bakr Amca pulled her back and held her protectively behind his arm.

The King of Elm had awakened.

CHAPTER EIGHTEEN

JAVIER

Javier had been to some really nasty places in his life. The brooding den of an *umma ghula* draped with the half-digested corpses of djinn and crawling with larval ghouls. The festering swamps of Tetzer Alanay and its bursting pustules of noxious, flesh-eating acid. The bowels of the immortal Bahamut. But the King of Elm's disgusting ear canal had to be top five.

Orange wax dripped and squelched all around him, falling from the green walls in huge, gelatinous clumps. For the first time, Javier was grateful to be nothing more than an amorphous ball of light.

He pressed into the King's brain—a squishy lump of gray matter. At first, his light wrapped around it, but soon he passed through, filling it up with himself, like water being absorbed into a sponge.

All at once, he was looking out through the King's eyes. Serap cowered before him, the tip of a sword pointed at her belly.

Javier tightened his grip on the brain and everything ground to a screeching halt. Bones locked up, and the heart and lungs stopped their unceasing work. Javier had a distinct feeling that any mortal creature would have died in that moment, and likely the King of Elm would have died too, given who was inside his brain messing with his motor functions. But the king wasn't really there.

The King of Elm—with his emerald skin and supernatural beauty—was not real. He was a projection, albeit a tangible and virtually flawless one. The magical illusion was so perfect, it could consume food, feel pain, and even father children. The King of Elm had put so much of himself into it, living through it for so many thousands of years, that there wasn't but a handful of souls left alive who even remembered what his real self looked like.

But now that he was inside the projection's brain, Javier saw it clearly. Papery green skin wrapped around frail bones. A face as ancient as it was damaged. Cracked and chipped horns. He lay in silken sheets, wrapped in sparkling clouds to keep him safe and comfortable, and locked away in a secret location deep in the bowels of his sprawling palace.

At last, he knew where the king really was. And in his incorporeal form, Javier cleaved himself to the line that connected the puppet to the ancient, sleeping body.

He touched the magic tether which snatched him up and sling-shotted him between worlds, through a thousand layers of fire barriers, and into the most protected chamber in all of Qaf.

Anger was his anchor in the tempest, having just witnessed the bestial green djinn pressing the double-pronged tip of a monstrous sword into Serap's tender flesh.

Her cry of fear echoed in Javier's ears as he slipped his wispy body into the brain of the King of Elm—the *real* King of Elm with all his thousands of years worth of wrinkles. The eyelids of the frail figure twitched, and Javier heard a familiar voice calling to him, begging him to stop. Promising him anything and everything if he would let him live.

But there was no stopping. Not after what he had just seen. For all his posturing, the immortal litigator had proven himself a monster, and the Immortal Killer had run out of patience.

The brain expanded like a souffle in a steamy oven. It pressed against the inside of the skull, quivering and cracking. A bubble about to burst. Gazing out through the King's eyes, Javier saw the limbs shaking and the torso rolling about wildly. Then there came a loud pop like the blast of a small cannon. The King of Elm's fragile, ancient brain exploded, leaving behind nothing but goo.

Riding the wave of his final heartbeat, Javier's intangible body of magic was thrown across the border between worlds, and back into the mind of the King's avatar just in time to witness that explode as well.

Javier swam through the gelatinous brain matter, arms and legs forming on his formless body with each stroke. He had no idea what had changed or how, but no longer was he a mere shapeless blob. His light had split into two sections, a head and a rounded body with limbs attached. He still could not feel or smell the world around him, for which he was exceedingly grateful at the moment, but his vision focused to the front. And as he slipped through the sinuses into the back of the throat, he realized he had much greater control of his movement.

He rolled down the black, slimy tongue, then got to his feet and pushed open the clamped teeth. He strolled down the tongue and hopped off onto the floor moments before the King of Elm's fabricated body began to decompose rapidly. The tight rigor of the body released, and the limbs spread out, then deflated until it was nothing more than an ashy, sticky pile of black bones.

His books lay in tatters all over the hallway, his carefully constructed piles destroyed with abandon. There were holes in his floor and cracks in his doors, furniture smashed, rugs smeared, and glass lantern casings shattered. Javier sighed and shook his head. Everything was falling apart, his entire life upended in a single afternoon.

And for what?

"Gordito?" Serap leaned down to him.

He turned to look at her, slightly disgusted with himself for answering to that name. She got on her knees and put a hand out to him. He looked at her fingers, then back up at her eyes, so large they overwhelmed her face. The fear and trepidation in them were rivaled only by their gentleness.

Javier walked into her hand, his little belly of light bouncing with each step.

Zayne peeked out from inside the tall man's shirt. *Is he really dead?*

Yes.

Zayne's light flashed with a rainbow of colors. *What happened to you? Are you okay?*

I think so, said Javier, patting his tiny body with his fingerless hands.

How did you do that to yourself?

I don't know. I just really wanted some arms and legs, so here they are.

"What just happened?" asked the man with the sword, looking down at Serap.

He appeared to be in his early twenties, with a checkmark scar on one cheek, another that split his eyebrow, and a large slash that wrapped around his neck. Rough stubble covered his face, and his hair was short and black. Simple soldier clothes hung from his broad shoulders, and the sword he held wasn't anything special—a double-handed broadsword that he wielded with one hand as if it weighed nothing. He was also disturbingly handsome, preternaturally so.

He wasn't human, and he wasn't djinn. What was he? And who was he? How did he know Serap? And how had he managed to teleport into his house?

Who is this man? Javier asked.

Zayne chirruped sweetly and raced down the man's shirt, rubbing himself all over his chest and stomach so he laughed, then slipped under his belt and down his leg before emerging from the cuff of his pants.

He's Bakr, the wisp sighed.

What is he? said Javier, his instinct to kill rising in his gut.

He's half-lilu, and a completely wonderful person, Zayne said with a quick flash. *And he's Serap's uncle. Don't you even think about doing anything bad to him. And stay out of his ears, you hear me?*

The word *uncle* caused a knot in Javier's stomach to release. This pulchritudinous sex demon of a man was Serap's uncle, not her husband. Javier chastised himself for being relieved, but that didn't stop him from feeling it.

Isn't he the cutest thing? Zayne flew back up to settle on Bakr's collarbone and nuzzled into his stubbly chin. *I could gaze into those eyes for centuries.*

Javier sighed and shook his head, refocusing on Serap, whose eyes were still pouring over him.

She turned her hand this way and that to examine his body. "What are you?"

He blinked his newly-formed eyes. He tried to open his mouth to speak, and a little hole formed. A giddy joy swept through him.

It's me. Don DeMario, he tried to say, but all that came out was a series of squeaks. The hope that had just surged through him dissipated.

Serap giggled at the sound, covering her mouth with her free hand. Though incredibly irritated by the development, watching her smile, he couldn't help but smile back.

Bakr leaned in for a closer look at him. "Where did you say you found that thing?"

Serap's pink lips puckered to one side. "In the field of wildflowers out front. Chupkin seems to think he came from this house, which I'd quite believe. There seems to be no shortage of strange creatures here, Don DeMario included."

Bakr tapped his ring against his chin in thought. "Don DeMario... now why does that sound familiar?"

Serap shot him a sheepish smile. "Pasha says he's known in dark circles as the Immortal Killer. *Alqatil alkhlid.*"

Bakr's eyes widened. He snatched Serap by the forearm. "We're in the house of the Immortal Killer?"

"Er... yes? It doesn't make that much difference to me. I can die by falling down a hole. But I'm sorry you ended up here. I didn't think about how I'd be putting you at risk."

Bakr lifted his eyes, scrutinizing the house with renewed energy. "Have you completely lost your mind?"

Javier's stomach sank. This man knew a lot more about him than Serap had. What horror stories was he going to tell her? As if she didn't have reason enough to hate him.

Her rosy cheeks warmed to fire red, and she cast her eyes to the floor, her bottom lip poking out. "You don't understand. I had to come. I had to. He's the only way...."

"The Immortal Killer is the craziest son of a snake to ever live!" Bakr cried, throwing his hands in the air. "They say he was swallowed by the Bahamut, half-digested, and still managed to come out the other side, sword in hand. He cut the eyes from the Seven Gorgons of the Ishmaki Hills. He slayed the festering King of Rothfar and his twenty-seven blood-sucking concubines. And he's human! He's just human."

Anxious to hide, Javier hopped down from Serap's palm. Light streamed behind him like the tail of a comet, and he landed with a soft plunk on the floorboards.

"I think you're scaring Gordito," she said, watching him. "And are you mad that I'm in the Immortal Killer's house or that I met him first? Because it sounds like you have a man crush." Serap giggled, poking Bakr's arm. "And I will risk whatever needs risking to reach my goal or else nothing I ever do will matter."

Bakr covered his mouth with his hand, laughing in his chest as he shook his head. "What exactly are you trying to get out of him? Do you have some immortal monster haunting you that I'm unaware of? Because if you do, I'm a bit hurt you didn't come to me first."

Javier stashed himself behind a few volumes of Livy's History of Rome but poked his head around the edge so he could watch and listen. If he'd had a heart at the moment, it would have been in his throat. He leaned in, desperate to learn the truth which he had been seeking ever since Serap first appeared at his house.

"I might have a few monsters in my shadow now that I've been in this house, but it's a different matter, entirely." Serap paused, her foot mid-air over the next step. "How did the *lilitu* become immortal? Or were your kind made that way by Allah from the beginning?"

"Only the divine knows the answer to that." Bakr narrowed his eyes. "You've got the human blues, don't you?"

She looked away from him, the red on her cheeks spreading down her neck. Chupkin swirled down from his perch on Bakr's collar and stroked her cheek. "You wouldn't understand."

Bakr's face softened and he laid a hand on her shoulder, "Poppyseed, anybody who has ever looked into the future and not seen themselves in it can understand. I spent most of my life not knowing that I was, you know, what I am."

"But you always thought you were at least half-djinn. You've never been just a human. A lump of walking death. Did you know my life is basically half-over? And everyone I love except Balian and Yousef will live long after I'm gone and forget my name? And no one wants to marry me except because I'm a princess and only because I'll die soon while my title remains." A plump tear formed in the corner of her eye, and she wiped it away angrily. "He said those words, Amca. Paco said that. I hate being human."

Javier sighed and let himself fall down onto his bottom. She wasn't the first person who had come to him not looking to destroy immortality but to create it. A cold pall settled over him. Once more he tried to bring up his voice, to try to answer her doubt, but all that came out was a squeak.

He let his round torso fall towards his legs.

"You are not a lump of walking death. What a horrible thing to call yourself." Bakr's voice was noticeably softer than before. "You're just human, like everybody else on Ard. And you're constantly surrounded by magic and healing potions and all of that, so I find it really difficult to believe that your life is half over. You're only twenty. *Inshallah,* you will live to be a hundred, maybe more."

Her shoulders hunched, and she turned away from Bakr, arms stiff. "You're right. I'm just being horribly silly. Who cares when I die? No one will remember, anyway." She pulled her headband further down her forehead. "If you want to be helpful to your dying niece, I have a favor to ask."

Bakr groaned and bent at the waist, hanging his head between his knees and mumbling incomprehensibly to himself. "Fire away."

Javier sat up, looking at her face as he waited to hear what it was she wanted. It occurred to him that he really shouldn't care, that everybody wanted something. But he couldn't help that he genuinely wanted to know.

"Ayelet told me a story," Serap said, "about you and Zan Hala and the Seal of Sulayman...."

"The Seal is incredibly dangerous." Bakr straightened and looked her in the eye. "There were one or two things we had to use it for, then we put it right back where we found it. And Zan did some research and found a bunch of spells to cast over it to help keep it safe, not the least of which involves spilling a lot of blood over the container in order to get it back. So not impossible, but certainly not something I'm overly anxious to break out."

"I was wondering if it could bind death, too?" Her eyes fell to her boots.

"I doubt it, Poppyseed. The ring works in this world. I don't know about the next. And I'm pretty sure it can only bind beings. Last I checked, death was just a natural process everyone goes through."

"Not everyone," she mumbled, then cast her glance back up the stairs. "Do you think the King of Elm is really dead?"

He shook his head. "I doubt it. I mean, he's immortal, right? And it was just some fat, little wisp that blew his brains out, not Don DeMario. His magic is probably reforming somewhere back on Qaf."

Javier wanted to speak up and tell them the truth, that the King of Elm was absolutely and unequivocally dead. He wanted to go mark that on his calendar but gave a little growl when he realized he was too small to hold a quill.

"Are you expecting the Immortal Killer back soon?" asked Bakr. "Is he going to be mad? I've heard he has quite a temper."

Serap looked about the room and sighed. "I honestly didn't think he left his house much. And our past encounters would indicate he has a temper." Her face fell, and she wrung her hands. "And yes, he will be mad about all his books. He'll probably never help me now. Just throw me back in his dungeon with Evil. Did you say you've slain some immortals before?" She asked with a hint of hope in her sad eyes.

"I mean, one time." Bakr's voice faltered. "But those were very particular circumstances. As far as I know, only the Immortal Killer has the power to kill any immortal. And, just so you know, he leaves his house all the time. The guy's all over Qaf and half of Ard slaughtering monsters every other day. I never would have taken him for much of a reader."

"That's what I said."

And how exactly am I supposed to learn the weaknesses of all the monsters I fight if I don't read? Javier bristled. He should have been used to such assumptions by now. All his life people had taken him for big and tough and nothing more.

"Just goes to show." Bakr shrugged. "And I do not have a man crush on him. Though I have to admit, I am just a teeny tiny bit jealous right now."

"Ah." Serap nodded. "Don't let Zan Hala hear." She chuckled softly, but her voice was tight around the edges. "If he's fighting monsters all the time, maybe he won't come back at all." Her shoulders slumped farther.

"Are you sure you don't want to talk to Jahmil and Ayelet about any of this?" said Bakr. "I'm sure they'll be understanding—"

"No!" Serap waved her hands out in front of her. "If they found out, I'd be doomed. Then I'd have to call you just to leave the palace, and there would be no way I'd find a way to keep living. I'd probably die of loneliness in a bed somewhere, and the maids would just roll me off and brush me under a rug and no one would be the wiser."

Javier felt a twitch somewhere deep in a blobby body. How many times had he imagined a similar scenario for himself? Though, of course, there would be no maids. He'd die alone in his house and his body would slowly rot until only his skeleton remained, after that treacherous feline ate his face, of course.

"You know, you've got some serious darkness in you. I never realized." Bakr scratched the scar on his eyebrow with his thumb. "So, what you're saying is, you want me to leave you here. Alone. In the house of the Immortal Killer, whom you admit has a bad temper. And you're doing this because you want to live *longer*?" He shook his head. "That seems a silly plan to me."

Javier scoffed in agreement, and it almost sounded like a proper scoff, though high-pitched.

Serap shrugged. "Abi Jahmil rarely has a plan, and he's done alright."

"Because he has Ayelet and me looking out for him."

"Do you have a better idea? What's the difference between one and fifty years to people like you and the djinn? My life doesn't matter so much when it's fated to be short."

"Obviously, you've got some stuff you need to work through." Bakr sighed heavily, his whole body aching towards the ground. "Umm... can you at least tell me that you don't think Don DeMario is going to murder you?"

"Do you need to just hear the words?" She gave a pained smile. "Probably not? He fed me breakfast today... let me out of the cage and sort of gave me a picnic. Maybe if I clean up his books, he won't shake me so hard this time."

Javier pressed his face into his tiny hands and rolled over onto his back, his big bulging belly pointing to the ceiling. He hated himself for that little bite on her lip.

Bakr sucked a harsh breath through his teeth. "I don't like this...."

"How does Zan Hala get you to do things you don't want to do?"

"It's not appropriate to discuss with children."

Serap blushed beet red. "So if I can convince her to convince you for me—"

"Stop right there," he laughed, cutting the air in front of his chest. "Look, whether me and your folks want to admit it or not, you are a grown woman and you are free to make your own mistakes. Just know I am going to be keeping close to my bell. I swear on my children's twenty-six eyes that I will be here the moment you call, okay?"

She sniffled once and wound her arms around Bakr, pressing her face into his shirt. "Thanks, Amca."

"No problem, Poppyseed." He patted her head and rearranged her headdress and necklaces so they laid flat. "If you get a chance, maybe you could introduce me to the Immortal Killer someday."

"Sure," she laughed, pulling away, but her smile fell. "I don't want you to fight him, though. Or maybe I do. No." She shook her head decidedly. "I do not. Your life means too much. I won't call you for that."

"Thanks for the vote of confidence," he sneered. "Alright, I need to get back. Zan just had triplets, did I mention? All girls. So stinking cute. She was super thrilled about me leaving her alone with them all, let me tell you."

Serap chuckled. "Wait a second."

She jumped the last two steps and disappeared into the kitchen. After some cluttering about, she came back with a loaf of bread and some fresh butter, both of which Javier had made for his breakfast tomorrow. Not only did she come into his house and poke his bread, then talk about bread incessantly while she was in his dungeon, but she also seemed perfectly happy to steal it and give it away to...

Oh, what's the point? Javier thought with a heavy groan. It wasn't like he could eat it anymore, anyway.

"It's the least I can do," said Serap. "Don DeMario is already going to be furious about the books, what's a little food on top? Tell Zan Hala thanks for the help and that I'm happy to watch your kids if you ever need a break. You know, if I survive this."

Bakr smiled and took the bread, then gave her a quick peck on the forehead and blinked out of the room, leaving nothing behind but the scent of agarwood.

Serap groaned and sat on the steps, putting her face in her hands. "What am I going to do, Chupkin?"

The little wisp laid across her lap and let her pet him, then dipped around her side and poked Javier.

Go on, Mountain Man. Now might be a good time to try being nice. Or did you change your mind about that?

Javier grunted, which came out as a squeak, and he walked closer to Serap. He grabbed the fabric of her pants and climbed up onto her knee, his little legs squiggling. Tilting his head to look up at her, he wished he could say something. But even if he could, he wasn't sure what he might say. The conversation he'd just heard was swirling through his brain, and he was still waiting for all the implications to land.

He sat down cross-legged on her knee and patted her lightly with his fingerless hand.

Her brown eye shone through a crack in her fingers. Then she ran one down his back and up to scratch behind his barely-formed head. He shivered at her touch, wishing he could feel it with skin instead of just light.

"You're sweet," she said. Then she scooped him up in her hands. "I don't know where you came from, but you're welcome to stay with me and Chupkin." She smiled wide, but her eyes still clung to sadness. "I would like it very much, even if I'm not around so long."

There was so much he wanted to tell her, but nothing would come out. And he seriously doubted if she would listen to him, especially once she found out that he wasn't a sweet sprite called Gordito, but the horrific Immortal Killer who had chased her down like a wolf, shaken her, imprisoned her, starved her. He pushed his mouth closed and nodded.

If he ever found a way to get back to himself, he was going to have a bit of explaining to do.

With that thought, Javier hopped down from her hand and scurried off toward the kitchen. Perhaps now that he had some semblance of a hand, he would be able to work the amulet again. The sooner he got back to his old self the better. When she looked at him—at Gordito—with those soft eyes and that trusting smile, he felt like the most despicable liar to ever live.

CHAPTER NINETEEN

SERAP

Serap stared at her golden boots, now scuffed and dirty from the fight with the ghoul and her run through the woods. From her fight, too, with the King of Eastern Elm. She sighed, exhausted just thinking about it.

Talking with Bakr Amca had left her more confused than anything, though she was grateful he had answered her call in the nick of time and agreed not to tell 'Abi Jahmil where she was. Based on what Bakr Amca and Cova said, DeMario wasn't a monster—he slayed monsters. But he had also given Bakr Amca enough pause to stand on guard the entire time they were in the house and even suggest reinforcements. He would keep her secret, she knew that, but his wariness had to mean something bad, didn't it?

How she spoke of the man probably didn't help. He did chase her down in the woods, grab her and toss her about gruffly, shake her and throw her in a prison cell. He had also left her a blanket, saved a girl, let her go, and given her food for the journey. So what did that make him? Ayelet would have said *complicated* with a laugh, which was no help at all. And Jahmil?

She sighed.

'Abi wouldn't have listened to her past the point where DeMario chased her through the woods, instead inflaming his fist with white fire. And Bakr Amca seemed to admire the man more than anything. If she called him to fight DeMario, would they devolve into a strange comradery that can only form between men who have killed a lot?

The thought was strangely comforting, and she pressed her knuckles into her eyes until she saw spots. There were more than enough people in Qaf—all of Vespar for starters—who would call Bakr Amca a monster. A murderer. And yet she knew he was a loving father, a desperately devoted husband, and the kind of uncle who would show up right after his wife had triplets to help his niece. And she loved him. So maybe DeMario could be the same.

She dropped her hands and nodded. "I should try to give him a second chance," she said to Chupkin, who flew about wistfully over where Bakr Amca had disappeared. "Though, I suppose I shall first have to learn whatever protocol he was talking about when he found me. I'm certain I shall never love him, though. The only thing I felt when I first saw him was fear, but perhaps we can find some sort of comradery that works for us. An understanding. Then maybe he will help me."

Chupkin dipped toward her, circling her ankle and riding down the rivulets in her silky, torn pants.

She laughed dryly. "You're right. That was an absurd thought. I think I got caught up in the sadness in his dark eyes when he handed Cova and I the basket. Like he was sorry even if he didn't say it, and like maybe he wished we wouldn't go. Isn't that strange, Chupkin? But you know how easily I feel the hurt in others. I'm probably just desperate for any sort of kindness after hearing all that Paco had to say." She stood up and caught Chupkin on one of his slides down. "Let's find Cova. I'm sure she's terrified after everything that just happened."

Serap walked around the staircase and headed down the hallway to the back room Cova had disappeared into. Halfway down, she froze. Dangling off one of the high shelves that lined the hallway peaked two creepy eyes and a black beak.

She raised up on her tiptoes and put a foot on one of the lower shelves to climb up. Then frowned. There was too much clutter to scale the shelf properly. A cold voice down the hallway dropped her back down to her feet. She hurried across the smooth wood floor and burst into the room.

Cova sat in a chair stock-still, eyes round and staring at Najima, who must have been the Queen of Western Elm, standing motionless across from her.

"She's innocent," Serap said, though she wasn't sure what accusation she was defending against or what the Queen even wanted.

"Yes." Najima's liquid red eyes stared at the child, unblinking.

"Then why are you holding her hostage?"

A slight crease formed between Najima's brows. "Your presumption is groundless. She chose to sit and stare at me. I would not ask for such a thing."

Serap side-stepped toward Cova and put a hand on her shoulder. "Are you okay?"

Cova nodded, her eyes stuck on the gloriously smooth queen. Even her cool gray dress rippled like starlight on a shallow pool that flowed seamlessly into her skin.

"You didn't tell me your husband knew you were out." Serap turned once more to Najima with a thousand questions on her mind. "Or that he was the infamous King of Eastern Elm."

"At the time we last spoke, he did not know. But he visits this house frequently, and he hates me ardently. It could only be inevitable."

"You could have warned me." Serap crossed her arms. "He almost skewered me."

Najima's loose braid slid against her skin as she tilted her head. "Yes."

Serap rubbed a hand over her cheek with a sigh. "Maybe you could be a little more helpful this time, seeing as I'm the one who let you out of your prison. Will he be coming back? He sort of collapsed back there on the floor and then vanished."

The first shadow of a smile appeared on Najima's face. "You have slain the un-slayable."

"He's an immortal, he can't be dead," Serap scoffed, but the queen's words blew into her like acrid smoke. Why would she lie? "I didn't mean for him to die. And it wasn't me, Gordito—"

"And why should that trouble you at all?"

"It doesn't." She crossed her arms tightly, ignoring the claw that squeezed her chest at the very mention of death. Even for someone as awful as the King of Elm. "What about you? I thought you wanted him alive?"

"I do not mourn his passing. While it does not satiate my pettiness, it has relieved me from my burden of revenge. I may now die in peace."

Her words shattered Serap's hope. "But he's dead. You can live now and not be bothered by him. Get both kingdoms back together. See the sun. You'll be happy, soon. You just have to give it time."

Najima's clear eyes drank her in, and she felt as if she swam in an ocean of liquid misery. Everything about the queen, from her passive stance to the pink tip on her wide nose, gave her the appearance of just having sobbed her heart out though her eyes remained dry.

"Time is all I've ever had. Time and a stolen kiss from a love that can only be after death. I wish only for this," she said.

Serap parted her lips, vehemence coating her tongue with bitterness. "Ungrateful. That's what you are. Six thousand years of ingratitude. If I had the chance you do, I would drink up every moment. How could you want to give up everything for the nothingness of death? It's absurd."

"To the unknowing, it must seem that way." The queen said, then disappeared, her body folding into a tiny star in the blink of an eye.

Serap stood in the middle of the room, the sun casting blocky shapes of light across the floor and catching the shimmering threads in her jacket. "You waste a gift!" she cried at nothing. Then muttered, "She's wasting immortality." She turned to Chupkin, nose scrunched in frustration, but he wasn't there. She furrowed her brow and turned. Cova, too, had vanished.

"Cova?"

She trod down the hallway, wary of whatever oddity awaited her around the next corner.

No answer.

"Chupkin? Gordito?" She rounded the corner into the living room and into a haze of green, a hint of blue light in the middle. "Evil?" she tried again.

The familiar green clouded her vision of the room when the door to the kitchen swung open. Serap flinched, but no monster appeared. Just Gordito, his chubby belly swaying as he marched across the room toward her. She couldn't help but half-smile even as the haze thickened about her. "Come on, little bear," she said and held out her hand.

He looked over his shoulder at the kitchen, then seemed to sigh in his tiny, high-pitched voice, and climbed up into her palm. The green in the room was now a thick blanket, which meant Evil was about to take her on a trip. But it was her own doing this time. So desperate not to be alone and to do something that mattered, she had once again called to Evil, not the other way around.

She brought Gordito to her cheek and rubbed him against her skin. "I can tell you don't want to come with me, but I'm glad you will. It's much nicer going where Evil takes me with a friend and Chupkin seems to have disappeared."

The chubby, little wisp crossed a hand over his chest and bowed his head.

She giggled. "Don't tell Chupkin, wherever that rug rat got to, but you're a bit more expressive than he is. Almost like a little person lives inside."

She tilted her head and stared intently into the sparkling white of his misty body. Then shrugged with a sigh.

"Okay, Evil," she said. "I'm ready."

This time, the room bent inward like fingers squeezed it together, then pinched out in black. No falling sensation. Just a quiet warmth before a light emerged in the darkness.

"Ready?" she asked Gordito.

Tiny, nearly invisible, and pearlescent eyes blinked. He nodded. She nodded, too, finding great comfort in the little wisp's presence and feeling decidedly strange about that.

She walked toward the light, which morphed into a white hole big enough to climb out of at shoulder height. She hoisted herself up and out onto a wide mountaintop, wind blowing over the heads of yellow and pink flowers as clouds dashed across the Atacama blue sky. She could smell rain in the air, a hint of honeysuckle.

Where were they?

Gordito scurried up the front of her jacket onto her shoulder. He held to her headdress with one hand, leaning out over her collarbone like a sailor on the bow of a ship as he surveyed the landscape.

She bit back a smile at his antics. Such joy seemed inappropriate when on a journey with Evil. "Do you know where we are?"

He looked back at her, the line of his mouth curving into a tiny grin, and nodded.

Serap put a hand to her brow and surveyed the bucolic landscape. A tiny house sat in the distance on the edge of the wood, looking out over a great valley. It appeared abandoned, the door worn and off-kilter, the windows wide open and the garden in front overgrown, but she headed over, encouraged by Gordito's wispy smile.

"Do you think it's safe to go in?" she asked, standing on the threshold.

Blinking a few times, Gordito did not answer. Then, he mimed rolling up his sleeves.

She puffed her cheeks with air. "You're right. Might as well just get it over with."

She looked at him sideways, getting that eerie feeling once more she was talking to a person instead of a ball of magic. Yes, she felt that way with Chupkin sometimes, but it had taken a couple of years to get to that point, and still, he wasn't so... featured?

She dipped her head and slipped inside. Dust sparkled in the sunlight that streamed through the window, and an overwhelming sense of nostalgia swept through her. The home was Turkish. Bright, multi-patterned blankets hung over a chair and draped the bed. A woven rug, worn by age and a leaking roof, kept back the cold on the floor. Beautiful dishes lined the shelf, only a few broken, and several cerulean charms against the Evil Eye spun excitedly in the breeze.

"What is this place?"

Gordito hopped down from her shoulder, a mist of light trailing behind him. He took slow steps across the wooden floor, slowly turning in circles as he went. He squeaked out a few little blips as if he were trying to say something. The voice struck her as sad and joyful all at once. Which was exactly as she felt.

"Is this where you came from?" she asked, running a hand along the neat stitching of one of the blankets.

The chubby wisp nodded and scrambled up the tassels of the blanket, then fell face-first on the soft fibers.

She giggled and joined him, sprawling out on the bed that smelled of sweet hay. "I didn't know you were Turkish. No wonder we get along so well." She scooped him up into the crook of her neck, admiring the amber and salmon, sage and blue paintings that sprawled across the ceiling, placed there by a delicate hand. "It's beautiful. But what's a wisp doing in a place like this?"

He looked up at her, his face open and simple. He brought his stubby arms together at his chest and mimed cradling a baby, then he pointed to himself and then at the floor.

At first, images of tiny bits of baby lights filled her mind, but she shook her head. Wisps weren't people, so they couldn't be babies. She cocked her head and took a harder look at the little guy.

"You're not a wisp, are you?"

Gordito shook his head, then he looked down at himself and shrugged.

"I'm in a bit of trouble myself," she said with a sigh. "I'm afraid I may have thought myself a bit more capable than I am, and the world a bit more friendly. Did you see the man who lived in the house we were in? The one with all the books?"

Frowning, Gordito nodded.

"I frowned, too, the first time I saw him. He was very mad when he caught me. I think I rather offended him, though I'm not sure what I did. Well..." She sat up and wrapped her arms around herself. "I guess I did sneak into his house. But I've never been so scared in such a long time. Not since I was a little girl captured by slavers. I think living in Shihala made me forget."

Tiny eyes watched her face for a while, then the wisp pressed a hand against the side of her neck and bowed his head. When he looked back up, he tapped the bottom of her chin and showed her a soft smile.

And for the first time, Serap felt the twinge in her heart that Ayelet had talked about when she first met Jahmil. Serap scurried to the edge of the bed and jumped off, her heart beating against her chest like the wind on the walls of the house.

"You're a wisp. Or not a wisp. I don't know who you are. I've just been referring to you as a *he* in my mind. *Oha!* I don't even know if you *are* a *he*?" The thought, the feeling, squirmed inside her chest, painful and pleasant. She had always thought of him as a *he*. Why?

She shook her head.

"Evil. I'm ready to go."

The air grew darker green, and the tunnel appeared once more, this time a black circle instead of white hovering against the far wall. She scooped up one of the blankets that smelled of must, cinnamon, and sweet grass. She was about to scoop up Gordito but stopped. Too soon.

She wiggled her way into the hole and beckoned him to follow. With a final lingering glance at the small, colorful home, he hopped after her and jumped up to rest in the folds of the blanket in her arms. She slid into the darkness, careful not to look at the little being of light who had so quickly won her over.

"I'll help you," she said in a tiny whisper, "get back to who you are. And then maybe we can still be friends."

The words came out somewhere between a question and a statement, one out of fear and the other of hope. And it was all she could do not to run back to the little Turkish home and curl up on the bed. But she couldn't. She had to go back into the house of the person who had acted like a monster before acting like a man.

CHAPTER TWENTY

JAVIER

Before the green mist had whisked them away to his childhood home, Javier had been focused on finding Serap's amulet. He remembered precisely where he had left it. On the kitchen table, laid flat. But when he'd leapt up to see if he could use his newly gained wisp arms to work its magic, he'd found himself staring at a dirty tablecloth and nothing more.

He assumed Serap must have gotten to it first. She'd had ample opportunity. But when he returned to her, he quickly realized that was not the case. Which meant someone or something else did.

Javier had just begun to panic about that when he looked into Serap's deep brown eyes and became distracted long enough to be whisked away to that illusory field. And there every concern for the future fell out of his brain.

The sight of his mother's paintings on the ceiling and her old dishes and blankets further rendered his globulousness until he felt little more than a warm puddle. In a sense he was grateful he could not smell or feel at that moment. For if he'd had full use of his sense he likely would have burst into tears.

For all the sweet nostalgia of the place, Javier was caught in the moment like a butterfly in a net. Serap's smile and her gentle, whispered promise to help him become whole again. When she was close, he felt as if his heart would burst from his chest. Not that he had a heart. Or a chest.

Oh, to hell with it.

When they arrived back in the present, Javier ran from Serap, bolting like lightning up the stairs. He scurried through the door of his office, his body becoming intangible with a single thought. Once inside, he double-checked that the door was locked, then jumped up to draw the chain across it as well.

He needed to be alone. It seemed years since he'd last been alone. And he was always alone.

He didn't want to think about Serap and the pain in her voice when she spoke of dying long before everyone she loved. Because the people she loved were djinn and lilitu, and heaven knows what manner of other magical beings. And she was human. Like him. A lone lump of clay in a world of fire.

She was also so young—in body and in spirit. She did not yet recognize how lucky she was to be loved at all, no matter how fleetingly. Time was not what mattered, because nothing remains the same and all beauty is ephemeral. Some creatures can live to be a thousand and never once impact the heart of another being. And some survive but a scant few years, yet their lives bloom in the hearts of those they touched for all time.

But how could he tell her any of that when he could not even speak? And should he ever learn to speak again, would she listen?

Not to the monster Don DeMario. Once he turned back into himself, if he ever turned back into himself, he was certain her kind eyes would never look at him that way again. Not as they had today. Not at the face of a killer.

And that was for the best. He was not meant for such softness—for innocence, or kindness, or even friendship. He had given that all up long ago when he sailed into the lair of the Eternal One, deep in the Sea of Bahamut, and became the first being ever to deny her venomous kiss. As a reward—or perhaps as punishment—she had made him what he was now, and there was no running from it.

Javier climbed up onto his desk and peered at his calendar, determined to pretend everything was normal. That his time as Gordito, the lovable sprite, was temporary and any moment now he would revert to his old self—capable, powerful, loathsome.

But how, without the amulet? He would be trapped this way forever.

Javier shook his head and focused on the calendar. Anything to get out of his own brain, which was spiraling into even darker places than usual.

Today, he was scheduled to face the *arak hunak* tree of Izrak. It was on the calendar, which meant he had committed to do it, and therefore it had to be done. But he hadn't sharpened his ax. He hadn't laundered his fighting costume. He hadn't even had dinner. The fact that he was a pot-bellied sprite somehow seemed secondary to all these things for a moment, as if he would be ready to go out and face anything if only he scrubbed the bloodstains from the previous battle out of his shirt.

Considering what he had managed to do to the King of Elm, maybe he could take on the Izraki tree precisely as he was. After all, he was not powerless. He was just different. Still very much himself, and still with the power to kill the unkillable. He had to find a way to be flexible.

Maybe it would be best to remain as Gordito the Wisp. He could move in with Zayne in Serap's belly button. It would be far from the worst living situation he'd ever endured.

"*That such innocence consorts with Evil...*" rasped a cold voice, falling upon his ears like a curse. "*A crime of nature, most natural. Nature, your goddess. Nature to which you cling, O immortal hunter.*"

Javier closed his eyes but did not turn. There was no point. The voice could never be seen, only heard. And smelt.

"*How the burden of spring's vapors fall upon the winter's ice,*" the voice went on, "*stirring the dead to rise and rise. Nature, most natural. A white-haired shadow that stalks the sunlight, a memory of the moon forgotten in time's infinite sorrow. And falling, always falling, beyond the grasp of spring's bloom. Even for such a bud forgetting she is spring, seeks the winter.*"

Javier did not respond, not with his voice and not with the vocalized thoughts he used to speak with Zayne. He pressed his hands into his knees and leaned back, determined to let the words wash over him like rain.

"*To this gray shadow, once a man. A flower among such flowers. How he does raise a fist and command the sun to give him light, even as it burns his flesh. Even as he is set aflame and always screaming more.*"

A fool, nothing more, Javier at last replied. *A fool among fools is not to be commended but pitied. A fool that flees fools sighting their foolishness is to be forgotten. I forget you, Khayin.*

The voice laughed, a noise that scraped over his back like a hot strigil. *"But the buds return every spring, always in shades to match their forebears, and always with fresh petals. Soft, fragrant whispers of beauty. And how the white-haired fools of winter breathe in the dew of spring's first bloom. To revel in the scent of innocence, to the neglect of all else."*

Javier scoffed and opened his eyes. *Spring blooms without husbandry.*

"Dear Persephone, of pale skin and plump cheek, hears the call of the hounds of Hades. Frightened by ghosts she cannot see, she flees the bosom of her mother too soon, forsaking the embrace of love to hide among the briars. Never knowing that he must be her husband. That he always has been her husband."

Enough! Javier's light flickering red in the din of his windowless office. *What interest have you in her? Speak plainly, beast, if only your twisted tongue remembers the taste of honesty.*

"Persephone is the goddess of all who hunger. Every stomach that pangs in winter longs to consume her breath. As every tongue upon which bread turns to ash aches but to speak her name. Is she not your goddess too, my dear Don DeMario? Does not Persephone bring her Hades such pangs?"

The words of Khayin settled over him as they always did, with far more weight than he ever should have given them. But his heart was not a scale to weigh and measure the meaning of words, but an open vessel taking in every ounce of substance until it spilled over the sides. And he had yet to run over.

You cannot harm her.

It sounded hollow, but he knew it was true. Khayin was trapped in Ashkult Prison, though somehow could use magic to project his voice and a touch of illusion to the world beyond.

How? How did he do it?

"*I cannot harm her.*" A cackle wrapped around Khayin's voice like the pop of a dying fire that had consumed the house of an innocent man while his family slept inside. "*But you can.*"

Javier pressed his face into his hands. Nothing substantive changed after that moment, but he knew the voice had gone and that it would not return that night. He had become so accustomed to it, he recognized the tone when Khayin had finished saying his piece. And he never loitered about to say any more than precisely what he had come to say. Verbose he may have been, but meandering he was not. Every syllable was planned, every word delivered with precision.

Persephone, the name of spring. It stuck in his brain like a song, round and round with no destination. Beautiful spring, a breath of hope to warm withered bones. That was what he had felt when she smiled at him, when she laughed. When she ran her finger over his back like a pet cat and he ached to press into her touch. To linger and to pretend.

Serap: an equally beautiful name with an equally profound meaning. *Mirage.* The fluttering of light that appears in the desert to a desperate man, that transforms the sands of death into the hope of water.

What a fool he was. She had only touched him, only smiled at him because she did not know the truth. When his flesh was restored, when he was able to look into her face with the eyes his mother had given him, he knew that she would shrink. That she would scream and press herself into the wall to get away.

Javier stayed like that for some time, hunched over himself on the desk, looking down at the space between his legs. In that moment what he had longed for half in jest became a painful reality: he did not want to be himself again.

Picking himself up, he quickened out of his office. Nothing had changed, he told himself. All was precisely as it had been before Khayin's voice swept over him, cutting into his soul with knives of sincerity. Serap and Cova were still in his house. The King of Elm was still dead. And most importantly, a certain *Evil* in his house was showing Serap strange visions, visions of his own childhood. And dear Pandora was rising to every occasion. Curious and gentle, and perhaps a little too confident.

Javier strolled about his house, the same questions swirling in his head. He found the hallway at the top of the stairs where the King of Elm had made his stand, and where Serap's uncle had torn through his poor books with reckless and barbaric abandon. But the mess had been straightened somewhat.

Serap sat on the floor among the scattered books, carefully arranging them back into stacks. Piles of paper laid in a semicircle around her knees, organized by size and type.

More than trying to clean up the mess, she was making an effort to fix the tomes that had been torn apart. He walked closer, approaching from behind so she did not notice him, and flicked through one of the piles of paper. She'd put the loose pages in numerical order.

Unbidden, a tiny squeak of joy filled his throat. Serap started and looked down at him, putting a hand to her chest. She drew in a quick breath.

"Gordito, you startled me." She slipped the book she was working on off her lap and held out her hand for him to climb on.

He should have hesitated, but he went to her like a loyal dog and climbed into her warm palm, his gratitude to be near her outweighing his shame.

"I'm sorry about earlier." Her brow folded in a soft crease and she looked askance. "About jumping off the bed at the house. It was rude of me."

He shook his head and patted the ball of her thumb.

A gentle smile formed on her lips. "Thanks." Then she looked around at the mess. "Do you think he'll forgive me? Don DeMario?"

At the mention of his own name, his smile fell a little but did not fade completely. What was to forgive, he wanted to say. He contented himself with nodding.

"I am not so confident as you. And he is not so kind as you, I should imagine, though he does have soft eyes." She held him close so her nose almost touched his amorphous belly. "What turned you this way? Did you anger a witch or something?"

He chuckled, which came out of his throat as a ridiculous little squeal. Still, it had the vague impression of laughter. He shook his head and pointed at his own chest, then smacked himself on what might be called his temple.

She tilted her head. "Stupid choices, huh? I hear you. I think that's all I make, though I try very hard not to. I just get such grand notions of adventures and family and... and love. Have you ever been in love, Gordito?"

Javier sat down cross-legged on her palm and slumped his shoulders. He had not been expecting such a conversation.

He had experienced many, though not all, of the different kinds of love in his life. As the Greeks would have it, he had known *storge*—unconditional, familial love—for his parents, his cousin, his sister. He had known *philautia*—compassion for himself—when he finally admitted that he could not save everyone and that that was okay. And he had known *philia* for his fellow mortals and the strange, uncomfortable position they all shared in this infinite cosmos.

But *eros*? Romantic and passionate love that people fall *into*? There were no memories to sort through, no long-ago glances of old flames. A few blurry faces, some unrequited feelings of friendship. But love? Never.

He shook his head.

"Me neither," she sighed. "What about the beginnings of it, though? I think I may have felt that... once." She flicked her gaze away from him and at the bookshelf.

He smiled, imagining it. She had confessed to her uncle that the suitors who pursued her only did so for her position, but he had to assume there were dozens, if not hundreds of young nobles of Shihala vying for her hand. What lucky djinn had caused her to feel even the whisper of such a feeling, and what had he done?

Javier balled a lazy fist and rested his chin on it, considering her question. What were the beginnings of love? What did they feel like? He'd read about them in a thousand poems by a thousand of history's most articulate lovers. And he'd it happen first-hand many times, not the least of which to his cousin, who from the moment of maturity seemed to fall in love every other Sunday.

Every heart sings a song, incomplete until another heart whispers back. That was what Plato said about love. Had any soul ever whispered to his? Even for a moment?

When he looked back to Serap's large, dewy eyes, the answer became clear.

He nodded slowly.

"*Oha*," Serap said with half a smile. "A lucky woman awaits you when you're human, then. Or... a woman?" she asked, eyes suddenly wide. "Are you a boy? A man? And do you like women either way?"

He glanced down at his featureless body. It was a fair question. He nodded, then stroked his chin with one hand, encouraging the phantom of a beard to form at the end, just so there would be no further confusion.

"A beard, huh? Very Turkish of you." The rose of her cheeks deepened, and she puckered her lips to the side like she did whenever she was thinking. "A man who made a stupid decision." She chuckled dryly. "You may be a stereotype, Gordito. But I shan't let that taint my opinion of you. I'm quite fond, you see."

He clasped his hands together and bowed his head to thank her. Then he pushed himself up to a stand and took wobbling, wispy steps to the tips of her fingers. Nerves tried to build up, but he reminded himself that he didn't have any nerves. Or cheeks to flush. Or a heart to beat too fast. All the embarrassments that had worked in tandem with his misanthropy to keep him alone all his life were no longer a part of the equation.

Knowing that gave him the courage to lean in and kiss the tip of her nose.

Her cheeks bloomed in a deeper shade of red that spidered down her neck in a wave of heat. She set him down and stood abruptly, dusting her pants off though they were clean. "Perhaps I should call *you* Chupkin."

His light pulsed bright and quick with a shade of gold. He wished it would stop. Was this what djinn felt like when their emotions flashed in their eyes? He'd never thought about how exposed that would make a person feel.

He should not have done that. She would be horrified if she knew the person that was hidden inside this flashing, featureless body. And if he had been himself, he never would have had the guts to do it.

She turned aside, her arms wrapped tightly around her body, and looked at him sideways. "And what will the lady you wait for think? You'll turn back into a human and whisk off happily while I'm still cleaning up these books." She furrowed her brow and then slouched her shoulders, pinching her arm hard. "Sorry. I have a tendency toward pitying myself. I am very glad for you."

She averted her gaze, busily shoving books back onto the shelf.

The lady he waits for? Javier's white mist shivered. He had accidentally given a very wrong impression of his intentions. Eager to correct the mistake, he folded his arms across his chest and tried once again to speak. More unintelligible squeaks. In hopeless dread, his gaze swept over her. He needed to tell her the truth, or whatever little kernel of truth he could manage without his voice or his identity.

Over her shoulder, he noticed a particular book sitting askew at the top of one of the undisturbed piles. Inspiration. He hurried towards it and scaled the spines. He seemed to have lost his ability to fly with the addition of his appendages. But that was alright. All the zipping around was making his nebulous blob queasy.

He reached the top of the pile in no time, then pushed the book off the top so it smacked the ground with a hard thump and fell open. Javier leapt on top of it and flipped through the pages.

"What's gotten into you?" Serap turned toward him with hands on her hips. "What are you looking for?"

The pages slipped by, illuminated Arabic script in shades of gold and red. Frustration curled his tips into knots. Had he misremembered which volume of the series the lines he wanted were in? At last, he came to the page he sought. His non-nerves were back, nipping at his non-brain and calling him a fool.

Better to be a fool in the open than to hide in the shadows pretending to be something else. Besides, there was no going back. He looked up at her and tapped the page. A short work, only two lines.

Serap bent down and lifted the book with him still on the pages.

He tapped it again to be sure she would read the right stanza.

"Because my love for you is higher than words, I have decided to fall silent."

Her eyes grew wide. They flickered shortly to him before snapping back to the words. The pink in her cheeks faded to a soft rose. She plucked him gently from the page and set him on the nearest pile, then tucked the book under her arm. Without another word, she rushed through the hall and down the stairs until she was out of sight.

Javier slumped onto his backside and let his head fall limp.

She knew now. For whatever that was worth. A twisting pain tried to assail him, but with no flesh, it was difficult to quantify. He had known he would frighten her off sooner or later. Perhaps, it was better to do it with poetry.

CHAPTER TWENTY-ONE

SERAP

Serap hurried into the kitchen, for once not tempted by the smell of spices and bread. What was she thinking? Or worse, feeling? He can't have meant those words for her. He couldn't.

She flipped the book open and read them over and over, imprinting them on her mind while telling herself she had misunderstood. She was always doing that.

Serap pressed a hand over her heart to try to soften its rapid beat. She didn't even know who he was. Not really. Her head jerked up. Should she run back upstairs and have him write down his name for her? Could he spell? She squeezed her shirt and dug her fingers into her skin. Of course, he could. He was showing her poetry, *aman tanrım*.

Serap set the book aside, open to the infernally beautiful lines, and walked over to the bucket of water by the sink. She splashed her flushed cheeks three, then four, then five times. Nothing helped.

For all she had dreamed of falling in love after watching Ayelet and Jahmil and seeing the heat burn between Bakr Amca and Zan Hala, she wasn't ready for this. It didn't sweep her off her feet or happen in an instant. It was slow, painful, and aching. Bitter-sweet. And she wondered if the bitter was not knowing how they could be.

She didn't know how to turn him back. With her amulet gone she had no magic. And Ayelet controlled magical wisps, not humans disguised as wisps. And if he turned back into a human—a sick dread clenched her stomach. What if back in his human form, he wasn't so fond? Maybe she was the only person who had talked to him in a century? It wouldn't be the most absurd thing to happen in this house. Or worse, what if she turned him back, and the Immortal Killer found him in his house and did what he does best?

Serap removed her headband, set it gently to the side, and dunked her whole face in the water. She counted for as long as she could hold her breath, then came up for air. The full dose of cold helped structure the spinning threads of her mind enough to grab hold of a thought. No matter what he did when he was human again, she had promised to restore him. And she had an idea.

Sopping from her shoulders up, she peeked out of the kitchen. When the coast was clear, she moved her way to the basement stairs. She twisted the handle, so it made no noise and slipped down into the dark. She didn't know if she needed to be down there to talk to Pasha, but at least her words would be hidden from Gordito, whoever he was. The man who kissed her without lips and moved her heart with poetry without saying a single word. Her cheeks flushed again, and she jumped the last few steps, nearly falling.

"Pasha." Her voice rasped with excitement and so many other things. "Pasha, are you there?"

The sound of a full-force gale blustered into the basement, though there was no wind. "My girl," Pasha's cheery voice crackled through the air. "Find the crow's beak?"

"I'm doing well, thanks for asking." Serap pressed her lips together with a sigh, a mixture of resigned and irritated at Pasha's single focus. "I've seen the beak, but I don't have it. If I did, I'd be talking to you in person. But I do have a question about wisps."

"Isn't that a question for your mother figure? She's the one who commands them all, right? I've always been a fan."

Serap stumbled for words, her heart still racing from running down the stairs and… other things. "I mean, I have a question about turning men into wisps? Or wisp-like creatures."

"Hmm." Pasha's voice was far away and up close all at once. Serap could practically hear her eyes narrowing. "You finally snapped from loneliness and are hoping your pet wisp can be your new boyfriend, is it?"

Serap's cheeks flushed a deep red. "No. This isn't about Chupkin." *Yet.* "It's about—It has to do with a different wisp I found. And I didn't say anything about a boyfriend. You owe me for dumping me hear by myself."

"Sure. I believe you." Pasha smirched a few times. "I might be able to help. But that falls under Pasha's Spells and Witchery services and comes with a price tag, even for friends."

Serap groaned. "Fine. I agree. I just need help turning a turned man back. Is that how you say that?"

"You can call it whatever you want. Most people don't actually turn back, so there's not a lot of chatter on the matter. But it can be done."

Serap's heart crashed against her chest like waves on a beach. She desperately wanted to meet him, the man inside Gordito, and was terrified of it all at the same time.

"How?"

"Crow's beak, first."

Serap's eyes narrowed though Pasha couldn't see. "I thought that was for getting me home."

"It has many uses."

"Are any of them to get me home?"

"No," Pasha quipped unapologetically. "You got me. But now we have an even trade. An item for a service."

Serap groaned, entirely unsurprised at Pasha's admission, though the betrayal stung. What had she gotten herself into?

"This is why Jahmil doesn't want you hanging around, you little liar."

"I'll take that as a compliment," Pasha said smugly. "But I didn't lie exactly. Finding the crow's beak would have gotten you home because I would have to come and get it. And I'd never let you come to harm. You can trust me that far."

Serap trusted her about as much as the Killer who locked her in the basement, but she had to get out, and she did know where the pair of beady eyes and black beak hung off a bookshelf upstairs.

She bit her lip. "The beak... it doesn't kill or hurt people or anything like that does it?"

"Of course not," Pasha laughed. "Of course not."

She wasn't convinced, but the ache in her heart no longer cared what her brain thought at all.

Serap sighed so her shoulders slumped. "Okay. I'll be back soon."

She trudged up the stairs and turned the corner at the top of the landing, bumping into Cova and Chupkin. It was silly, but for whatever reason, she couldn't make herself look at Chupkin. Like she was worried he was a person, too, and she had never offered him freedom. Or like he could see the flush of her cheeks and piece together what had happened. Or like she had been caught with a torch over a pile of dry hay.

"Where have you been?" she asked Cova. "Did the queen come back?"

Cova shook her head. "No sad queen. What are you doing? And when will DeMario be home?"

Serap glanced between the basement and the shelf behind Cova with the bird's beak sticking out up high. "I'm fetching something. And I'm not sure about De-Mario. I've recently learned he travels a lot."

Cova's forehead knit into concerned curls. "He's okay, right?"

"I wouldn't know." She shrugged with a sigh, then licked her lips, eyeing the beak again. "Would you like to help me with something?"

She wanted to steer the conversation away from the Immortal Killer and the pall he cast over her otherwise bubbling thoughts.

Cova nodded. Chupkin swirled back and forth, though she refused to follow his pattern or try to understand what it was he had to say. She guided Cova to the shelves she needed to climb.

"Ever been an acrobat?" Serap asked.

"What's an acrobat?"

Serap chuckled. "Nimble things with no fear, as my trainer said when I started. But I prefer to think of us simply as highly capable and extremely driven. It all starts with a desire to reach something unreachable." She pointed to the beak high up on the shelf. "Like whatever that gross thing is. If you were an acrobat, how would you get it down?"

Cova frowned. "A ladder?"

Serap couldn't help but laugh, some of the tension she had built inside her easing. "Go fetch, then."

Cova looked up and down the hallway, scoured the rest of the first floor, and even went and checked the barn before returning. "The only ladder is nailed to the hay loft."

Serap nodded, keeping her face neutral. People learned half as fast when their teachers were patronizing snobs. "So, how would you get it now?"

"Climb?" Cova shrugged. She placed her hands on a few shelves, but there wasn't much room for her toes and the dust made her grip slide off the wood. She grumbled in frustration. "Can't you just show me?"

"Oh, I can't reach that without a ladder, either." Serap shook her head. "Chupkin. Go fetch." Remembering that he might be a person, the words caught in her throat. "I mean, will you get that for me, please?"

The little wisp darted up to the top shelf and whipped the air until the beak slipped off the side into Serap's waiting hands.

"That's cheating." Cova curled her lip into a pout and crossed her arms.

"It would be if acrobats were solely nimble things with no fear. But highly capable and extremely driven people don't waste their time on solutions that don't work."

"What is it?"

Cova relented with a sigh.

Serap took a closer look at the creepy, dried bird. The back of the head and what would have been the neck were wrapped snugly in the flaking soft skin of a donkey nose, and seven-colored strings bound the two tightly together, then braided off into a little tether that could attach around a baby's foot.

"A charm against evil, I think. Or grossness. Or something that a witch would want. Or all three."

Cova cast her a glance at the witch one, but she shrugged it off.

"Thanks, Chupkin. Have you been with Cova this last while? I couldn't find you. It was just Gordito and I." The heat found her neck and cheeks again, and she cleared her throat.

Chupkin swirled up to face her and floated like a cloud, frozen in space right in front of her. The heat only flared more. She swore she could feel non-existent eyes boring into her own, judging the color in her face and the look in her eyes.

"What?" she asked, at last, turning away in a huff. She clenched the nasty crow's beak in her palm and let it go just as quickly as she remembered what it was. "Go find Gordito."

Chupkin continued to hover, his clear judgment floating closer and closer. She swatted him away.

"Go. Shoo." She waved her fingers through his sparkly body. "I'll come to find you, shortly."

When he finally slunk off, Cova still stood before her, eyes wide on a tilted head. "You're acting funny."

"Nu-uh," she said, then groaned inwardly at how childish that sounded. She inched her way toward the basement.

"Evil told me to tell you not to go down there anymore."

Serap snapped her head toward Cova. "What?"

"He says it's not safe."

Serap slipped the braided cord around her wrist and frowned. She couldn't tell what bothered her more, that Evil was getting in the way of her plans or that he was talking to people other than her. The second one was ridiculous, but her pride still stung.

"Did Evil have anything else to say?" She folded her arms.

Cova nodded. "He said to hold my hand."

"That doesn't sound weird to you?"

Cova shrugged and held out her palm.

"Did he give you any gifts?" Serap asked, suspicion pressing her eyes into slits.

Cova's large eyes misted. "He showed me my brother."

The little girl softened some of Serap's anger. "Why didn't he come to talk to me himself? He usually does. I don't understand why it would be any different than normal."

Not that she expected Cova to answer, or Evil for that matter. With a sigh, she grabbed Cova's hand.

The air shattered with dim, blue light that faded quickly to green. Her vision filled with little thin stalks, like dried corn falling down towards the earth and collecting into nothing. When the stalks faded, she was in a different room in DeMario's house. It could only be his house, what with all the books and bric-a-brac. Brass urns with stars on top. Bedouin capsules with hanging bells. Sculptures of fat faces and curled hair. A bird of dimpled copper, flecks of blue paint still clinging to the wings. There were odder things, too. A pair of jade dice that winked even when there was no light. A ruby ring that looked far too large for any human finger. A bronze hand she swore twitched every time she looked away. A bone-carved box with images of *effrits* and sirens, and an azure tassel that hung from the top over a rusty iron lock.

Strangest of all, a large mirror leaned against a wall on the far side. It reflected her image in a faint hue, like the front-facing side of a clear glass window with its back side covered in a map of Qaf. Celestial constellations encircled the frame. The moons stretched across the galactic sky, and purple and pink leaves shimmered in the starlight. In the distance, a gnarly forest jutted out in sharp angles and groaned in the wind with knots that looked like mouths.

A strange warmth radiated from the glass, beckoning her to touch it and join the scene within. Considering the house she was in, and Evil, and how many times she had vanished and reappeared into nothing, she did not doubt that the invitation was real.

This wouldn't work out for her, she could feel it in her bones. One of those situations that was driven by stupid decisions that seemed right at the moment, like the ones she had told Gordito about.

But it *did* seem right at *this* moment, so....

"Coming?" she asked Cova. "I ought not to leave you with an Immortal Killer, just in case."

The little girl stared doe-eyed at the magical mirror and tightened her grip on Serap's hand. She nodded.

Serap smiled and stepped through the mirror. A cool viscousness washed over her skin until she burst out the other side. Muggy heat enveloped her, a cedar-scented breeze brushing against her nose. But her feet never hit the ground. Her hand remained stuck on the other side of the glass where she held onto Cova's. Her legs dangled, and her grip began to slip from the girl's. She tried to scramble up, swinging her toes toward the frame to catch hold and flip inside, but her feet wouldn't go back through the other side.

Cova's face fell into frantic wide-mouthed expressions, but Serap could hear nothing. Her grip gave way to the clammy sweat of fear and Serap fell, landing in foul-smelling mud that oozed over the sides of her boots. Cova banged against the glass, crying at her about something. That she'd get help? That everything would be okay? It meant nothing. Especially when the creaking groan of thousand-year-old wood twisted nearby, and a faint orange glow erupted in the forest.

Why did she have such terrible ideas? Terror settled into her heart like a hundred prickly needles of an *atalya kemer*. And all she could think was that she would not know Gordito's real name or be able to look into his eyes. His true, human eyes. Not if she died in this place. Though it shamed her, she opened her mouth to call for Bakr Amca once more when a rough bark-laced vine wrapped around her throat and squeezed.

Cova's face blanched as the forest dragged Serap away through mud and bramble.

She would never find someone who loved her now. She had always known she'd die too soon.

CHAPTER TWENTY-TWO

JAVIER

Javier traced the grain of the wood floor with the end of his squidgy arm. Part of him said he ought to get up and do something. But what? All the energy had been sapped from him, and yet he had no urge to sleep. No urge to read, or eat, or drink. There was nothing to do. So he just sat, occasionally looking at the stairs down which Serap had disappeared and enjoying the smile that tugged the corners of his mouth when he remembered the color in her cheeks when he had kissed her.

The flowy cloudiness of Zayne appeared at the end of the hall and rushed towards him, at his side in an instant. He looked different. A little bigger and more substantial with a faint trail of golden glitter following behind him. *What did you do to Serap?*

What are you talking about?

Zayne floated down, pointing the tip of himself closer as if boring into his eyes. *How did you make yourself look like that?*

Javier shrugged. *I'm not sure. I just really wanted arms and legs, so here we are.*

I want arms and legs! This isn't fair!

I don't know what to tell you.

The wisp stretched himself out making little groans of effort that trickled into Javier's brain. He twisted and wiggled and squirmed, and then eventually gave up.

You look different too, said Javier. *When did you get so sparkly?*

Zayne shifted in the air a bit. *I guess I just really want to be sparkly,* he said, then laughed nervously.

That's very strange.

Mind your own business, Gor-di-to. *What have you been doing to my Serap?* He maneuvered his mist to point at Javier like a knife made of light. *She's keeping something from me, and I know it's about you.*

Javier tried not to, but he couldn't help smiling guiltily. *I was able to tell her that I'm not really a wisp, and she promised to try to help turn me back. That's all.*

What!? Zayne's light burst out like smoke being blown by a harsh breeze, then just as quickly reformed. *That is not fair! I have been trying to get back to normal for—*

Five years. Yes, I know.

I cannot believe her!

It isn't Serap's fault. It's your fault for not being a little more creative with your communication. If she knew you were human, she'd help you. And if I ever get back to my old self, I'll try to help too. I promise.

Zayne grumbled, his light drifting lazily back and forth. *Okay.*

The sound of wind blasted through the hall, as loud as a hurricane without the effects. Not a single piece of paper was disturbed. Zayne rushed to hide behind Javier's back.

A little hole opened above him in the air—a slit in the very fabric of reality only about the size of a human palm, and inside black as coal. A hunk of metal dropped out and smacked him on the head, then bounced to the ground. He shook his head and his eyes focused on Serap's amulet.

"Third row left to right, fourth column bottom to top," a voice said. Female, rusty, and a little bored.

Don't trust her! cried Zayne, though his voice was so riddled with trembling, it was hard to understand. *She's the one! That witch that did this to me!*

"Don't get any ideas, *little Chupkin*," the woman mocked. "It won't work for you."

Who are you? asked Javier, his eyes scanning for any physical evidence of the voice, though he should have known better. He had to deal with so many disembodied voices on a regular basis. *Why are you helping me?*

"Because a deal's a deal." The sound of the scraping wind redoubled, then as quickly as it had come, it faded away. Javier waited a moment as the last of the whistles died down, then he walked over to the amulet and flipped it over so he could see the symbols.

Zayne rushed him, whirling himself around him over and again like a cyclone. *She never helps anybody. She's a horrible, mean, lying, moody witch. She probably just told you how to kill yourself or make a big arm grow out of the top of your head.*

I have to try. Javier shooed him away. *It can't possibly make my situation much worse.*

He swiped the amulet in the combination the witch had told him.

A sensation like painful gas filled his guts, then spread out into his chest and limbs and finally to his head. The ground rumbled, or perhaps it was just his body shaking. He couldn't be sure. Then like an explosion, his senses were assaulted by white light and the burst of thunder.

He blinked in the new light and looked down at himself. Huge, calloused hands. Hair on his chin. A crick in his back. The same clothes he'd been wearing when this mess started. Laughing, Javier snatched up the amulet and put it in his pocket, then he pulled himself to a stand.

Zayne flashed to the amulet and rubbed himself furiously all over it.

"Fat chance, Chuppy," the cold voice blew through. "The amulet can only change you back if it was what changed you in the first place."

I hate you! Zayne screeched out a flustered high-pitched harrumph, and the witch chuckled before her voice and presence faded into nothing.

Can you still hear me? asked Zayne, sounding very little and unsure.

"I can still hear you."

The wisp did a quick loop-de-loop. *Well, at least that's something. I guess your brain has been reworked for wisp-speak.*

"Is that a thing?"

It is now.

A desperate scream struck his ears and bit into his skin. Javier straightened, eyes scanning the hall.

"Cova?"

He raced downstairs, taking the steps two at a time. When he realized which room the cry was coming from, needles pricked his heart. "My mirror."

What mirror?

"The portal I use to get back and forth to Qaf."

You don't keep that locked up?

"Of course I do!"

Javier tore open the door with so much force, one of the hinges was ripped from the frame. Little Cova had her hands pressed against the mirror, tears streaming down her face as she gazed at the sky of Qaf.

"*¡El árbol se la llevó!*" She spoke so quickly, all of her words ran together. "Don DeMario! Serap! The tree took her. It was strangling her. I tried to go in. I tried to hold on. You have to help her."

"Get back from there." He pushed her behind him as he approached the mirror. It was one of the first honorariums he had ever received—a magic portal that could take him anywhere on Earth or Qaf, right into the lair of a beast so he could cut down on all the tedious traveling time. He had figured out a few years ago how to coordinate it with his calendar so the mirror automatically formed a connection to his next written destination.

What had been scheduled for that day?

Javier looked into the mirror. His guts twisted and sank all at once. The *arak hunak*. The man-eating *I-see-you-there* tree of Izrak. And Serap had fallen right into its virgin-murdering clutches.

There was no time to prepare properly. His gaze snapped to the corner of the room where a large trunk sat open, overstuffed with weapons. He snatched up a *tabar*: an Ottoman fighting ax with a long, metal handle and a single blade. Its curve was designed to cut flesh, not wood. But he was in a hurry. He grabbed a *janbiya* dagger, one and a half cubits long with a curved blade and a tip like a needle, with an ornate golden sheath inlaid with jewels and ivory. He'd never used it before and he hoped it wasn't just a showpiece.

Javier shoved it in his belt and jumped through the mirror. Passing through it was always the same, cold and inexplicably slimy.

When he came out on the other side, he was already falling.

His feet burrowed into the mud when he landed and popped when he pulled them free to take a step. The sky of Qaf blazed above—moons and stars and impossible beauty, but it meant nothing to him.

His eyes scanned the thicket, which he knew was actually all one super-organism. He'd seen drawings of it but realized now they were little more than line sketches. This was no loose collection of saplings. It was an entire forest with limbs as sharp as barbs and leaves coated in biting acid. At the center rose the core of the beast, three times higher than his own house and just as thick. The branches that clung to it wiggled as freely as an octopus's tentacles. There was such sharpness to them, they looked like they could cut flesh.

"Serap!" he called, praying she could hear him and that she would be able to call back.

He closed his eyes, trying to calm his thoughts and bring his body and his brain into the time and place where it was. Where it needed to be. The gentle swoosh of leaves, the scrape of wind. A *marleki* bird overhead screaming its horrible call. And then the soft whimper of a woman.

He reeled towards the sound. Through the tangle of black, spiked branches flashed a hint of golden fabric. Javier put his head down and ran. The underbrush nipped at his unarmored skin, cuts like razors making streaks on his shoulders and shredding his pants.

He snatched a branch and yanked himself up. Finally, he got a clear look at Serap. One of the spine-covered, tentacle-like limbs was wrapped around her neck and mouth. The skin of her cheeks was bright red, her eyes bleary and bulging.

The great tree at the center of the forest was only some fifty cubits out, covered in pods the size of mattresses—huge yawning mouths filled with black teeth where prey was deposited to be digested, often while still alive. The branch lifted Serap towards an open maw.

Javier grabbed a nearby vine, holding tight as tough, tiny spines like a young rosebush tore into his palms. He kicked off a branch. Bringing up his ax, he swung at the limb that coiled around Serap.

It snapped and her body plummeted to the ground, landing with a thump in the mud. She kicked up her legs and struggled out from the murderous embrace. Javier was so distracted watching her, trying to assess if she was okay, that he didn't see a branch the size of a battering ram hurtling towards him.

The club slammed into his stomach, knocking him into the air and sending him flying. Another branch caught him by his ankle and slapped his body against a trunk. The air snapped out of him. He struggled to turn and swung his ax, severing the limb that held him. He fell, but another vine snapped him up before he hit the ground. He sliced it open with his dagger, revealing pink wood that dripped pinkish-red dew. Finally, the prickly, green whip dropped him.

Javier tucked in his body and turned in the air to land on his feet. Eyes darting in all directions, he tried to regroup, to remember the plan of assault he had initially concocted. He had to get to the heart of the forest. The vines, the other trees, everything else was superfluous and could be cut back time and again, only to regrow. In the core lay the heart, a great pulsing organ hidden behind bark as thick as whale skin and as strong as steel. But there was a weak spot.

A scream cut into his brain, and he turned. A hundred vines as thick as fingers were tangled around Serap, tying her wrists, wrapping her torso, yanking at her hair. One snatched her ankles and swept her feet so she slammed into the mud.

Javier bounded towards her, hacking away vines as he went. Little screams went up all around him—tiny, genderless voices. Like filthy pigs squealing as they were slaughtered in the wet markets of his homeland, but fainter and more numerous.

He reached Serap. He snatched her ankle in one hand to hold her still, then used the ax to hack through the tangle of creepers. She bit down on the vine that had gagged her mouth, thrashing her head from side to side until it broke free, then spat it out and took a heavy scream of a breath.

Javier worked quickly to yank the rest of the vines from her. Little suction cups had already adhered to her skin, leaving tiny, red marks where he pulled them away. She winced with each pop. Her breathing was labored, bordering on hysterical. He set a hand on her shoulder and looked into her face until he captured her eyes.

"You need to run," he said. "Run as fast as you can to the edge of the forest and then keep running. Don't stop. Do anything you have to do to get away from this place."

She shook her head hard, her eyes darting all around as her body trembled. He grabbed her hand and opened the clenched, sweaty fingers, then he took the amulet from his pocket and set it into her palm. She looked down at it and narrowed her gaze before turning her wide, frightened eyes back to his.

"Take this too." He offered the dagger. She reached for it with slim, shaking fingers. What had been a large knife in his hand looked like a short sword in hers. He smiled at the sight, then he picked up his ax and rested the head over one shoulder.

"What are you going to do?" she asked.

Javier's face slumped with a grin. "My job."

With a final lingering glance at her mud-covered figure, he turned and darted back into the forest.

CHAPTER TWENTY-THREE

SERAP

Serap watched as DeMario, the Immortal Killer, slashed his way back into the thick of the woods. Where had he even come from? He must have come home and found Cova screaming into the mirror—his mirror, of course. Only a psychopath would keep a portal in his house that led to a murderous forest.

Or maybe he was headed here, anyway. Bakr Amca said he was always about somewhere killing something.

My job, he had said with the start of a cavalier smile.

A vine slithered up her leg, and she hacked it back with gusto, each sore from the little tentacles throbbing with pain. When at last the woody tendrils dropped lifeless to the ground, she looked again into the shadows of the deeper forest. He had told her to leave at any cost, and she had half a mind to obey.

Although, it grated her nerves. He was here because she had been foolish enough to walk into a magical mirror. She made a lot of messes, yes, but she always cleaned them up afterward. Besides, she wasn't weak. Nor were her hands too soft. She had already fought a ghoul and made friends with Evil. She could do this, too. Even if he had smirked at how she struggled to hold the dagger. She'd show him how tough she was.

She huffed and marched after him into the woods. The dagger was as long as her arm and made keeping the sappy branches back much easier. But with every step, the bottoms of her feet collected prickly, little seeds. She couldn't help but wince whenever she took a step. The tiniest of vines began to blow against her body like the silk of a spider's web, making it harder to cut any one thread. Woody fingers grabbed at her clothes, beckoning her to stay. To lay. To die.

At last, she made it to a giant log with glowing purple mushrooms that illuminated a patch of forest beyond. Don DeMario battled a wide, whorled tree with bark that wrapped the trunk like the corded muscles DeMario himself had sported shirtless earlier that day. Every rivulet of power beneath his skin was imprinted on her mind. A gaping black hole lived in the center of the trunk, sucking in dry leaves and twigs with a rasping, raking sound.

The Immortal Killer held his ground, his back to her with feet spread apart and his ax raised high in the glowing purple of the clearing. Even his silhouette sent shivers down her spine; an impossibly fearless man made of muscle and stone.

The wind left her lungs. Why had she come here? Silliness. Pride. But even pausing long enough to call herself a fool allowed the grabby fingers of the trees to poke through her pants and slither around her ankles. She shook her foot in hasty jerks, sawing away at a gnarly knuckle of wood that jerked her knee. Free at last, she grabbed the stubby stem of a glowing mushroom, ripped it from the trunk, and barreled forward.

Serap sprinted up behind DeMario and swung her dagger down so it cut through a pair of splinter-tipped bark toes that had come up from the ground behind him. The *thwack* of metal hitting the rustling earth snapped his head back to her. His eyes widened before cinching together in a tight V.

"What are you doing?" He turned back and slashed through a heavy branch that stabbed at his thigh. He swept an arm back and pointed aggressively. "The way out is that way."

"Rude. I know which way is out." Serap stomped on a duo of roots that snaked together to trap her foot. "And I came to clean up my mess. You can't fight a whole forest by yourself."

"Yes, I can. And I could do it a lot easier without having to look after you."

A branch came sailing towards his head. He turned, but not in time to move. It slammed into his face, sending him flying back until he slammed into a trunk and fell face-first in the mud.

Serap winced with both impacts, then ran to him, kicking back hungry vines and hacking at the sapling that bent overhead with razor-like leaves. His words stung like the bite of winter, but he may have been right.

She brushed several twigs from off his back using her boot, still too afraid to touch him. Then leaned over with the purple mushroom to light his bleeding face.

"Sorry," she said, cringing. "Do you want help up?"

He growled in pain like a bear as he rose. His nose was clearly broken, and yellow bruises had already formed under his eyes that would purple with time.

His eyes widened. He snatched her shirt by the collar and yanked her down into the mud as a walloping branch sailed a finger's width above her head. She cried out and crunched into a tiny ball, unfurling only when he let go to battle more branches.

This mess was definitely too big for her to clean up. "I'll call my Bakr Amca," she said, feeling like she needed to ask permission. "Do monster slayers accept help? Er, real help, not whatever pathetic sword-slinging I can offer?"

"No," he snapped. "The last thing I need is more damn people." His eyes darted between her and the great sentinel tree that loomed over the rest of the forest. Then he got down on his knees, his back to her. "Climb on my back. You can keep the little ones from tearing my flesh off."

She eyed him and his taut muscles warily. His words had once again stung her heart. Was she not one of those "people" he so clearly despised?

She could see little alternative. Serap bit her lip and charged, jumping onto his back in a leap. She wrapped her arms around his neck and held her breath.

He leapt to his feet and sawed his way into the treeline, the ax out ahead hacking through branches and vines like a dervish. Dozens of smaller vines, as sharp as daggers and quicker than wind, snapped at her from above. Each tip sported a tiny beak-like mouth searching to bite. She gripped the collar of his shirt in one hand and swung her blade with the other, cutting the mouth off just below its neck.

With DeMario's every twist and turn, she could feel his muscles moving beneath her. His shoulder blades pulling in tight and swinging wide. The heat from his skin. The smell of summer in the sweat on his neck. And even in the middle of the nightmare she had thrust them into, she wanted to lean in and breathe more.

Another sharp mouth darted for them. She fought the urge to flinch, bringing her sword up instead so the green vine burst open, pink droplets oozing from the wound as the head fell to the ground.

"How much farther?" she asked, trying not to let her voice pitch with desperation.

He gestured with his chin towards the massive black tree at the center of the tangled forest. Only some thirty paces away, but every step was hard fought. The degrees stretched out as he tore his way through, and the assault of the sharp mouths grew more frequent and frenetic with every step. Several times, he had to throw himself hard to one side or duck into the mud to avoid being smashed by a branch as thick as an elephant's leg, and she clung to him to keep from being thrown.

The thicket ended as they came upon the center, a calm in the eye of the storm. DeMario fell to his knees.

She tumbled to the earth, landing on her bum and completely out of breath. "What are we going to do now?"

He held out the ax. "Trade me."

She shrugged and offered him the dagger. When she took the ax, it fell to the earth, her tired arms angry at even the thought of lifting it.

"You want to help, right?"

No one ever asked her to help. Her chance to prove herself had finally come with a man-eating tree. She nodded.

"You see those pods?" He pointed up the trunk. Several pods were attached to the sides; giant flat mushrooms hanging open like mouths and tangled with sharp black teeth, some dripping with red and brown ooze like old blood. "Climb up there and chop them up. Keep it distracted while I get its heart."

She looked between the ax and the height she had to climb. She had a mind to protest when she remembered what she had told Cova. She was highly capable and extremely driven to reach the unreachable, and as an acrobat, she would. She gave

DeMario a sharp nod and swung the ax blade up, so it caught between an old snarled knot in the wood and the crook of a branch. Then she swung her legs up between the ax and the trunk.

Again and again, she did this, using the handle to gain ground and shimmying up in between. Each time she pulled herself through, her nimble toes found purchase on rivulets of bark or old nicks in the wood.

Serap scanned the ground below when she was some twenty cubits in the air. DeMario had vanished. Hopefully, to the heart of the monster. She found good footing and hefted the ax to shoulder height, afraid if she lifted any farther, she would fall straight back to her death.

She dropped it, letting gravity and the ax's own massive weight do the work. The purple of ground mushrooms glinted off the sharpened edge. The blade slid through the flat heads and black teeth like butter. The tree shook and hissed as red and brown ooze splurted from the wound. The smell of festering polyps and decaying oranges filled her nose as spores with spitting mouths and no eyes burst towards her with every slice. She kept hacking, determined to distract the tree as long as necessary. Someone finally wanted her help, and she wasn't going to fail now.

She hacked at sharp-toothed, eyeless creatures until putrid stickiness covered her hands and her muscles raged. The groan of the tree shifted into a terrible, ear-shattering cry. A heavy branch swung toward her with the force of a gale, and she could do nothing but watch.

The impact crunched something inside her and sent her tumbling out of the tree and onto the ground below. The ax teetered in the branch overhead, then fell. She couldn't even hold her breath, so completely pummeled were her lungs from the impact.

The ax smacked the ground mere inches from her head. With a gasping shiver, her entire body quaked at the nearness of death. The throb of pain consumed her.

The tree screamed again, the wail of snow in winter and the rush of a waterfall in spring. The man-sized branch raised up vertically, the needle-like sharpness of the fluff on its twigs catching beautifully in the light, like the tip of each was lit with the fire of the stars. Her breath picked up; tiny, excruciating little gasps that did little more than tease her body with the breath of life while slowly draining it from her. The tree groaned. The branch fell.

A great mass of black spines and tentacles broke through the bark on the trunk and hurled itself toward her. It snatched her up, coating her in hot, sticky tar that scalded her skin. She screamed as the monster wrapped itself around her and rolled her out from under the crushing force of the massive branch.

The oozy, black figure came down on top of her like a cage, shielding her as sharp-tipped vines whipped around like tall grass caught by a cyclone. The forest gave the great moan of an old ship being sucked into the depths of the ocean. The weight of the tar-covered mass pushed her deeper into the mud, wincing and hissing with each lick from the vines. Slowly, the outline of a face and two brown eyes buried deep in the black goo took shape, staring down at her.

She took a stuttering breath, grateful that her lungs would finally fill with air. And as chaos raged around them and DeMario took the brunt of the forest's dying rage, she breathed in the cocoon of safety provided to her by the man people called a monster.

The ground shook with a low rattle, like a final breath of wind scraping through barren rocks. The furious shaking of vines and branches slowed and then stopped altogether. Silence rushed over her like a wave until all she could hear was her own breath, and his. Rasping, exhausted, and in pain.

He rolled off of her and lay on his back.

She lay beside him, enjoying the bite of silence without the rustling of deadly trees. "*This* is your job?"

He started to laugh but it quickly devolved into a cough. "I know."

"I don't know how you do it. For all your effort to save my life, I think I shall die here. My body hurts too much to move, and I'm too tired to even want to." She sighed and winced. "Take care of my wisp, Chupkin, for me."

Wiping some of the muck from his face with both hands, DeMario let his head roll to the side to look at her. "Not bad for your first time."

"Second." She tried to tilt her chin up in pride but regretted it instantly. "I fought a ghoul yesterday."

"I heard" He laid his hands on his chest and closed his eyes, taking long slow breaths. "Are you hurt?"

"Only when I breathe." She tried to sit, but pain zipped through her spine and down through her limbs. "I think I broke something when I tangled with the tree. I don't think it liked me much."

"Immortal monsters are like that." He rolled up to a seat and shook some of the muck from his arms. "Moody."

The bubble of a laugh started in her chest, and she nearly cried in pain. Why was he being so nice?

"I have some healing potions back at the house. Do you think you can stand?"

"What part of 'take care of Chupkin' did you not understand?"

He pulled himself to his feet. Then with a guttural groan, he leaned down and picked her up, cradling her in his arms. She held her breath, not out of pain but of shock. Shock at his warmth, his confusing bit of kindness, and how much she enjoyed being tucked snugly against his chest while he lumbered through the woods, carrying her like she weighed no more than a picnic basket.

He spoke a few, very foreign-sounding words, and a rush like a cool breeze brushed by them. When she looked up, a wobbly mirage of the magic mirror floated above the tangled mess of dead vines.

Grunting with every step, he carried her through. The bright coziness of his house enveloped them, and her heart hurt with a different kind of pain. He would put her down now and tell her to get out. Or get mad about his books. Or look at her with distrustful eyes. And she would have no choice but to look back at him the same way. Because in that world, the one they actually lived in, she could not forget the anger in his voice or the fire in his eyes as he chased her down in the woods, even now as she felt safe in his arms.

CHAPTER TWENTY-FOUR

JAVIER

Everything hurt even more so than usual.

Setting aside the bear, Javier couldn't remember the last time he had gone out on a job without his magic armor, which protected him from cuts and punctures as well as cushioned him from blunt blows. His eyes were blurry, his chest stinging. The sharp pain in his face from where the branch had caught him full-on told him that his nose was broken, if not his cheekbone. Serap weighed very little, but his chest burned, suggesting a rib or two may be cracked. He desperately wanted to put her down, and at the same time, he never did.

It crossed his mind to scold her for breaking into his private room, going through his magic mirror, and refusing to get to safety when he gave her the chance, but the lecture caught in his throat. She had stuck by him through all the horror of the battle. But why?

Yet another thing he didn't understand about her. And the urge he had felt earlier, back when he was a lovable wisp that she looked upon with utterly trusting eyes, flared in his gut once again.

He carried her to one of only three rooms in the house that had a bed, the others being his own and the one where she had ripped up the floor with his two-hundred-year-old atlas. It crossed his mind that he ought to block that room off, lock it up, and never go in it again. No matter what happened, he would never be able to step inside of it without remembering the night when he had thrown Serap down on a mattress and she had looked upon him with utter terror.

He laid her on this bed and averted his eyes so he wouldn't have to see that familiar fright on her face.

"It's okay," he said, straightening. "Rest. I'll bring you medicine."

She opened her mouth, but he turned and walked out, leaving the door wide open behind him.

What happened? Zayne's voice hit his ears before he saw the figure of the little wisp rushing towards him.

Javier groaned and kept walking.

The devoted little sprite rushed into the room with Serap.

He lumbered down the hall and into his bedroom, squeezing through stacks of books to try to avoid coating them in the noxious pink and black tar clinging to his body. He peeled off his clothes and tossed them into the rubbish bin. He badly needed a bath, but that would take time to prepare—boiling water and carrying it to the tub. It sounded like a nearly impossible task at the moment. So, he wiped himself as well as he could and yanked on a long kaftan with holes in the elbows because he didn't care if it got ruined.

His own bed called to him, but he ignored it and went into the kitchen to boil water. As he waited by the counter, he knocked back a couple of healing potions. He wished their effects were quicker. Perhaps he had taken so many through the years that he had built up something of a tolerance. It seemed he needed more than he used to.

"Don DeMario?" a little voice asked.

Cova stood in the doorway, somehow looking smaller than ever. Thinner, her cheeks more sunken, her fingers more delicate. But the way her big eyes stared at him was like a breath of fresh air.

She took a nervous step closer. "Are you okay?"

He wanted to laugh, but it hurt his ribs so much. What a question. And the truthful answer was no. He wasn't remotely okay. Everything hurt, inside and out. He was used to fighting monsters, but the battle with the *arak hunak* had taken more out of him than usual. It wasn't just because he'd taken so much damage. He was emotionally exhausted from the panic that had flooded his mind through every moment of the battle, worrying about Serap and if she would make it through. Having to worry about other people was so much work. And there was a part of him that wanted to shove it all aside, to tell Cova and Serap that the time really had come for them to leave.

The pain in his chest redoubled.

"We're okay." He forced a smile for Cova's benefit.

The sound of horse hooves outside drew his attention.

"God loves a duck! What is it now?"

He limped to the window and peered out. The outline of two white horses blotted out the brown of the road, identical riders on their backs. His stomach turned.

"*Dios mío*, no." He wiped his face with his palm "Not now."

Two women were dressed stylishly in long velvet dresses, leather boots, and riding cloaks. One wore red, the other blue, hoods drawn up over their dark hair. But their faces were the same. Tawny skin, dark eyes, heavy brows. Moon-shaped with flat noses. They rode around the side of the house towards the kitchen door, chatting with each other as they went.

"What's the matter?" Cova moved closer as timidly as a rodent. "Who is it?"

He groaned so deep, it shook the floorboards beneath his feet. "My sisters."

Cova smiled and lifted her brows. "You have sisters?"

He checked his reflection in the shine of a copper pot hanging on the wall. He had known it would be bad news, but it was even worse than he had expected. Smeared in black slime, his nose cocked far to one side as if it were pointing at something, and huge purple bruises surrounded both his eyes, threatening to seal over and steal his vision. Ramona and Cecilia had misgivings about his appearance on the best of days. What were they going to say when they saw him looking like this?

Far too much, he was certain.

"Get down." He laid a hand on Cova's shoulder and pulled her with him to crouch on the floor.

Voices approached, going back and forth with their impossible-to-follow twin banter as they wandered onto the stoop and knocked at the door.

"What's going on?" asked Cova.

He shushed her and closed his eyes, vainly hoping that if he couldn't see them, they wouldn't see him.

"Javier?" called Ramona and rapped on the wood.

The two identical twins had virtually the same voice, but he could tell them apart with no effort. Ramona spoke a little deeper in her throat, lending more authority to her words. She always wanted to make sure everybody in shouting distance heard everything she said.

"*Hermanito?*" she called again, knocking harder. He glanced up and saw a single brown eye peering at him through a break in the curtain. "I see you there, baby brother."

Javier moaned and stood slowly, forcing a smile as he turned towards the door. "Go hide," he told Cova through clenched teeth.

"I thought you said they were your sisters."

"Who's that you've got with you?" asked Cecilia. Sweeter and always with more laughter at the edges of her voice.

He walked to the door and pulled back the curtain on the window. "Now is not a good time."

"Javier!" cried Cecilia, her big brown eyes widening. "What happened to you?"

Ramona folded her arms, tilting her head far back so she could look down her nose at him even though he was a full foot taller. "Open the door, *hermanito*. We came all this way to see you."

He bit his bottom lip, then immediately regretted it when he realized that it, too, was bruised and swollen. "You didn't send word you were coming. I... uh... I haven't had a chance to clean."

That got a big laugh out of both of them.

"Let us in," said Ramona one last time in her no-nonsense voice. With a painful sigh, he relented.

Ramona swept past him into the kitchen. Cecilia followed quickly behind, but she paused to clasp his hands and mimed kissing his cheeks.

"What happened to you?" she cried. "You look awful."

"A cow kicked me in the face."

"Oh, you are so full of *mierda*," snapped Ramona. "As if we don't know what you spend your time doing."

He almost laughed. It would curl her hair if she ever found out what he actually spent his time doing. Though, he supposed, she knew enough to assume he had gotten into a fight.

Cecilia's soft gaze fell on Cova. "Hello there, *niña*."

The little girl drifted towards him and tucked herself behind his back.

Ramona frowned, deep lines forming between her eyes. "Who is this girl?"

"She's... uh..." He faltered.

It hadn't once crossed his mind what he would say should he be forced to try to explain why some random twelve-year-old was living in his house. If anybody else in the entire world had asked, he would have told them to shove their questions up their own asses.

"I found her living in my stable. She was hiding in the hay and eating scraps, so I let her come inside."

"Another stray cat?" Cecilia laughed, but Ramona put her hands on her hips and narrowed her eyes.

"I told you we should have come to see him over Easter," said Ramona. "You see how much worse he gets when we skip a month."

Cecilia twitched her lips. "What's your name, *pequeña*?"

Cova grabbed his finger and looked up at him with big eyes like he was supposed to have the answers.

He stared down at her blankly, though he could never quite control the way his face twitched when he was around his sisters.

"Are you going to offer us tea, or aren't you?" Ramona pulled out a chair at his little table, then used a lace handkerchief to wipe the seat before settling herself into it. She shot a glance at Cecilia, who obeyed without a word and took a seat beside her.

"Of course," he said, but the healing potion was growing sweaty in his hand. He peeked down at the sparkling blue and then back at them. "Stay here for a moment. I'll be right back."

He grabbed Cova's hand and pulled her out of the kitchen. All their unasked questions swirled around him as he plodded back up the stairs to the room where he had left Serap. Her voice drifted down the hall towards him, airy yet secretive, then stopped at the sound of his footsteps.

He tapped on the doorframe before stepping inside. Serap sat on the bed, caked in equal parts mud and exhaustion, talking to Chupkin.

You... The wisp flashed.

Serap slipped back to the corner of the bed like the first time he had thrown her there, only more slowly, pain etched across her face.

Cova ran to her and jumped up on the bed. She threw her arms around Serap's neck, smearing them both in mud. "You're okay!"

"Ah, ah, ah," Serap said, a cry on the edges of her voice. She placed a hand on the girl's head and gave her a kiss. "I'll be a little more okay if you loosen your grip."

Cova let go and sat back on her knees, a guilty expression filling her eyes, but it did not wipe away her smile. "Sorry."

Javier fiddled with the potion in his hands, then, keeping his eyes on the floor, he crossed the distance to the bed and held it out to her.

Her eyes fell upon the vial and then slid up to his face. "That's a healing potion from Qaf. Why do you have that?"

"Why wouldn't I?"

"That's not some peddler's potion. Not with a glow like that. You're not a prince. So why do you have a potion like that?" Her eyes widened, and she wrapped her arms around her knees. "Did you—"

He shrugged. "My job comes with its perks."

Her arms loosened in seeming acceptance of his words. She reached forward slowly, her breath in short, pained rasps, and snatched the bottle from his hand.

"Thanks."

Her eyes met his, soft for once, wide and honeyed like the ones she had used to look at Gordito. She held the potion close to her chest and slipped her gaze to the bed.

"For the potion and for saving me from the moody tree."

One corner of his lips tipped up quickly, then he looked down at the floor and grunted, "*De nada.*"

He turned to leave when a face popped around the side of the door.

Cecilia smiled guiltily and straightened, then gave a little wave. "*Hola.*"

"I told you to wait," said Javier.

She shrugged. "Looks like you got a few new boarders since the last time we were here." She turned her gaze to Serap, her expression curious and concerned. "Nice to meet you. I'm Javier's sister."

Javier clenched his teeth. "She doesn't speak Spanish."

Cecilia frowned and pressed her lips together. "Where's she from?"

He almost answered, then decided against it. Her and Ramona trying to talk to Serap could only cause trouble.

"Well, her clothes look Turkish." Cecilia tilted her head, tapping her chin with a single finger. "*Sen Türkçe biliyor musun?*"

He clenched a fist and pressed it into his thigh. How did she always do that?

Serap's eyes perked up. She nodded and tilted her head to the side, her gaze still flickering to him every so often. "*Ben* Serap," she said. "I didn't know the Imm—Don DeMario had a sister."

She laughed and clasped her hands together. "He has two. Though, I don't think he likes to talk about us much. Or... anything." She went up on her tippy toes to pat him on the head. "But we love him."

"Are you two coming back?" Ramona called from the base of the stairs. "I really do not appreciate being left here on my own."

"Then, come up!" called Cecilia. "There's someone you should meet."

"Will you stop?" Javier snapped at Cecelia in Spanish. "Just leave her alone. She's had a hard day."

Cecilia twitched her lips, ignored him, and walked towards the bed. "So, how did you come to be here? Don't tell me he found you living in his stable?"

Serap smiled just a little, the skin around her eyes tight and her gaze assessing. "I was hungry and smelled bread."

She was still clinging to that tired excuse. Javier started to smile, but when a shadow fell across Serap's face, it disappeared.

"Are you alright, dear?" Cecilia knelt down to face Serap.

Serap looked down at her knees and then back up. "I could use some fresh clothes."

"Of course. Do you not have any? I think I packed an extra dress in my bag that would fit you."

Javier brightened. Maybe there was some advantage to his sisters showing up.

"How on earth did you end up like this? You look like you lost a wrestling match with a pig." Cecilia slapped a hand over her mouth. "What an awful thing to say. I didn't mean that. I only meant, look at you. You poor thing."

Serap's mouth opened and closed a few times before settling back into a tiny smile. "It's okay. I do look like that. I was climbing a tree and... fell."

"Somebody better come down here and tell me what is going on or I am going to get very angry," called Ramona.

"Just come upstairs," Cecilia shouted back.

"You know I don't like walking around this creepy house."

Javier crossed his arms and looked at the wall. Everybody was always picking on his house.

Cecilia groaned, then turned her gaze back to Serap. "I'll get you the dress, and maybe we could draw a bath for you."

Serap brightened. "That would be lovely. I thought I'd be stuck in these dirty things forever."

"I'd never hear of it." Cecilia tapped her hand affectionately, then stood and rushed towards Javier, her face contorting with a conspiratorial smile. "Let's go boil some water." She glanced over her shoulder at Serap. "Just sit tight, dear. I'll have you cleaned up in no time."

She grabbed his arm and led him quickly from the room, holding tight enough to add more bruises to his collection. "She's pretty," she said in Spanish, wiggling her eyebrows. "I want you to tell me absolutely everything."

Javier pressed his face into his hand. The healing potion was beginning to work its magic, but he was in more pain than before.

CHAPTER TWENTY-FIVE

SERAP

Serap leaned toward the door, trying to catch what the voices were saying as they vanished down the hall. It was no use. They had switched back to whatever language they spoke in España. *Espanese*? Who knew?

She looked down at the potion in her hands. It really was the best there was. The kind Jahmil kept stored away for emergencies only, and then still gave away begrudgingly. Bakr Amca had used a ton. She popped open the cork and drank the silky liquid. Her body tingled with the magic it missed from Qaf. The pounding in her head lessened.

"What happened to you?" Cova's curious eyes combed over every scrape and scratch and pool of ooze that was drying on Serap's clothes. They had been her favorite—her special festival wear so she could glitter like the djinn and still do tricks without flashing everyone in her silky pants.

"Exactly as I said. I climbed a tree and fell. I just left out the part where it strangled me and tried to eat me with its razor fangs."

Cova's face paled. "How are you alive?" A look of realization donned on her and she settled into a superior smirk. "It was DeMario, wasn't it? He saved you from the tree like he saved me from the bear."

Serap plucked at a bit of pink, sappy liquid that clung to her arm, afraid to even touch the thick glops of tar. "Yes," she managed to say, though it stuck in her throat and the 's' sound lingered longer than necessary.

"Why don't you sound happy about that?" Cova asked, voice flat.

She did not want to talk about what she couldn't even understand.

She shrugged and forced up a smile. "You ask so many questions, you'll be fine no matter what you choose to do in life."

Cova was too sharp to miss the evasion. She frowned and leaned in. "You can talk to me. I'm not a child. I understand stuff."

Serap chuckled, and Chupkin emerged from inside her shirt. He twisted about as if wringing off the filth before flapping himself like a wet blanket being hung out to dry. Then he settled on Cova's shoulder, waiting as expectantly for an answer as the little girl.

"Gug," Serap groaned. "What do you want me to say? He yells at me and shakes me one moment and then lets me go the next. Chases me down like deer and then gives me a picnic. Is angry when I refused to leave him to fight the tree alone and then asks for help. What am I supposed to say about that? I'm confused?"

"You definitely are." Cova shook her head.

Serap scowled. "I thought you were trying to be helpful."

"Why *did* you come here?" Cova wrinkled her snub nose. "You don't look skinny enough to break into someone's house for bread."

Serap looked over the young girl's boney frame, protruding cheekbones and lips that cracked when she smiled. Cova was right. It had been a long time since she looked as hungry as that. Guilt washed over her. Did she even deserve all that Shihala had given her? She was no better than Cova. Worse, probably. Maybe she didn't deserve to live her life in Qaf, much less make it longer. She had told 'Abi Jahmil that living in Shihala had done nothing for her, but that was the biggest lie she had told yet.

"I wanted him to kill an immortal, what else?" She expelled the air from her lungs over ten seconds; a trick she learned as an acrobat to regain composure after a bad fall. "I'm just like Najima or the King of Eastern Elm. No wonder he hates me."

Cova patted her knee and Chupkin her hand as if they were in on the pity together. "DeMario doesn't hate you."

"He wouldn't even look at me when he came in the room." She wrapped her arms around her chest and squeezed as hard as she could, wishing for one thing. "Where's Gordito?"

"I don't know." Cova shrugged, her bony little shoulders like tiny pyramids on each side of her neck. "I haven't seen him since before you fell through the mirror."

Chupkin retreated slowly, drifting behind Cova. He had already gained a bit of gold sparkle she couldn't explain. What else was he up to? Serap narrowed her eyes.

"What are you hiding, Chupkin?"

He stayed hidden.

"Chupkin!"

He pooled around Cova's back, like lava flowing so slowly it cooled as it went.

"Where's Gordito?"

He shook his wispy head.

"Show me."

Chupkin swished about in a sad little circle then up to her face where he ran a little tendril across her cheek. His glimmer dimmed to a faint glow. Serap knew what that meant, even if she wanted to claim that he was a wisp so his twirling could mean anything, and what did he know anyway?

A hard ball formed in her stomach as sticky and putrid as the sap on her arm. But she had not given up on hope, yet. If Gordito was missing, maybe Pasha had fulfilled her promise and changed him back. Maybe he wandered out of the house while she and DeMario were fighting the tree. Or maybe, he was still a wisp and Pasha was working on it right now. Either way, as the Witch of Eternal Finding, Pasha would know the answer.

She plucked Chupkin from her cheek and set him atop Cova. "Go on down and talk to DeMario's sister. She seems very nice and could be very helpful to you. Don't let her see Chupkin though."

The wisp sharpened his edges with indignation.

"I know you know, I just thought I'd remind you since we're on Ard."

"What are you going to do?" Cova's large eyes narrowed into slits.

"I'm going to the basement."

"But Evil said—"

"I don't care what Evil says," she snipped.

The girl's face fell, and guilt became another tarry blob on the ball in Serap's stomach.

"I'll be fine. Now, off with you."

Cova slumped off and thrice looked back at her with sad eyes on her way out the door. When the last of her footsteps quieted down the hall, Serap slid off the bed. She removed her black and sticky headscarf—praying Allah wouldn't mind her not wearing something so soiled—and dropped it to the floor. Then she removed her jacket and set it neatly on the bed. There would be no salvaging it, but it still deserved a little respect while she mourned its loss. With a glance down the hallway, she crept down the stairs, cringing whenever a floorboard creaked.

The door to the basement stood ajar just past the kitchen where DeMario's sisters were chatting up a storm. How different they were than him. Another thing she found utterly confusing. They clearly loved and doted on him, and he had appeared no more chatty or friendly than normal. She bit her top lip and waited for a bout of laughter before making her move. It didn't take long.

In three wide steps, she passed the kitchen door and made it to the basement stairs. But something held her back. Foolishness, probably. She had recently come to the realization that she had that in spades. For having grown up on Ard, she was terrible at living there. She paused mid-step and leaned back until she could just see into the kitchen.

DeMario stood at the stove, boiling water, a clean, ripped kaftan over his muscled back. His tanned skin peaked through a large hole in his shirt, marred with a deep cut that shimmered with a hint of deep cobalt blue. Something no one would notice if they weren't familiar with Qafian magic. She could feel her own healing potion working inside her, like honey melting into warm tea. The potions were expensive, even by royal standards. Why had DeMario shared something so precious with her for a couple of bruised ribs and deep scrapes?

Cova sat at the table nearby, swinging her legs back and forth as she listened to twin sisters talk in their foreign language. A piece of bread sat between her lips, and her eyes wandered trustingly to Don DeMario. She looked happy. Safe. Probably for the first time in her life. And when he looked back at her, there was a kindness, a softening of the dark brown that took in everything, even under all his bruises.

Serap straightened and squeezed the doorknob beneath her fingers. If she had not snuck into this house, if she had not broken whatever protocol seemed so important to him, would she have learned to look at him that way, too? The ball of stickiness in her stomach grew, rubbing its awfulness against her heart. She wished, just a little, that he would look at her like that. With that deep warmth and bit of twinkle. But what did that matter? He would not, and she would not accept it. He was volatile. As prone to fickleness as the *januub* wind. And she had broken his trust first.

Gordito, on the other hand, had only shown her kindness. Had only been gentle and had caused that pinch in her heart. The first pinch of its kind. She would not give up on that.

Serap tiptoed down the rough stone and sucked in a quick breath. The sad-eyed queen sat on a cracked wooden bench at the back of the basement, an ethereal glow radiating from her wintery skin. Her hands clasped each other in front of her, and her red eyes stared at Serap as if she had been waiting for her in the dark the whole time.

"What are you doing down here?" Serap kept her voice low, glancing toward the ceiling.

Najima's eyes shone like dead embers even though they glowed. "Waiting."

Serap did not ask what for. She already knew, and it nipped at her like the little beaked plants—a comparison she could not have made that morning.

"Maybe instead of waiting, you should do something about it."

"Shall I?" Najima's eyes moved from an aimless spot on the wall to Serap's. "I may kill the Immortal Killer?"

"No. You don't even need to kill him now; the King of Elm is already dead."

"A promise was made."

"You can't kill him," Serap said forcefully, a sudden desire to protect the man who had saved her rising.

"Then I shall wait."

"Why?" Serap flung her hands out to the side. "You can go do anything you want. You've lived for thousands of years and have so much time left ahead of you. Why are you wasting your life?"

"Why are you?"

"I'm not. I'm trying to save it."

"You are running," Najima said, her tone as frustratingly uninterested as usual.

Serap lifted her wrist so the crow's beak twisted back and forth on its string. "I'm not running from anything."

"Toward something, then."

"Is that so bad?"

"True love is a fool's errand. It can fool you into thinking it's real, like I did with my treacherous husband, blooming and then fading just as quickly. Or worst of all, true love can blossom in dark loneliness, fill you with unmistakable light and joy, then disappear forever. Hearts split in twain, leaving you wondering where your love went or if the ache you felt was ever real at all."

Serap smacked the crow's beak so it spun in furious circles. "You don't even love your life, how could you love another?"

Najima's smooth brows creased, cracks in mud. "Loving life and loving people are two different things. Neither is dependent on the other."

"I disagree." Serap snatched the beak and used it to point at the queen for emphasis. "What's the point of living if you can't have love and what's the point of loving if you're going to die and have no one remember you in the first place?"

The placidity returned to Najima's face. "She already did it."

"Who did what?"

"Your witch. She already turned you sprite back into a man."

Serap's heart beat against her still-healing chest, each thrum pained with hope. "Where is he?" she asked, the agony too much to bear.

"I do not know. I have been busy waiting."

Serap scrunched her face at the cryptic woman, wishing for once the visitors in the house were a little more direct and less ominous. Still, she had half the answer she was looking for. Now she could ask Pasha for the second.

She stepped into the cell DeMario had thrown her in, rubbing away the chill of memory.

"Pasha?" she called, then she glanced at Najima who sat still in the corner, looking at nothing without a blink.

The wail of wind surrounded her. But instead of Pasha's voice, the air turned green and wavy.

"Evil?" The ice of dread coated Serap's stomach. She had never disobeyed Evil before.

"Serap?" Pasha's voice broke free.

Before she could answer, a yawn in the floor opened up, each stone cobbling on top of the next like a builder piecing together a wall on either side. Serap fell through the windy black with a yelp and landed on her bed upstairs just as quickly.

"*You grow bold, young one.*"

"I need an answer." She hit the mattress, looking about her for some indication of where to turn her head.

"*In time.*"

"Now," Serap said, her gnawing eagerness to find Gordito—the true man behind the chubby wisp who had touched her heart—driving her argument.

"*A present,*" Evil said.

Another hole opened up above her, and a large, cloth-bound tome fell onto her stomach with so much force, she grunted. Then the green faded from the room like the sun behind the mountains. She clenched her fists and looked down at the book.

It was in Qafian Arabic with several thousand pages to read. She must not have been working fast enough to fulfill Evil's command to read the books. She had only been there two days. The spirits in this house sure were temperamental about their time frames.

Moody, DeMario's voice said in her mind, thick and deep and tinged with humor. She shook her head and opened the cover, all too ready for her bath.

"Pasha?" she called, figuring it was worth one last shot. "Pasha, are you there?"

Nothing.

Of course.

Everyone in this house decided when they talked to her and not the other way around.

She glanced out the window, wishing she could ride on the breeze and find Gordito. He was the only one who listened.

CHAPTER TWENTY-SIX

JAVIER

He brought water and boiled it to pour the bath, showed Cecilia where the soap was, then went out to the stream to clean himself off. He didn't often bother with warm baths, usually only after a nasty battle, but he was happy to concede the tub to Serap and any of the other females in his house who felt like making use of it. It was the perfect excuse for him to get away and be on his own.

Normally, he would have been very nervous with so many people in his house—far too nervous to ever dream of leaving. And his skin did twitch as he made his way toward the small, freezing mountain stream. The King of Elm was dead, but Khayin and all the other spirits were still in fighting form. And he vaguely remembered Serap mentioning a specter that she had named *Evil*. That couldn't be good.

None of that changed how badly he stank. He kept his ears peeled and stayed close enough that he would be able to hear a scream should one cut through the relative calm of purple twilight.

The potion had sealed up most of the wounds, and the pain in the bruises was beginning to fade, even if their appearance hadn't. He peeled off his clothes, rubbed himself with lye, and scrubbed his skin in the freezing water until it stung. Then he sank down and lay on the rocks, relishing the tickle of the cold washing over his abrasions and burns.

Serap's very worried about Gordito, said Zayne, drifting lazily over the tall wheat that grew in the field nearby. *She thinks her little love sprite has abandoned her.*

Javier sighed and laid his head back in the water so it bubbled and giggled through his hair and beard. "I can't very well stay a wisp forever. It's impractical. Besides, for all the skills I may have had in that form, I doubt I would have been much help against the *arak hunak.*" He laid his forearm over his eyes. "I don't want to lie to her or win her affections through trickery any more than I want to force her or intimidate her."

Are you saying you do want to win her affection? Zayne asked, sounding cautious, excited, and optimistic all at once.

"Thus it will be." He slowly rose to a seat in the water. "*Slender arrows are lodged in my heart, and love vexes the chest it has seized. Shall I surrender or stir up the sudden flame by fighting it?*" Javier trailed off and shook his head. "*A burden carried willingly is more light, is it not? Or in dreaming, shall I transform the fragile weight of tinder carried into a heavy cross upon which to hang myself?*"

Zayne didn't say anything for a while, but the lazy drift of his body paused, and he began to spread out over the top of the hay like a glittering, golden fog. *We're still talking about Serap, right?*

"It's Ovid."

Can you just be normal for a few degrees? Are you in love with her or not?

He shrugged and cast his gaze out toward the purpling sunset, beyond the sea of golden wheat that shivered in the first chilling breeze of autumn. "I'm not sure I would be able to recognize the feeling. I've read about it, and I have seen it written on the faces of others, in their deeds and words. My parents loved one another very much, even if my father never quite understood what my mother was saying half the time." He chuckled and shook his head. "She was much smarter than him, you see. But you could always see in his eyes how he admired her and longed to please her, to give her everything she ever wanted and more. He died trying to give her more."

How did he die?

"An ordinary death." Javier turned his gaze back to the sunset. "We were in the Persian Sea when a knot slipped, and he fell from the rigging. He broke his thighbone so violently that it protruded through the skin. An infection took hold. He never made it back to port."

That's awful. It was clear from Zayne's tone that he was uncomfortable discussing serious matters. But Javier was only partially speaking to him. He had been alone with his cat for so long, he'd grown accustomed to conversation partners that did not reply.

"I held him in my arms as he died. He had an opportunity to say everything he wanted to say, and he did not waste it." Javier smiled sadly and shook his head. "He told me what he needed to say to me, and gave me messages for my sisters, and for his brother. He told me what I needed to do to tie up his business affairs. But of my mother, he said very little until the end began to close in around him. His last word was her name: Fatima. He just said it over and over until all the light had faded from his eyes."

Zayne drifted closer and floated down onto a river rock at the edge of the stream. *Taeazi,* he said, the Arabic word used to offer condolences. *What happened to your mother?*

A hard spot formed on Javier's heart just hearing the question, let alone trying to form the answer. He didn't know that he particularly wanted to confide that information in the chatty little wisp, but it also occurred to him that Zayne, for better or worse, was his only friend.

"I spent most of my youth as a sailor, following in my father's footsteps and doing what I could to provide for my family. But with the discovery of the New World, the old routes to India no longer seemed like the best way for a man to make his fortune."

Why did you need to make a fortune?

Javier smirked at the ground. "You must've been born rich."

So?

"Not me. My mother was an Ottoman, as you may have gathered. Born in Ankara. She was a Muslim who fell in love with a Christian, despised by her own people and by his. With what was going on in this kingdom at the time—everything that is still going on."

Javier cleared the tightness from his throat. "I wanted to take my mother and my sisters away from this place, back to Anatolia, where we'd be safe. My cousin had just joined the *Armada Española*. He had it in his head that we'd be gone for nine months, a year at most, and we would come back dripping jewels." His eyes blurred and he shook his head. "He could always talk me into anything."

It sounds like a good plan to me.

His skin twitched on its own and his lips curled. He clutched a fistful of stones from the water and squeezed them until his palm hurt. He rose from the frigid water and dried himself with the *peshtemal* towel he had brought and pulled on clean dry pants.

"I was gone for nearly three years, and when I came back... I was alone." He cocked his head to one side, refocusing his eyes on the sunset, the beauty left to be seen. "When I made it to Seville, my mother and the entire community of Arabs and Turks living there had been put to death. My sisters survived because they'd married well and had good standing in the church. Their husbands protected them. But my mother was alone. Neither of those men did anything for her because she wouldn't convert."

He pressed his palms into the back of his head and turned away from Zayne, unable even to look at a faceless puff of cloud while he spoke of such things. His mother had been on his mind these last few days. If not at the forefront, then nipping quietly at the back. Going with Serap to visit his childhood home in the plains, seeing his mother's dishes, the blanket she had knitted, and the paintings she had made. It had all been pulsing through him ever since. Perhaps, that was why he was being so sentimental, why he had allowed himself to try to connect with Serap, not only as Gordito but as himself. She had such kind eyes—wide and trusting and so much like a pair of eyes that he missed more than anything in all the world.

It started when he was still in Qaf. When he had to watch every man on his boat die—men he had known and lived with and fought beside for three years—until only he and his cousin were left. One day a sphinx swooped down from above, and then only Javier was left. But for as broken as he had felt at that moment, he hadn't lost hope. Not for nearly a year later when at last he washed up on the shores of his homeland and learned the horrible truth of what had happened to his mother while he was gone.

Since that day, Javier had felt no desire to love. In a world that would not even spare such a gentle and intuitive soul as Fatima bint Khadija DeMario from a fate of torture and humiliation, what hope was there for love? He had lost any desire to ever draw close to another living soul, knowing that no matter how good they were and no matter how much he cared, the day would always come when they would slip through his fingers.

He did not fear death. It was an inevitability, so much a part of life and living that its eventuality almost seemed inconsequential. But to take another soul into his heart only to lose them...

It was not so horrible to be alone. A twinge before he went to bed, or when he gazed across an empty table. A pang of envy when he went to the market and saw newlyweds entwined and laughing. It hurt, he did not deny it. But all the seclusion and desolation in the world could not hold a candle to the sharp, stinging pain of loss. Without love, there can be no broken hearts, and a broken heart was worse than the cold, inevitable, touch of the reaper.

He was fine alone. He could watch sunsets on his own.

"Please go," he said, not looking back at Zayne.

He didn't turn to watch, but he could feel the departure of the wisp, who fled from him like a rabbit from a fire. Like a songbird from darkness.

Alone again, Javier let himself take a knee in the wheat. He sat down and picked a stalk, running his finger over the golden grain that was almost ready for harvest. His heart was hurting, and he had no one to blame but himself.

Draw her close, said one beat. Send her away, said the next. Never let her leave. Tell her how you feel. Kill how you feel. Confess about being a wisp. Die without ever speaking a word.

His heart had no logic, no sense of right and wrong. Which was why he did his best to ignore it. But he could never remember it having beat so loudly in his ears before. Every sentiment made some level of sense, but he could not trust his own judgment. Still, one thought kept running through him that could not be denied, one thing he needed to say to her no matter whatever else he chose to do, or not do. And no matter how she might respond to it.

He turned and looked at the ruined pile of bricks that had been his home these last five years. It was strange to see smoke puffing from his chimney and two horses that did not belong grazing in his grass. Inside were four heartbeats—four women milling about and doing things that he couldn't control.

Serap was chief among them. Not only could he not control her, but he also could not control himself when he thought about her. It was absurd, ridiculous, painful. Yet he could not stop thinking of the color of her cheeks, the spider veins of blush that rushed down her neck and over her chest when he had given her that immaculate kiss. The image was stuck in his mind, blotting out all else, and changing the rhythm of his confused heart.

He went into his house through the kitchen door, pausing at the pantry just long enough to check if he had any pistachios.

He did not.

Women's voices filtered through the halls, down the stairs. His dreary house suddenly felt alive, and he couldn't deny that the sound made him smile. It also gave him a stomachache.

He snatched a shirt and jacket from a pile as he passed, sniffed the pits, and decided they were good enough. As he made his way back to his mirror room where he kept all the strangest and most volatile magic items he had ever been given, he took a blue scarf and wound it over his hair a few times before tying off the ends and letting them dangle to the side. He stuffed his pockets with gold coins from a massive pile in the corner—one of many such piles in his house.

In the end, he had returned from his final voyage very rich. Though of course, the money had meant nothing by then. And none of it had come from the New World.

He walked up to the mirror and pressed his palm against the glass, speaking the incantation to change its destination and thinking hard about the place he wanted to go.

The image swirled quickly, transforming into a glittering image of Hagia Sophia. A crescent moon shone beyond the white dome, stars pricking the sky all around like holes in a canopy. It was later at night in Istanbul than it was in Spain by a couple of hours, but he still felt confident he would be able to find what he wanted. The bustling city never really went to sleep, especially not the ports.

The world was ephemeral, as was everything in it. How house was alive now, but it would die again if he made no effort to change it.

He was ready to take a chance on being alive. At the very least, he was ready to come clean.

CHAPTER TWENTY-SEVEN

SERAP

Serap lay back in the hot tub, what was left of her wounds weeping with joy as the heat undid their knots and soothed her still-healing skin. She dunked herself beneath the water and came up with a gasping breath. A hot bath had never ever felt so good, even if it was in a wide metal tub that filled up the tiny, dusty room instead of a palace *hammam*.

She sunk so her lips were just below the sage-scented waterline and blew bubbles. When the sheer relief of heat on her skin and the tingles it sent across her scalp had subsided, leaving her in pleasant warmth, she reached for the nearest book. The one she had set there for just this moment, and the one which Evil had dumped upon her in his moodiness.

"I'm reading the dusty old tomb now, Evil," she said aloud. "So you don't have to hit me with it again."

She flipped through the book bound in blue cloth and covered in gold letters, careful not to get the pages soaked for fear of upsetting DeMario, and still getting them wet. She was in a bath, it couldn't be helped. The crinkly pages smelled of grass and must, and some of the lettering had faded. Old, it was. And a little too delicate for her patience. It was the story of a family she didn't know. What did he want her to do with a bunch of dead people's names and histories?

At least it was an interesting read, as far as dry tomes went. It was a royal family, so each branch had its own unique magic. And this family, in particular, happened to hold a cornucopia. The treat of inbreeding, that. Visions. Teleporting. Bridges between worlds. There was also longevity—*of course,* she scoffed at the bubbles—the ability to cast spells, and oh, a dozen or so more.

Why hadn't she heard of people with these abilities until now? Where had they all gone? She scrunched her nose and then nearly dropped the book in the water as she read the ability of a particularly spoiled brat, Prince Demarus, who could turn people into wisps.

Serap scanned the page in a frenzy, leaning over the sides of the tub so the cool metal pressed against the soft skin of her chest and her arms hung over the side. Five hundred years ago. Was Gordito that old? She muttered to herself as she did the math and looked closer. With a wet finger, she traced the family lineage down, the water leaving a dark path through the generations printed on the page. Demarus to Aamas, to Abdullah, to Gamil, to Kaiden who failed to produce a son. The lineage jumped to a Sheikha Cyra and a Sheikha Marana, twins who split the powers, the older gaining more of the Celestial magic before the younger was born just moments later. She decided to follow Cyra's line first and flipped the page to see who was next in line.

She choked.

Faris Khayin D'Jaush.

A dainty hand knocked, and one of DeMario's sisters popped her head in past the door—Cecilia, maybe?

Serap dropped the book on the tiled floor and jerked back into the tub. She slipped down and hid most of the way beneath the bubbles, her nose just above the water. With the door open, a fantastic smell wafted into the room. A smell so familiar, so achingly a part of her, that her stomach hurt with equal parts memory and hunger.

"Dinner will be ready soon, Serap." Cecilia slipped into the room and set a soft-looking purple dress on the nearby chair with a white headscarf. "I'm sorry they don't match. As a Christian, I didn't have any head coverings in my wardrobe, but I managed to fasten something together."

"Thank you," Serap squeaked. She still wasn't sure what to make of DeMario's kind sisters, and this one's comfortability with barging in on a stranger only made it harder. Bathing with others was common enough, even among the djinn, but with skin so different from anyone in Qaf, Serap had always preferred to bathe alone.

The door shut, and Serap scurried out of the tub, careful not to splatter water over the book. The lineage chewed at her mind. Was the traitor Khayin the same one as in the book? He was immortal, so being nearly five hundred years old—well past a djinn's average two hundred—wasn't absurd.

She dried herself off with a rough towel and slid the light purple dress over her head. It fell a little past her feet so she'd have to walk on her tiptoes not to trip, but the fabric was well-made and the stitching strong. The shape of it, too, was far more form-fitting than she was used to, following her curvy shape that Paco had called soft. And while she'd normally care, fretting about too many eyes gliding over her and the judgment behind them, it didn't matter right then, not when the burden of knowledge was too great. And not when the state she had been in before the bath had been far worse. At least she had a headscarf, *alhamdulillah!* A tender mercy in the comfort and modesty of the thin square of cloth.

She opened the door, her mind drifting elsewhere. If Khayin could change wisps to people, had he been the one that turned Gordito? Or had that power transferred to the twin sister's line? And if that was the case, would he know who did? Or who Gordito was? If Pasha didn't know, would the only way she'd ever find out be to use her question?

Love for life? If she could even call it that. The thought was absurd, right? If she lived much longer, she could feel that pinch again, couldn't she? Even it was just a tiny pinch.

She huffed and slid the hair cover on, then stepped out into the hallway. She nearly stumbled down the stairs as she tripped on the hem of her dress, already forgetting to walk on the balls of her feet. As she drew nearer the kitchen, all she could think of was how hungry she was for the delicious food in the kitchen and for home. What she wouldn't give to be sitting at a table with Jahmil and Ayelet. With steel-eyed little Tabor and laughing baby Lalam. Experiences and memories she wouldn't have because she was here where she wasn't wanted reading dusty books.

Serap tilted her head to look into the kitchen. DeMario stood at the stove, his broad shoulders now in a clean shirt and the bruises on his face nearly gone. He seemed happier, somehow. There was a bounce to his step and a glimmer of something other than ferocity on the corner of his lips. His hands moved expertly, familiar friends to the tools in his kitchen and the food he prepared. He diced, chopped, sauteed, and stirred with nary a glance at what he was doing. The smell of melted butter, lavender, and roasting nuts stirred a gurgle in her stomach. He slapped a ball of pastry onto the wooden counter and went about rolling it out, humming quietly to himself as he went, his hips dipping slightly from side to side.

She slid her feet one after the other into the kitchen and folded her hands in front of her, not sure what else to do with them.

"What smells so good?" she asked, hoping she already knew the answer—*baklava*.

She felt a sudden rush of shyness and searched for somewhere to rest her eyes other than on him and focused on the ball of creamy white butter he carved from on the counter.

He turned to look at her, a strange softness on his face. His nose had snapped back into place, though it was still a little swollen with red and yellow bruises clinging under his eyes.

"I thought you'd be asleep."

"I was bathing." She pressed her hands into each other. "And then I was hungry and smelled... well, whatever amazing thing you're making. I swear it smells like Edirne as the sun sets in here."

"Istanbul." He turned back to rolling out the silky dough into sheets so thin they were transparent. "I was worried the markets would be closed in Edirne."

She tilted her head. "You sound like you popped off for some shopping, but I don't even know where Turkey is in relation to this strange place you call España."

"Several days journey on a fleet vessel. Several months on camel. But that's what magic mirrors are for." He set down his rolling pin and walked to the stove to stir a pot. "I have something for you. Please, have a seat."

She hesitated, then took a slow seat at the table, watching him from under her lashes. She couldn't help how her heart had picked up or her hands grew clammy. What in Ard would he have to offer someone he hardly knew with such genuine eyes? And where was the anger they had glittered with yesterday?

He took a cup from the cupboard and poured some white liquid into it from the pot, then sprinkled it with a generous helping of cinnamon and set it down in front of her.

"*Oha!*" she breathed, a smile spreading wide across her face. She recognized the smell immediately: *salep*. The expensive-even-for-sheikhas Turkish drink of hot milk and powdered orchid root she always craved but had only ever had a few mouthfuls of in her life. "Where did you get this?"

"Istanbul." Dusting his hands, he walked across the kitchen and grabbed a parcel wrapped in white linen from where it lay on the bookshelf. He dusted off some flour, a twitch in his hands as he walked closer and set it down on the table in front of her. He took a step back and pushed his lips together, then quickly turned back to the counter and picked up the rolling pin.

Serap stared at the linen, lips parted in surprise. She looked at him fervently stirring a mixture with his back to her. Then back to the linen. At least three times she did this, unsure of what else to do. But then curiosity roused its head as it always did. She took the parcel in her hands, grateful to grasp onto something so she would stop shaking. The fabric dimpled under her fingers, whatever was inside soft and yielding.

"Is this for me?" Her voice felt dusty and dry, but she had to confirm, to make sense of this whole thing before she opened something that was clearly for someone else, and he got upset again.

He looked at her over his shoulder, turning the rolling pin over in his hands, and nodded.

She slipped her gaze back to the shiny white and pulled the edges of the linen. Inside, she found a black jacket made of thick wool and embroidered with gold thread. Under that were pants made of folds of silk with a vibrant pattern of red and yellow. Almost like the ones she'd lost, but so much better.

"Your clothes looked unsalvageable," he said.

A desire to throw her arms around him swelled in her throat and tugged at her arms, but she sufficed with pulling the wool close to her chest and breathing it in deeply. It smelled like cardamom and honey. She squeezed harder and harder and buried her face in the shimmering gold threads of the jacket.

He twisted the fingers of one hand into the curls of his beard, his gaze shifting around the room. "I wanted to... to apologize."

She pressed her nose harder into the thick fabric, afraid he would see her eyes. Afraid to see his. Where did such tenderness come from? Where did it hide in a body and heart trained to slay beasts? An absurd urge to cry thickened her tongue and stung her eyes.

"I'm unaccustomed to anything coming into my house uninvited that is not trying to kill me, or steal from me, or manipulate me. If I had known what you were, I mean, *who you are*, I would not have behaved as I did." He sighed and rolled his head on his neck, which sounded like the crunch of broken concrete. "I'm not accustomed to humans anymore."

She pulled her eyes from the safety of the Turkish fabric and tried to look at him. First his boots, then up his black pants that clung to his calves and the braid of his thigh muscles. Farther still, taking in his solid frame, his muscles honed so they could lift her like nothing, up past his square jaw and finally to his eyes, dark as night and lit with stars. He was unequivocally handsome in a rugged, yet reserved way.

Heat bloomed across her cheeks. "They're perfect."

She wished to say so much more and knew she needed to get out of the kitchen before she made a fool out of herself. "I should change promptly out of these silly clothes that cling to me so. I couldn't even do a handstand in this thin dress."

He smiled and turned his gaze askance to the floor. "I can see how that would be a problem." He tapped the rolling pin in his palm a few times then turned back to the counter. "If they don't quite fit, I can adjust them for you. One of many skills you learn living on your own."

A tightness squeezed her chest. He was so capable, handy, and independent. The opposite of everything she had turned out to be. If he found out, he'd laugh at her helplessness and despise how little she had to offer. Why wouldn't he? She could do nothing for him but juggle.

The noose around her lungs tightened even more. Why? Why did she care so much? She brushed her hands over the jacket again and again as if rubbing her callous-free and useless hands against the rough wool would somehow make them worth more.

"I'm sure they'll fit just fine," she managed to say.

She grabbed the cup of salep and took a heavy swallow before she realized what she'd done, how ungratefully careless she'd been with such a rare gift. Silky warmth and a melody of gentle flavors washed her tongue. She moaned a little in pleasure and again felt a ridiculous urge to cry.

She turned her head abruptly, undeserved sweetness still coating her tongue. "You don't have to do this. All of this."

"All of what, *señorita*?" He lifted up a sheet of dough as long and wide as a bolt of fine fabric, so thin she could see shapes on the other side, and carefully layered it into a shallow dish. "It was my fault your clothes were ruined. I should not have left the mirror open to that place. I hope the potion helped."

She nodded but couldn't shake the heavy feeling from her chest. Like she was guilty of something. He did not seem like the type of man who would care at all to be a sheikh. So what was he getting out of being so nice to her? He was sure to be angry once more when he learned she had little to offer. Paco would have been. And all the other courtiers in Karzusan.

She looked at her bare feet. "I'm sorry. For breaking into your house and the mirror and everything."

"Please, there is no need." He turned to look at her, the dough still hanging from his buttery forearms. "I do make excellent bread. It is little wonder you were tempted by it."

Her eyes grew wide and swam with tears, but a giggle whisked them away. She slapped a hand to her chest and inhaled sharply. Once again she felt that twinge Ayelet spoke of. The one she had only ever felt before with Gordito. She cast her gaze to the door. Something in this house was playing tricks on her. A ghost. Or an apparition. Why else would she fall so easily and twice when she had never fallen before?

"You will have to teach me your protocol." She stared at a spot of mud on the floor. "So I don't make you angry while I stay."

"I am confident that you are not here to kill me, so I won't be getting angry with you again." He finished layering the dough into the dish and turned to look at her, but his eyes only brushed her momentarily before dropping to the floor. "I don't like being angry. I never used to be, before... well, before I took this job, frankly. I hope someday I can convince you that the way I behaved when we first met is not who I really am. But I understand if you are unable to forgive me. You are welcome to stay either way. And if you do have some particular request you would like to make of me—I mean, in an official capacity—then I think it is only fair I allow you to bypass the usual protocol and speak with me directly."

She shoved her face once more into the jacket. Gug. These stupid tears. What was wrong with her?

"I have nothing to ask," she said thickly through the fabric, the fine embroidery scratching her cheek. "Because I have nothing to give."

The chair scraped as he pulled it out and sat down at the table across from her. He rested an elbow on the table, the butter on his arms shining in the light cast by the fire. "I don't actually get paid for this job. I charge a fee to listen to requests, but all the work is pro bono. And I have been known to wave my honorarium for special cases. Like when the leader of a very poor village comes to me with a ghoul problem or something like that. And I've been known to turn away royal envoys dragging whole caravans of precious gems just because I thought their cause was petty, or I didn't like their faces. It's all on a case-by-case basis, you see."

She smiled into the fabric, pressing the salty water into the wool so her face would come up dry. He was such a strange mix of serious and silly and terrifying.

"Are you saying you like my face?"

He took a deep breath and met her eyes. "I do."

Her smile fell, and her cheeks burned hotter than the heat on the stove. She couldn't deny how much she liked his eyes lingering on her, swimming in light and so soft around the edges. "I do not understand you, Don DeMario."

"I'm a complicated person." Smiling through one side of his mouth, he stroked his beard. "And you may call me Javier."

She shook her head quickly without thinking and winced. It was too much. Such informality with someone who seemed a million years wiser and a thousand times more complicated than anything she was. As if he had lived centuries and she had just been born. He would not want her either—a useless, foolish girl who would fall to death just as easily as a flower to the frost of winter.

"Or you can keep calling me Don DeMario. Or you can call me The Immortal Killer. Or you can call me the Digestive Biscuit of the Bahamut." He shrugged. "You can call me Maria if it makes you happy."

Again, a smile crept onto her face, and she yearned desperately to change the conversation to something other than herself. Her chest would stop crashing around with feelings she didn't know what to do with. She took another sip of the delicious salep and set it down with a harder thunk than she intended.

Taking a breath, she looked into his eyes once more. "Do you own a wisp?"

His lips parted and his jaw twitched. "I don't think so. Then again, I own a lot of things I'm unaware of."

"Have you seen one around, then? He's small—" She sized him up from the table with her hand. "A little tubby and... well, kind, I guess?" She couldn't help but smile, casting her eyes to the side.

Standing, he went back to the stove, lifted the pan of roasting nuts, and began layering them onto the pastry. "There are wisps of magic around here, of course. But the only one I have seen that I might comfortably call a *he* is your own little Chupkin."

"How do you know about my wisp?" She flicked her gaze up to him. "And why would you be comfortable calling him that?"

"Because he... she, it, they... has a personality. It's no ordinary wisp."

She narrowed her eyes. "And how much time have you spent around Chupkin, exactly?"

"Hmm," he said, then wiped some sweat from his brow on his bicep. "He followed me out to the river earlier this evening."

"And?"

He shrugged. "Bounced around. Wiggled a bit. Spun in what looked like very deliberate circles. Not to mention Cova had him in her pocket earlier. He is your pet, isn't he?"

"He's not a pet." A familiar sense of unease was creeping back inside her, taking up residence above her clavicle and cooling her body.

"Then what is he?"

"You tell me. You're the one who is comfortable with calling him *he* and who thinks he's no ordinary wisp."

"Do you think he is ordinary? I don't know how much experience you have with wisps, but most of them are just *things*."

"I have an inordinate amount of experience with wisps."

Serap scrunched her brows together. Something about the whole thing wasn't sitting right, even though his points were valid. Logical. Reasonable. But the fact that he had them in the first place felt funny. He seemed so plagued by strange creatures in this house, he barely glanced at them anymore. So why his interest in Chupkin?

"Is something the matter?" Javier glanced over his shoulder. "Was I not supposed to know about him?"

"Chupkin decides who he'll show himself to. I do not make the choice for him. I just don't know why you care."

"I suppose because I thought he was your pet, and you were asking me about wisps."

"Logical," she muttered under her breath.

He glanced over his shoulder, one eyebrow raised. "Do you not like things that are logical?"

"I rather find the emotion behind a statement to be of more importance. Logic can hide things just as much as nonsense can."

"A wise observation. In point, fact, logic, and nonsense often work in tandem. That is when they are at their most dangerous." He lifted a pot from the stove and poured it over the pastry he had made. A smell of butter wafted towards the table. "So, I suppose I'm meant to elucidate my emotional investment in Chupkin?" He laughed and shook his head. "Chupkin."

"You laugh at me," she said, a twinge of hurt in her chest. "Because I think about things differently. Because I care how people feel."

"I agree with you. But you're still angry with me," he said. Not a question. "That's completely understandable. And who am I to judge anything you say, or do, or feel?"

"But you do judge me. That's why you laugh." She pushed herself up from her chair, still clinging to the beautiful clothes from her home. "You think I'm silly. Someone to be chortled at and told how I feel."

"I did not remotely chortle. I only laughed because I think Chupkin is a silly name. Isn't it meant to be?"

Her bottom lip pushed out, and she turned so she wouldn't have to see him and his calm face and smug smile. "I'm going to go change." She marched toward the door, then paused, turned around, and grabbed the cup of *salep*. "Thank you. For the... the gifts."

He smiled and nodded slightly.

"Stop smiling," she grumbled, then hurried out the door muttering under her breath. She had completely lost that conversation and hadn't even realized there was something to lose. He may not be the monster she thought he was, but he was... and...

She growled and threw herself into her room. He was impossible.

CHAPTER TWENTY-EIGHT

JAVIER

The baklava baking in the oven filled the air with delicious smells that soothed Javier, but the exchange with Serap had left his stomach unsettled.

"What exactly do I think I'm going to get out of this?" Javier asked Sappho when she hopped up on the table to lick up a little blob of butter that had fallen from his elbow. "I'm sure that's what you must be wondering."

He rooted through his bag for a bag of dried, salted lamb he'd bought in Istanbul and held a gray piece out to Sappho. She licked it and pawed at it but wouldn't take it into her mouth.

"That is a very good question, my poignant little panther. And the answer?" He pushed his lips from side to side, trying to find words. Then he heaved a sigh and his shoulders dropped. "I have no idea."

He drummed his fingers on the table. Dinner was brewing slowly in a small cauldron over the fire—lamb stew mixing with the sweetness of the baklava. It should have been ready some time ago, but he had accidentally let the fire die down.

"*Así es la vida*," he said, shrugging. "What are you gonna do?"

Sappho nipped the tip of his finger, finally capturing the lamb in her mouth.

"Why did I lie to her, you ask? She gave me a perfect opportunity to come clean. To tell her that the sweet globule who chastely kissed her nose was in fact the same man who had shaken her so hard that her own tooth pierced her pouting lips."

Javier slumped down into a chair and the kitchen table and let his forehead rest on the tattered, greasy red lace tablecloth. "Why indeed? Why does any man lie but to shield the weakness in his own heart, to protect the whitened liver and the shimmering-smooth bowels of cowardice?"

"Who are you talking to?" Ramona stepped into the kitchen with an accusatory sneer on her lips. Cecilia was, as always, close behind, as bright and sunny as her twin was glum.

Javier grumbled and patted his cat. "Sappho."

"*Puaf.*" Ramona waved a hand and wrinkled her nose. "Get that vermin off of the table. Why do you let that thing live in your house?"

"Do not speak of the great poetess in such a manner." He bristled and sat up straight. "And the singular of vermin is varmint."

Cecilia narrowed her eyes at him. "Is everything okay?"

Ramona crossed her arms across her chest and leaned back. "I think it is a very... interesting? Let's call it an *interesting* development that you now have two young women living in your ridiculous house."

He bowed his head sarcastically. "I accept your endorsement of my continuing ability to arouse interest."

Suddenly, a man blinked into existence in the kitchen with no fanfare—not even the puff of smoke or colored fire that typically preceded djinn manifestations. Javier immediately recognized the Apollonian figure of Serap's Uncle Bakr.

Cecilia leapt back in shock and tripped on the hem of her dress. Bakr snatched her in his arms as she fell, one hand wrapped around the small of her back and the other on the nape of her neck, like a dancer dipping his partner. Cecilia leaned back to meet his eyes, and her lips parted in what could only be described as awe.

"I'm so sorry." Bakr's smile shined down on Cecelia. "Are you alright?"

She opened her mouth to answer, eyes sparkling and cheeks flush. Her tongue darted out to lick her lips. "Oh."

Bakr whipped her up to her feet and spun her out gently, then turned to face the table. When his eyes met Javier's, his smile widened to almost impossible heights.

And it was a charming and welcoming smile, which only served to make Javier
squirm.

"Is it you? The infamous Immortal Killer?" Bakr stepped closer and extended his
hand. Javier looked at it. The sandy brown skin, the calloused fingers, the nicks and
scars of a man trained at combat.

He took the man's hand and shook.

"What a handshake! My fingers feel like they're being crushed by five giant thumb-
screws. Amazing." Bakr laughed and clapped him on the shoulder with his other
hand. "Do it again, *efendim*."

Javier released his hand. "You must be Serap's uncle."

"Bakr al-Eayima zawj Sezan."

"Javier, who is this man?" Ramona stood to back away from the table. "He doesn't
look like a djinn. And I thought you put up protections so they couldn't pop into
your house anymore."

"He's not a djinn. He's a lilu."

"A what?"

"Male lilith."

"*Bismallah.* Demon." Ramona clasped his cross with one hand and made horn
hands with the other to frighten back the Evil Eye. If he had tried to explain to her
all of the contradictions in that single movement she would have looked at him like
he was insane.

"He doesn't look like a demon." Cecelia was still staring at him like she'd been
caught in a literal halo. He imagined that's the same way Zayne would have looked
at him had he eyes to look.

"I'm here to see my niece, though it seems my aim is off." Bakr rubbed his chin
and narrowed his eyes. "Where is Serap? You don't have her in the dungeon again,
do you? Because I need to have words with you about that."

"You locked that poor girl in your dungeon?" snapped Ramona.

"It was one night. I'll show you to her room." Javier turned to Cecilia. "Please be
sure the baklava doesn't burn."

"Sure." She blinked dreamily, her gaze fixed on Bakr's backside. "I'll grab it when it's... on fire."

"Thank you," grumbled Javier. "That's very helpful."

He walked to the cauldron and spooned up a bowl of stew, then sliced a large chunk of bread and set it on the plate before turning and walking out of the kitchen. Bakr followed, his hand resting on the pommel of his long sword. Every time Javier passed through a tight space between stacks of books or other cobbled piles of his possessions, he'd hear a crash from behind, and Bakr would swear and show him a guilty smile.

They came to Serap's door, shut tight and perhaps locked. Javier could not help a small sigh. Everything had been going so well until he brought up Zayne, also known as Chupkin.

It was a silly name. That wasn't his fault. Though choosing to be cagey and not come clean, when that had been the entire purpose of the gifts and the baklava. But under the pressure, he froze.

Javier had never understood men who seemed to lose their senses around beautiful women, and he'd born witness to more embarrassing foolishness than he cared to remember. Alessandro alone he's seen lay in the gutter and sing Florentine love songs for a pretty merchant's daughter he'd met two days before, interrupt a theater troupe performing for the King of Sicily so he could declare his undying affection to a particularly attractive scullery maid. And that wasn't even including the tremendous fool he'd made of himself in Qaf over that fire-breathing sphinx woman.

Javier had always thought himself above such nonsense, but when Serap's warm eyes gazed into his and he felt her sweetness down in the depths of his aching soul, he suddenly understood. He was frightened to lose her, so he couldn't tell her the truth.

Pausing by the bedroom door, Javier rapped lightly. "Serap, your uncle is here to see you."

The door swung open. Serap smiled wide and threw her arms around Bakr. "You've returned for a visit so soon. Is everything okay?"

"That's a categorical no, Poppyseed." He rested his big hand on the top of her head. "Actually, everything is pretty messed up."

Serap pulled back, her arms still half-draped around her uncle, and her eyes distinctly turned away from Javier. "What happened?"

"There really isn't an easy way to say it." He bit the inside of his cheek. "Qaf is in anarchy."

"Anarchy?" Javier echoed.

Bakr tightened his lips into a long line to show his teeth, then looked back at Serap. "You remember the other day when the King of Eastern Elm kind of died, and I said there was no way he was really dead, he was probably just re-materializing somewhere because the King of Elm is immortal and can't be killed?"

The pink drained from Serap's face. "Yes."

"Yeah. Well, I was wrong. He is dead. And it turns out that killing him kind of... what's the word? Nullified? Yes, it nullified every contract that had ever had his seal placed on it in the last six thousand years or so. So basically, every legal document in Qaf is no longer valid."

Javier choked as dread seized his every fiber. "That can't be true."

Bakr made an apologetic face, then walked past Serap into her room and flopped down on the mattress. "Obviously, no prince of Elm has ever succeeded to the throne before. You know, because the king was literally older than dirt. All the Elmaran lawyers are losing their minds trying to figure out what's going on and what to do about it. Meanwhile, the peasants of Watali are in rebellion and trying to overthrow the monarchy while the throne is still empty. Jahmil sent in troops to back up the Grand Vizier, but he also had to deploy troops throughout Shihala because the people are all losing their minds now that the rule of law has basically gone out the window." Bakr wiped a hand over his face and sighed. "I've never seen such a mess, and I've seen a lot of *alqarf* in my life."

Serap shook her head slowly in disbelief. "Doesn't he have an heir? Someone who takes over his magic abilities or whatever."

"He must," Javier said. "The vulture had literally thousands of children."

"That's true enough. And I guess the king did set up an elaborate, paperwork-heavy, Elmaran-style system for his heir's succession like four thousand years ago. A way for his heir to smoothly inherit his power, including the maintenance of the Seal. But here's the thing..."

Bakr set his elbow on his knee and leaned forward. He talked with his hands, as generous with all his gestures as he was with his smiles. "A billion years ago, the king made a deal with his ex-wife that he did not get to choose which of his children would be his heir. This was supposed to save the family and the kingdom from infighting by leaving the choice to chance and in the hands of the Almighty." Bakr paused and chewed on his cheek. "The problem is, the current heir has been missing for over five years."

"Dead?" asked Javier.

"We don't think so." Bakr shook his head. "A lot of princes have been born with the sealing power over the years, but the King of Elm's children are birthed by ordinary djinn women, so they're not immortal like he is. Long-lived, but not immortal. So when one dies, the power of the seal passes to a new one. If this current one were dead, another of the King's children would have taken on the power of the Seal.

"The Grand Vizier thinks the prince is alive somewhere, but maybe incapacitated, or in hiding. The best Finders in seven kingdoms have not been able to locate him. And unless he magically reappears, it looks like there is going to be a lot of war, famine, and general death and destruction on Qaf for a very long time."

"Oh, God. I'm going to be sick." Javier set the soup down on a nearby table and pressed his face into the door frame.

"Nobody knows what happened to the king, obviously." Bakr's gaze turned serious, moving slowly between them. "Whoever—or whatever—killed the king is currently the most wanted being in all of Qaf."

Serap eyed him, her hands twitching as they clasped together. She glanced at Bakr. "I should go home, shouldn't I? I'm probably just adding to Jahmil's worries by being on Ard. And if I'm at the center... If I'm the reason Qaf is on fire, I should own up to what I've done."

Javier's head snapped up, a twinge of unexpected and unwelcome panic ripping through his bowels.

"I don't think that's such a good idea." Bakr twitched his nose. "If the Elmarans find out a Shihalan princess—you—and the High General of Her Armies—me—had a hand in the death of their king, Grand Vizier Devran Al-Zahrani will declare war. And have no doubts, Shihala loses that war."

Serap cringed. How could her simple desire to live longer turn everything into such a terrible mess?

"We can't let that happen," she said quietly, guilt knotting her stomach.

"Exactly." Bakr nodded. "Which means we can't tell your 'abi the truth. He's a terrible liar. It also means you shouldn't tell *me* the truth because I am likewise terrible at lying to him." Bakr cocked his head to one side, his smile tight and exasperated. "Are you starting to understand my problem?"

"But how did Gordito kill the king, anyway? I thought he was this ultimate immortal thing, and then one wisp in his ear?"

Bakr bit his bottom lip. "You raised a good question. And that's kind of what I came to talk to you about. How *did* a random wisp manage to kill an immortal that has been around for thousands of years? And do it so easily, like it was nothing..."

Javier felt Bakr's eyes on him, silently accusing him. The *salep* he'd drunk earlier was in his throat, sweet and bitter. His hands were cold, but his neck was sweating.

Why hadn't he told Serap the truth when he had a chance?

"It seems especially odd," Bakr continued, "considering whose house we're in..."

Serap's eyes widened and darted to Javier. She took a step back, hand on her chest. "Where were you? Yesterday, when we fought the king. Where were you?"

He looked up at her, at her eyes filled with dread, and his stomach lurched even harder. He wrapped his arms over his chest. "It was an accident."

Serap stumbled back, taking shelter behind Bakr. The look in her eyes told him so much, and none of it was what he wanted to see.

"I was just looking at your amulet," he said quickly. Too quickly. "And I accidentally turned myself into a wisp. I tried to talk. I tried to tell you what had happened, but I couldn't speak. And then that green *madre* showed up and he was going to kill you, and I..."

"No." Serap shook her head, so the ends of her headscarf whipped back and forth. "No, you can't be... You can't be Gordito!" She turned wide, betrayed eyes on him as her voice rose with anger. "I talked to you. I held you. I... And you just lied to me at the table. You could speak then, couldn't you? I know you could because you laughed at me for being worried. You laughed. And you lied."

He wanted to step toward her. Instead, he backed away. He'd been frightened to lose her—too frightened to speak. And now because he couldn't speak, he would lose her forever. "I wanted to tell you. I was planning to tell you. My confession was to come in stages..."

"And what stage was kissing me? And showing me poetry?" Her fingers wrapped tightly around her uncle's shirt, like she was afraid he would hurt her. "I feel like such an idiot."

"Serap, please. I wasn't trying to manipulate you." He turned away from her, unable to look at the terror on her face a moment longer.

There was nothing he could say. She would always hate him, always be afraid of him. He felt like such a fool. He wanted to run, hide in his basement, and never speak to another person as long as he lived. But that was precisely what was about to happen whether he ran or not.

"I think you should come back with me to Eayima, Poppyseed." Bakr wrapped his arm over Serap, protecting her from the monster in the room.

She pulled away from Bakr, fire in her eyes. "I can't go back. I haven't accomplished anything. I've changed nothing. If anything, I made things worse. I ruined all of Qaf because I unlocked a door. I... I..." She clenched her fists. "I know now why no one thinks I'm worth their time. Why people and djinn lie to me." She flashed her eyes at Javier.

"I'm the one who killed the king." Javier tried to force himself to stand up straight and look her in the eye, but he managed the straight part. He could face a lava-spitting *eimlaq* and never once would his nerves fail him. But one look from those brown eyes and he crumbled to ash. "You didn't do anything," he said. "This is my fault."

"Oh, no. This *is* my fault. Because I'm a gullible little girl who believes whoever is talking to her at the time. Who trusts everyone when she should trust no one. I am impulsive and childish. 'Abi was right."

Javier wanted to argue. To tell her that her trust in others and the kindness she showed even to people who didn't deserve it was one of the most beautiful things he had ever seen. But there was a foul-tasting lump in his throat, and he couldn't speak past it. Before in the kitchen fear had stilled his tongue. Now it was despair.

"The son of a snake was coming at us with a sword," Bakr said testily. "It's his own fault he got himself murdered." He turned to Serap, gentleness returning to his expression and his voice. "Some messes are too big to clean up on your own."

"What good is asking for help when you can't trust anyone?" Serap sulked.

"You don't trust me? Or Ayelet? Or Jahmil?" He scoffed and shook his head in disbelief. "Or have you become so obsessed with death, you no longer see the people in your life who love you and would do anything for you?"

"Of course, I trust you." She dropped her gaze to the floor as her neck brightened to the color of her cheeks. "I just think you're wasting your time and will realize that pretty soon. But I trust you, Bakr Amca. You're the one I call when I need help." She seemed to shrink into herself, arms wrapped around each other tightly.

Javier wanted to wrap his own arms around her, but he was glad that her uncle was there to comfort her. She deserved to be held and loved, even if he could never be one of the people to hold and love her.

"Please listen to me," Bakr said. "Making mistakes is the only thing all living creatures have in common. Human, djinn, immortal beings. We're all just making it up as we go along. It doesn't make you useless. And trusting people is a good thing." He sighed and pressed his hand over his eyes. "But this is a really big problem. Jahmil has me running back and forth like a *naeama* with no head. I can't keep track of you here the way I promised."

She pulled back from him, her expression tight and defiant. "I'm not leaving. I don't belong on Qaf. Not until I finish what I came here to do. And I will find a way to do it, even if I can't trust anyone in this house to help me."

Her words finally pulled Javier from his frozen hell and he managed to slink off into the hall. He took a few steps, energy leaking from his bones, then pressed his back against the wall. His heart seemed to be beating too slow and couldn't get a deep enough breath.

For years now he had wanted to kill the King of Elm. His name had been put into Javier's hat dozens of times, which meant Javier had reviewed and verified dozens of offenses committed by the king which were monstrous. It was the one name he would draw and then put back, waiting for the day when he might find an opening.

He hadn't been thinking about any of that when he killed him. He'd only been thinking about Serap and the terror on her face as he pressed that ancient double-pronged blade into her side. Nothing else had mattered. The king had to die.

"Why would you want to stay here?" Bakr's voice drifted down the hall towards him, concerned and quiet, yet tight and irritated. "Are you punishing yourself? Because I have been down that road and it leads nowhere."

"I'm staying because if I go back now, I'm a soft-handed failure, and I refuse to be that anymore."

A great vocalized sigh. "What about Shihala? Do you mean to never go back? I don't understand. I thought you liked it there."

"You wanted to leave Qaf before you found out you were special and got a wife who loves you." Serap's voice grew sharper than he had heard before, like a dull knife sparking on a whetstone. "But I don't have secret lilith blood or wisps that do my bidding or even the ability to kill stuff given to me by a giant fish. And I can't stand being a pawn for the stupid courtiers, having them smile at my face and laugh at my back. At least here, Evil wants me. And I know the liars for what they are."

"Again with this *evil*," Javier cursed under his breath. If nothing else, he would find the identity of this specter who'd taken to leading Serap by the nose through unknown visions and get it out of his house.

"I'll grant you your problems with the courtiers," Bakr said, "and Shihala is no place to be right now. But you can come to Eayima. Nobody to laugh behind your back there, and all the sunshine you could ever want."

"Why do you want me to leave so much, Bakr Amca? Are you worried I will mess things up even more than I have? That I'm childish and impulsive just like 'Abi Jahmil thinks?"

"I told you. I can't watch after you the way I promised, and I don't want you to get hurt. It sounds like you and the Immortal Killer have an... interesting relationship." His voice tightened. "Something about kisses and poetry?"

"Don't speak to me of either. Those sweet nothings turned out to be the bitter tonic that cured me of my naiveté. I know what and who Don DeMario is. The Immortal Killer. A liar. A thief—" Her voice cracked. "I am at no risk of falling prey to idiotic fantasies here. Not anymore."

Javier couldn't take it anymore. He pushed himself up from the wall and hurried down the hall not stopping until he was in his bedroom with the door shut and locked behind him.

Idiotic fantasies. That's all it was, all it ever could be. And he had let it happen. All his life he had been safe behind his walls in a womb of his own creation. Untouchable, unmovable. Free in his heart and mind and never a prisoner to the wills of others.

But she had cut through his defenses. Without an ax, or a sword, or a well-practiced series of platitudes. All it had taken was a smile, a few tears, and a promise she need never fulfill.

What had he allowed himself to become?

And now instead of leaving—what he thought had been his worst fear—she wanted to stay and torment him with her hatred, like a hideous mirror held up to his face so he could never forget and never be free.

He had told her she could stay, whether she forgave him or not, and he would not be made a liar again. Perhaps he had lingered too long on this particular island. It was attracting immigrants and fortune hunters. People who despised him so much they wanted to steal the only thing he had left that meant anything—his solitude.

First Khayin, then Serap. What next?

A fool that performs the same task twice expecting a different result is a fool unworthy of life. He had allowed himself to become such a fool. And in the process, he had upended the delicate balance of laws that held all of djinn society together. The Immortal Killer had become the destroyer of worlds.

It was time to remove himself from it, once and for all time. Remove himself from the constant litany of sadness and misery that had become his everyday life—the people and creatures that came to him, expecting him to solve all their problems and never once showing any concern for his.

He was a commodity, a service rendered. Not a human being. Not a soul with a heartbeat, with desires and fears and joys that were all his own. Not unless those could be manipulated. Nobody cared about him, and if he were gone, only the economy might notice.

"Good riddance to the immortal legislator and to his seal of death," Javier said aloud, wishing he had a glass to raise to the occasion. "Let Qaf learn how to build a society based on trust instead of magical penalties. Let them try, and then see if they still scoff at we humans in our disorder."

He slammed a fist into his knee. "To hell with the djinn. To hell with the shadowy monsters that plague them. To hell with love and hope and broken hearts. To hell with poetry and the lies it tells. To hell with everything."

"You were not meant to kill him."

Javier jumped at the unfamiliar voice—female and light, low and enervated. A woman had materialized at the foot of his bed. She was tragically beautiful. Blue lips, blue veins under white skin, and eyes of pure red. A djinn? Perhaps not. Her miserable expression sucked the remaining blood from his heart.

"He was unworthy of such mercy," she said.

"Who are you?"

"Another selfish soul who comes seeking your help." She lifted her hand towards him. Between her thumb and index finger, she clasped a tiny coin that sizzled and popped against her pale skin.

A djinn indeed.

She tossed the coin to him, and he snatched it out of the air. A single chip of copper, barely enough to buy bread.

"Will you listen to my proposal?"

CHAPTER TWENTY-NINE

SERAP

Serap fought with Bakr Amca like she never had before. He had always been her bright spot. Someone as happy as she was despite circumstances. But she wasn't happy anymore and neither was he, and so, they bickered until he threw his hands up in the air and winked out of the room.

She cringed, shoulders up tight around her neck and her eyebrows furrowed, waiting for Jahmil and Ayelet to appear and take her away. But they didn't come.

No one came.

Because no one wanted to invest in her.

To pour into a cup that would soon be empty.

She was just a pawn to be manipulated. Pasha was using her. And despite her defense of Evil, she knew he wanted something from her, too. Chupkin, too, had been leaving her more and more for fresher ground and a younger face in sweet Cova. And then there was Don DeMario. *Javier*. Gord—

She grabbed the closest book and tried to tear the cover, but its spine held strong against her trembling fingers. The edge of the book cut into her palm. She pulled away and looked down at the red.

She did have soft hands.

How could the Killer be her sweet wisp? How could he do that to her? Oh, it was all so mortifying. She pressed her hands to her cheeks to cool them down and embraced the sting of the cold. He must think her an idiot. Was he playing games the whole time? Seeing just how far she'd expose herself as a naive little girl before he turned back into a man and laughed at her?

Why had he laughed?

She threw herself on the bed, but her eyes burned too much to weep. He didn't deserve the tears. He deserved... He deserved...

Serap growled and shoved her face into the pillow. She tried to tell herself it hurt so much because she had been made a fool. Because he lied. But that wasn't true. It hurt so much because he had been so kind. As Gordito, her wisp. And as Javier Don DeMario, the baker of baklava.

But he had also lied. He had pretended. He had laughed and lectured.

And he had also been infinitely more romantic than anyone else she had ever met without saying a word. Most of all, he made her heart feel so good it hurt. Twice. Without her knowing her wisp and her captor were one and the same.

That had to mean something. Didn't it?

She had searched so desperately for Gordito because she wanted to see his face. His eyes. To meet him and see... see if he still cared. And hadn't she done that? Did it change how she felt that the man turned out to be Don DeMario? The man who threw her in a dungeon and then apologized profusely with a taste of home and tender gifts?

Serap wanted to dismiss it all as a plea for forgiveness, a way to save face now that his sisters had shown up, but her mind wasn't in it. Perhaps because her heart continued to splutter between waves of anger and waves of—

She bolted up from the bed, hands balled into fists. She had wanted love to knock her off her feet, and it had, just not in the way she had expected. Still, two yanks on her heart were more than the none she'd had before. And she had done nothing useful for him. Had nothing to offer him that would make him say he liked her face and look at her in a tight dress with a blush on his cheeks. He had been right, too, in that annoyingly simple way he had. He would think she hated him.

She had treated him that way on purpose, unable to forgive. But he had time and again proven he was not a killer of innocents. And that he could be sweet. So sweet, her heart pricked in a strange new way. A way that made her chest ache for more looks from his soft eyes and made her body yearn to be carried in his strong arms. She wanted more nervous hands and adorably averted gazes.

The blanket from the bed fell to the floor as she scrambled out in a hurry. All of Qaf burned with the pettiness of people who could not let things go. She would not be one of them. No. She would go and ask him directly how he felt about her. And if his words made her heart ache once more, she would put the rest aside. It is what Ayelet would do. And Zan Hala. Even Yousef Amca was the same. She would trust love to handle the rest.

Huffing out her nose several times, she worked up the courage to open the door and jog down the hallway.

"Don De... Javier?" she called with a little more timidity than she had intended. The name felt odd on her tongue, rare and sweet and curious like *salep*. Her steps slowed, but she continued forward. "Javier? I need to talk to you."

"He's in his bedroom," said Cecilia, stepping out from the end of the hall. She was dressed in a long nightgown with lace at the neck, her hair done up in a twist. A coy, sad little smile played on her lips, her big brown eyes brimming with concern.

Serap paused, realizing she had no idea which of the dozens of strange rooms in this house was his. Her stomach did strange little flips at the idea of his sister knowing she was headed to his room at night, but this could not wait. "Could you point the way?"

Cecilia ran a hand over the banister. "Are you okay? I overheard bits of your fight. Mostly tones and... tears. I know my brother can be a little rough around the edges."

"I'm okay. Thank you." Serap said, keeping her voice and thoughts as neutral as she could.

Cecilia's thin brows curved together. "He wasn't always this way. Back before he left home to follow our cousin, Alessandro, on his quest to the New World to seek his fortune. *Idiota.*" Her upper lip furrowed like she wanted to spit, but she pulled it back, closing her eyes quickly. "He was gone so long, we thought he had been lost to the sea. I think part of him was lost because when he returned he was different. Harder. Then he found out how our *anne* died, and we lost more of him."

"*Taeazi.*" Serap dipped her head in condolence, remembering his words. *I'm not accustomed to humans anymore.* Neither was she.

"I'm glad to see you here, though, as long as it's of your own free will," Cecelia added carefully. "You and Cova have brought out a softness in him I haven't seen in a long time. I hope he's given you something in return."

"Of course," Serap said. "A bed to sleep in and food to eat."

"I meant something softer." Cecilia's kind eyes held her own in a knowing sort of way. "His room is in the east wing, a large walnut door with a *nazar* over the door."

"Thank you."

"*İyi geceler*, Serap."

"Good night."

Cecilia disappeared into the dark room behind her just as Serap's stomach growled. The smell of lamb and broth still lingered in the air. She had not yet tried the delicious stew Don... Javier had made earlier. And after he had gone all the way to Turkey to make it just for her. She pressed a hand to her stomach and descended the stairs.

A strange, wriggling hope had seeded in her stomach. Perhaps, she did have something to offer him. Even if her happiness was small. She was soft, and maybe that wasn't such a bad thing all the time. Maybe it could be good.

She approached the door at the end of the hallway and knocked. "Javier, are you in there?"

The lock clicked, and the heavy wooden door creaked open. Backlit by the fluttering of dim candlelight, Javier gazed down at her. He didn't say anything. And he didn't smile as he had before. He folded his lips on each other, wrinkling the skin around his eyes.

Her heart sunk low to rival her recent high. Maybe she should go. Maybe she had misinterpreted everything he had done. But that would fix nothing. She had come to ask, to learn the truth if he was a monster, a wisp, or a man.

"Can we talk?" she asked, forcing herself not to fidget.

His gaze turned to the floor, and he nodded, then stepped back as he drew the door open to let her inside. She felt a nervousness walking into the room of a man after dark. A man she had recently realized she yearned for. The room of someone who she used to fear but now... didn't?

She clasped her hands together until her knuckles turned white and, for lack of anywhere else, sat on the bed. The mattress was long and narrow, built for one tall man and no one else. The pillows looked fluffy and clean, dressed in a thick wool blanket that had a similar design on it as the one she and Gordito had found in that quaint little house.

With a deep breath, she patted the bed beside her and looked at him with hopeful eyes.

He left the door wide open and came to sit on the far opposite end of the small mattress. The bed dipped to one side, popping her up like a seesaw. The room held the unmistakable, musty odor of old books, but he still smelled of fresh, melted butter, honey, and crushed lavender.

He pressed his hands into his knees and took a slow breath. "I should have told you the truth when I had the chance."

"Yes."

They sat in silence for a moment, the warm, delicious air soothing her nerves like syrup filling the holes in apricot cake.

"I haven't been entirely honest with you, either." She ran her fingers over the patterned blanket. "So maybe I deserved it."

"You said you did not trust me, so you were not going to tell me the truth." He stroked his beard and shook his head. "That is about as honest as one can be."

"You heard that?" She dropped her eyes to the stitching in the sheets, a horrible hollowness sneaking into her stomach. "Sorry."

"I haven't given you a reason to trust me. And now, I feel like a thief."

"A thief?"

His shoulders slumped and the volume of his voice dropped. "I stole secrets from you that you would not have given if you had known with whom you were sharing them. And now I cannot give them back."

A rawness scraped at her throat. She wanted to look at him, to see what his eyes held. What they did not.

She took a sharp breath and forced herself to look at him. He twitched, and his eyes glanced at hers before shrinking away.

"You're right," she said. "You cannot give them back. What matters now is what you do with them. So, what do you, Javier, plan to do with my secrets?"

"Hoard them."

She breathed out a tiny giggle. "I don't think you have any more room."

"It's deeply empty inside of me, in the place where I intend to keep them."

Those words broke a piece of her, a piece she wanted to fit inside his lonely smile. She scooted closer. Her soft hands ached to touch his rough ones. To connect with the only man who had touched her heart. She took a deep breath and set trembling fingers on his knee. Warmth. Giddiness. A pinch of all things good.

She cleared her throat, speaking through the tingling that spread from her hand and up to her brain. "The truth is, I'm glad I said them, my secrets. I'm glad that you know."

He gazed at her hand on his knee, his eyebrows drawn together to form two deep lines. For what felt like an excruciatingly long moment, he said nothing, just watching her fingers. "I am sorry for a great many things but I am not sorry that I kissed you."

The nascent heat she felt around him returned, and this time she welcomed it. "I'm not sorry you did, either. Though it doesn't really count."

"I was, rather unfortunately, a nebulous globule at the time." He rubbed a hand over the back of his neck, his gaze shifting between her eyes and her fingers on his knee. When he spoke again, his voice was quiet and nervous. "I should like to do it in such a way that it counts."

She bit the corner of her bottom lip and smiled, the waves in her chest surging into a sea, pushing her closer, closer toward him, and then yanking her back with greedy hands of nervous fear. Not of him. But of everything else in between.

"Is there a protocol for that?" she asked, scooting a little closer.

"It's never come up." He turned to look at her at last. His clear dark eyes shined like a mirror under the moon and his bottom lip quivered. He lifted a hand towards her face, then hesitated before tracing a single rough finger down her jawline so delicately that it gave her a chill. "You have such expressive skin."

She closed her eyes, enjoying the feel of his touch, drinking it in thirstily.

His finger moved excruciatingly slowly, wandering to her down to the edge of her neck. "I can read your emotions in it like a djinn's eyes."

Serap opened her eyes. He gazed intently upon her, his dark features serious. Serious and soft and fixed only on her. She would have blushed, but her skin was already afire.

"And what story does it tell now?"

"You are written in a language I am only just learning to read." The edge of his thumb brushed over her bottom lip. "And I do not want to make a fool of myself. Again."

"I never took you for a man who cares what other people think."

"I don't." He clasped the back of her neck and gently her closer, leaning in until his lips nearly touched hers. "I care what you think."

Serap could hardly breathe. The waves returned and pushed her closer. She leaned in and kissed him. A small thing, soft and gentle, afraid he would turn away and leave her.

He exhaled a short, hot breath, then pulled her closer. Still gentle, still soft, but more intense and lingering. He breathed her in, his hands and his breath trembling. She pressed her fingers into his knee and brought the others to join them, leaning fully, eagerly into his lips.

She moaned sadly when he, at last, pulled away. "You are not a fool," she said and looked askance.

"You are so delicate." He breathed audibly, closing his eyes and tilting his head to one side, a quiet smile on his closed lips. "I fear I will break you."

She gave in to his pulling like the shore to the sea, crawling closer, hoping to breathe him in more. Kissing him—it had been as fantastic and breath-taking and intoxicating as she had always hoped her first kiss would be. She was enticed. Drawn in. And wholly committed. Whatever she had heard from Zan Hala and Ayelet had not done it justice.

She was still confused. Still caught up in thinking one thing and feeling another. But the clash of emotions inside her wasn't really a clash at all. It was an awakening. A surety that left no doubts.

She had no idea what the future would hold, but she knew she wanted to hold him for it.

Always.

CHAPTER THIRTY

JAVIER

It took every muscle just to keep breathing, to pull more air into his lungs. His body was shaking, the smell of her filling up his senses. Overwhelming, every ounce of it. How was she here? And why would she kiss him? And why did he need to kiss her with every fiber of his being?

Blush colored her cheeks, beautiful spider veins of red and pink devouring her. He ran his fingers over the curve of her hip—that curve that had awakened him to feel like a man for the first time in his life. Then drew his fingers back, terrified to move too quickly and miss a single moment.

He touched her face, and her eyes flinched to his, the candlelight dancing on the soft curve of her cheek. Her lips were the sweetest flavor he had ever known, yet he pulled back so he could look at her and push clinging strands of cypress brown hair back from her forehead.

Whatever she said, her body seemed to him as fine as a butterfly's wing. He wished he could see her in the sunlight, to take in her color. Yet he never wanted the moment to end, precisely because it was impossible.

He stroked her face, gazing into her eyes, and again he tried to speak. A thousand words seemed to jumble in his throat.

Was she his wife now? For he would never kiss a woman who was not his wife, and he knew Serap was one of the faithful who would not give herself to a man who was not her husband.

Did this kiss mean he got to keep her?

Serap ran a slender finger over his ear and down his neck. "The radiance of his face beneath his locks was like a moon rising on the dark night," she said in Arabic. "While the scorpion on his temples halted at his cheeks afraid of their fire and water. A moon, I beseeched time to bring him back to me one day, but he spurned my pleas."

The breath stilled his lungs. "Oh, Serap. I pray your name is not prophetic. Should you fade from me like a mirage in the sands, I will cease to search for any oasis."

"And what heartwarming wine could ever be more intoxicating than the fluency of the Bedouin?"

"None." He smiled, overcome by the fluency of her satin tongue. "Poetry so pure it is profaned even when it is written down. It should always be spoken and heard. And your voice, more fleet and sure than the wings of Mercury."

"You woke my heart with your silence."

"Then I shall always be grateful for the spell that stilled my tongue."

She smiled and kissed his nose. "My little Gordito."

"I should not ask, but I can't stop wondering...." He bit the tip of his tongue. His hands were shaking from nerves. He wanted to kiss her again and again and always, but he could no longer move.

"What?" She placed her hands on the sides of his face and tilted his head to look at her. "What is it you wondered, then bit back in your cheek?"

"I was certain you would hate me forever. Why did you change your mind?"

She sighed, her chest falling. "I have felt the beginnings of love only twice in my life. And they have both been with you. If you could steal my heart with the silence of a wisp and the hands of a man, I would be a fool to turn away from you. For you would take my love with you, and then I would be empty."

A stirring in his stomach, and for the first time in as long as he could remember it wasn't at all painful, but like a new bird taking flight. He turned his face from her again because his eyes felt hot and wet. "I am a clumsy thief."

"Only if you lose the treasure you have taken."

"That is a terrifying proposition." Laughter trembled through his lungs. "I lose everything or cling too tightly. "

She gazed up at him, pure trust like honey in her eyes. "Then make sure I'm the latter."

"I would not make of you a prisoner, but I will remain your captive as long as I live."

"Then I wish more than ever that I could live for eternity and you with me."

He rubbed the fabric of her veil between his fingers, his smile fading. "Yet more secrets that I stole from you. Twice I've heard you tell your uncle about your desire for immortality. It is the reason you came to find me."

"Your tone and words are too heavy for this moment, I think." Her voice sounded light, but she turned away from him and drew her fingers back from his knee.

"Forgive me, but I would not insult you by being flippant or dishonest."

"More logical statements that hide an emotion. What is it you really want to say?"

"Logic and emotion are not so extricable in my character, I'm afraid. But I wonder when you were learning about me and making the decision that I could somehow help you with your problem, did you ever ask how I came to be the proverbial Immortal Killer?"

"I did not." She smiled sheepishly and bit her chapped bottom lip. "Your name was only spoken of in hushed whispers. I do know you entered the Bahamut and returned alive, a gift in your hands that slays the ancients. But I will ask now. How did you come to be bound to a job that haunts your eyes and wears your body down so it aches and trembles under the softest touch?"

He frowned at her observation, overcome by the implication. It was not a story he told often. In fact, he had never told anybody the whole truth. He probably never would. It was too long, too complicated. But he felt like she, of all people, deserved to know. Strangely enough, he wanted to tell her.

"When I was twenty-three, my cousin joined up with the Royal Navy, and I followed him because... I don't even know, anymore. We were supposed to find our fortunes in the New World and come back and live like kings. It was going to solve all our problems." He sighed and shook his head. "My cousin always had a way of talking me into things, getting me excited about things I knew were terrible ideas.

"Six weeks to cross *océano Atlántico,* and all we found was a portal to a strange world with no sun, just stars that shined day and night, filled with rainbow-colored fire-wielders. We had sailed directly into the Sea of the Bahamut, and for years we were lost, our ship tossed from island to island until the day came it shattered on the diamond shoals of Far Jasraib. I could tell you tales of our journeys until the day I died and still fail to relate every detail."

She ran the back of her fingers along his jaw and down his beard. "Then tell me the one that matters most."

Her touch was like a bolt of lightning through his soul. He had to take a few breaths to refocus himself.

"There's only one that really matters. After four years, every other man on my boat had died. All of them, except me and my cousin. He was..." He pressed his tongue to the roof of his suddenly dry mouth and tried to swallow, but it wouldn't come. "His name was Alessandro. He was my best friend. I lost him, too."

Serap leaned forward and kissed his forehead. "That's awful."

The touch of her was like a cool mist on a hot day. It gave him the strength to keep speaking.

"I was left alone, floating through the eternal sea on a raft with no sail, wasting away and certain I would die too and become food to the seven-tongued sharks of the high waters. And it was precisely when I had lost all hope that the Bahamut found me. A shadow and a shimmer, little more, but as large as the world itself. The great one engulfed me, and I was swallowed, pressed down its celestial esophagus into the belly of the omnipotent fish."

Javier paused, pulling himself back from the memory he sought to recall. He did not want to feel it.

"There in her stomach, with the acid of infinity gnawing at my flesh, I came face to face with the Eternal One. She is the Bahamut herself, a manifestation of her that appears differently to each man or woman. And she offered me her gift, the Kiss of Eternity. The same gift that gave Khayin his impossibly long life. Her kiss is the truest, and perhaps the only, road to eternity that is open to mortals."

"Did you take it?" Serap whispered, her body tight in his arms.

"No." His wandering gaze met hers again. "I turned her down. And so, she made me what I am today. What I will always be until the day I die."

"Miserable?"

He chuckled and shook his head. "She gave me the power to end immortal life, even immortality she herself had bestowed. I admit it is a yoke I've languished under, but I am grateful for it. For the ability to offer succor to the people I have helped by slaying immortal monsters, and perhaps even more than that, the immortals I have freed from their prisons, which all too often are self-inflicted."

"Najima." She jerked and scooted back from him on the bed, brown eyes wide and panicked. "You haven't talked to her, have you?"

He nodded slowly. "She came and spoke to me this very night."

Serap wriggled further from him and stood. Her fingers went to her hijab, and she straightened it. "What did you do?"

"I have not killed her yet."

"*Yet*?"

"She asked to die with the dawn."

"You can't do that." Serap shook her head fiercely, a ring of the fear he dreaded to see resurfacing in her eyes.

It made him want to relent, to tell her what she wanted to hear. But that was one thing he could not do. "I made her a promise. And she is deserving."

"She is innocent. How can an innocent person deserve to die?"

"Death is not a punishment, not in her case. She has no desire to continue living. Why would you want to prolong suffering?"

"She's been in a prison for two-thousand years. Of course, she's unhappy. She hasn't even given life a chance to get better, and yet you're willing to kill her? If I'm no longer happy, will you come and slay me?"

"The Queen of Elm has given life six thousand years of a chance. But as to your other question, if your life ever became so miserable, if you were so sad and in such a great amount of constant pain, and I knew in my heart that you were of sound mind when you made the request, then I would honor your wishes the same as any other soul."

"Then kill me now, Javier." She opened her arms to bear her chest. "Because if you will not help me live forever, and if you are not just an Immortal Killer but a killer of innocents, then I have nothing left."

His heart stung at her condemnation and at her sudden change. After everything that had just happened between them—the silent marriage they had just undertaken—how could she so quickly switch back to hatred and fear?

He had laid himself raw before her, and she balked at what she had discovered.

"I do not kill innocents. There are certain souls that I help on their way." He pressed his lips together, wishing he could go back in time and not say anything. But he refused to lie anymore. "*The gods envy us. They envy us because we are mortal and because any moment may be our last. Everything is more beautiful to us because it is finite, because we are doomed. You will never be lovelier than you are now, and we will never be here again.*"

"So you will not help me live forever because I will be less beautiful, and you will not kill me because I'm not deserving?"

His eyes crossed at her conflation of Homer. "More than any mortal, I have seen the ravages of immortality. I know the idea is seductive, but Allah tells us immortality is a curse that separates us from paradise. But as mortals, we cannot know exactly what will happen when we die and so we fear like children fear the dark."

"You didn't answer my question," she said, her lovely face tight with clenched teeth.

Javier stood to face her. "I will not help you live forever because I know that it is a fool's errand. And I will not kill you because you do not need me to. My hand is only given to those who cannot open their own veins." His voice cracked, and he had to clench his teeth. "Though I cannot begin to describe how painful it is for me to imagine you doing such a thing."

"I thought it was beautiful?" she whispered, a glimmer of a tear forming in each of her eyes. "But you're right, I do not need your hand. You were a clumsy thief after all, and now neither of us will have my heart. Bakr!"

"Serap, please." His deep voice cracked, a mountain splitting apart. "Premature death is not beautiful, but neither is unnaturally long life. Life is meant to be experienced in its fullness, and then death is meant to come at the end. And there are tremendous consequences for those who go against this."

"So because you refused immortality, you get to be the judge of when everyone else gets to live or die? Stop lecturing me. You are not my judge. You do not speak my language. And you *are* the monster I thought you were." She slid off the bed and slapped at the wrinkles in her pants. "Bakr Amca!" she yelled to the room.

Javier shook his head and pressed his face into his hands. There was a part of him that wanted to take it all back, but the pain in Najima's voice when she told him her story—an epic of two loves that both were fated to end in tragedy.

"I will not prolong the suffering of an innocent woman because you have yet to come to grips with your own mortality, Serap." Javier's voice hurt to say the words. "That is not logical, and it is not fair."

"Am I not also an innocent whose suffering you prolong? Please, forget logic, Don DeMario. Listen to me. Listen to what I'm feeling, instead of how I say it. Because if you don't, if you refuse to help me ease the pain of mortality because you cling to logic instead of me, I don't think I can bear it." She buried her face in her hands, hiding crimson cheeks and wet eyes from his sight.

The figure of Bakr and his long sword popped into the room. He was dripping wet, his hips wrapped in a bath towel. "What? What's wrong?" He turned this way with fiercely alert eyes, then he slowly straightened. "What is going on here?" He turned to Serap and whispered, "Did you mean to call me?"

Javier kept his eyes on her, his skin tightening as his heart begged him to take it all back. But doing that would be turning his back on everything he believed in.

He loved her as he never thought himself capable of loving a woman. He wanted her to be his wife and stay with him forever. But was that even possible? Could the Immortal Killer ever have a wife?

Not what he wanted to believe, the purpose of his existence had changed when he was swallowed by the Bahamut. He was the merciful hand of God that helped foolish immortals reunite with the divine. He was the protective hand that relieved Allah's worlds of monsters and ancient evil. She said she was sturdy, and she had thrived while living in his house, even as a captive. He'd begun to hope that maybe he could have a companion. That Serap could be the one sitting on the other side of his table.

But if she did not believe in his work, then how could she love him? Was a monster killer always fated to become a monster himself?

"I do not cause you suffering," he said at last.

"Nor will leaving stop my suffering. I'm certain it will linger long after I am dead."

"I don't feel like I'm supposed to be here," Bakr whispered.

Serap turned her wide, pained eyes to her uncle. "I called you, Amca. I cannot stay here to be hurt anymore, though I shall carry an arrow in the place of my heart until I die, which is his wish. Take me home with you." Her jaw trembled. "Please."

Bakr squished up his nose. "Okay. No problem."

"Don't go." Javier's voice cracked and he couldn't be sure if she even heard him. For at that moment, she and her uncle blinked out of existence, leaving him alone in his cocoon of candlelight.

Javier wanted to slump down on the bed, to let his bones melt under the weight of what had happened. But the sky was beginning to purple with morning, the last stars fading beyond the dirty window. And he had made a promise.

Javier dressed in silence. His brain was playing over a scene of him crying, or begging, or falling to his knees, but none of that happened. It was as she had said. The cavity in his chest had been emptied and nothing remained. Numbness, emptiness. Very much like she must assume death would be. He had no concern whenever it should come to him because it had already happened.

But as he took a step, the pain that radiated up his leg and through every bone in his body—fire and lightning and crushing blows more intense than any he had ever known—reminded him there was still much left to endure.

He grabbed a sword from where it rested in one corner and trudged outside, the tip of his weapon dragging on the ground. He breathed the crisp air of morning through his nose, but the fight with Serap twisted violently within. He paused in his walk, grabbed his stomach, then threw up on the grass. Very little came out, and he dry-hacked for a while before he managed to straighten himself. He continued toward the figure standing at the edge of the wheat field.

He was his job. It was all he could ever be. And he had been a fool to believe he could ever have a life outside of it.

Najima didn't look at him as he approached, her gaze fixed on the dawn. The wheat shined like gold and autumn clouds illuminated in the same color twisted across the sky, shadows of night still clinging to their edges.

Javier stepped up beside the immortal queen.

"I've always enjoyed your sun," she said, not turning to look at him. "How the sky here changes so much every day. It is so different from Qaf."

Her red eyes looked liquid, as if they were about to slip right down her face. Her white hair blew behind her in the soft breeze. It grabbed his shirt too, causing it to billow. There was cold in the air today, the first he had felt since the end of spring. Winter would be upon the land soon. Clean, white snow, ice, and biting chills. The leaves would turn and fall, like they did every year. The seasonal death that always came.

Hades embracing Persephone, holding her prisoner.

But there was beauty even in the cold, reassurance. The birds would go on singing, and the sea would continue to rush to shore. It made no matter that his heart seemed to have stopped beating when Serap left him.

"Are you sure you want to do this?" he asked.

Najima nodded slowly and got down on her knees, pulling her hair to one side. "I have wanted this for a very long time."

CHAPTER THIRTY-ONE

SERAP

Serap collapsed upon herself and curled into a tight ball on the floor of the temple of Eayima, the floating island of Sulayman's Seal and her amca's home. She felt hollow. Empty. Devoid of love and missing Chupkin. Bakr Amca shooed his screaming children from the high-ceilinged room, and Zan Hala came in chiding, strands of sparkling hair peaking out from hijab.

"What did you do to poor Serap?" She hurried over on pink, slippered feet. "You said you were going to keep a good eye on her after leaving her in that killer's house. Just look at her. Look what you've allowed to happen."

He scooped Serap up, carrying her over the chaos of children and down a hallway painted in chipping reliefs of *effrits* and men. His arms felt safe and warm, but not what she needed. Not what she wanted. He smelled too much of agarwood and not enough of lavender and honey. Though his hands were rough, which meant he was far more capable than she.

Bakr adjusted his hold as he side-stepped through a door. "First you piss at me and call me overprotective, and now I'm in trouble for letting her be. Make up your mind, woman."

"I have made up my mind," Zan Hala quipped. "You did a terrible job. How big do we have to make your bell for you to show up on time? All of Elm is in chaos because you missed the first time she rang. You could have brought her home after the ghoul and spared everyone this nonsense."

"Excuse me, but I remember a certain someone clawing at my hand and screaming, *don't go, Bakr. How could you leave me like this, Bakr? I'll scratch your eyes out if you take one step towards that door, Bakr.*" He kicked open the door of a bedroom and carried Serap inside to lay her gently atop an overstuffed feather mattress. "And this time I was in the bath. Considering how mad you were the last time I answered my bell buck-naked, I thought I should take a moment to throw a damn towel on."

"Don't get smart with me, Bakr," Zan said, her voice a mix of tight and playful. "The reason I had these triplets in the first place is your fault. No more hot springs for you until you admit I'm right."

Bakr stomped over to Zan Hala, snatched her by the waist, and yanked her body flush with his. "No hot springs for me means no hot springs for you, *ayuni.*" He moved in close like he was about to kiss her, then quickly bent down and bit her neck.

Zan Hala giggled and wrapped her arms around him, pulling him in for a kiss—deep and passionate.

Serap watched blankly on the bed, eyes strained and heart scraped empty. Normally, Serap would giggle or egg them on, but now it all felt so distant. Like something she had within her reach that got snatched away and tossed into a hurricane.

"Get out of here. I'd like to speak with your niece, and you walking around in that little towel of yours is not helping anything."

Bakr slapped his wife's butt before walking out of the room. "I'm going to go finish my bath. Everybody leave me the hell alone."

Serap crinkled into a smaller ball on the bed, tired of watching them. They bickered, yes, even full-out fought sometimes, but their love was palpable to anyone around them. Suffocating even. Not like her and Don DeMario. They did not have the history, the foundation that her uncle and aunt did to help weather the storms. They were only at the beginning of such things when everything fell apart. And Don DeMario did not have the passion. Bakr Amca would never stop fighting for Zan

Hala, but the man she had foolishly trusted with her own heart had just watched her slip away without once asking her to stay.

She was grateful for the sheets Zan Hala tucked around her and pulled them up over her head. No tears came this time. And why should they? She was not confused, not feeling the gentle pangs of spring love. In a single day, he had raised her higher than she ever thought possible and then obliterated her with the bitter bite of winter. Even Paco would be better than him.

Serap decided then that that was entirely and utterly true.

"I'm going to marry Paco."

"Who, dear?" Zan Hala walked back over to the bed, her satin yellow dress like the shine of sun that rippled in waves from her eyes. Things always seemed warmer and softer when she looked at Serap with those eyes. "That's not the Immortal Killer, right?"

"No. He's a courtier who asked for my hand in marriage. At the time, I thought it was silly because we hadn't even kissed or held hands. Because he wants me only for my position and because I'm soft, but none of that matters. He at least never lied to me. Or lectured me about loving death. I might as well stay at home with 'abi and Ayelet whose love is constant."

The words fell from her mouth with a pain in her chest. It was the truth she had just spoken. Guilt filled her up. She did have a lot more growing to do, for she hadn't understood love when she had it, even if it wasn't the romantic kind she had been so keen to obtain. Ungrateful, yes. Childish, yes. And now hurting from her impulsivity.

"He is the best I shall ever get, I think." Serap sighed so deeply, it made her sick. "Yes. I shall marry Paco, and that shall be the end of it."

"Woah, woah, slow down." Zan Hala sat down on the edge of the bed, hands out and wide towards Serap. "Nobody's marrying anybody. Especially out of desperation. Let me tell you that does *not* turn out well for any party involved."

"This isn't the same thing as you and that Ahmaran prince," Serap huffed and squished down tighter in the sheets.

Her hala's tale of almost marrying a shiny, yet backstabbing, prince to get back at her uncle was well-known even beyond family circles. Stories of a demonic lilith, lies, unread contracts, and her cousin, Izkander's, baby fire being bounced about between djinn. It was the stuff of fantasy and absurd circumstances. Not the mundane end of humanity like her own tale.

"Oh, okay. I get it." Zan pursed her lips. "You had a fight with a man."

"Exactly."

"A man you like a lot, if not more, seeing the state you're in."

Serap blushed, hot skin against cool blankets.

"And the fight went poorly," Zan Hala continued, "and now you're hurt and think you have no options and are just going to marry some royal bumpkin so you don't have to think about it anymore."

Serap's shoulders tensed. "He ripped out my heart, and I am empty inside. So, what does it matter, anyway?"

"A lifetime is a long time to be married to someone you think so little of. It is hard enough when you're married to someone you do love."

"My life is not long at all."

Zan Hala grinned with a sigh. "We may not share blood, but we are more alike than you think. And with the way my doting husband speaks of your Killer, I should think they're similar men at their core. Bakr Amca is drawn to people of passion. Jahmil with his sweet Ayelet. Me with him. And it seems like this Don DeMario and you. Don't think for one second that getting engaged to someone else will brush by the man without a second thought. You're asking for trouble."

Serap wrapped her arms tightly around her chest. "He told me I will never look more beautiful than at that moment because someday I will die. He talked about how any moment could be our last and that that's a gift. And then he waved me off like he was already ready for that moment to come."

"Ah, he's an Achilles. I see." Zan Tezyi chuckled and touched a hand to the ruby that draped across her forehead. "Men are the worst. They attempt to be poetic and deep, and really they're just tying their own nooses."

Serap hurt too much to even nod.

"May I ask what the fight was about?"

"You don't want to know," Serap muttered through the sheets.

"I do not ask for me, Serap. Sometimes it's just nice to have the argument over again with someone on your side."

Serap shoved the blanket from her face and stared at her aunt. "He kills people."

"His name *is* the Immortal *Killer*. And you knew that going in. So what specifically about the killing is bothering you?"

"When I first showed up, I thought he killed whoever and whatever. But slowly, I convinced myself that he was soft and kind and that he only killed monsters. And then right when I gave him all my trust, he told me he was more than willing to kill people who haven't done anything wrong at all. And that he was going to do just that when the sun rose."

Zan Hala ran her turquoise fingers across Serap's forehead, brushing away stray hair. "That is awful."

"And he told me what I wanted was foolish and ignorant and that I wasn't in my right mind. And all that right after I... right after we..." She stared at her hands, too ashamed to even look at her aunt.

Zan Hala laid a hand on Serap's shoulder and gave it a soft pat. "What is it about men and opening their big fat mouths immediately after a woman trusts him with her body and soul? Though my problems were having to listen to your Amca talk about a demon and a bird." She pursed her lips, then added, "And sometimes Jahmil." She sighed even deeper. "And now maybe this Immortal Killer."

"We kissed," Serap whispered, disquiet rinsing her brain with the realization. The moment she had dreamt of and dreaded had come and gone with little fanfare and lots of fighting. "It was my first kiss, ever. I wasn't thinking," she stammered. "And then it just—"

She swallowed hard.

That wasn't true, not entirely. She had been thinking, hyper-aware of his breath on hers. His lips. The tickle of his beard against her soft skin.

"I just wanted to tell him how I felt, and then we were clinging to each other and reciting poetry, and then we were fighting."

"Poetry, huh?" Zan Hala shook her head and ran her finger through Serap's hair. "I'm surprised a man called the Immortal Killer would be into that. You ask your Amca to read anything, and he... I digress. Your amca reading poetry is the most utterly absurd thing I can imagine. Continue, please."

"I've never been so close to a man before, Hala. I never knew I could feel that way even though I've dreamt of it for so long. And filled up with all that love, I told him I wanted to be with him forever. I don't understand why he wouldn't want that after we... after I..." She bit her lip and looked away. "I thought he had felt it, too. The beginnings of love. So why does he despise me so much for wanting that?"

"'Despise' is far too strong a word, *aziziti*." Zan Hala sighed. "You're both just trying to communicate in the way you know how. It's normal at the beginning of a relationship, though it doesn't make it less painful. It takes time to write a book together, and until then you can only pull from what you know."

"Why does everyone keep calling me a book?" Serap soured.

Zan Hala laughed. "Because you have a lasting effect on people, Serap, and are something we want to carry around with us and open up again and again. And everyone has their own book of idiosyncrasies and desires and stupid remarks. Some are just bigger than others, and it has nothing to do with how long you live."

"Then his book is full of lectures," Serap said bitterly. "And mockery about how I like the name Chupkin." She bolted upright in the bed. "Chupkin! He's still at *his* house. He'll never forgive me if I leave him there."

"I'll send your Amca to go get him."

"I have to do it." The words tasted dirty. And true. A common feeling for that day. "I didn't just leave Chupkin, I also need to retrieve Cova, and a book, and..." Creepy crow's beak covered in donkey nose? "And a charm that I hid away." Her stomach squirmed as if an infestation of *zulāl* worms had just burst from the icy snow that now coated her heart. "I have to go back and get those, too."

"Are you sure you want to go right away?" Zan tucked another strand of Serap's loose hair back under her headdress. "Chupkin will be fine if he has to wait a couple of days. I always thought the little squirt was a bit prissy, myself. Just another creature that fawns over your amca."

"You fawn over him, too." Serap raised an eyebrow.

Zan Hala smiled coyly and opened a drawer. "Hush you. It's no bother to have Bakr take you back. But don't linger. I know there's a temptation to jump right back into terrible fights. It's the martyrdom that runs in your family. You'll heal fastest if you get in and out and never think of it again. But first, you'll probably feel better if you slip into something comfy."

Zan Hala pulled out a green shirt woven with fluffy threads and twined mohair and held it out to her. Serap nodded and stood, slipping it on. The softness of it against her skin brought up feelings of Javier's beard against her cheek. She rubbed her arms furiously to chase away the memory. Would he haunt her like that every time she heard the whisper of a breeze or felt a gentle touch?

"You look nice in green," Zan Hala nodded in approval. "I thought you would with those honey-brown eyes and that ring of red around your irises. Quite fetching, though I do have a weakness for human eyes. Let me go get your amca."

The worms were back, wreaking squeamish havoc in her stomach. She couldn't face Bakr Amca right now. Not after all the shame he'd seen her in. He took it well enough, but the sad glance he'd tossed her way was a rock tied to her drowning soul. She grabbed Hala's sleeve. "Can you take me back instead?"

"Me?" She raised an eyebrow. "To the house of the Immortal Killer?"

Serap nodded, scuffing her bare foot on the red and gold rug beneath her feet.

"You are aware I just had triplets, right?"

Serap hung her head glumly. "Yes."

"Then you'll know how much I need a break." Zan Hala grabbed her wrist and lit her hand with a sweet rose fire. "But you have to promise me you'll wait a good month before you decide to marry anyone. At least a month. Maybe a year. Or Three. And no contracts, dead King of Elm or not."

"I promise," Serap said.

It mattered little. She'd still be just as broken and empty then as now.

"Good." Zan opened the door.

An expanse of endless clouds peeked through a key-shaped hallway window. Only air and sun and sky, no land to anchor it down on their floating island.

"Bakr," Zan called half-heartedly, "I'm taking Serap back to grab a few things." She turned toward Serap with mischief in her eye. "He's been so busy putting out Jahmil's fires, he should be in the bath for a while, so we should be fine. But let's go before he realizes what I said."

Zan Hala dragged her to a full-length mirror that hung on hinges that swung back and forth. She pressed the top against the wall to form a triangle.

"We must pop through to Qaf before we can circle back to Ard."

She pulled Serap through. In a puff of rose, they landed in Serap's room in Karzusan Palace. Jahmil stood with Ayelet in the center, faces drawn in concern. When they registered her appearance, both of their faces flooded with relief.

"Serap?" Jahmil's fists exploded in white fire. "Sezan!"

"Oops," Zan Hala said, and they were gone in another puff of sparkling pink.

Guilt shoveled a hole in Serap's heart. Her fingers twitched to rub the amulet that hung once more on her neck. To send a message to her parents and tell them she was okay. But it was far too late for that, now.

Serap's feet touched rough, wooden boards. The smell of lamb and vegetables lingered in the air. *Home*, she thought briefly, then mourned the loss of that, too. How could she return to her parents when she had wounded them both so? Especially since she had accomplished nothing? And how could she ever stay here after Javier judged her so harshly? Just as 'abi had.

The difference was, she could learn not to be so childish. To think things through. But how could she learn to be okay with death? The desire to live was woven into the very fabric of her being.

Zan touched her arm as the smoked clear. "You must have been missing your parents and thinking of them for us to have popped into the palace. Jahmil is going to kill me." She smirked and touched a finger to her full red lips. "The controlling, little brat. He's probably going insane."

Serap grimaced at her hala and 'abi's rivalry. "This is the place." Serap sighed and led her aunt into the living room.

Zan Hala's eyes lit up. "So many books," she said, but not in the stuffy way Serap had when she first saw the place. It sounded more wistful and jealous.

"You can look around." Serap shrugged. "If Don DeMario sees you, just tell him you came for bread and that he's a thief and a liar, and he'll leave you alone."

"Okay..." Zan Hala gave her a worried side-eye. "Hurry, though. I honestly don't know if Bakr can keep his pretty face from checking on me. And since your parents saw me with you, they'll be ringing his bell incessantly to find out what's going on. He hates that. A lot. And since the King of Eastern Elm died, everything has been in chaos, anyway. Jahmil has never looked more stressed."

The pit in Serap deepened. She nodded and hurried upstairs, her heart thudding with every step as she glanced over her shoulder and around every corner before making a turn. To look for Chupkin, she only half-lied to herself. Fortunately, Don DeMario was nowhere to be seen.

She rushed into the room he had kept her in and grabbed the book Evil had given her from a stack by the window. She glanced between the open shutters and her breath caught. Don DeMario walked through the grass, the sunrise morphing his body into a broad-shouldered shadow. New slivers opened up in Serap's ragged heart.

She turned away, forcing herself toward the bed where she pulled the crow's beak out from under the pillow and shoved it in her pocket. But she couldn't heed Zan Hala's advice to let it be. She wanted one more look at the clumsy thief who so poorly stole her heart.

She crept back to the window and peered out once more. Her eyes widened. She clapped a hand to her mouth, suppressing a scream as he raised his blade to the morning sun and ended the life of the innocent queen.

Serap stood there, frozen, vision blurring, room tumbling and fading in and out. She did not know how long she stood for, but eventually, the rabid beast inside her lungs tore out of her throat in a horrible scream.

"Serap?" Zan Hala's voice carried up the stairs in alarm.

Chupkin appeared first, swirling around her neck and brushing her cheek. He *had* noticed she was gone. That tiny comfort was all that kept her from breaking into a thousand ugly pieces.

She fell back, the book and Chupkin with her, but did not hit the floor. Instead, she kept falling, first like a leaf caught in a breeze, then one whipping through a torrent. Her head snapped back and forth. Chupkin stretched and flapped in the whirlwind, clinging to her in the storm. She thudded against dry earth, gasping when her ribs cracked from the force. Bits of dirt and dust flew up around her, and she stared into an empty dark. Chupkin floated down upon her chest, thin and flat like a protective blanket.

"Silly child, silly child who released my Queen and hunted a hunter."

"Evil," Serap gasped through short, painful breaths. "I am no longer hunting Don DeMario." His name stuck in her throat. "I will never go back to that house again."

The raspy voice snickered. *"He has already been snared."*

"But I didn't read your book." She kicked at it where it lay by her feet. "And he walks around slaying immortals even now."

"The hunter owned the book; the book was for the bear."

She pulled to a sit and brushed gray dirt from the cracks in her fingers and off her shirt. Her copper necklace twisted around her neck, choking her. She untangled it and pulled it free from her hair, then righted her veil. Chupkin ruffled indignantly as she rearranged his hiding spot, exposing him to the open when Evil was about.

"I thought Don... I thought the hunter was the bear."

"No. The bear draws closer. It is out for blood. And honey."

Serap pinched the bridge of her nose in her fingers. Why did the days seem so much longer since she'd come to España?

"Okay, I'll watch out for the bear. May I go?"

Silence.

"Evil?"

Nothing.

She jumped to her feet, claustrophobic in the pressing blackness. Only a hint of gray broke the bleak monotony. "Evil!"

Serap kicked the earth with her bare foot, toes stinging from the impact. She called Bakr several times to no avail. She swiped at her amulet, but no wisps escaped to ask for help or bear tidings of safety. Nothing happened at all. Not even seal hands or Jahannam's harpies.

Serap curled into a crouch and wrapped her hands around her knees. Chupkin left and returned, flitting one way and then the next, venturing as far as he dared in hopes of finding something and always returning with nothing.

She did not need Evil's help to relive visions of horror or to visit places of light this time. What she saw out the window already plagued her. As did the fight that happened before that.

And as the two flashed as memories before her, mixing and mingling in a poisonous concoction that killed the worms in her stomach and left a festering hole, she concluded that wherever she had landed seemed just about right. In her quest for life, she had only found the nothingness of death.

It was as cruel and stinging and awful as she'd thought.

CHAPTER THIRTY-TWO

JAVIER

Javier's sword sliced through Najima's neck as easily as it would have any other, the blow precise and the metal sharp. She felt no pain, or if there had been any, it would have been brief.

A faint scream reached his ears from somewhere inside the house. He turned but didn't see anyone through the foggy windows. He had forgotten that Cova and his sisters were still home. Had one of them witnessed this act? Try as he might, he could not bring himself to care. There was no end to his work, so there was no hiding who and what he really was. They would all know eventually, and then they would leave him. So why prolong the inevitable?

He rifled through his pocket and took out the copper coin that the queen had given him, her honorarium. Tarnished, small, and worth next to nothing, it was perhaps the most important piece of metal he owned. It was the death of hope, a hope that had bloomed so large and so bright in the night. When he closed his eyes, he could still feel Serap's lips against his, taste her sweet saltiness. Just a moment, like all the others, that had passed and would never return.

The words he'd spoken—the words of Achilles—smarted like needles in his guts: *The gods envy us. They envy us because we are mortal, because any moment may be our last. Everything is more beautiful because we are doomed. You will never be lovelier than you are now. We will never be here again.*

They rang truer to him now than when he had first read them, when his heart had pinched with sorrow and joy all at once. And truer still than when he had spoken them in hope to a woman he loved. A woman who had no desire to hear them, or to hear how he yearned for her to simply be.

It could never be enough for her.

He mumbled those words over the rapidly decaying body of what might have been the most ancient creature he had ever slain. They stung his soul with exquisite pain. He had not taken for granted a single moment that Serap was in his arms, for even as they spoke soft promises of forever, he had always known such things were finite. And it *had* made her lovelier—her body, her breath, her trust, and her sweetness.

Her kiss had made him worthy of envy from the highest king of any land or the most powerful immortal to ever live. She had chosen him. From a deck stacked with princes, she had drawn a grumpy peasant living in a haunted house and smiled—however briefly—at her selection.

It had not lasted. It never could have, and he had made a fool of himself in the end, because when she was in his arms, he had longed for forever.

The Queen of Elm's body was gone, melted back into the soil after so much time away. He knelt down and dug a small hole with his hand, then set the coin inside and covered it. It was Najima's grave. It was also the grave of his fantasy of ever being loved.

He stabbed the sword into the earth and turned away.

Serap did not resent him for being a liar. She hated him because he had failed to provide her with the refuge she sought—a safe place to pretend. In a way, that was what this house had always been for him. He could see that now.

She wanted to hide from the truth even as he hid from the world. But he had refused to let her.

A breath of cold wind rushed over him so he shivered deep in his marrow. The chill of autumn and the promise of winter crept in through his pores, and his mind drifted back to the events of yesterday. To the words of Serap's uncle and the anarchy that his own actions had caused on Qaf. They fell on his back more heavily than the ox's yoke he used to till his fields. He had slain an immortal, as was his sacred duty bestowed upon him by the Bahamut. But did that mean it was also his responsibility to deal with the consequences?

No, he decided.

He didn't care. Furthermore, it was not his fault. His nature was that of a hunter. A wolf need not worry about what becomes of the doe and her fawn after he has slain a stag. Like so many of Allah's creations, a wolf could not survive without killing. It is his *modus vivendi*, and to go against it would only bring death. He hardly needed to apologize for doing precisely what he was created to do.

He walked back into his house and stopped cold at the sight of a turquoise djinn standing in his foyer, casually perusing a stack of books that was taller than she was.

His temper flared, but remembering everything that had happened with Serap—the way he had allowed himself to behave and the horrible consequences of his rashness—Javier swallowed his rage and took a deep breath.

The woman started and turned to look at him. She was very beautiful—thick, dark red lips, eyes that shimmered like the sun that peeked through the window. And her silk and gossamer clothes fell around her frame like the robes of a queen. Perhaps she was a queen. She would not be the first.

"Does this look like a library?" Javier asked.

The woman took a cautious step back, holding the book to her chest as if it were a shield. "I was told to tell you I'm here for bread and that you're a liar and thief. That said, what's the matter with you?"

"Serap sent you." He drew his brows together, then sighed and shook his head. "You've come to collect her things, I suppose."

"I'm sorry, did you not hear my question?" She snapped the book closed with a puff of dust.

"I don't have any bread. Tuesday is bread day. But I have some baklava nobody's eaten. You are welcome to it, and anything else you want. Borrow a book, have some bread, enjoy a cup of tea with an immortal demon." Another heavy sigh. His shoulders drooped toward the ground. "It doesn't matter anymore."

She pursed her full lips and narrowed her shining eyes. "I don't see why my husband is so impressed with you. Nor Serap for that matter, but she must be, because you've crushed the sweetest soul I've ever met."

He loped past the djinn and dropped himself into the chair at the center of the room. "I cannot take full credit for that. Her soul is fractured under the weight of mortality. I fear, for all the posturing in the world, no single man may take responsibility for that."

"No, any such man would be foolish in pride and a sense of wisdom he had none of. But that is not why she is shattered."

He set an elbow on the armrest, then rested his cheek on his fist, eyes blurry as they gazed past the djinn woman to nothing. "I feel certain you are going to elucidate whether I ask you to or not."

She set the book gently back on the shelf, her finger lingering on its spine before coming to stand in front of him, arms folded tight, all tenderness gone. "When you draw a woman close to you and lay her soul bare, no amount of sophistry can save you if you say something stupid immediately following."

An argument formed on the tip of his tongue, but was quickly scattered as all of her words slowly sank into his mind, like rain into wool. He covered his eyes with his hand.

"You *are* an idiot," the woman continued with a healthy share of vitriol. "And you have no right to be so presumptuous and take advantage of an innocent woman. What do you know about her? You lecture her on her fear of death after taking a gift she has guarded most carefully her whole life?"

"What gift?"

The djinn groaned. "Her first kiss. And do you think your hard words will suddenly change her mind? Do you think that is what she wanted from you?"

He stroked his beard as he considered her many questions. "The gift of a kiss leaves both the giver and the receiver—should he have any honor whatsoever—exposed with nothing but their raw hearts with which to communicate. The heart is foolish and brash, whereas I am... shy." He looked up at the djinn's eyes of yellow and amber. Reading djinn eyes was not as straightforward as it seemed, for while their emotions flashed in colors within them, they each had unique backlights—a natural color to the eye like humans—that tinted their every emotion. Did this djinn have naturally yellow highlights in her amber backlit eyes, or was she just that disgusted by him?

"What I know of Serap is immaterial at this juncture." He snatched his worn and abandoned copy of Celestina from the back of his chair and shoved it under his nose. "I will never again steal her secrets."

"That is not enough." The djinn grabbed the nearest book and threw it in his lap. Then another and another. "You hide in these. You consume others' thoughts and expound them as your own. You claim you make your mistakes when overcome with emotion and then defend them with logic. It is incongruous. And saying you will not press her for more when you've already taken everything is delusionally selfish. You will never make it right with Serap that way. Or do you even care to?"

"She wants nothing to do with me. Not because of anything I say or do, but because of what I do. Who I am. That cannot be overcome. Not by a friend. And certainly not by... what might have been a wife." Javier hesitated.

It was hard to say out loud, though only moments ago, he'd been screaming with all his heart that he had finally found the only woman he could ever want as his wife.

The djinn woman *tsked* at him like he were a child. "The entirety of who you are is not bound by what you do, nor is it inextricable from it. But I think that is a wisdom you have overlooked in all your scholarly pursuits. Yes, she is struggling with mortality, but that is something you should empathize with, not be critical of."

"My very existence plagues her psyche."

"Ending the lives of immortals, innocent or not, is the lot that has been bestowed on you. But you need not shove it in her face at such a moment. She was aching. Thinking that no one would love her because she would die soon. She wanted your affection. Your sweet nothings about how you could live a thousand days or one and she would mean the same to you, always. She wanted a kiss. A sympathetic word. Not a lecture, you stupid man."

"I did kiss her..." He cut himself short and growled in his throat, irritated by the conversation, yet undeniably stimulated by it. "I was simply trying to tell her that mortality and its ephemeral beauty was part of what draws men and women together.

I wanted to be sympathetic, and empathetic, of course. But when the entire reason she sought me out goes against everything I believe, what recourse have I but to be critical? Granted, the timing was perhaps wrong—"

"Perhaps?"

"It was certainly wrong. But I am unaccustomed to the unstructured and tangential nature of human conversation. As you have so mercilessly pointed out, my dearest friends are dead poets."

The djinn scoffed, the tips of her sparkling hair brushing out from beneath her hijab. "For someone so sure of their philosophies, you blame a lack of control far too often. You heard her secrets and could have discussed them with her before you accepted her gift. Then again, you claimed you were swept up in illogical passion at the time, right? So, none of this is your fault?"

The djinn moved closer, her eyes flashing like the sun on water that hides a current. Was that blue in her heart—a possibility of hope? "You speak to Serap as if she were you, a hermit of a man who hates people and talks with dead poets. That is not her."

"I know that."

"Any wise man would know that a person can only understand what they're ready to understand. Yes, she knows the words of lovesick poets, but she is not learned like you and meI. Not in the depth and darkness of a mortal soul. She is a ray of light that floats on the breeze, and you tried to drag her down to Bahamut and called it sympathy."

Javier pressed his hands into his knees and cracked his neck to one side. This entire conversation was utterly humiliating, and there was no way to get away from it. Deep in his heart, all he wanted to talk about was Serap.

"A lovers' kiss should always be a meeting of equals, never an exchange of goods." He paused, moving his lips from side to side so that his beard twitched. "I *was* swept up in illogical passion, an experience entirely uncommon to me."

He clenched his teeth, wondering why he was speaking so freely with this stately djinn woman whose name he did not even know. Not that he wanted to stop, not when he was so seduced by the cathartic experience of an intellectual duel with someone who seemed capable of both parry and riposte.

"I am not some lascivious calculated fiend," Javier said. "Quite the opposite. I have very little physical experience with a lover."

"Sensuality was not the gift I was referring to, though thank you for illuminating your sexual prowess, *hermit*. I'll lock that away for later."

"I have no sexual prowess," he barked, then sighed and let his shoulders drop. "I had never kissed a woman until Serap walked into my haunted house and... poked my bread."

"Who poked what now?" The djinn's lips pinched in clear disgust.

She shook her head, shoulders, then arms as if getting rid of the chills. Her soft silks *swished*, wafting the scent of lilies toward his nose.

"Nevermind. I don't want to know. And I was being sarcastic, you impossible man. When I said her kiss was the gift, I really meant her trust. Not the wide, honey-eyed trust she bestows freely on everyone, but the deep trust she must have given you to allow her heart to open so. She has been scarred time and time again by cold courtiers who woo her and then espouse her failings, so much so she has become guarded, burying her fears in her Amca's djinn-burning necklaces. And then you come along and win her over in days. Days! And then do the same exact thing: tell her you care and then tell her a great part of who she is is not good enough for you."

"It is precisely because I do not wish to abuse her trust that I spoke in the manner in which I did." He scoffed and shook his head. "And what of *my* trust? She snatched my soul from the glass jar where I had quite deliberately left it to desiccate, rehydrated it without my permission, and then carelessly spilled it over the earth so that with every breath the soil leached me dry. Does that mean nothing?"

"Not if she doesn't know about it." The djinn smirked. "And maybe that *does* make you feel cheapened. I don't care, because I'm not here for you. But what is love if it is not shared? What does it do but torment the holder if it is not set free? If your soul pulls away from you, where does it push towards? If the answer is Serap, stop pontificating and do something about it."

He clenched a fist and cracked his knuckles. He wanted to throw knives at her to get her out of his house, which is precisely what he would have done had she shown up just a few days ago.

"I pity your husband, *señora*." He released his fist and laid his palm flat on the armrest. "He must constantly be covered in snakebites from your tongue."

"It is my snakebites, as you so kindly call truth, that remind him I am not to be taken for granted. And it is his snakebites that remind me of the same. I suppose that is poor Serap's problem. For she never bites anyone, and you will devour her."

"You speak of her as if she were a child that had yet to cut her milk teeth." Javier's shoulder twitched. "She is a grown woman. Sensitive and brave and sweet. Her fangs are sharp and have sunk deep into my musculature to loose her slow-acting venom. Her hatred has already been the death of my heart and liver, and someday will consume the rest of me."

He shook his head hard and stood, his own words sinking like anchors in his bloodstream.

"You should find her and take her from this place," Javier said, his eyes tightening on the djinn woman, "this house of horrors that has so damaged her fragile spirit. Take her somewhere bright and beautiful so she can relearn to shine and let her forget me and this darkness. For you are right, I cannot but yank her down into Hades. She should be free to walk amongst the flowers forever. And I will stay here with my poets, my shadows, and my beloved misery."

The djinn's eyes flashed into narrow slits. She crossed the space to him in three sharp steps and grabbed his cheeks in her hand. He flinched as if at the bite of hot irons, and his body froze.

"It seems as if only the touch of another person reminds you that you are human, so listen closely, for I do not wish to touch you again. Serap does not hate you. She yearns for you. She hurts for you, but it is not hate. It is love. And if you are too cowardly to show her you feel the same way, then fine, go to Hades forever, but know that she is already there and only you can bring her out of it."

She released his cheeks and snapped her hand back with regal precision. He flinched, worried she would slap him.

Then a scream sounded from somewhere above in a voice more precious to him than any other.

"Serap?" The djinn's gaze darted to the stairs.

Javier bounded past her and up the steps, taking them three at a time. When he came to the top, his eyes scanned the hall for the source of the sound. He rushed to the room where Serap had been staying and yanked open the door so the hinges pulled from the wall.

"Serap?"

The room was empty, but not in the usual way. Not simply deserted as a vessel without water. There was a deliberate, aching quality to the emptiness. And a smell—the stench of rancid meat and sulfur. The hideous taste of dead, rotten teeth, and the noxious fumes that rise from a dead body days after it has breathed its last.

Khayin. He had been there. Perhaps, his invisible form still lingered in shadow. The smell intensified, and a hot wind like the breath of a predator swept over his body. The voice echoed through the wind like a whisper in a cavern.

Persephone has tasted the seed.

"Who is that?" the djinn asked as she peered past him in the room, her voice taut and wary. "Where is Serap?"

"It is Khayin."

And at that moment, strange words Serap had spoken over the course of several days filled his ears, growing in volume until they reached a deafening crescendo.

"It is Evil."

CHAPTER THIRTY-THREE

SERAP

Seventy times seven times she had relived the argument with DeMario. The intimacy before. And the fear before that. And seventy times seven times she had come to the same conclusion: love was a gift only the rare few would ever find, and it tormented the rest. That her attempt to find it ended with her in this dark place devoid of anything but a muggy breeze and Chupkin made perfect sense. Love had struck her family thrice, defying the odds; it was justice that the pendulum had swung the other way and landed her in misery.

The acknowledgment of her fate didn't keep her from being stupid, however. More than once had she caught herself longing for the gentle pat of Gordito or the brush of Javier's hand on her neck. Her heart swung like a pendulum between rage and love, happiness and sorrow, and her mind tried its best to salvage the memories of the sweet wisp and gentle man from the wreckage of who they both turned out to be. Reeling, she grasped for any string to pull her from the carnage, and she remembered Javier's caginess about who Chupkin was before she learned the truth.

Her sweet wisp swept back and forth in front of her, a faint echo of his dim light on the shadowy ground beneath.

"Chupkin?"

He twirled in a lazy whirl and came to rest on her knee. Why had she never thought to ask him if he was something more than a wisp? He was certainly loyal, affectionate, and even a scaredy-cat at times. And far more of a companion than anyone else she had. Bile rose in her throat at the thought of a suffering person trapped for so long at the side of as ignorant and selfish a girl as she.

Serap scooped his little cloud into her hands and brought him up before her eyes. She tucked both her lips in, then scraped them loose. "Are you a person?"

His light dimmed to almost nothing. Then he rose up and dipped up and down twice before settling again in her lap.

She drew up her shoulders and tucked her elbows in with a grimace. He deserved begging apologies. Tears. But she was bereft, and all she had left was a whisper.

"I'm sorry, Chupkin." Her eyes trailed to the dark before turning back to him. "I should have figured that out long ago. I'm a terrible friend."

Her head drooped, and Chupkin's gentle light brightened. He wrapped himself around her neck and pressed into the spot below her ear.

She nuzzled him back, completely undeserving of his loyalty and comfort. And even though she had given up hope for herself, a familiar desire to push through and keep fighting surfaced for Chupkin. After all his years of sticking by her, didn't he deserve the same?

"Maybe we can find someone who has the power to change you back. The magic to wispify djinn was in the book Evil gave me to read. The one about Khayin."

The tome she had pulled from Don DeMario's house still lay at her feet. She scooped it up and flipped the crispy pages to where she had left off.

"From what I can understand of the magical ancestry of Khayin's family, they had once been powerful rulers all over Qaf, each with their own power. And every time one of the holders of a particular strain of magic—say the ability to turn men into wisps—died, the power imbued itself in the closest living relative."

Chupkin bobbed, sliding around her back and over her shoulder to read the pages with her.

"It looks like over time," she continued, rubbing a finger over the page, "the family lines died out. Powers jumped to second, then third cousins, crisscrossing and falling away due to plague, or war, or impotence, or super suspicious deaths—there were an inordinate amount of those after Khayin was born, surprise surprise. Eventually, all the powers funneled into one person, except two that had managed to squirm their way down a different line and disappeared."

Chupkin's dim light illuminated the final corners of the page, flickering over the lost lines.

"You're right. The power to change you back was one of those. But I don't know where it went.

She took a closer look and her stomach tightened.

"The person who absorbed all the magic was a man of seven siblings who all died young. A man whose powers were said to come from his travels abroad slaying strange beasts and visiting mystic lands. A man who became the Traitor of Shihala."

A gust of wind wailed in the darkness. She covered her face, awaiting an onslaught of thick air, but none came. She lifted her eyes to the sky, turning her head around. Chupkin's light dimmed, and he ducked into her shirt.

"Serap?" came a tunneled voice.

Serap jumped to her feet, relief and irritation an equal wash over her mind. "Pasha? Pasha are you there?"

"Who else would it be, sweetie?"

"How did you find me? I couldn't even call my amca from this place."

Pasha's voice crackled overhead with an annoyed puff. "What part of me being the Witch of Eternal Finding are you not getting?"

"The fact that I've been doing all the finding for you here on Ard," Serap offered dryly.

"Did you get the crow's beak?"

Serap opened her mouth, then slung it closed. She had been able to barter a little before when trying to facilitate Gordito's return to Javier. Could she do so for Chupkin now? Or something more? Her stomach twisted up in acrobatic knots. Not here. She was already at Evil's mercy and in a place of little power. She needed to wait until she had more leverage.

"No, I did not get it." The lie tried to stick in her teeth. She cringed, once again hoping the witch couldn't see. "I've seen it, though."

A deep, growly sound cast through the wind, and she wasn't sure if Pasha was muttering or if whatever connection carried the voice was having difficulty.

"Seeing does me no good. I'm not a patient witch, you know."

Serap raised an eyebrow and cast her gaze to the black nothing overhead. "You can't see where I am?"

"I'm using a tether I put in your wisp. I can't see you at all. I can just push and pull voices and, if necessary, you through Celestial strings that connect the universe. It's not an exact magic, child, and is very difficult to pull off."

Serap's brows furrowed, and her lips puckered. She shot Chupkin a glance.

"My apologies. But I'm currently caught in a dark nothingness, so I shan't be able to get your beak anytime soon."

"A black nothing... Who put you there? I bet it was that son of snake..." Her angry voice dipped into a spell of hashed mumbling. "Did you tell anyone about it? The beak?"

"No. Why?"

"Because it's a bad idea."

"What does it do, Pasha? I have very good reasons to never return to the Immortal Killer's house. I won't go snooping there again without an excellent reason."

Pasha hissed. "You won't be searching in anyone's house if I leave you in darkness."

Serap winced and almost caved, tempted to switch to a pitiful begging to get her out of this prison. But where had being weak, compliant, and *readily suggestible* gotten her?

Oh, yeah. Here.

She ignored the pain in the back of her throat and squeezed her soft hands. "Tell me or no beak."

More sharp crackling scattered through the air about her, and she half-expected lightning to break the sky and fry her.

"You crack me up. But I'll let you in. The beak is a gateway to Ashkult."

"What?"

"Ashkult, sweetie," Pasha said, the nickname like venom. "The impenetrable prison. No beast, no teleportation power nor spell can break its walls. No enchanted items even. Except one."

"The beak?" Serap fought the urge to press her hand against her pocket and feel the dried bird's head, a little wary that Pasha had lied and watched her even now. "Why?"

"Why does any magical thing do what it does? Because the creator wanted it that way."

"The *wali*?"

A cackle and a sigh. "Yes, the *wali*. It is said the quicksilver lake was made from his tears. The barrier that keeps evil from the human world and the grave of his baby reside on the island that is now Ashkult. Because its magic existed before or in conjunction with the barrier, it works unimpeded through time and space."

Serap dug her toes into the dirt, enjoying cool relief from the muggy air. The weight of Pasha's words dripped down her neck as sweat.

"So why do you want it?"

"Do you want me to get you out of your prison or not?"

"Pasha." Serap pulled her shoulders back and glared at the sky.

"I don't know why you're fighting me on this so much, Serap. You should want me to have the crow's beak, too."

"Why?"

"Why did you start this whole quest?"

Serap bit her lip "To find a way to kill Khayin so I could use 'Ab's final question to achieve a longer life."

The words felt strange in her mouth. Almost wrong. Like calling someone you've known forever by a new name. Speaking her desire now, after Don DeMario's cruel judgment, made her feel petty and small.

A popping, snipping noise broke on Pasha's end of the wind. "And where is Khayin?"

"In Ashkult." Sweat dripped down her neck in large drops. "Are you going to take Don DeMario there to kill Khayin?"

"Bingo." Pasha's voice turned bright once more.

"For me?"

"Sure, honey."

A lie. But why else would Pasha care about the traitor?

Pasha's voice began to fade, and an urgency kicked up inside Serap. "Send me back."

"You already owe me for the favor I did with your little wisp friend."

"You needed Don DeMario in human form, too." Serap clenched her fists and jerked her head towards the sky. Pasha's games were no fun anymore. "Just like you need me free to find your beak. If I lose, you lose, too."

The realization sat like rancid stew in her stomach, for the reverse was true, too.

A smirching noise bounced around despite the lack of walls. Or solid surfaces. Or the physical presence of Pasha. "Alright. I'll send you back. But whoever put you there—" More bitter muttering. "—is going to be pissed. So, I suggest you hurry and get the beak. Fifteen degrees tops, before I come looking for you. And I'll be the least of your worries."

The wind picked up to a hurricane, flinging dust in Serap's eyes and over her skin. She coughed and spit dirt from her mouth, but the cyclone only grew stronger. She crouched into herself, Chupkin under her shirt and against her chest and Evil's book clutched against her chest.

When the coating of dust seared her lungs and clung to every pore and vein in her body, the wind ceased. She opened her eyes, and dirt fell from her lashes. The dungeon. She had four finger's-widths of the sun passing to figure out what Evil wanted, what Pasha did. And to find a way to get ahead of it all so she could figure out how to save Chupkin. The key lay in the book in her hands. In the beak in her pocket. In Khayin. And, inevitably, in the man who had won her heart and scoffed.

She bent low and rubbed the pain in her chest. Her arms felt heavy, her neck stiff. Each heartbeat made her feel like she would burst as she relived his betrayal. His broad sword flashing against the light. Najima's hair hanging loose over her delicate shoulders. One motion. Silence. The death of a living thing, a beautiful ancient woman. And then him walking away, head up like he was right. Because he always thought he was.

He did not care at all what she thought because she did not cling to logic as he did. Because she valued feelings. Because she was not some dead poet in his books. And that realization ripped through her body more than the gruesome images that played over and over in her mind.

Javier *would* cherish her more if she were dead.

Her shaking shoulders begged her to be a coward and call Bakr Amca once more. To keep running and never come back to this terrible place. But the cool touch of Chupkin against her chest sealed her throat. He was the only one who had been there for her no matter what, and she had treated him terribly. As a *pet*, Don DeMario had said. Not as a friend. And she would not abandon him.

"Stupid child, stupid child. Thinking you could run."

Serap shot up straight and dove for the stairs, hoping to outrun a being who was everywhere and nowhere all at once. She scraped her knees against the stone as she stumbled and fell up the basement steps. Gasping in pain, she burst from the door and right into Cova.

The girl fell backward and landed in a heap. Her soft eyes rounded, eyebrows hiked high up on her forehead. "Where have you been? Don DeMario came and told us all to leave. His sisters are already gone."

It was calm on the main floor, a world apart from the madness in the basement. Serap cast a nervous glance over her shoulder and slammed the door shut. "I don't know where Evil's powers started or ended, only that he is in this house. We've got to get out."

"He's looking for you."

Serap's heart seized. "Who?"

There was no *he* that could be looking for her that would be a good thing. And despite the demon on her tail, there was one other she dreaded even more.

Cova shrugged. "Evil."

Serap grabbed the girl's hand and dragged her toward the door in the kitchen. "Don't talk to him, anymore."

Cova giggled and put a free hand over her mouth. "He said you'd say that."

"I bet he did."

Cova followed Serap's hurried steps willingly, but her voice dipped somewhere between curious and accusing. "He said you've joined the bear."

"Nonsense," Serap chided, but fire burned in her chest, clouding her vision and filling her lungs so it was hard to breathe. "I don't even know who the bear is."

She reached the threshold, and Cova pulled back.

"Come." She tugged, pushing open the door.

"I can't."

"Why not?" Serap bit her lip, her eyes darting between the girl's pale face and the door to the hallway behind her.

"He said not to."

"Even more a reason to leave."

Cova shook her head. "He said leaving is a trap."

Serap groaned, tempted to yank the girl through the open door. But what if Evil was right and leaving was a trap? She had no idea what his motivations were or why he had left her to sit in blackness. He had helped. He had hurt. And he couldn't be trusted, after all. Just like everyone but Chupkin. And that meant leaving.

But she didn't want to hurt Cova. Serap glanced between the kitchen door and the outside. Maybe if she stepped out into the yard and nothing hurt her, Cova would follow. It seemed the only way.

Chupkin brushed against her neck, yanking on her headband in the direction of the door.

She nodded and brushed a finger against him. "Are you sure you want to come? You've done enough. You don't need to risk any more for me."

His little light surged, bright and steady and strong as ever.

She grinned, her heart full of his loyalty. "I love you, Chupkin. I'll keep you safe."

Wisp on her shoulder, she let go of the girl's hand and turned to the sunlight. Then took a step into the unknown.

CHAPTER THIRTY-FOUR

JAVIER

Before doing anything else, Javier donned full armor. He had no expectation of really needing it, but after the bear and *arak hunak*, he would never leave his house in anything less than full armor as long as he lived.

He found his sisters and Cova all together in his kitchen, eating the baklava and the stew he had made for Serap. Laughing in the warmth of a fire that smelled like roasted chestnuts—the kind his mother used to make.

Javier stepped into the doorway with heavy feet. "You have to get out."

"*Hermanito*?" Cecilia raised from the table.

"This is the last time I am going to warn you. If you don't get out of my house now I will not be or fiscally or even hypothetically responsible for what might happen to you, up to and including a violent death."

He turned and walked briskly away until he was in the room that held his most precious treasures, including his mirror.

He ran a finger over the frame to tell it where to take him, then stepped through onto the white shores of Ashkult.

His boots crunched on sand. Thick dust of white coated the barren landscape like snow—snow found in the mountains of Ankara and Zabriya, snow that occasionally fell in the south of Spain in the darkest months of winter. But despite the painful chill in the air, the white held no moisture. He bent and took some bleached sand into his gloved hand. Powdery shards of broken glass or crystal, so spiny it seemed as if it were soaked in acid.

Straightening, Javier's eyes scanned the flat terrain. He was no djinn and had no magic in his blood. All his mortal frame carried was the singular gift of the Bahamut which rode on his soul so discreetly it was almost forgettable, but even he could feel the barrenness of this land. The cloying nothingness and smell of metal seeped into his skin.

He had never been here before. A few times individuals had come to him with proposals, asking him to break inside to kill one horrible creature or another, but he had always refused them. Why should he concern himself with a monster that was already so well-contained?

He had dressed in his armor before leaving the house this time, his daggers tucked in their holsters concealed in his jacket. His gun in his boot, and his katar strapped to his arm. He had not come seeking a fight but refused to enter the djinn world without protection when at all possible. A black turban was wrapped over his hair, the loose fabric pulled over his face to cover his mouth and nose.

As he walked toward the lifeless lake of silver, the shape of a djinn man appeared, standing on the crystal-like sand. The Shihalan's clothes were immaculate and expensive, but with no ostentatious decorations or jewelry except for a single opal ring on his finger. His skin was a vibrant shade of sapphire blue and his eyes shimmered with the facets of an expertly cut diamond. Diamond eyes have no backlight and the flickers of their fire shine through with no perversion. A mist of black fear and miserable purple coiled around his. The sadness in the djinn's face snaked down Javier's throat and into his already aching guts.

Javier cleared his throat and asked in Arabic. "Is this where one gets passage to the prison?"

The blue djinn nodded slowly and turned towards a small, wooden shack near the shoreline. "You must speak with the boatman."

Javier gave a curt not and stepped past the man, then knocked on the rickety door. He had not meant to put much power in his fist, but the decaying wood splintered.

"What?" a raspy voice shouted. Then a short, very fat Ghaluman answered the door. His fiery red skin looked stark beneath thick, twisted black hairs growing from his ears and over his knuckles. "*Aleamaa*! You don't have to break the door down." His phosphorescent yellow eyes swept over Javier. "Human?"

"You noticed." Javier snatched him by the collar, lifted him up, and slammed his back against the door.

The Ghaluman rolled his eyes with a sneer. "Please. Like I haven't seen that before."

The boatman's name was Almurakibiu and he was a known immortal, at least in certain circles. He had been the ferryman of Ashkult for at least a thousand years. Little was known about him and even his immortality was a secret from most. He was most famous for being the only djinn alive that was impervious to the effects of metal.

Javier shoved the tip of his katar up under the djinn's jowls. "You think you have nothing to fear from my blade."

"I am threatened with death nearly every day." The boatman yawned.

"But I am *Alqatil Alkhalid*."

The djinn's eyes widened and flushed with black. Javier threw him back so he broke his own door and crashed into the shack.

"Get your paddle," snapped Javier. "We leave now."

The Ghaluman scrambled to his feet and did as he was told.

Javier turned and walked back to the shore where the rickety boat waited. The blue djinn stared at him unabashedly, no more fear in his eyes than what had already been there.

Javier took his waterskin from his hip and emptied it onto the white shore, then bent over the lake of quicksilver and refilled it with the frozen, shimmering liquid. Then he stood and corked the bottle with a satisfying *pomp*. He would be mad to go into Ashkult without bringing any special protection, and this was as devastating a weapon against djinn as was possible to create.

The ferryman lumbered over, giving Javier a wide berth, then climbed inside his boat and cast off the line.

Javier drew his gaze back to the blue djinn and remembered the pain on his face. "Come. There is room for two."

The Shihalan bowed his head and followed. They pushed off and began the slow journey across the quicksilver sea toward the looming figure of the ancient and impenetrable prison. That Khayin was able to force his influence beyond the contaminants of such a place was a testament to just how dangerous he was. Although Javier was loath to admit it, he could not stop the nervous bile in the back of his throat.

The blue djinn played with his ring of shimmering opal, watching Javier with unabashed intent.

"What?" Javier asked when he was unable to handle the silence a moment longer.

"You are human." The djinn's voice was as refined as everything else about him.

"You noticed."

"What purpose could you have at Ashkult?"

He folded his fingers together in his lap and ran his tongue over his front teeth. "Why should my race have any bearing on my business here?"

"Ashkult is a prison utilized exclusively by the kings and queens of Qaf, and it does not tend to hold human prisoners. As far as I understand there has only ever been one."

"I am here to visit an old acquaintance. What more do you need to know?"

"Visit?" The djinn's eyes flashed pink and yellow. "The prisoners of Ashkult do not receive visitors."

"There are always exceptions." Javier cracked his knuckles, irritated by the slow progress of the boat. "What is *your* business here?"

The djinn's solemn, symmetrical face hardened so much, the contour of his jaw was visible under his trim black beard. He turned his eyes to the sea of quicksilver. "I've come to interrogate a prisoner."

"Perhaps interrogation is a better word for my business, as well."

"May I ask whom?"

"What concern is it of yours?"

The djinn shrugged. "I'm merely making conversation. A transparent attempt to distract myself from the liquid death that surrounds me."

Javier pushed his lips together, grateful in some small way to engage in meaningless talk with the sad djinn. "I have come to see Faris Khayin D'Jaush."

The djinn's eyes flashed white, and his head snapped to attention. Colors flowed through his eyes in a brilliant kaleidoscope—light and darkness and everything else. The beauty of it drew Javier in, but the anger and suspicion that flooded the djinn's features pushed him back.

He almost wanted to laugh. What was it about Khayin that caused such a reaction in so many men?

"Who are you?" snapped the djinn. "What is your business with the traitor?"

"Who are you? And what concern is it of yours?"

"My name is Almalik Jahmil al-Shihalai. Khayin is my prisoner, and no one sees him without my permission."

"The King of Shihala?"

So this was Serap's adoptive father. The one from whom she had been hiding, whom she refused to answer to.

"And who are you, *human,* who threatens the ferryman and presumes to interrogate my prisoner?" King Jahmil blustered.

Javier's first instinct was to refuse to answer, or to lie, or to tell the djinn that he could go straight to Jahannam for all he cared. His second thought was what a very vulnerable position the king found himself in. A single jostle of the boat, a little quicksilver spilled over the side, and the noble would die a horrible, fiery death, whereas Javier would feel a bit cold.

Then he remembered he didn't give a damn. He had come here to do a job, long overdue. And he had never once let a king or queen or emperor or anybody get in his way.

"I am Javier Don DeMario, *Alqatil Alkhalid.* And I do not need your permission."

The muscles in King Jahmil's face tightened, like a hundred little ropes being pulled all at once. He clenched his fists. "*You.* This is all your fault."

"What exactly is my fault?"

"You murdered the King of Elm!"

"It was more of an execution." Javier paused and furrowed his brow. "Wait. Who told you that?"

"What difference does it make?"

Would Serap have told him that? Or was it her Bakr Amca, who had happily declared he couldn't keep secrets from the Shihalan king, who Javier supposed was his brother somehow.

He still had no idea how that half-djinn half-human family worked. He felt sure the story behind it was complicated.

Bakr had said Jahmil finding out that he and Serap were involved in the King of Elm's death would be a big problem politically for Jahmil. Logically, that meant Bakr simply gave credit where it was due and said the Immortal Killer had whacked the big green rubbery bastard.

"Fabulous," Javier grunted. "All I needed are a bunch of assassins from Elm showing up on my doorstep."

"I ended his disgustingly bloated existence and, in so doing, preserved the life of an innocent."

"You have plunged all of Qaf into turmoil."

Javier cleared his throat. "Good."

"I beg your pardon?"

"A society built on the hubris of a magical seal deserves to be in turmoil. Perhaps this reckoning will force you djinni to reforge your civilization on more stable ground."

"Hundreds of thousands of djinn will die all over Qaf. We will face famine and war as we have never known." King Jahmil snarled. "And you—the murderer—walk into Ashkult expecting to be shown anything other than a cell to rot in?"

Javier stroked his beard as he thought. Bakr clearly had not mentioned Serap's role in anything or the King of Shihala probably would have been trying to throw him overboard.

That was likely for the best. However, he could not have this big blue bag of hot air getting in the way of his purpose.

"You would do well to see that does not happen, *malakiun*."

"I am going to make sure it happens."

"Because if I end up in a cell there is no telling what may happen to Serap."

"Serap?" Without warning, the Shihalan king pounced and snatched fistfuls of Javier's jacket. "You dare to threaten my daughter?"

"It is Khayin who threatens her, you fool. Why do you think I'm here?"

"Explain yourself."

Javier growled and looked down at the blue fingers on his leather jacket. "Let go of me."

The king stared hard into his eyes. There was white-hot anger in those gemstones, but Javier could see the black mist of fear pooling in the background. "How do you know Serap?"

"She's merely an innocent who has become a pawn in Khayin's never-ending games," Javier bit back all the other words that bubbled in his throat. "I am here to put an end to them."

The King's expression contorted as if he couldn't decide if that was true but hoped that it was. "You mean to kill Khayin?"

"That depends on how he answers my questions."

King Jahmil stared daggers at him as he settled back into his seat. "Tell me how you know Serap?"

"She sought me out." There was no reason to lie. He didn't care what anybody thought, so why lie? "She was looking for help with something. I sent her on her way."

"What did she want your help with?"

Javier sighed and straightened his shirt. "Her secrets are not mine to divulge."

"What secrets?" Jahmil scoffed.

A thorn twisted in Javier's gut at the condescending sound. A memory of Serap covered in mud as they battled the man-eating Izraki tree filled his mind. At the time, he had not understood her refusal to run to safety, her desperation to prove herself, to clean up her own mess, to show that she was useful.

Now, it made sense.

"What reason could she possibly have to seek you out?" The king wiped his lips. "Was it to do with Khayin?"

Javier shook his head and looked away. They were nearly to the glass-smooth, black walls of the prison, the stone dock manned by four red guards, each with a long obsidian sword strapped to their hips.

"Why would Serap seek out an Immortal Killer if not to kill an immortal? And what immortal would she have any reason to kill but Khayin?"

Javier wanted to brush those words away like flies, but they gnawed at him. "Why would she have a reason to kill Khayin?"

The king hesitated and Javier found himself all but hypnotized by the dizzying dance of colors in his eyes. "I made a pact with him long ago that he would answer three questions and then I would kill him."

"And he believed you?"

"I suppose a man with no hope will cling to even the most unlikely fantasies." The Shihalan's gaze once again slipped to the bleak horizon. "I asked one question and my half-sister, Sezan, asked the second. One remains. And once that question is answered if Khayin does not die..."

"You will. Or, you would have until I broke the Seal of Elm." Javier smirked and tilted back his chin. "You're welcome."

The king snarled and clenched his teeth. "Is that what she wanted from you or isn't it?"

"Serap? She never got around to asking."

"Immortal Killer," said the king, his voice so sure and soft that it caught Javier off guard. He looked up at him, at his crystalline eyes that swirled with purple and pale blue. "I believe fate brought us together at this moment. Allah, the merciful and compassionate, sent you here to free me of my burden and to reunite me with my daughter."

"What are you talking about?" Javier sneered.

"You are going to kill the traitor and you are going to do it in my name."

"And why in the Seven Circles of Hell would I do that?"

The king folded his fingers together and leaned back in his seat. "I have a proposal for you."

CHAPTER THIRTY-FIVE

SERAP

Serap held her breath and stepped out into the grassy field behind Don DeMario's house. Before her foot hit the pebbled path, little hands grabbed her shirt and yanked her back.

"Don't go," Cova begged, innocent eyes streaked with fear. "It's a trap. Evil said it was a trap."

"Cova." Serap sighed and turned to face her. "Please, I—"

She froze. The kitchen waved with green light. Blurry and translucent as if she was drowning, looking up at the room from the bottom of a pond.

"What do you want, Evil?" Her voice trembled.

The green thickened into a smog. Serap coughed. The door slammed shut behind her. She grabbed Cova's trembling hand and dragged her out of the kitchen and into the main room of the house. The little girl's fingers tight in hers, Serap weaved and zig-zagged through the piles of books toward the front door.

She wrenched the rickety thing open and yanked Cova out with her. The second her foot hit grass, a whipping wind erupted, tugging her clothes and hair and stinging her eyes. The sky darkened, blotting out the sun. Larger and larger, the gusts churned into a ferocious storm that pulled trees from their roots and knocked down a row of small boxes built by the road. A raging storm out of thin air.

"The trap!" Cova shriveled down onto the ground, making it impossible for Serap to drag her further along. She scooped the girl up and stumbled, her mind torn between which fate was worse. Evil or death by some mysterious bear?

Fear of the unknown won out, and she let herself fall back into the thick, green haze inside the house. Cova tumbled from her arms and tripped back into the yard. Already the storm had died down, the sun shining and the torn limbs of trees fluttering in a gentle breeze. Serap jerked her head between the sky and herself. She jumped up and stuck her foot out. Again, the sky darkened in a flurry of wind. She snatched her leg back and slammed the door shut with Cova still outside. Her desperate pleas pounded on the door, but Serap did up the iron locks with shaking fingers.

Whatever Evil wanted, she would keep Cova out of it.

"*Yes, child, yes. Come back to me.*" Evil snickered.

Chupkin popped up from her shirt and whipped toward the stairs. Serap followed, knocking piles over as she went. A flickering image of blue appeared halfway up the steps, clinging to the air like cobwebs. She chased Chupkin, trusting he knew a better way than she did, and jutted to the hallway that led to Don DeMario's room.

"I can't," she cried after him, pulling back. "I can't go in there. Not after the fight."

Chupkin whirled around her hair, brushing her skin, then conceded, plummeting toward the kitchen. They both skidded to a halt. A hideous face hovered in the doorway, sharp, smiling teeth framed in folded skin and topped with death-black eyes. A hand with crooked nails and cracked skin reached for her from nothing. She yelped. Tripping over herself, she ran back the other way. Trapped.

The hand flung toward her, and she scrambled in the only direction she had left. Up. Up and up the piles of books, hopping from one to another as they collapsed beneath her. Over the old, stained chair in the middle of the room and with a flying leap onto the bookshelves. Her hands slipped on the dusty surface, but her frantic feet found purchase. Step. Lift. Hold. Jump. Slide. Repeat.

She had nearly made it to the second story landing when she lost her balance. Three-shelves-worth she fell with a cry before Chupkin flashed brightly over the hammered sides of a thick, brass pot spilling out over an edge. She aimed and caught the rim, metal slicing into her skin. She gasped and clung, desperate to live and completely out of ideas.

The pot shivered beneath her fingers. A glowing hand appeared from inside it, clawing and reaching over the side in frantic bursts. She screamed and let go.

Agony. Fire. Her ankle definitely sprained. She lay splayed across three piles of demolished books, the large spine of one of DeMario's wretched atlases stabbing into her spine.

The monster cackled. Spots littered her vision. Chupkin whipped anxiously about her, batting away the green fog that tried to envelop her. Serap reached her hand around her neck for Ayelet's amulet. She smashed her eyes shut and swiped the surface, hands shaking so hard, she hardly knew what she had done or what would come of it.

Serap opened her eyes to putrid, blackened nails swinging down toward her face. She flung her arms out in front, heart pounding and death certain.

"Serap?"

She cracked open a twitching eye. The hand had vanished. Instead, a soft, white cocoon encased her, swirling gently with glitter.

"Chupkin?" Her heart stammered. The little wisp appeared from her collar.

"Serap!"

She started and sat up, listening for the voice and hearing the soft lilt of an unseen breeze.

A face appeared in the mist, ruby-black hair and gray eyes soaking up the light.

"Ayelet!" Serap tried to crawl for her, but her ankle gave way in a searing twist of tendons.

Ayelet rushed to her side, flinging her arms around her in a tight squeeze. She kissed the top of her head, her cheeks, then scooped up her hands and kissed those, too.

"Where have you been?" she asked through all the kisses. "We have been so worried. Jahmil, Bakr, and Sezan. Even Balian and Yousef. We have scoured half of Qaf and Ard, each. Then *finally*, you send us a wisp to let us know where you are. For all of Allah's mercy, I do not understand why you have tortured us so."

"I'm sorry, Ayelet." Serap hunched her shoulders, leaning into the affection she didn't deserve. "I'm so sorry."

"Shh," Ayelet's eyes sharpened, darting around their cocoon. "The magic is off in this place. Someone is listening."

Serap shuddered. "Evil."

"Probably. Disruptive magic usually is."

"No, not evil. *Evil*. Or, at least I call him Evil."

Ayelet looked at her, head falling to the side. "*Do not talk to strangers. That is what we always taught you. I assumed you especially knew that included anything named Evil.*"

"Sorry?" Serap's neck shrunk into her shoulders.

Four streaks of blue lightning raked through the white overhead, tearing the magic like fabric.

Ayelet flicked her wrist, and a fog of white billowed toward the wounds, covering them up. "Sorry, indeed. But we can discuss that later. Any idea what this Evil may be?"

"I don't know," Serap sighed. "A spirit? He shows me things and takes me places and gives me gifts."

"Sounds kind of like a boyfriend." Ayelet raised her eyebrow.

Chupkin flashed indignantly, and Serap's mouth fell into a lop-sided smile despite the fear drying in her throat. "Paco doesn't seem so bad, now."

"Never say that." Ayelet shot her a wink, then pulled her to her feet.

Serap winced with the slightest shift in weight. The throbbing pain in her ankle rushed and stung in waves.

"I don't know what he wants. He's obsessed with the Immortal Killer and Khayin and started talking to Cova, and I don't know what to do about it anymore."

"Then it's definitely time to get you out of here." Ayelet patted her pockets until she pulled free a large, orange feather that smelled like a campfire. "Teleportation for humans, courtesy of your Bakr Amca's Fajar."

Serap grinned, eager to get away from this place and be at home.

The smokey billow of the rukh bird's eternal flame encompassed them when a shot of green fire exploded Ayelet's shield. Grey, white, and green fought and swirled around them, yanking them toward Qaf before pulling them back to Ard. Back and forth in jarring jerks until the feather in Ayelet's hand caught aflame.

Ayelet yelped and dropped it, Evil's fire nipping her skin.

Wide-eyed, she grabbed Serap's wrist. "Plan B. Which way was the door?"

Serap shook her head so hard, the copper coins on her necklace clacked together. "Whenever I try to leave, a tornado happens."

"Hmm." Ayelet's mouth twisted to the side. She looked up, tilting her head to and fro. "We may have better luck with the cyclone."

Two gnarly, clawing hands dug for them, black nails tearing through pure white.

Ayelet winced with every slash, like each hungry scrape on the magic shell tore at her skin as well. Serap's fingers twitched to do something. Anything.

"Time to go." Ayelet raised her hand. "Ready?"

Serap looked to Chupkin who twined himself into her hair with a nodding bob. She joined him, and Ayelet winked.

The cocoon popped, and a hundred little wisps broke out into chaos. Serap pointed toward the door. Ayelet nodded and grabbed Serap's hand. They made a mad scramble for outside. With every step, Serap took a book and flung it at the hands wherever they appeared. She leaned into each stack to help take the weight off her ankle and did not limit herself to the dusty covers. Not with Chupkin darting about, lighting the best objects for throwing.

She lobbed an urn. A loom. A strange box covered in cracks that burst with spiders when it hit the wall. And with every toss, she winced with regret and smiled with glee. Whatever happened to her, Don DeMario wouldn't be able to forget her now. Not with the mess she left in his house.

They reached the door, and a great crack shook the house. Green fire erupted around the frame, instantly hot and curling out towards them in little licks.

Ayelet flung her arms in front of Serap. The fire reddened her cheeks and singed the hems of her dress. Serap stared, frozen in guilt and horror, as one of the people she loved most in the world risked their life for her. A tight weave of wisps descended like a waterfall between them and the fire, but the flames only grew brighter, eating the magic with chomping, green teeth.

The glowing evil tendrils burst through the protective net and rushed toward them. Ayelet flung herself over Serap. They clung to each other, bracing for the burning impact. Smoke engulfed them. The scent of *alyasmin*. The glitter of Shihala, all wrapped in a rosy pink.

Zan Hala appeared next to them in a puff, hands on hips. "What in the world is going on? Bakr's up to his ears in work just trying to hold the kingdom together while Jahmil's away doing heaven knows what. Then you vanish. And I came back to—"

Her words dissolved, eyes flashing amber at the scene of horror. She clenched both her fists, and fire erupted bright around them, flame fighting flame. She grabbed their arms and dragged them to where the ratty chair had tipped back against a still-standing stack of books, forming a triangle—an escape with Sezan's djinn fire.

"Go," she cried, then shoved them in front of her.

Evil's angry green roared forward and lit the books in an instant flash of cinders, demolishing their escape.

Zan Hala and Ayelet stood, shielding Serap once more from all the hardness life had to offer. The green-toothed fire rose up as the blue hands and shining, black eyes of Evil took shape before them.

Serap pulled back, fear trembling in her bones, when a cool touch brushed her cheek. She looked at Chupkin, looked into him. And though she couldn't see the shape or features of the person he was, she knew who he was. He was loyal and sweet and cared for her. She swallowed, taking strength from all the years he stayed with her and whatever good things he must see in her, too.

Between his shining light and the horrific face of Evil fully formed before her, something lit up inside Serap, catching her heart afire.

She refused to take it, anymore. Not her family's sacrifice. Not her pathetic self-doubt, nor her paltry excuses and refusal to be grateful for what she did have. She would not let anything happen to the family she loved so much.

For what was forever without them?

Serap crawled out between their feet

"Serap!" Ayelet reached for her.

Serap grabbed Ayelet's hand and gave it a quick kiss. "I don't want to live without you."

Then she dropped it, turned with a soft smile, and threw herself at the green blaze.

Zan Hala blasted a hole in the fire with a burst of rose, leaving nothing for Serap to collide against. The lack of impact sent Serap stumbling straight for the grasping black of waiting hands. Every muscle seized, bracing for torment when a shadowy hole zipped open between her and her fate. The rush of windless wind. An annoyed hiss. A thin green hand with painted purple nails grabbed her shirt and pulled her through.

She expected to tumble and float in a free-fall as she did with Evil, but her face smacked instantly into a wooden table.

Serap thrust herself up, disoriented, and fell off the back and onto the floor with a *thwump*. Her lips throbbed. Her ankle stung. Her lungs cried for air. And her head ached from the very back to the ridge above her nose. When her double-vision unified, she started and fell back, a creepy set of faceless eyes rolling around indignantly before her.

A light green face with a rosebud nose and purple-zinged hair appeared above her, a casual sneer of pearly white shining through her confusion. "Hey, girl."

Serap swiped a hand over her face, the lick of flames still hot on her skin. "What just happened?"

"I saved your butt. I told you worse things were coming, didn't I?"

She bolted upright. "Ayelet. Zan Hala. You left them!"

Pasha waved her hand dismissively. "I'm sure they're fine. He was only there for one thing, and I got it first."

"Get them," Serap demanded. "Save them."

"I can't." Pasha shrugged. "Your wisp is with you, right?"

Serap pushed a hand against her chest. Chupkin shivered just below her sternum, his courage in the face of Evil gone in front of Pasha. She felt only relief and gave him a reassuring stroke.

Then, she pushed up from the ground with shaking hands. "I have to go back."

"The only place you're going, sweetie, is to Ashkult."

"What?"

"Crow's beak." Pasha held her hand out to the side, fingers flippantly loose and her eyebrow raised.

"And why would I go there?"

"To make sure the thing trying to eat your family stops."

"Evil?"

"Khayin."

Serap's ankle gave out, and she fell hard to her knees, pain shooting through her nerves and up to the top of her head. "Khayin is Evil."

Then she laughed bitterly, each sharp chuckle a shard of glass in her brain. How could she have been so stupid? It was gullible enough to fall in love with the altered form of the man who threw her in prison, that becoming friends with the very creature she was trying to kill and who was trying to kill her in return only made sense. Her laughter grew more and more hollow until it racked her chest painfully and without sound.

She placed her forehead on the dirty floor of Pasha's magic shop and dug out the crow's beak. With a heavy sigh, she held it out. After all that had happened, she'd get to face Khayin, after all. Not to kill him; she could not without Don DeMario. But most likely to be killed by him. To save her family, the people who mattered, the people she cared for the most.

A small, painful hope burned inside her, the embers of fire ready to take to flame.

Maybe, just maybe, her brief stint in each of their lives would make her just a bit more beautiful before they forgot her altogether.

Maybe it would make her more beautiful to Javier if she accepted death as he so wanted her to.

CHAPTER THIRTY-SIX

JAVIER

Six massive Ghaluman guards drew open the heavy iron door and led Khayin into the interrogation room. Each red djinn held a heavy wooden rod attached around a gold collar, securing it to the prisoner's neck. They guided him like a dog to the center of the room where they sat him down in a golden chair and strapped in his legs and arms.

Javier had never seen even a picture of Khayin, but the creature before him was everything he expected from the rancid smell. Rubbery, grayish-green skin, long pointed ears that drooped out to the sides, eyes of pure black set in folds of his face like marbles placed on a loaf of moldy bread, and his sharp teeth covered in brown and orange moss.

He had seen a face like Khayin's once before—these were the twisted features of a monster who believed himself above the common experience of death.

Until of course, he didn't anymore.

Serap's soft features flashed through Javier's memory, bright and wholesome before the image of her rosy cheeks and unassuming brown eyes twisted with such ugliness. He clenched a fist, the bite of his katar on the back of his hand helping to clear the vision.

The familiar smell of the voice washed over him, and he wrinkled his nose. Javier fought back the urge to vomit. How long had it been since he'd eaten anything or drank water, or slept? He was running on stores of energy from deep inside his bones, an exhausted, frenetic rhythm to his heart that made his eyes burn and his skin tremble.

The guards released their poles from the bulky collar and filtered out of the interrogation room, shutting and locking the door behind them. King Jahmil stood in the far corner, his arms folded across his chest. His narrowed gaze flicked between the Immortal Traitor and the Immortal Killer.

Javier stepped closer and sat down in a creaky wooden chair set across from Khayin, their knees a few stone tiles apart. Khayin raised his chin and parted his lips, intensifying the revolting stench of his breath.

"At last," he said with a putrid exhalation, "Hades has come for me."

"What have you done with Serap?" Jahmil snapped from the corner.

"Is that your final question?"

Javier shot the king a cold glance. "No. It is my question."

"I have made no such arrangement with you," Khayin quipped, his voice as rusted and befouled as his face. His words came out muffled as if his tongue were swollen and his cheeks filled with rancid saliva.

"The release you have sought for so many years will soon be yours." The corner of Javier's mouth lifted into a sneer. "Provided you do not anger me with riddles. Refuse to answer my questions, and the king has agreed that he will not ask his. Then we will both leave this place, and you will return to your familiar cell for at least another ten years."

"How easily you have made allies." Khayin laughed, turning his gaze between them. "And how easily has noble Zeus forgiven your abuses of his beloved daughter?"

"Abuses?" sneered the king. "What is he talking about?"

Javier shook his head and leaned back in his chair, his gaze never leaving Khayin. The trickster could only be counted on to make things difficult. "You just can't help yourself, can you? Even when your goal is within reach, you would rather stir up resentment than reach for it. Is the joy you take in tormenting others reason enough to live?"

332   KYRO DEAN & LAYA V SMITH

"What abuses?" King Jahmil repeated harshly, stepping across the space to stand beside Javier. "Answer me."

Khayin cocked his head far to one side, gazing into his eyes as he spoke, "As swift and gentle as a rabbit, did the child flee her pursuer, screaming in terror and begging the hunter to relent. As barbarous as he is powerful, the hunter snatched the hare from her burrow and dragged her back to his cave, as cries for mercy fell from her bleeding lips. Keeping her prisoner in his fortress, he showered her with lies until, in her innocence, she succumbed and showered him with her charms, which the hunter then consumed with ravenous appetite until she was left crying softly into the tangled mats of her own hair."

Javier jumped from his chair. "That is not what happened!"

Lighting flashed from the King's eyes. "I'll kill you!"

The djinn balled a fist and swung at his face. Javier tucked his chin so the blow landed on the top of his skull. A swirl of stars formed in his vision. Jahmil hit harder than he'd expected from such a slim, sophisticated djinn.

Javier still hit harder.

When a second punch slammed into the side of his neck, he tucked his shoulders and lunged at the king. He swept his feet, so Jahmil's body flapped to the ground on the flat of his back, his skull slamming hard against the stone floor. Javier moved in to pin him, but the quick king kicked him hard between the legs.

Javier's eyes bulged, a shock of pain racing through him that started in his testicles and radiated out through his entire body with crackles of lighting. The king rolled out from under him and leaped to his feet. Setting one hand on the ground like a racer at the starting line, the king snarled and lunged, spearing him in the gut with his broad shoulders. Javier wrapped an arm over his opponent's torso and spun with the impact, then fell back, holding the djinn's head tight so the top of his skull hit the floor.

The king lurched and twitched, the power of the head injury visibly zipping down the rest of his nerves. Javier clasped him around the throat and raised a fist but stopped with his hand cocked back.

"Listen to me. That is not what happened. The traitor is just trying to goad us."

The king's eyes flashed lightning, sending another crash of thunder to clap against Javier's ears, dazing him.

The king landed another punch in his eye. Javier's grip on his neck loosened.

Guards threw open the door and rushed inside. Two snatched Javier by the arms and pulled him up, their grips as tight as vices. Chain mail gloves dug into his skin. He didn't struggle. Two more guards hefted the spitting and snarling king from the floor and dragged him to the opposite side of the room.

"This interview is over," a fifth guard boomed from the doorway.

"No!" Javier cried. "It has not begun."

"I will not tolerate brawling," the guard snapped.

Javier turned his gaze to the king, whose glowing, white eyes were swirling with fury. "Is this what you want? If we get thrown out, we will never know what happened to Serap."

He growled, baring his teeth. "You are a monster. Why should I believe anything you say?"

"Why should you believe anything he says?" Javier snapped, jutting his chin at the traitor.

Khayin's cruel chuckle snaked through the room, growing like an impending storm until it filled the space. "The Throne of Olympus battles the Throne of Tartarus, each fighting for the honor of a lady who has forsaken them both." His laughter redoubled until he leaned over his knees, his inhalations scraping and frantic. "What fools these mortals be!"

Javier puffed up his chest and threw off the guards in a single thrust, then stomped across the room and slapped Khayin's face so hard that the golden chair toppled over and crashed to the floor.

"Where is she?"

Khayin coughed, black blood trickling from his lips. "The rabbit has chosen the bear."

"Enough with your rabbits." Javier kicked him in the stomach. "Speak plainly."

"It is irony, all of that," Khayin rasped. "For she has scurried into the trap laid for her, into the very mouth of *true* evil. As evil sent her to you, so shall evil take everything from us all."

Javier kicked him in the face. Several cracked brown teeth scattered across the floor. "How do I get her back?"

Khayin coughed out a lump of gray, followed by droplets of blood. "The foolish rabbit runs towards her own death."

"Death?" Jahmil echoed.

Javier grabbed the chair and righted it, then leaned down into Khayin's face. "What death?"

"To be beautiful to her Hades, she will dwell in the land of death for all time."

What was left of Javier's heart cracked open. The words the stately djinn woman had snarled into his face as she clenched his cheeks in her hands leapt into his mind.

Serap does not hate you, she had said, and, perhaps, she knew. *She yearns for you.*

Yearns. That was the word she had used. But was such a thing possible? That a soul such as hers could yearn for his, even now? That Serap could yet feel some small flicker of love, hidden in the darkness of a brooding pool of hatred and self-pity?

If you are too cowardly to show her you feel the same, then go dwell in Hades forever. But know that she is already there, and only you have the power to bring her out.

Javier tightened his hold on the now-bent chair. Perhaps, there was still hope if he could repair himself in her eyes by giving her the gift she so desperately wanted.

"Tell me the answer to Serap's question," he said in Spanish, knowing that only Khayin would understand. "How can she become immortal without having to suffer the consequences of pain and ugliness?"

"Death is not the greatest of evils. It is worse to yearn for death and not be able to die."

"That is not what I asked," Javier growled.

"Release me," snapped the king, yanking himself free of the guard's grasp with a heaving shake. "*Tahadath bialearabia.* What are you saying to him, you filth?"

Khayin lifted his gaze to Javier's. "How weak you are to force such a fate on an innocent rabbit."

"She is not a rabbit, you condescending, double-talking piece of magic trash. She is not a child. And she is not Persephone. She is only Serap. She wants what she wants, and I..." He trailed off, his tongue heavy in his mouth. "I will give it to her."

"It will mean your own death."

Javier swallowed the bile in his throat. "Even better."

Khayin cackled before spitting up more blood. "As you wish. And since this question is for the benefit of the King's daughter, I will count it as the King's question. After I answer, you will perform the promised deed, forthwith."

Javier's brow twitched, his gaze darting to the figure of Jahmil whose face still purpled with fury. The djinn king could not possibly hate him more.

He looked back at the black, limpid eyes of Khayin. "I will kill you. I promise."

"As you killed the one I loved." The gray face softened and the black eyes filled with ruddy light. "Thank you."

In that instant, those black mirrors filled with gray mist. Pictures flickered across the slick surface, and Javier took them, each image imprinting an entire novel's-worth of information into his brain. Serap's answer was not so complicated. It was magnificently simple, in fact. Though, it would not be easy.

When the images subsided, Khayin blinked. Javier's gaze refocused on the entirety of the face. In it, he recognized an expression of both hope and desperation.

The cruel mirth left the traitor's face. "Now, it is your turn."

Javier nodded and leaned forward. He plunged his katar into the emaciated stomach of the Immortal Traitor. Khayin's eyes bulged, and his lips twisted into a smile. A gasp of pain and pure joy fell from the cracked, rubbery lips.

The guards and King Jahmil rushed closer. Javier finished the job, drawing the blade across the stomach, spilling Khayin's bowels.

"Die well, Faris Khayin," he whispered.

Sometimes Javier wished there was more flash to his gift. A light or a sound when he killed, anything to show that the magic of the Bahamut was at work and that a soul was being set free. But no matter how old or how powerful his victim, death—the greatest transference of energy possible—remained both silent and common.

Khayin fell over himself, gagging and wriggling in pain. He laughed hysterically with every breath left to him.

The guards drew their black blades and rushed Javier. He snatched the waterskin from his hip and poured a splash of quicksilver into his hand.

"Stay back!"

Every djinn in the room drew back in fear. Javier flicked a few drops in front of him. The guards all moved back.

King Jahmil's expressive eyes flashed yet again, then simmered with copper. "I will be the death of you, Immortal Killer."

"Get in line." Javier flicked some silver at him, which the king narrowly dodged, then darted from the chamber into the suffocating halls of the prison. Guards rushed him, but a smattering of the lake's tears kept them back.

Javier made it outside and leapt into the boat, quicksilver sloshing over the sides and frightening the fat ferryman so that he jumped to the safety of the shore. Javier took up the paddle and pushed off into the lake. His powerful arms and shoulders propelled him quickly through the waters, his human skin immune to the effects of the thick liquid as it sloshed into the boat. Guards rushed to the dock, bows and arrows in hand. Javier lifted the paddle from the lake, careful to gather a large scoop at the end, and tossed it towards the dock. The guards screamed and scattered. By the time they had regrouped, he was out of range.

When he reached the shore, he leapt out of the boat onto the stinging white sands. Then he spoke the words to bring up his mirror and disappeared into the mist.

CHAPTER THIRTY-SEVEN

SERAP

Serap never had figured out how magic could pull beings between worlds faster than a blink of an eye. Perhaps, it was because she had no fire or gift of her own, but the movement between the fabric of space always left her queasy. So when she landed with Pasha in a dank hallway that smelled of human waste and rotting flesh, she nearly lost her stomach.

Chupkin pulled around her waist in gentle circles to keep her from keening.

Pasha did not seem to share her qualms. As soon as their feet touched moist rock, she released her grip on Serap's arm and darted forward into the cell. A screech erupted from her throat, followed by vitriolic cursing that sent Chupkin diving for cover in Serap's hair.

"That immortal-killing leach! That life-sucking parasite! I was owed a question. An answer! And he stole it from me!"

The tiny room wore a rough dress of thick gray stone laced with iron, silver, and gold. Serap's eyes refocused in the dimly-lit gloom. Her stomach curdled at the revolting body of a djinn prostrate on the floor, his hands still bound to a golden chair and bleeding glops of congealed, pitchy blood.

The fading creature's eyes flicked to hers, and a horribly recognizable grin surfaced on his thin lips. "Persephone, silly child."

"Evil?" she inhaled and gagged. "Khayin."

It was strange to hear his voice in person instead of in the silence between breaths that lingered in a room. And while his ugly, molding body repulsed her, she crept forward. After all he had done—the visions, and gifts, and the last act of rage—she still had a strange familiarity with him. A longing to return and an unwillingness to leave. Like when a toddler reaches for her mother's breast the last time, and then pulls away confused, awareness replacing innocence and instinct.

The sound of angry men sounded from deep within the hallways of Ashkult. Guards? Were they headed to this room because of what happened to Khayin? What *had* happened to Khayin?

"He speaks," Pasha gasped, shoving Serap aside as she flung herself toward the traitor. "Tell me the secret to immortality," she said, spit dribbling from her chin as she yanked at Khayin's spoiling black cloak.

"You forget that I yet live, witch." He sneered cruelly, blood leaking from where several mossy teeth had been knocked free, marring his gums. "Step back," he gurgled, "or my last breath will be to end you."

Pasha hissed and stood, raking Serap's neck painfully as she retreated. Serap gasped and pulled away. With a glare, she moved next to Evil.

"Why did you give me that book?"

"To reveal the bear." His inky black eyes darted to Pasha. "To show what it wants and what it has the power to do."

Evil's telling glance fizzled inside her. Serap had suspected before Khayin had said a thing that Pasha carried a far larger role in all this. She crouched and shuffled as close as she could stand in the face of such putrid smells. The closer she drew to the horrendous man, the tighter a ball Chupkin made himself, pressing against her skin. But she had to get the answers before the growing din of guards in the prison grew louder and pulled her away. Not again. Not when she was so close to finishing her quest. And not when so much weighed upon her mind.

"Why did you have me release the queen?"

"To free her from her suffering."

His words wrapped like leather straps around her stomach, cinching it tighter. "That can't be the only reason. Everything you do is a game."

"Because I loved her." His chest seized, and his body twitched in waves of agony, eyes rolling back into his head. When his limbs finally settled, his gaze flickered back to her. "I found her in her prison while traversing the plains between worlds. Hers was a beautiful soul that never ceased to suffer. We were separated, my powers no match for the pure djinn power of the King of Elm. I was expelled. She remained. Her death was a gift, all I could offer her in the end."

Serap snapped her teeth together and ground them so they crunched.

"The Immortal Killer did this to you, didn't he?" she asked, anger rising up in the back of her throat.

Khayin nodded once.

Air sliced through her lungs in a sharp inhale, only the pounding of boots keeping her grounded in reality, a warning that her time for answers was up. Don DeMario had solidly refused her proposition for help and then fulfilled the request without her. Out of spite? To make sure she could not follow what he deemed her childish folly? She wrapped her fingers tight into themselves.

"And King Jahmil's final question?"

Khayin chuckled, drops of blood splattering out between the gaps in his teeth. "Stolen by the hunter."

Serap punched her hand against the stone. She felt no pain but pulled her hand back with the odorous stick of Khayin's blood. "Where is he now?"

"It is thanks to you, Persephone, that death has come for me at last. So I will answer." Air scratched inside Khayin's chest, bubbling out in horrible pops from deep inside his throat. "He has gone to the Bahamut. Once upon its gaping maw, a soul must enter. Beware lest the bear arrives there, too, and plunges the worlds into darkness."

His dark gaze once more slid to Pasha, then he turned back to Serap.

"I have died as I have lived." His whole body quivered, and the shine in his eyes dimmed. "For far too long."

The last of his raking breaths left his chest.

Serap shivered as Chupkin slid down her back and hid under her armpit. Evil was gone. Why did she feel sad?

Pasha's angry growls turned into pointed laughter. A dark glow, like rainbow fires mixing with black, rose up from Khayin's smoldering body. The cold colors blew through her and upon Pasha.

The witch raised her fists, a triumphant sneer upon her lips as the muddied power soaked into her skin. Her laughter filled the prison and echoed beyond them.

Serap stumbled to her feet and turned to face the glowing witch.

"What did you do?"

"Received my birthright, sweetie." She flashed luminescent teeth.

The truths Evil had tried to warn her about in his dark and twisted way clarified in an instant.

Pasha was the bear.

Pasha was the lost descendant squirreled away from Khayin's line, in hiding and waiting to receive all his powers when the immortal being finally died.

Pasha was the monster.

"You used me," Serap said, stepping back. "From the start. You suggested I kill Khayin so you could take his powers."

Pasha's rage over Khayin death resurfaced, the fuzzy parts of the picture solidifying.

"And you wanted my question, too."

"Bingo." Pasha raised the crow's beak she carried on her wrist. "You were fantastic, by the way, though I'm upset you didn't leave the house and come when my whirlwind called you. We could have been here in time. But you can make it up to me."

"What more could you possibly want from me?" Serap asked, exasperation breathy in her voice. "I've done everything you've tricked me into doing."

"I want you to come and talk to your boyfriend with me."

"I don't have a boyfriend." She clenched her teeth as a dull ache filled her lungs. A bitter regret. "I'm not going anywhere with you." Serap scooted her way toward a dark doorway at the end of the room.

She had no idea where she was other than the soul-sucking prison of Ashkult, but anywhere else was better than here with Pasha. Chupkin agreed, poking out the end of her outstretched sleeve to light the way.

The witch smirked, the wrinkles around her eyes tight. "Would you prefer I call him your captor? Your hunter? Your Hades? Your husband? Don't be like that. I said I wouldn't let you get horribly hurt, and I've kept my word. You were about to barge into Khayin's flames, and I plucked you right up. You're welcome, by the way."

"You didn't do that for me; you did it for your precious teleporting bird head."

The distant ring of alarmed guards and angry prisoners percolated down the hallway.

What would happen if they found her? A human girl with no business being there, standing with a witch and a dead body? She couldn't help but ache for the simple days when her biggest threat was idiot suitors. After everything that had happened, she begged for them.

Her innocence was gone, given willingly and eagerly into the hands of a thief. And she would never get that back. But as much as that hurt, she didn't regret it. Not when she could still feel the brush of his gaze on her cheeks, his breath on her lips, or the strength in his kiss.

No... even though she still burned with hurt and anger, she didn't regret being wrapped in his arms. How capable he made her feel when her name was on his lips or how vulnerable she felt when his lips were on her own.

"Oh, sweet, unsure, little Serap," Pasha sneered. "I thought you wanted to be helpful? If that dead old goat on the floor was telling the truth, then the Immortal Killer awaits at my current destination with information I need. You know how much of a pill he can be. I need a little assurance that he won't cause me any trouble."

"You want to use me as leverage?" Serap scoffed. "You'll be sorely disappointed to learn that he fancies me dead as much as he does alive. Maybe more. He embraces death and has no qualms when innocents die."

Pasha's mouth broke out in an uneven smile, her pink eyes flashing with hints of green and amber, envy and disgust. "Then you'll be fine coming along with me to test that theory. On my honor as the Eternal Witch of Finding, if he doesn't try to save you, I won't harm either of you and will leave without complaint."

Serap recoiled at the thought. Her fate would be the same either way. If he tried to save her, Pasha would kill one or both of them. And if he didn't, her heart would finish breaking, which would be a pain worse than death. That thought dug deep into her core.

Pasha smirked and popped her lips. "Don't make me ask again." She held out her bony fingers, black blood speckling her purple nails. "I'm not a patient witch. You don't want to see what I'll do if I get mad."

Chupkin quivered against her belly button, the uneven pulse of his light visible through her shirt. Under the acrid spit of Pasha's threat, another realization clicked inside Serap's mind.

Pasha was the missing genealogical line. The line that could turn people into wisps. And she had found Chupkin in her shop.

"Is that what Chupkin did to get turned into a wisp?" She crossed her arms and raised her chin. "Made you wait?"

The smirk on Pasha's thin lips faded. "Let's just say the brat had it coming."

Serap's lungs tightened, the cold sweat of fear and an angry, bubbling fire colliding within her. "Turn him back."

"No."

"Turn him back, or I won't go."

Pasha rolled her eyes. "I don't need your permission. Haven't you noticed? People can make you do whatever they want. You're weak. Pathetic. And what did that boy say? Ah, yes, *readily suggestible.*"

Heat spidered over Serap's neck and cheeks. Did everyone see her the same way as Paco and Pasha? Never again.

The shouts of guards picked up in the hallway behind them. Pasha's eyes darted to the doorway. Serap bit her lip. Then, she pulled back her shoulders and stepped toward the door.

She tilted her chin up and looked Pasha in the eye. "Change him back, or I'll run. And then the guards will have me. I know that crow's beak takes you in and out of this place, but your magic is limited here, and you are not as practiced and powerful as Evil Khayin. You won't be able to free me from their hold, which means you'd have to face the Immortal Killer on your own. How easily do you think he can cut through mortal flesh when his blade is meant for the unslayable?"

"You'd stay here in this awful place to be tortured until your swift, inevitable death?" Pasha scoffed.

"Yep."

"What of your quest for longevity?"

"Pointless if I can't save the ones I love."

Pasha stared at her, breath growing heavy. Serap stared back, a new sense of power taking a place in her heart, however fleeting.

At last, Pasha broke with a snarl, her eyebrows crunching together in dark green lines. "Fine. I will return the disgusting little wisp to his human form as soon as I am free of the Immortal Killer's grasp at the mouth of the Bahamut."

"Swear on your fancy witch title."

"A swear?" Pasha sneered. "What is this, kiddie play time?"

"If you're a witch of Eternal anything, your power comes from the stars. And from what I understand of the Celestials, swearing anything on their name is binding."

Pasha's lips twitched.

Serap smiled, cold and unfamiliar.

"Fine," Pasha muscled out through clenched teeth, "I swear as the Witch of Eternal Finding that I will turn him back when I have arrived safely at my destination without the Immortal Killer on my trail."

The clatter of guards was almost upon them. Serap's heart beat in her throat. She was crazy following Pasha to the Bahamut, she knew that. But there was little choice left in the matter. She needed to make things right and follow things through. For Chupkin. And for Javier, too. But not just to see if what Pasha said was true about him saving her. She wanted to warn him about Pasha's powers, concerned for the life of the mortal Immortal Killer.

Serap shivered. Most of all, she wanted to show him she could be brave about death, just like he wanted.

Chupkin poked his head up by her neck and gave her a *you-don't-have-to-do-this-for-me* pat that poured the honey of courage into her soul.

She brushed his glittering, pulsing back and nodded resolutely at Pasha.

"Deal."

Pasha cackled and ripped a black tear in the space between them. "Babies first."

Serap winced and stepped toward the black.

"Serap?" a painfully familiar voice called to her from the doorway.

The weight of a thousand moons crashed into her lungs.

She whipped her head around and clutched at her heart, fingers squishing straight through Chupkin. "'Abi?"

"What are you doing here?" He looked tired, his face bloody and his usually luminous blue skin ashen and gray.

A desire to fling her arms around him and hide in his strength flooded through her. The glint of purple, white, and blue shone haggard in his diamond eyes. Sorrow, anger, hope. It was too much to see, knowing she had placed it there. But she couldn't return to him. Not yet.

She stiffened her arms and fought the urge, taking a step back. "I'm sorry, I have to go."

"Wait," 'Abi Jahmil called, reaching for her.

"I'm sorry," she said again, a pathetic offering for all she had done. She was sure it crushed his heart as much as it did hers. "I can't. I can't let you do things for me anymore."

Pasha snickered behind her, driving a nail into her temples. But it didn't change what she had to do. She tried to think of something she could tell the only father she had ever known to help him forget her. Something that would make him stay and not follow or rage about, alone in a prison full of death.

"Serap, wait," Jahmil reached out, his face broken with pain as clear as the First Moon's break on the horizon.

She forced her eyes to his, her hands trembling. "Go to the Immortal Killer's house with Bakr Amca. Ayelet and Zan Hala need you."

Then she snatched Pasha's cold hand and leapt between worlds, leaving behind a broken bond between father and daughter.

CHAPTER THIRTY-EIGHT

JAVIER

Beautiful Jasraib—white sands that changed in iridescence with the rising of each moon, crystal blue water filled with luminescent fish so it glowed brighter than the sky, a thousand colors of shimmering palms.

Birds with wings of starlight sailed the trees, and turtles with mirrored shells shuffled across sand so fine it squished like white flour underfoot. The brightest, most brilliant land in all of Qaf, no question. And the land he had spent the most time in since the archipelago of the visible kingdom was located in the Sea of Bahamut.

Standing here, it was tempting to forget that the water he was looking at was not ordinary water, but the entrance into both the edges of this world and the beginning of a new plane of existence. A plane where immortals the size of stars floated through dimensions that the eyes of humans and djinn could not perceive.

Jasraib was the end of the known Qafian world and the beginning of Bahamut. Home to the equally beautiful and elusive *baharia*—djinn of the water—with their shimmering metallic skin, amphibious fishtails, and secretive nature.

The first time Javier found the Bahamut had been after four years of sailing these mysterious and deadly waters. He could ill-afford to take the same path now. This beach was as close as the mirror would bring him.

There were some fringe advantages to the line of work he'd entered into since then, not the least of which was that many of the most powerful djinn in Qaf owed him favors. Two years ago, the Sultan of the Jasraib, Sidi Moussa, had come to him and asked for his help in slaying the *wahash bahriun 'usturiun*—a squid the size of a city with a beak sharp enough to crush diamond—that had been tormenting his borders. As an honorarium, the Sultan had offered a singular promise.

Javier didn't usually accept IOUs, but the Sultan of Jasraib did not owe very many people favors. It was worth more than gold.

With a deep breath, Javier closed his eyes and spoke the words the Sultan had told him: "*Taealaa li*, Sidi Moussa. *Ana muhtaj.*"

He waited, the salty breeze wetting his face and drying his lips until the water before him bubbled. The heads of four sharks, each the size of a large bull, broke the surface. Their eyes shined a disconcerting red, and a series of fins ran down their backs like points on a dragon, gaping mouths overstuffed with teeth as long and sharp as daggers. A chariot emerged behind it, the black shell of some massive mollusk, glimmering with diamonds and luminescent starfish. And at the forefront, with seaweed reins in his hand, was a man with skin that shined like silver. His black beard hung down to his waist, his torso unclothed so that his bulging muscles caught the light of the sea as well as the moons. His fishtail curled under him, bright white, covered with dozens of sharp fins, as long as Javier's own body.

The Sultan of Jasraib, King of the Baharia and all creatures in their sacred waters, maneuvered his chariot nearer to the shore. The imposing and stern figure raised a hand in welcome. Javier took a running leap to jump aboard, the water splashing over his legs when he landed.

"Don DeMario." Moussa hit a clenched fist to his chest, his voice deep and clear. "*As-salam Alaikum*"

"*Wa 'alaikum-as-salam*," said Javier respectfully. "I have come to call in my favor."

"Of course. It is my honor to fulfill my obligation, *shaqiq*. What is your destination in my kingdom?"

"The Bahamut."

The Sultan lowered his gaze and pressed a palm to his forehead. "*Bismillāhir rahmān ir rahīm.*" *In the name of Allah, the most gracious, the most merciful.*

"Will you take me?"

The Sultan's glowing blue eyes met his, their expression solemn, almost worship-ful. "The baharia never commit to a promise we would not fulfill, for hearts build lives on promises, and broken promises are the gateway to sin."

"Indeed." Javier twitched at the sultan's well-intentioned words of promises and sin, truth and lies.

"And you of all men know the gravity and the danger of the creature which you seek."

"I do."

"*Alhamdu lillāhi rabbil ᶜālamīna.* There is such resolve in your eyes, *shaqīq.* I fear even the falling of the First Moon could not dissuade you."

"No."

"Then we shall do away with words, and I will take you to your quarry. Though I cannot linger in such waters."

"I do not ask your help to bring me back."

The Sultan raised a feathered brow before nodding. He lifted his hand, speaking words under his breath in the secret language of the baharia, and a tendril of white fire shimmered from his fingertips. When next Javier drew breath, the fire was pulled into his lungs, opening and expanding them. The wind of the Second Moon, Javier knew from his battle with *wahash bahriun 'usturiun.* Three hours of breath granted to him by the ocean so he need not come up for air.

The Sultan flicked the reins of his chariot, and they dove under the water. Javier glanced down, hoping to catch a glimpse of one of Jasraib's glimmering cities, but they were already on the outskirts of the underwater kingdom. Tremendous Sev-en-Tongued Sharks swam at great speed, pulling them deep into the luminescent ocean. Javier stood straight against the powerful current, watching the water bubble all around him. They passed beyond the glimmering water and into the stark dark-ness of Bahamut.

For an instant, his resolve faltered, and he allowed himself a brief moment of abject self-pity. Why did she need this? Why could his love not be enough?

His lungs were beginning to burn for want of a breath when the Sultan turned his chariot towards the surface. The sharks broke through first, creating a bubble that moved over them before the heavy chariot burst through the top of the dark water.

He gazed at the dark, formless sky, vaguely shimmering in iridescent shades like the surface of an opal, and a chill ran through his bones. It was no sky. The entirety of the horizon was filled by the impossibly vast body of the Bahamut.

"Thank you," Javier said.

The Sultan put a hand on his chest.

"Take one of my steeds," he said, then snatched a bone knife up from inside the chariot and cut the ropes that hitched one of the massive, terrifying sharks.

"Will it allow me to ride?"

The Sultan nodded slowly. "*Fi Amanillah.*"

"Thank you." The freed shark swam up beside the carriage, and Javier hopped down onto its back.

He managed an awkward grip of the beast between his thighs and held tight to one of the sharp fins. The Sultan nodded again, fist once more on his chest. With a final lingering glance at the shimmer before him, Javier reared the chariot around and dipped back under the water, disappearing from sight as quickly as he had come.

It took a few moments of swirling blue and turquoise and cream for Javier to get his bearings. He watched the water, looking for the natural flow of the current to try to determine which way the Bahamut was moving. Decided, he urged the shark to follow the strange arc of the non-sky. The mount responded to him quickly and easily, skimming the surface as it swam so he was not submerged. However, the sandpaper fins fomented the waves into a steady churn that splashed upon him, making it difficult for him to catch a breath.

He had not been seeking the Bahamut when he first found her, floating aimlessly on his unmasked raft, waiting for hunger or thirst to separate his soul from his body. Darkness had simply overcome him. Death, he thought at first, but soon he was moving through a massive, pink hall until he found himself standing on a carpet of guts and gazing up at ribs like ceiling beams—higher and more spacious than the most glorious building he ever could have imagined. And there, trapped and warm, screaming into a muted nothing, his body had wasted away to the very edge of nothing.

That's when she came to him, the very breath of divinity. An angel, perhaps. Javier had not been able to lift his eyes to look at her, her light so consumed him. And then she had spoken his name.

Hands of pure light had wrapped around him and lifted him into a soft embrace. She had said his name again, and that time, he had heard the warning in his heart. Her shining face before him was so bright he could not perceive it, making him the offer. The curse. The test of all time cloaked in the softness of her voice. He had not managed to squeak out a single syllable but had found the strength to shake his head and pull away from her.

Her light had consumed him.

He had awakened back on his raft. Whole, healthy, as young and spry as he ever had been. And her message was implanted in his soul. She had created him as something new, something with a power that would be needed and despised, a power to balance her own, if but for a time. A power that had never existed in the world before. For while she was a curse in the guise of an angel, he would be a blessing in the clothes of a monster.

If the only option for giving Serap what she desired had been to place her before the Eternal One, he would have refused. The Bahamut's promise of eternity was a sentence of pain and aching—an opportunity to be reviled and despised and unable to find an end. A punishment fitting for a creature that so feared the Divine's plan, it flew in the face of it.

The desire for immortality was a sin of arrogance and fear.

But that was not the only option. There was a way to spare Serap that fate, to absorb the consequences and absolve her from punishment. A way to offer himself as the sacrifice.

He sighed deeply within his chest, remembering her honeyed eyes and gentle smile. After one thousand years, or three, or six, when at last she grew tired of life, would Serap look back and remember him?

Darkness rose on the horizon, a sunrise moving in reverse. The moment had come. He braced himself and closed his eyes.

One cantankerous man.

One sacrifice to the divine.

One wounded heart to cease its beating.

And perhaps, the smile that he had broken would be mended.

CHAPTER THIRTY-NINE

SERAP

Serap and Pasha zipped from ethereal place to ethereal place. Black depths of swirling galaxies shimmered into the navy blue of evening skies, then brightened into white light that made her squint and shelter her eyes with her hands. At one point, they fell through a sky that glittered with rivers of green lights, then ran through silky nothing as two suns crossed her vision.

"How?" she managed to gasp as shooting stars streamed about her in a sky of charcoal gray.

"Ursa Major." Pasha shrugged. "It is how I became the Witch of Eternal Finding. I struck a deal with the constellation so she would lead me, light to light and star to star, wherever I need to go. Though, each find has its price."

The streaking light of falling stars hit unseen earth and bloomed into an orange haze around them. Serap held her breath, but there was no need. Wherever they were, whatever they saw, it did not affect their bodies, though it stretched and pulled at her mind.

"Price?" The word felt like an unripe persimmon in her mouth, making her lips pucker. "What price do you pay this time?"

Pasha looked at her sideways. "Hmm? Oh, it's different every time. The harder something is to find, the bigger the price. It is why my finding fees are so high. Sure, sometimes the fiery immortals of the galaxies just want power, a taste of emotion, or odd magical trinkets. Once, Hercules asked for snow from the highest peak in Zabriya and the kiss of a woman." She smirked. "But other times, they want something far more serious. Pain, death, innocence."

The witch's words sent chills spidering through Serap's veins, despite the sparkling fire of the stars that encompassed them.

"How hard to find is the Bahamut?"

"Very hard when you're trying to time your arrival with its location and that of another."

"And how long do you have to pay your price?"

Pasha surveyed her nails, flicking off a speck of dust. "A full cycle of the First Moon from the first offer to find, or a quarter turn after the finding. Whichever is sooner."

Serap swallowed sticky spit. "And if you don't?"

"Servitude." Pasha shrugged, but her lips twisted into a grimace. "And let me tell you, playing slave to the stars is not as glamorous as it sounds. I missed the delivery time for an egg of a particularly barb-finned baharian princess by two degrees once—a minor fee for helping me find an ex-boyfriend so I could destroy his life—and was forced to do their bidding for a decade." Pasha's thin frame twitched. "Never again, sweetie. Now, I always make sure I get what I need to pay the price, no matter what."

Serap clamped her jaw tighter and tighter until each individual tooth begged for mercy. A plan and a price Pasha was willing to pay no matter what. Serap had been a fool once again, thinking only of the next step and not of the fifty after that. What had she walked into? Worse, what had she put at risk by coming at all?

She prayed to Allah, asking that Pasha be wrong, that Javier wished her dead and would not fight for her. That he would let her go as he had so easily done before. Or that he would not be there at all. But she struggled to form the words on her mind's tongue. Why would Javier go to the Bahamut as Khayin said? What could have driven him to deal with the blessing he called a curse? Was he so determined to stop her that he would slay the Bahamut? Was that even possible?

"Ah ha!" Pasha snapped her finger. "Found it."

The last of a spinning planet cloaked in translucent rings of purple and yellow swept past them, and their pace increased. Whether from above or below, she could not tell, but they came in from the sky like a comet. And on the waves below, before a twinkling sky clouded with darkness, balanced on the back of a shark, stood Don DeMario.

Javier, she forced herself to think his name. To accept the intimacy that had bonded them together for a beautiful, agonizing moment. To accept what he meant to her even if she was nothing to him but a silly, foolish child.

His silhouette was as strong and sure against the glowing sea as when he fought the *arak hunak* for her. When he cooked for her in the kitchen with a hum and swaying hips. And when he pulled her close to him and they breathed each other's breath.

"Just as I suspected." Pasha smirked. "Come, little Serap. Let us see how much your Don DeMario does not care."

Serap tensed, and she scooted herself behind Pasha's lithe frame as they blasted to a halt beside him. She held her breath, expecting to splash into the cold, gray waves, but a smooth circular platform that shone like obsidian formed between her and the ocean, sparking flames of yellow and green and blue that shot up from around the edges. The sky rapidly descended from light to dark, and a great moaning shook her body even though the air about them maintained a prickly silence.

"Javier Don DeMario. Immortal Killer," Pasha said with an aggrandizing flourish. "I have something to show you."

He turned, and his eyebrows drew together into hard lines.

His voice floated across the *shashoosh* of waves. "Serap?"

She winced, unable to look him in the eye. Maybe if she were cold to him, unkind, he would wish her dead and spare them both Pasha's wrath.

"Well, go on." Pasha used her sharp elbow to shove Serap forward.

Serap scowled at the witch and looked to her feet. To the sky. To the quickly approaching doom on the horizon. Khayin said once the Bahamut arrived, a soul must enter. Who would it be?

"Why are you here?" she asked, at last, forcing her lips flat despite how each heavy beat of her heart pulled their edges down.

"To see the Eternal One."

Her hands fidgeted nervously against her pants. "You have already seen her. It seems a fool's mission to come again. Or have you come to laugh at her also?"

He looked down and shook his head.

Unbidden and cruel, her heart pinched in the way it did only for him. She could not stand to see the sadness on his face, could not stand not knowing why he felt so in the first place. But she couldn't ask. She couldn't bear to hear the answer she so desperately wanted, and feared she'd hear the answer she didn't want at all.

"Please," he said, his gaze still downcast into the inky water. "Please spare me your hatred. I need no reminders of it. And please, spare yourself this journey. There is no need for it. You shall have everything your heart desires, I promise. I have accepted your proposal."

Sweat broke out across her palms and chilled her back. "What?" Then she shook her head and glanced at the grin growing on Pasha's face. "Leave. Go home, Immortal Killer. I rescind my proposal. I want no—" A ball of pain stuck in her throat and choked out the words. She swallowed it down. "I want nothing from you."

"But you shall receive it, nonetheless. And perhaps in the fullness of eternity, you will again think fondly of me, however rarely."

"Eternity?" Serap blinked. For the first time, the word sounded like poison.

Pasha giggled, her voice like bubbling lava. "Are you saying, my debonair Don DeMario, that you plan to save Serap from her very mortality?" She turned to Serap. "I definitely won this bet. Sucks for you."

"You're wrong. He does not mean to save me from mortality. He cannot. It is against his very being. Against nature. He said so himself." She wanted to turn beseeching eyes upon him but felt sick at the thought of what she might find.

"And yet, Hades seeks for you eternal living," Pasha sneered gleefully. "His very kingdom for his dear Persephone, and without him in it."

"I know your voice..." Javier's eyes shifted from the water to Pasha and Serap. "You're that witch, aren't you? The one in my house. The one that turned Zayne into a wisp."

Chupkin stirred within Serap's shirt in a flurry of movement, then coalesced in a tight ball under her shoulder blade.

Serap glanced between Pasha and Javier, her knees shaking. She should continue de-ribbing her soul, pushing Javier further away until she folded in upon herself. But her curiosity was an insatiable monster.

She tried thrice to speak and found only a name. "Zayne?"

Pasha waved her hand dismissively. "The wisp you were whining about earlier. Though I'm curious how you came about that information." She narrowed her eyes, then snapped. "It was when you were deceiving poor Serap as a plushy bit of magic, wasn't it?"

Javier turned tired eyes on Serap. "Is this witch holding you against your will?"

Serap's eyes widened. Would he kill Pasha if she said yes? Could he? Or would Pasha kill him now that she flowed with the power of the stars and all the gifts of Khayin? She froze, degrees ticking by in the fading light. Then she shook her head slowly. Chupkin—*Zayne?*—burst from her shirt in a tizzy, whipping towards Don DeMario and tugging at his shirt.

"Chupkin, stop!"

"Slow down." Don DeMario's eyes followed the ball of light. "I can't understand you... She what? The witch?"

"Are you talking to him?" Serap retreated, looking between the two.

"But how? Who is she?"

Pasha groaned. "You have always been a thorn in my side, you know that?" She shot a ball of lime fire at Chupkin. The little wisp... no, person... slipped into DeMario's pocket to hide.

"Khayin...?" Don DeMario narrowed his eyes at Pasha.

"Fantastically dead, thanks to you," the witch chuckled. "Though you could have waited until I showed up. Still, it seems you and I had the same question, so I'll forgive that rugged face of yours. I do, after all, owe you for my recent expansion of magic."

Javier grunted. "I thought knowledge of the Eternal One was common knowledge in magical circles. Or are you generally disliked by other witches?"

Serap cringed. If Pasha flew into a murderous rage, he would probably be fine, but she had no idea how to fight anyone. And then she would be dead.

"All witches dislike other witches." Pasha smirched. "But how would you know that? You're just some self-loathing commoner so lonely, you turned away Allah's greatest gift. Still, I'm not so stupid as to accept the kiss of the Bahamut to gain eternal life. Did you see Khayin when he died? Disgusting. I don't want to look like that. Do you, Serap?"

She shrunk, unsure of how to help the situation and desperate to do just that. All she wanted in that moment was to help Chup—Zayne and Javier live as themselves. If being here and enduring this would allow for those things, then she would endure. All she had to do was get Javier to leave Pasha alone.

"You already look disgusting," Javier sneered.

Pasha bared her teeth.

"And I've known a lot of chatty witches. You must not be invited to their parties." He let his head fall lazily to one side. "But if you didn't come for the Kiss, then why are you here?"

"For unblemished eternal life. Something whispered of only in the corners of the universes. I stumbled upon it when searching the stars and thought I'd ask Khayin how to make it so. But then you showed up, and I found my answer. I always do, you see. It is not a *how* at all. But a who." She smiled widely and tossed her shoulders back. "I've come to accept your sacrifice."

"Sacrifice?" Serap ran a hand over her cheek, cold on hot and utterly unhelpful. "What are you talking about?"

"And if I refuse?" Javier asked.

"Why do you think I brought an innocent?" Pasha snaked her arms around Serap's shoulders and squeezed. "Well, *your* innocent? Though if you don't care for her, I may have miscalculated. You see, she assured me in no small terms of your desire for her to die. An interesting way to woo a young lady, don't you think?"

He shrugged. "I fear I have been misquoted. Catastrophically so."

Serap folded into herself. She needed to do something. Anything. But what? She bit her lip hard and thought.

Javier rolled his shoulders and looked Pasha in the eye. "And if I allow you to sacrifice my life to your futile and blasphemous endeavor, you will let Serap go free?"

"No!" Serap cried, clutching at her heart. "What are you talking about?"

"Sure," Pasha said, a cloudy gleam in her pink eyes. "She'll be free."

The Bahamut's roar grew so loud that Serap clasped her hands to her ears. It did nothing to quell the resonating chaos. Darkness stole the light completely, and a wavy haze overtook them. Soft mist over gentle waves became shiny scales, each the size of a grown man, opaque and translucent at the same time.

The sea and sky trembled around them. The witch flinched and cast an annoyed glare across the pitch of waves. The ghostly Bahamut approached, as large as an island and ten times larger still. Javier, meanwhile, stood immovable, his shoulders taut, the last of the moonlight at his back, and eyes of hate upon the witch.

"The mouth of Bahamut awaits," Pasha said.

He closed his eyes and took a shaking breath. "Swear that you will take Serap from this place and allow her to live her life unassailed. Swear that you will never interfere with her again."

"I said no." Serap ran to the edge of the slick platform and met his eyes for the first time since she had left him with the heat of passion still on her skin. "No one has to sacrifice anything. Please. I don't understand, and I know I never do. I'm simple and silly, and you must think I'm so—" She bit her tongue and winced. "But please, don't do anything. I'm not worth it."

His large, brown eyes gazed at her, glimmering in the darkness. The soft skin around them wrinkled as if he were in physical pain, and he reached for her cheek, tracing the line of it without actually touching her.

"You are worth everything to me," he whispered, his voice trembling.

Her pulse quickened with pain and fear and searing love for the man that stood before her so openly. And in that ephemeral agony, she realized how right he had been. How much time she had wasted being upset by death. By his acceptance of it. By his desire for her to just be. She longed to linger in that moment, staring at his eyes that had never been more beautiful.

She reached for him, standing on her tiptoes as waves hissed in the twinkling magic fire that encircled the platform. "I know I have to apologize far too often, but I'm sorry."

She dropped her gaze to her feet and took a heavy breath. Then she forced a smile and looked up, wanting him to remember her happy, beautiful, shining with the only thing of value she had to offer besides the beat of her heart.

"I always clean up my messes. Remember that, okay? And that the gods envy me because I am doomed."

Serap stretched to kiss his lips, suddenly shy at the smell of cinnamon and butter and the look of genuine softness in his eyes. She gave him a soft peck on his nose, her heart hurting so much it shuddered, and stepped back from the edge.

Her hand still lingering on his face, she tugged gently at his beard, then looked askance. "I love you, Javier. More than life itself, and far more than the eternities."

She pulled her hand away, wanting to keep the smooth heat of him on her fingers until the very moment she died. Then she turned away, ran across the platform, and jumped into the long-toothed and blue-scaled haze.

One soul must enter therein.

She was determined to meet the Bahamut, at last.

CHAPTER FORTY

JAVIER

Stop her! cried Zayne to Javier, shivering with desperation as Serap disappeared into the shadows.

Every muscle in Javier's body wanted to follow her, to stop her, to...

His heart cracked open remembering her final words, and he knew that no matter how logic screamed that it was insanity, he had to trust her. To give her a chance to clean up her own mess.

And with Serap out of reach from the witch, Javier saw his opportunity. The witch's pink and yellow eyes flashed as they followed Serap, and she lifted a hand, magic sparking from her fingers. Javier leapt from the back of the shark, the weight of his body crashing upon her. They tumbled together into the black water.

Green djinn fire blasted into his chest, bubbles hissing as fire met water. His armor deflected the blow like sunlight on a mirror, slamming the energy back into her and knocking her back. Javier kicked for the surface, searching for a breath of air, but the witch cast a tendril of magic from her hand that caught onto his ankle like a whip and yanked him down. He tightened a fist and stabbed for her neck with his katar. It bounced off a magic shield around her body, sparking with lightning.

Her tendrils wrapped around him, squeezing him like spider's webbing. Cutting into his flesh and crushing all the remaining air from his lungs. He turned his eyes to her, a confident, condescending smile on her lips. A bubble clung to the bottom half of her face, allowing her to breathe underwater.

She laughed.

A great wave crashed into them, sending them both reeling through the dark water like hurricane winds. An eye the size of the First Moon flashed in the distance. The Bahamut had closed her unfathomable jaws, sealing Serap inside and leaving them on the out.

Pasha released a tremendous scream. She kicked for the surface, a blast of magic at her back like the tail of a comet. For the first time, a hint of desperation flashed in her cold, calculating eyes.

He twisted his body, his back cracking painfully as she dragged him behind like a buoy. He turned his katar in and cut at the black tendrils she had wrapped around his body. They loosened just enough that his hand touched his boot. He yanked out the pistol and aimed at Pasha's back. Then found the trigger and pulled.

Djinn fire flared in the enchanted weapon, and a bullet whizzed through the water. It struck the witch between the shoulder blades. She screamed, and the magic buzzing around her faltered. The tendrils clinging to his body released. His lungs were tight, his skin stinging. The breathing bubble Sidi Moussa had given him trembled and popped.

The witch's body drifted down, but he couldn't go after it, every organ begging for air. His vision blurred, senses failing. A warm calm tried to settle over his brain, like a body succumbing to hypothermia.

He kicked for the surface, breaking through with a strangled breath moments before it was too late. He bobbed back underwater, pressed down hard by a towering wave. He threw up his arms and clawed to the top again for another yawning breath that filled his lungs to their very depths. His eyes scanned the horizon. The shifting scales were gone, the stars of Qaf shining in their place. The Bahamut had moved on, Serap trapped inside its gullet. There would be no getting to her before she reached the Eternal One.

A flicker of light by his eye, pulsing and twisting amongst the thronging water.

Serap! Zayne cried whipping about just above the water. *Where is she? What happened? Why did you let her go?*

Javier opened his mouth to answer when a sensation like a thousand needles seized his body, and he was dragged back below the water, his lungs caught on an exhale.

The witch's fingers dug into his leg, red blood blooming all around her. She held her free hand in front of her, claws turned inward as a great ball of flickering electricity brewed in her palm—lime green and shifting like the surface of a sickly sun. Her teeth clenched in pain, eyes flashing black despite her natural pink. He reached into his jacket and drew out his knife, blue fire erupting around the blade.

The witch snarled and cast the ball toward him. Javier ducked hard to one side and swung for it with his dagger, slicing it in half and sending slivers of it back in her direction. They cut across her face and torso, but he hadn't deflected the entire blow. Stinging magic wrapped into his arm, deadening it. Numb fingers lost their grip on the dagger, and it plummeted through the water, its blue light quickly eclipsed by the nothingness.

Pasha snarled and readied another glimmering ball. Javier's lungs were screaming, his body hunched with desperation for air. She cast, and this time the miniature sun slammed into his stomach and legs, driving him back and further down. It numbed his body. Legs useless, torso devoid of muscle. His one good arm clawed for the surface, but it was no use. He drifted down, down, into the emptiness of the ocean.

His vision blurred, the strange calm returning. The embrace of death, once again. He had been close to it so many times, it almost felt like a reunion with an old friend. But he was not ready to let it take him, not now. Not like this. Not knowing that this monster would be waiting for Serap when she emerged.

He reached into his jacket and drew out another knife, but a green hand seized his wrist and twisted with unnatural strength. The witch's face came into focus before him, fear in her eyes as well as anger, and he realized that she had no desire for him to die yet anyway. He was supposed to go into the Bahamut with her, to sacrifice himself so she could be young and beautiful forever. Only the sacrifice of the Immortal Killer could grant flawless immortality. Yet another of God's precious ironies.

Magic twirled below them, pushing them to the surface. They rocketed up from the water and landed on the obsidian platform. Javier rolled onto himself, unable to rise, unable to do anything but breathe and wait for his eyes to clear.

Fire sparked at the fiery edges, the substance under him solid and unsure. A creation of pure magic. He pressed the side of his face against it and coughed out a lungful of water.

"You shot me," Pasha gasped in huffing breaths. She forced a throaty laugh. "Unbelievable."

He rolled onto his back and gazed at the sky, at the twists of stars moving in the heavens. It was not like the rest of Qaf—beautiful pulsing galaxies and nebulas. Here at the edge of the world, he could see the great immortals moving in the space above. Creations of pure light, the closest to the Creator. Angels the size of galaxies, watching over djinni and men from afar. Distant sisters of the Bahamut.

Javier...? a tiny voice trembled in his ear.

He turned his head slightly and realized Zayne had been hiding under the collar of his armor, his amorphous body shaking like a leaf caught in a tornado.

Are you okay?

You must help me, Javier thought back.

I can't, the trembling voice replied. *I'm just a wisp.*

Pasha took a knee and leaned over herself, the damage from the bullet taking its toll on her magic. She turned her gaze up and scrutinized the sky.

"Because of you," she rasped, "the fish and Serap are gone. But I found the Bahamut before, I can do it again."

"There's no point," he choked out. "Serap is already inside receiving the Eternal gift. You cannot threaten me with her anymore. I will die before I help you."

Her head snapped to face him. She crawled closer to where he lay and lifted her hand. Sharp studs sprung from the flesh on her palm—bone spurs that looked like tiny daggers. Then she slapped him with the force of a tree branch. He lost his breath, his stomach, and momentarily his will to live.

"I don't need you to agree, Hades," she spat. "All I need is your body. It is the only part of you that has ever had any value, anyway." Her eyes focused on Zayne, and a cruel smile filled her face. "And you, Oh Prince of Elm. It's time you paid the price to the stars."

No! Zayne dove deeper into Javier's shirt. *You can't let her sacrifice me. Please. You have to help me.*

"Help yourself," Javier spat. With his one good arm, he snatched up Zayne and shoved him into Pasha's ear. The wisp screamed, trying to fight back, but Javier balled a fist and punched him inside.

Pasha stumbled back, clawing at the side of her head like a dog with water in her ear. She screamed and scratched at her own face, then fell on her side. Flesh came up under her nails, leaving long streaks of blood oozing on her face. Javier reached into his jacket for another dagger, but they had all been jostled loose by the fight. His numb body did not have the power to land a blow, anyway. He pushed himself up on his good arm and watched the witch convulse. Then it stopped.

She lay frozen, her claws digging into the side of her head, her legs kicked up, and her face a mask of pain and terror. But she was completely frozen.

"About time you stood up for yourself, you little coward," Javier laughed, dry and miserable.

He used one hand to pull himself closer to the frozen body. His eyes poured over her—the green skin, the red blood, the baubles and chains and sacks hanging from her clothes.

He fell in a limp heap at her side and used his one hand to yank free a pouch, then tore it open with his teeth and poured it out on the sparkling stone raft. He fumbled through blinking eyes and bottles of *god-only-knew*-what, searching for something useful. He had emptied every one of her pouches before he found a vial of familiar, flickering blue liquid. He yanked out the cork with his teeth and drank down the powerful healing potion.

He let his head fall back as the beginnings of it flowed through his veins, changing what had been numb flesh into painful tingles. It would take a little time before it restored him, though he had never been paralyzed by a witch before, so he couldn't be completely certain. An hour, maybe two?

"Stay in there, Zayne," he said through heavy breaths. "I know it's nasty, but you have to stay. At least until I have enough strength to finish her off."

There was no answer. He didn't even know if the wisp could hear him. Experience told him... maybe.

He released a deep sigh. He didn't understand everything that had just happened or who exactly this green monster was, but it didn't really matter. She had hurt Serap; that was all he needed to know.

A memory of her kiss filled him to the brim, and he swallowed hard. What would be happening to her now? What was she doing to herself? He wanted to believe in the words she had spoken before she raced off into oblivion, but as he played them over in his head, doubt began to creep in. When faced with the Eternal One, would her resolve falter? Would she accept the curse in disguise?

He shook his head, banishing such thoughts, and focused on her gentle immaculate kiss and on her final gift of words.

She loved him.

She had told him that she loved him. More than life itself.

As that memory echoed through him, he realized that even with his body broken and numb, trapped on a bizarre raft with a murderous witch in the middle of oblivion, he had never felt more alive.

CHAPTER
FORTY-ONE
SERAP

She is impossible to describe, as large as the world itself. A shadow and a shimmer, little more.

Javier's words filled Serap up as she wandered a mistless gray. She was grateful he hadn't followed. That he was the one person who treated her like she was capable. Who trusted her, though she may not deserve it. And who let her make her own choices, despite the concerned judgment that might linger underneath.

No acid stung her flesh. No faceless Eternal One moved in the Bahamut's breath. She was simply in a state of being and had no idea what to do with herself.

Javier had been close to death when he encountered the being. Was that her problem? Was she destined to waste away in nothingness until the gnaw of her own body upon her organs finally brought the angel? She shivered and moved forward through the gray. Every footstep pressed against what felt like water, though not once did she sink.

A miracle.

An illusion.

She kept walking.

But the thought of a painful, horrific, starving death made her bones twitch. What if she grew so weak, she was tempted by the Eternal One's kiss? The thought of immortality even now wet her throat with greedy hope. She worked to quench it with logic, with love. If she was in agony, gasping for her last breath, would she care that she'd look like Khayin?

She bit her lip hard. The answer was a solid *no*.

A sharp sensation stung her eyes and needled in through her tear ducts. It swept through her mind and down her spine, filling up her belly. Not with the acid of a stomach, but with memories. The Bahamut would not consume her body, but her spirit, her mind, and her heart. Her logic and her nonsense, which, together, were the most dangerous of all.

She could not deny it. She was tempted.

A shadow of Bakr Amca appeared, a bloom of light in the darkness. Her breath caught, and she took a step back. Then, gathering her strength, she reached for him, fingers gliding through his image as he smiled wide. He hefted his sword over his shoulder in one swing and tilted his head towards her.

Anybody who has ever looked into the future and not seen themselves in it can understand.

She pulled her fingers back and looked at them, expecting to see vibrant colors like paint on the tips. She saw only gray.

"You've come to ask me about your Kiss, haven't you?" Serap asked, eyes scanning the mysterious world she found herself in. The world on the precipice between life and something more. "To tempt me to do what Javier has warned me against. What we wasted time fighting about."

Zan Hala's image unfurled next to Bakr's, her turquoise skin as bright in translucence as the real thing. Her eyes were filled with the same pity and delicate sharpness as they had been on the floating island when Serap divulged her heart on a feather bed.

Sometimes it's just nice to have the argument over again with someone on your side.

"You think that living forever is a gift?" Serap asked the image, asked the Bahamut. "That Javier is wrong?"

Men are the worst. They think they're poetic and deep, and really they're just tying their own nooses.

Serap shook the déjà vu from her head and rubbed her eyes. "You're just pulling memories. Trying to trick me with arguments I've already had so I accept your proposal."

This time the body that appeared sent her eyes tumbling to her feet.

It's not just some proposal.

Ayelet's faded gray eyes looked at hers, almost one with the surrounding mist, her bemused smile perfectly recreated. She ran a flickering finger over Serap's cheek, and Serap felt nothing.

"Be gone and take your spirits with you," Serap trembled.

But we are worried. Ayelet's image continued, a look of immense sorrow filtering through her light-filled eyes. *We've been so worried. Jahmil, Bakr, and Sezan. Even Balian and Yousef.*

"Stop," Serap shouted, clapping her hands over her ears. "Go now and leave me be."

The next illusionary being to appear carried the cold eyes of Khayin. Of Evil. His wavering reflection came with a hissing snicker.

What is now? What is then? If you can't live forever?

She gritted her teeth, slamming her fists into her thighs. "Time doesn't matter. It can't. Or what's the point of life? And eternity? Of dying, or not?"

She had not meant for the gray of the Bahamut or the magic of the Eternal One to reply, but the voice of Khayin answered.

So that spring will never face winter.

Serap raised her clenched fists and flung them through Evil's image. "And what is spring if it's as bright as summer or as cool as fall? What about when its soul withers to the frost of winter and still it remains? It will not be spring at all."

She sank to her knees.

Explain yourself, said the staccato voice of Jahmil, her childhood savior, loving 'abi, and the one person whose judgment could shatter her very bones. She snapped her eyes up to his and felt a stab of pain.

What could she say to him? To his sharp gaze that saw everything even when he wasn't really there?

"I'm trying," she said, looking back down at the white of her knuckles as she pressed them into gray. "I'm trying to be good and accept my fate. To let go of the idea of being with you forever. I'm trying to accept that I'll die, and you'll forget me." She raised her pained eyes to the shimmering image of her father. "So why won't you let me? Why won't you help me when I need you most?" She took in a shuddering breath. "I am faced with an impossible question."

What is your answer?

His coldness cut her even though she knew it wasn't him at all, but a light puppet of his image. Jahmil would not treat her so. His remarks, his concern for her came from love. From her impacting their lives in a way he wouldn't forget, and he hers. Same with Ayelet, and Hala, and Amca. Even Evil, in a way. And that thought—the idea that whoever this mischievous angel was had used her love and theirs as a weapon to trick her—gave her the courage to stand.

"Get out of my head."

Oh, sweet, little Serap.

Pasha's fake hiss shot arrows through the mirage of her bravery. She turned and stumbled back, falling through the image of Jahmil as the witch and her cruel pink eyes stared through her.

You're weak. Pathetic.

Then a new voice, clear and bright like the ring of a fork on crystal, swept toward her from a ray of white light. "What will you be when you die but nothing?"

"A memory." Serap's shoulders shook with her pathetic answer.

"And when that fades? Because it surely will. Beings, immortal or not, cannot hold such inconsequential things in their minds for too long, lest they push out what's important."

Serap flinched.

"But if you live forever, you will never be forgotten because you'll never have to be. You will matter. And *you* will decide who is worth forgetting."

"I don't want to forget anyone." Serap's voice quivered.

"Not even the Immortal Killer?" The tinkling voice cut through her.

Serap looked away from the brightness and whispered, "No. Never."

"And how can you promise never if you don't know what death brings?" the Bahamut's ringing voice questioned.

"I... I..." Serap rested her face in both hands—temptation a fire that fed on all her doubts.

She didn't know what death was. She couldn't until it happened, and that fear had driven her to seek eternal life as much as it had the desire to mean something permanent to her loved ones.

"I hate you," Serap looked up at the gray with stinging eyes. "I hate this."

Do you not like things that are logical?

She gasped and flicked her eyes up to see Javier—a shimmering, light version—smiling at her with his kind eyes.

"You're not real." She backed away, heart thudding with each step.

He looked real, though. His built frame and massive muscles stretched his shirt so she could see every divot and line underneath. She could almost feel them on her fingertips, smell butter and lavender in the air.

Is something the matter?

Serap pressed her palms against her eyes, then looked at her hunter, once again coming for his prey. But he was not really there. None of them were, no matter how they smiled and sounded like home.

"You would tempt me toward the very thing you called foolish?" she choked out.

Who am I to judge anything you say, or do, or feel?

"Stop it," she cried, closing her eyes. "Stop sounding like him. He wouldn't want this for me."

There are certain souls I help on their way.

"Not like this. He helps people find peace with themselves, not fight nature. You're just evil. A temptation set to bring more victim's under your curse."

That is a terrifying proposition.

His voice filled her mind and sent her heart tumbling. She knew it wasn't real. It wasn't real. Merciful Allah, let it not be real. For how much longer could she resist the temptation to seize what she had so desperately wanted? How, when her resistance was anchored solely in the wisdom of the man she loved? Especially now, when he stood before her, telling her it was okay to give in?

"Let me leave. Let me die," she cried.

Should you fade from me like a mirage in the sands, I will cease to search for any oasis. Premature, unnecessary death is not beautiful.

She wrapped her hands around the back of her neck, squeezing tight as she tried to separate the fake from the real. She thought of his soft smile. His insistence on truth and how he would never deceive her again. His hand upon her cheek, his kiss upon her lips. *That* was her Javier. Not this voice who warped his truths into a path toward misery.

"Unnecessary death is not beautiful, but neither is unnaturally long life," she said, at last, taking a gasping breath as she clawed her way out of the depths of the illusion. "And I will not take it, the curse you call a blessing. I do not want it. I just want to be. To love. I want to be with those I care for and appreciate every second I have with them. I will find life by living it, not by fearing it."

A great rattling shook the air and her bones, groaning and deep so that it filled her up and left her empty. She clutched at her ears, tears filling her eyes.

The fake and smiling faces of her tempters faded from around her, Javier's last, and she reached a hand toward it wistfully. Her chance at immortality was gone. She had survived the curse. And by doing so, she would die and lose them all.

The crystal voice spoke, softer and sharper than it had before, like it was both pleased and irate. "You are certain?"

Serap nodded weakly. "I am."

"Then leave this place. And for your acceptance of all that is, may you see the truth in all things and bring them into being."

"Thank you," Serap said, but already the gray was fading into the bumpy tongue, sharp teeth, and choppy seas of the Bahamut. The groaning buzz of its mouth opened to let her free.

She walked out on unseen buoys, lost in how much time she traveled and not caring. A shining raft specked the distance, and she headed there. As she approached, she could see two bodies laying upon it. She broke into a run, everywhere her steps landed upon the waves shining like opalescent glass, so her feet did not get wet and she did not sink.

She opened her mouth to call to them, but her voice fell away as she more fully realized the truth in what she saw. Pasha lay unconscious, a glimmer of Chupkin coiled inside and around her heart. Serap blinked, unsure just what the Eternal One had done to her. She slowed her pace and drew up by the side of the raft.

Javier lay, too, an arm across his eyes and his breathing heavy under his drenched shirt. He looked exactly as himself, if not more beautiful with the water glistening off his skin. She smiled, then turned her gaze at Pasha and gagged. The witch looked transformed. Like herself but in the physical form of a monster, with folds of skin growing around her chin and her hair falling off in the oceanic breeze. Boils grew across her face in popping pustules. Her back hunched as she lay upon it, skewing her legs in an awkward angle, her skin cracking in the day's emerging light.

Chupkin must have sensed her from inside the beastly witch because he jolted from Pasha's body in a lightning bolt and wrapped himself around her. She felt a tugging from her heart, like the touch of the Bahamut leaking out to do just what it had promised. Bringing the truth into being. His tingly, wispy hug grew firmer, stronger, as white cloud transformed into lean arms, tight curls, light green skin, and dazzling blue eyes.

"Chupkin?" she breathed, pulling away to look at him, worried she'd gone insane.

"Hey, *fatati*." He grinned with the same sparkle in his eyes that had lived in his body for the five years she had known him.

A smile stretched across her face, and she flung her arms around him, squeezing him tight. She knew nothing about the young man in front of her, except what she had learned from his as a wisp. And that was all she needed.

"Serap?" said a voice so gruff, it rippled on the waves and echoed in her heart.

She froze.

Chupkin... er, Zayne, patted her back. "Go on."

She pulled away and offered her dearest friend an apologetic smile, then turned.

"Javier," she breathed, then threw herself toward him.

CHAPTER FORTY-TWO

JAVIER

Still numb from the witch's magic, Javier clung to Serap with his one good arm, her body draped over him on the sparkling, magic ground. The rest of him tingled painfully, and he had just the beginnings of movement, able to lift a leg at the hip, but unable to twirl an ankle. Her wet hair fell in his face, and he drew her further up his body, then gripped her cheek with one hand and looked into her eyes.

Tears rolled down her pink skin, a shiver in her lips, and bright eyes that gazed softly down at him. They looked the same as ever, yet entirely different, as if a new shimmer lived inside. White and secretive, moonlight hiding behind the cloud of her irises. The mark of the Eternal One. What had happened to her in there?

Javier opened his mouth to ask when a raspy moan sounded beside him. He and Serap both snapped their gaze to the side. The twisted, frozen body of Pasha began to twitch. His eyes flinched to the figure of the young man standing at the edge of the platform—pearlescent green skin, eyes of cerulean gems, a quaff of dark curls. It was the frightened, yet cocky curve of his oversized lips that told Javier exactly who he was.

In his excitement to see Serap, the little turd had given up his post. Javier lurched his body to grab a short length of iron chain from where he kept it affixed to the belt of his armor, then lazily draped it over Pasha's legs, hoping that it would be enough.

"What happened?" Serap asked, her eyes finding Pasha.

He sighed and let his head fall back on an exhausted neck. He tried to speak but coughed instead. "I don't like your friend very much."

Serap smiled and ran a hand down the side of his neck. "Me neither. But we must do something about her. If she wakes and gets her way..." The skin around her eyes creased. She looked down his body, padding a few pockets with gentle hands. "Sword?"

"Ocean." He gestured toward his dead hand with his chin. "There's a katar strapped to my wrist. Sorry, I'm a bit of a boned fish at the moment."

She pulled back his sleeve and worked to unfasten the blade, then stared at it in her little hands. "I suppose I should... That I need to..." Her face crumpled, and she looked to the witch and back. "If you can kill monsters, then I..." She bent her head.

"Here." He gestured for the dagger with his good hand. "I'll do it."

She shook her head and clutched the katar closer to her chest. "You are not a killer. Not in your heart. I wish to spare you from it whenever I can."

He breathed out sharply and cupped her cheek. "You've already given me everything I could have wanted. You came back."

The witch twitched once more, groaning. Serap's fingers whitened on the hilt of the blade. "I still have a mess to clean up." Then her eyes slid to his. "And I love you."

He smiled and pulled her closer, but Zayne's piped up as he stepped closer. "I'll do it." He touched Serap's shoulder. "She turned me into a wisp for ten years. Let me be the one."

Serap raised a brow. "And where was this courage a few days ago?"

He looked down, eyes shimmering with orange mist. "I guess I just found it."

She held out the *katar* for him but flinched when he took it. The skies churned overhead and the raft rocked beneath them. Javier tightened his hand around the small of her back as Zayne walked over to Pasha and knelt down beside her. He set the tip of the katar to her throat and took a deep breath, his fingers shaking.

An alarm penetrated his mind, unable to be ignored in its intensity without making a single sound. Serap and Zayne must have heard it too, for they turned their gazes with him to the heavens. Stars swirled to life behind the misty clouds, then grew

KYRO DEAN & LAYA V SMITH

in intensity, moving closer. The raft shimmered and rocked hard from side-to-side before the edges began to fall away like chunks of ice on a hot day.

"What is happening?"

Serap stood, her impeccable balance keeping her upright, and tilted her chin to the sky. "The stars have come to collect her debt."

"What?" Zayne's head snapped up, his eyes filling with black fear. He fell onto his backside and scrambled back. "They can't. Pasha is beaten. The stars can't take me. It's not fair."

With every ounce of strength, Javier rolled onto his stomach and pushed himself up with one arm, swinging the other under him like a broken table leg. He locked his elbow and pushed himself up, but his legs wouldn't cooperate. "We should get off of this thing."

Serap nodded and shifted herself under him to help carry the weight, sturdier, indeed, than he expected. "If we leave her like this and run, the stars will take her to pay off her debts. But she won't die, and after a decade or so of servitude..." She bit her lip. "I suppose that's a problem for our tomorrow selves. Where do we even go?"

"We can't just leave her," Zayne snapped. "She can't get away with this. She stole my body. She ruined my life and tried to take yours." Zayne's grip tightened around the katar, and he scrambled toward Pasha's twitching body to finish what he started.

Comets of light fell from the sky and crashed into the ocean, sending heaving waves toward them as Pasha's body began to glow in a haze of rainbow light.

"No," Zayne cried, stumbling forward, but the careening waves were too much.

The raft shook and slapped the water, knocking Serap into Javier, who wrapped his arms tightly around her. Zayne tripped on unsteady feet and tumbled into the water.

Javier scanned the tumultuous waves for him, relief breaking across his skin when curly hair broke free of the waves. But garish sparkles pulled his gaze back to the twitching body of the witch. The green of her skin had faded, replaced by shimmering blackness like the night sky. She screamed, but it was little more than an echo. Then a blast of light consumed the witch's body like liquid through a straw before fading into the gentle gleam of stars. She was gone. A slave to the stars before she would come back and exact revenge. Or not. But Serap was right, that was not his task for now. Loving her was.

"Help!" cried Zayne in a frantic burble that broke through the awe. "I can't swim!"

Serap left him and jumped into the choppy waves. She reached him, scooping him to her like she always had as a wisp, and tried to pull him back to the raft. But the waves thrashed higher, and she cried out as the ocean tried to swallow them whole.

Throwing all his weight to one side, Javier rolled to the edge of the platform. What remained of the platform cracked beneath him, and he plunged into the water.

His eyes scanned the darkness as he clawed for the surface with one hand, the other flapping uselessly at his side, his legs dead weight. He heard Serap and Zayne's frantic screams and gasps, but all he could see was a twirl of bubbles in the black water. He tried to move towards them, but his limp body only fell deeper and deeper, away from the faint, glinting light on the surface.

After everything that they had been through, it would end here in the infinite, bottomless waters where it had all begun, with him without the strength to rescue the only thing in the universe that mattered. Just as it had been with Alessandro. With his mother.

No. Never again.

His legs touched something solid and sharp, then suddenly he was rocketing back toward the surface. He shook his head, squinting in the water at the form beneath him, then lurched forward and snatched the sharp dorsal fin in his good hand.

The shark exploded through the surface of the water. Javier sucked in a deep gasping breath. "Serap!"

Her frantic response gurgled as her face slipped below the waves, a single hand the only sign of where she slipped away. He yanked the fish hard to one side and raced towards her, taking a deep breath before the animal dipped underwater. Zayne's green skin shimmered in the faint light, and he saw the glint of copper coins beside it. The shark lunged for them and as they passed, Javier thrust out his numb arm, sweeping Serap's waist nearer to him like a fish in a trawling net. Her fingers held tight to Zayne, flailing in a panic at her side. Her strong fingers dug into his shoulder, and he drove his heel into the shark's side. It turned back for the surface, sending a great plume into the air as its head slapped down atop the water. Serap gasped for air and spluttered, clinging to him, and burying her face in his neck.

Javier snatched Zayne by the back of his shirt and slapped his body down onto the shark behind him. He clung to its tubular body like a monkey on a branch. Javier pulled Serap into his lap, cradling her with one arm.

He pressed his forehead against the top of her head. "Are you okay?"

"I've had better days, I see that now." She nestled into his chest. "But I plan to savor every moment with you—even ones like this."

He smiled and pushed clingy, wet hair back from her cheek. "I'm so sorry. Perhaps someday, I will learn to keep my mouth shut, or perhaps to open it at the right time. Though somehow, I doubt it."

"It's okay, I have an amulet with a spell of silence I can use on you whenever I wish. And..." Her tender smile grew nervous. "I'm pretty sure I'm the one who will be apologizing. You have not seen the current state of your house."

His lip twitched. He bit down to try to stop it. "My house might be in need of a little renovation, anyway. You know, a woman's touch."

"Ah, yes. Gordito may have mentioned one such woman to me. One you were just starting to love. But she will have her work cut out for her."

"That's putting it mildly," he scoffed, then his chest pinched, and his eyebrows tightened. "I can't help wondering if you really understand what you may be getting yourself into. I am not an easy person to be around. I'm grumpy and antisocial, and I read too much. And I pontificate when I should be speaking sweet somethings. And my cat is a tremendous pain in the ass."

She grinned and coughed up a bit of water. "This is one of those times, my sweet, when you should be kissing me instead of talking. But never fear. I will give you another chance. Go ahead."

He pulled her closer and kissed her, thankful that Pasha's numbness had not spread to his lips. The ice inside his chest melted. She moaned, and she drew herself closer to his chest. After a moment, he pulled away and looked into her eyes again, searching his memory for some profound and beautiful words to give to her. Something from the bedouin, or the Greeks, or any number of enlightened men from enlightened cultures that expressed themselves as if their teeth were made of diamonds.

What came out was, "I don't think your parents are going to like me very much."

She laughed a whole-bellied and light giggle that filled the air. "Jahmil only loves his family. And you are mine, so he must love you, too. Ayelet is not so hard, just bring her a flower."

"I met Jahmil. He seemed nice... until he tried to kill me." Javier had to laugh at the absurdity of it all. Then he furrowed his brow as the words she had said washed over him. "You want us to be family? Does that mean you'll stay with me? You'll be my wife?"

"As readily as winter gives way to spring." She smiled. "But it does come with the burden of making you a Shihalan sheikh. And having to talk to people. And dealing with my Zan Hala... to whom I may have wept over you."

"Is that the turquoise woman with the snake tongue?"

Serap grimaced. "I see you met. I imagine the war of words that ensued was fiercer than locking blades with Bakr Amca."

"I found her utterly delightful," he said without sarcasm, his mind tumbling from one subject to the next. "A Sheikh of Shihala. There must be some irony in that. I will cling to it with all my might and find the strength to muddle through." He furrowed his brow. "In that case, I suppose I ought to care about all the anarchy going on there right now. Especially since I'm the one that caused it."

Serap leaned forward and peered behind him. "Let's hope Chupkin can find his place in all that as well."

"Chupkin? What could he possibly do? He can't even swim."

"I'm right here, you know," he snapped.

Serap squirmed from Javier's arms and wobbled her way over so she sat between the two of them, careful to avoid the spiny fins of the undulating sharks. "He's my family just as much as you are, Javier. And he's a prince. *The* prince. The heir of the King of Elm. I should imagine him very valuable in cleaning up the mess in Qaf."

Javier turned as well as he could on the shark's back and wrapped his arm around Serap's waist again, unable to tolerate even her momentary absence. "The prince of Elm? Really? Why didn't you say anything?"

"Ah, crap," Zayne sighed.

Javier blanched. "I killed your father."

"It's fine. No big deal."

"But does that mean that you are going to be the new King of Elm?"

"Ah, double crap."

Serap giggled and reached out a finger, hesitated, then poked him just below the ribs. "Don't worry. Javier can help scare all the mean people away, and you can hide behind my shirt, just like always."

"Girl, I know you're joking, but if I have to do this, you and the terrifying mountain man are coming with me."

She squealed and threw her arms around him, pulling herself a little from Javier's hold. "I'm still calling you Chupkin, though, I've decided. I won't be persuaded otherwise." Then she shot a glance at Javier.

He laughed and put his hand up defensively. "Hey, he's your wisp. Call him whatever you want."

"Be nice, you grump." Zayne slapped his shoulder. "Maybe I will be King Chupkin, and those upright bureaucrats in Elm can just deal with it."

"Or maybe just Chup-King." Serap's smile widened, lighting her whole face. "I love you two."

"Stop it, you're going to make me cry." The new King of Elm reached for her and hugged her tightly. "Thanks for being my friend." He pulled away and looked into her eyes, his own sparkling with blue and gold flecks. "And just so you know, your man here is a ridiculous human being. He tries to seduce roasted chickens."

She looked sideways at Javier. "Do tell."

He covered his eyes with his hand. "Don't tell."

"I'll tell you later. It is the stupidest thing I have ever seen. Adorable."

Javier sighed and grumbled, "I'm starving."

"Me, too," Serap said, clutching her stomach that growled right on cue. "I think I'll eat this shark if we are not home soon. Could Bakr Amca make it here?"

"You can't call Bakr with me looking like this!" cried Zayne.

"You're a djinn, aren't you?" said Javier.

"So?"

"So... you can just blink us back to my house."

"Oh yeah." Zayne smiled slowly. "I forgot I could do that."

"Okay, okay." Serap held out her hands with a chuckle. "We'll go eat and calm our nerves. But then I must also return home and make amends. And you must, too, little prince."

Zayne's shoulders slumped, and he looked off to one side but nodded.

Javier wrapped his arm around Serap and pulled her back into his lap. "Do I get to come, or do you want to do this alone?"

"How can I cherish every moment with you if you're not with me? You are the reward I get for coming to terms with my mortality. I shall keep you with me always."

"Then I shall cling to you far too tightly," he said, pressing his forehead against hers and breathing in her sweetness. "It's a good thing you are so much stronger than you look."

CHAPTER FORTY-THREE

SERAP

With the chaos that ensued after the King of Eastern Elm's death, Pasha wreaking havoc, Khayin's mess, and the Bahamut, Serap hadn't yet had time to formally introduce her fiancé to anyone. Chupkin's coronation, set the day after they had returned him to Elm, seemed as good a time as any, so she had begged and pleaded with her wide eyes and many kisses to get Javier to show up.

Serap couldn't help but grin at Javier, her giant, gruff, immortal-killing ball of gooey softness who couldn't stop running a nervous hand over his beard. She had even coaxed him into wearing formal clothes she and Zayne had commissioned for him, crisp pants and an embroidered kaftan that barely fit his bullish chest. Though he had refused to don the bejeweled jacket. There was a limit to his generosity that no amount of sugar could persuade him to surpass, and she wouldn't push. She was too happy savoring every moment.

"It's official." She swept towards Chupkin as he entered the room.

He wore a large ivory crown on his head that imitated the sweeping ram's horns of his father. A large, carved jade ring sat on one finger—the original and official Seal of Elm, the power of which had returned to Qaf in full force the moment he took the throne. The black and dark purple robes he wore drowned him, and there was a twitch on his lips that had grown more noticeable as the ceremony had drawn on.

She set her hand on her dear friend's shoulder. "How do you feel?"

He tapped the tips of his fingers together nervously. "I mean, it's amazing, of course. Elm is amazing. And it's amazing to be king and have everybody do pretty much everything that I say. Really just... amazing." He bit his bottom lip and leaned in closer. "But I kind of miss being a wisp, sometimes."

"I miss it, too. Sometimes." She gave him a hug and pulled back. "I miss having you with me always."

His eyes softened, and his anxious frown twisted into a gentle smile. "Me too."

The large doors to the room creaked open, and royal guests from all over Qaf streamed eagerly into the room, looking for Chupkin. His lips tilted in an uncertain sneer.

Javier clapped him on the back so hard that he stumbled forward. "Go on. Your public awaits."

Serap watched Chupkin wade through the mass of eager, bowing nobles and caught sight of Jahmil and Ayelet, one bright and laughing and the other sweeping the room with observant, diamond eyes. Jahmil leaned over Ayelet's shoulder and whispered something in her ear which made her laugh so hard she choked on her drink. He smirked and looked back up, continuing to scan the crowd.

Serap's stomach squished. She hadn't had a chance to sit down with either of them and explain herself after everything happened. Hadn't had a chance to apologize.

She slipped her hand into Javier's for support and churned out what she could of a smile. "Ready?"

"He's going to try to have me arrested," Javier whispered. "I know he will."

"I thought you liked living alone. A prison cell would be a vacation." She cracked a wry smile at him, then bit her lip when his serious eyes remained so.

"I'm glad you find this so amusing. I'm sweating like a pig."

"And in your Ahmaran silks." Serap sucked a breath through her teeth. "Just keep your arms down and stop worrying so much. Jahmil is with Ayelet. As long as you don't threaten either of us, he'll play nice... Probably."

"Last time I saw him, I bashed his skull on a stone floor. Twice." Javier groaned and rolled his head on his neck, churning concrete. Still, he squeezed her hand.

Serap opened her mouth to call them over when turquoise skin and shimmering silks blocked the way, accompanied by a wide smile and charming green eyes.

"Well, look what the Orkeshi namur dragged in." Bakr gave Serap a bear hug. "Finally found your way home from the backwoods, huh?" He balled a fist and tapped it to Javier's shoulder. "No offense, thumbscrew."

Serap squeezed him back and pulled away to give Zan Hala a hug, too. "You guys made it. And just in time. I was about to officially introduce Javier to Ayelet and Jahmil, and he's worried he won't survive the encounter." She poked Javier in the stomach. "So, say your hellos now."

"Poor bastard." Bakr shook his head and clicked his tongue, then turned a furrowed brow to Serap. "Have you even talked to Jahmil, yet? Might not be a bad idea to give him a chance to bite your head off in private before sacrificing this poor bastard."

Serap's smile fell, and she brushed one foot over the other.

"Now, look what you've done," Zan Hala chided. "This is a celebration; you'd be telling anyone else to smoke some hash and join you for a dive off the balconies. Leave the poor girl be. I don't blame her for not wanting to talk to Jahmil. He's not the most understanding soul in this family. Or this room. Or Shihala. Or Qaf. Shall I go all the way to Allah's both worlds?"

"You've always had it in for Jahmil." Bakr put his arm around Serap and pulled her close. "I know how to get your old man to forgive any sin. Do you believe me? You should because I have been sinning against him for fifteen years."

"Not just him," Zan Hala muttered playfully.

He waved a hand at her to shoo her off. "Now listen to me, Poppyseed. Just walk over there. Don't say a word. And hug him like you haven't seen him in years. That is literally all you have to do. He will melt like butter on toast."

Serap chewed on her lip and turned her eyes up to Javier. "What do you think? Will you be alright if I leave you here with Zan Hala? You said you liked talking with her last time."

Zan Hala raised a brow and smirked.

Javier opened his mouth, but Bakr cut him off. "Are you nuts? I am going to get this great lump of a man some proper food, and I will bring him back to you when I see that the coast is clear." He smiled wide and wiggled his eyebrows. "Deal?"

"You should have a private moment with your parents," said Javier and lifted his lips into a soft, encouraging smile.

Serap groaned, but Zan Hala shooed her in the direction of Jahmil and Ayelet. "Don't tell Bakr, but he's right," she whispered over her shoulder. "Get it done so you can be happy about this, too. They really did miss you. And I'll keep an eye on my lovely husband so he doesn't get your philosopher ox into any trouble."

Serap nodded and offered a small smile in thanks, then weaved her way through the crowd to where she had seen her parents last. Before she laid eyes on them, willowy arms draped themselves around her from behind.

"Serap," Ayelet breathed into her back as she squeezed her front. "Thrice you've disappeared from before my eyes, and I was yanked back to the empty dungeon I lost you in when you were a child. I was so worried. I have missed you so."

Unabated love and complete acceptance washed over Serap—pure, unfiltered Ayelet.

Serap winced, undeserving of her sweet and ready forgiveness, and grateful Ayelet couldn't see.

She spun around. "I'm sorry. I don't even know what to say other than that, except that I really truly am. I missed you so much, too."

Ayelet nodded and brushed the back of her hand against Serap's cheek. "I will take you any way I can get you, no explanation needed. Just promise me you will warn us next time you plan to go have a life-threatening adventure with ghouls and ghosts. Do not talk to strangers or Evil. And Bakr mentioned something about the Bahamut?"

"I didn't plan for any of that." Serap grimaced helplessly. "But don't worry. I have no intention of adventuring alone again." Then she took a deep breath. "Where's Jahmil?"

Ayelet's brow creased over soft eyes. "You nearly killed him, do you know?"

"I know." Serap looked to her feet before coming back to rest in Ayelet's warm, gray eyes.

"He did not sleep a wink. Not when you left the first time, or after he saw you with your Zan Hala. You owe her a thank you, by the way, for the tongue-lashing she took from him on that. But when he met that Immortal Killer and watched you vanish from Ashkult..." Ayelet pressed a hand into Serap's shoulder, pain creasing the corner of her eyes. "He is devastated."

"Should I just leave him be, then...? Is it too broken to fix?"

"Of course not." Ayelet pulled her into a gentle hug. "You're his daughter in every way that matters. He loves you so much it hurts. And you know how fiercely protective he is of those he loves. He will forgive you. I promise."

Ayelet gave her an encouraging smile, then pointed behind her. Serap turned as slowly as the tide comes in with the first moon. Jahmil stood in the middle of the busy room, his crystal eyes locked on her despite the courtiers vying for his attention. Even from this distance, she could see the colors playing in his eyes. Orange and white, pink and black, and all shrouded in the delicate purple of sorrow that seemed to run down his cheeks and color his entire face. He turned from her and looked into his water glass, and that hurt worse than any fire on his fist.

She opened her mouth, then snapped it shut. Taking Bakr Amca's advice, she smiled soft and wide, rushed forward, and threw her arms around him, hugging him as tight as she could.

His body stiffened, but slowly, he laid a hand on her back and pulled her tighter. "Serap," he breathed.

Perhaps, it was the gift of seeing truth that the Bahamut had given her, but in that one word, she heard so much more than he ever could have said. Sleepless nights sitting up worrying, twisting his fingers, and pacing in the dim light. Days standing on his balcony and gazing at the moons, wondering what he had done wrong to push her away, why she refused to trust him. The fury he had felt when he learned that she had been captured, imprisoned, abused and yet still refused to come to him, to accept his help. His love. And more painful than anything, the question he had refused to even ask himself out loud. Did she not care about him anymore?

She pressed her hands into his back and breathed in the crisp scent that had comforted her time and time again. "I missed you." She rubbed her face into his kaftan. "I love you so much. I'm sorry I left. I know it hurt you, but that's not why I did it. I just needed to do something for myself. It hurt too much being here. I wanted to be helpful and felt so helpless. And the thought of losing you... I'm sorry."

He stroked her veil, then pulled back and looked at her face, tears shimmering at the edges of his eyes. "Do you know what I thought had happened to you? I thought that..." He clenched his teeth and looked away. "Please, tell me that you're alright."

"I'm okay." She smiled and lifted her brows, then pulled him in for another hug. "I promise. I'm so happy to be back here with all my family. You and Ayelet and... and Javier."

He furrowed his brow. "Javier?"

She tried to think of how to describe him, tempted to just point at his hulking frame through the crowd, but if what Javier had said about the prison encounter was true, that would be a terrible idea.

She tilted her head and looked up at Jahmil, trying to loosen her tense shoulders. "The only other man in my life I care about as much as you."

"Really?"

The softness in his voice was like a drink of cool water. It was easy to forget sometimes with his scowls and hard stares and ruling the kingdom with an iron fist that he was a hopeless romantic at heart.

"Yes. And I wish for you to meet him. He... he makes me feel the way Ayelet said she felt about you the moment she saw you in the marketplace. He seems hard on the outside, like you sometimes, too." She smiled gently, remembering times when both men had broken their tough faces for gentle jokes and tender touches. "But he is kind and wise, and I wish to be with him until my days on earth end and my new adventure begins."

He smiled and straightened the corner of her headscarf. "I never liked that little prick, Paco, anyway."

She let her shoulders relax just a little with a laugh, but her hands still wrung and pressed against each other. "So you want to meet him? He's here...."

"If he's going to be with you for the rest of your life, then he's going to be my son-in-law one way or the other, which means I ought to, don't you think?"

"Son-in-law?" Serap's mouth twisted into a smile. "That's a very good point. But it depends on if you're going to be nice and not scare him away with your lightning eyes and sonic booms."

One corner of his lips twitched. "If he scares so easily, he has no business in this family."

"Oh, hush," Ayelet chuckled, swooping in from behind Serap. "We all know you're all bark." She hung herself on Jahmil's arm and leaned up to kiss his cheek. She tangled her fingers with his and squeezed them tightly. "Come, show us your chosen one."

Serap led them to the corner of the room where Bakr had headed with Javier, hands a tumbling mess of nerves. As he came into sight, she cringed and refused to look back at Jahmil, worried about what she'd see.

Bakr stood facing Javier, his back to their approach and in full-on lecture mode. "You see, I'm old hat at this whole marriage thing now, so I'm going to tell you the secret to winning any argument with a woman. Are you ready?"

Sezan choked on a laugh and put a finger to her chin. "Oh, I am dying to hear this."

Bakr flashed her a smile, then turned back to Javier. "You just refuse to have it. That's it. Don't engage. Just shut your mouth, even if you know you're right. *Especially* if you know you're right. Think about it. Would you rather sit cold and alone in your little corner of rightness or be making love with a woman who is convinced you're an idiot but likes you, anyway?"

Sezan laughed and shook her head, then leaned in and kissed Bakr's temple. "He's smarter than he looks."

Bakr growled and snatched her body to his. Gazing into her eyes, he cupped her cheek so she visibly melted into his hands. He kissed her, and they were gone into their own little world again.

Serap stepped next to Javier and slid her arm around him, though her hand didn't even come close to reaching the other side. Then she turned her eyes to her parents.

"Ayelet... 'Abi, this is Javier Don DeMario. The love of my life, however short it may be."

Jahmil's eyes widened painfully, but otherwise, he made no move.

Javier's jaw twitched from side to side. "It's nice to see you again, *malakiun*." He dipped his head slightly to Ayelet. "And a pleasure to meet you, *malaka*."

Ayelet beamed. "I'm just normal people, like you. You may call me Ayelet. And it is a pleasure to meet you. We really did not get much of an introduction from Serap before coming over. Tell me, how high do you think you can throw her? Your muscles are huge, and with her acrobatic skills... ah!" Ayelet brushed a hand against his arm. "Serap is giving me her wide eyes. I shall ask you about it later."

"Twenty cubits." Bakr Amca looked up from Sezan, though he still held her tightly to his chest. "At least twenty, I bet you ten dinar."

"No making bets." Zan Hala kissed his cheek, then rubbed a bit of her cherry lipstick off with a thumb. "You know better. Though I'd take those odds."

Serap grinned, warmed by how quickly they were taking to Javier in their playful way. She slipped an eye toward Jahmil, praying he would see what she did, what everyone else did. That Javier was worth more to her than eternity.

Javier let go of her and took a step towards Jahmil. "I know our courtship has been a tad unorthodox," he said, gazing fixedly into the crystal kaleidoscopes of her father's eyes. "I love Serap. I will never cause her any harm, and I will do everything in my power to ensure that she is happy all of her days. I swear to you."

Jahmil stared at him unblinking for a long moment, his face fixed like a stone.

Serap held her breath, aching to intercede and knowing they had to come to terms on their own. It didn't help that everyone else had leaned in to listen, or that Ayelet's brows dipped just so with worry.

"See that you do." 'Abi Jahmil nodded. He turned from Javier and walked behind Ayelet to wrap her in his arms. He laid his chin on her shoulder and seemed to breathe a sigh of relief. She whispered something into his ear with a sweet smile, and he snuggled deeper into her neck.

A grin like the first sunrise of spring spread across Serap's face, and she turned to Javier. "See, no jail."

She jumped up. He caught her and chuckled. "Pure luck."

"General Bakr," an official-sounding voice said. Serap turned to see one of the stoic guards of Elm approaching their circle. "His Majesty, King Zayne, requests your urgent presence."

"Me?" Bakr's smile widened, and he pressed a hand into his chest. Tossing his head to one side, he pouted at his wife. "Do you have any idea how exhausting it is to be so popular?"

"How could I not when you love me so much you take me everywhere you go?" Zan Hala pinched his side, and he pecked her lips before they followed the soldier, arms wrapped around each other.

Javier pressed his forehead into Serap's shoulder to conceal a chuckle. "Your wisp is incorrigible."

She laughed and nestled deeper into his arms, then kissed each of his cheeks, and finally his nose. "Life is beautiful, don't you think?"

His kind brown eyes moved over her face, and he smiled. "It is now."

The End

Want a peek into how Serap and Javier are doing in the future? Join them as they help Bakr's oldest son, Izkander, fight a bat monster and win the love of a stoic queen in the land of Fyre, the birthplace of Drakonte. Check out Book Three in the Fires of Qaf series, Eve of Fyre, now!

Thank you for joining us on this escape! We LOVE having you in the Community Fire! We also love hearing from you! If you enjoyed reading the books, please hop online and leave a review on Amazon and Goodreads. A star review is better than no review, a paragraph review is better than that, and a review with a paragraph AND your picture with the book is the best! Five stars means you liked the book and you're excited to read the next one!

ANY review helps the authors keep bringing you new adventures in Qaf! We'd also love to see you more! We're releasing new and exclusive content in our newsletter ALL THE TIME! Join us at the Community Fire!

GLOSSARY OF TERMS

QAFIAN TERMS:

Places:

Ard – the world of humans, Earth

Ashkult – an internationally utilized, inescapable prison. Built in an area of Qaf where there is no magic.

Buhayrat Alzaybiq – the lake of quicksilver that surrounds Ashkult.

Eayima – floating island located on Ard. Legend claims it is where the Seal of Sulayman is housed.

Ghaluma – one of the Nine Kingdoms of Qaf, located on the Lower Continent. The location of Ashkult.

Izrak – one of the Nine Kingdoms of Qaf, ruled by Queen Mapenuk

Karzusan – Capital of Shihala.

Qaf – the world of the djinn.

Shihala – one of the Nine Kingdoms of Qaf, ruled by King Jahmil.

Vespar – one of the Nine Kingdoms of Qaf, now a vassal state ruled jointly by Ahmar and Shihala.

Zabriya – one of the Nine Kingdoms of Qaf, located on the Lower Continent. A mountainous
region.

Miscellany

Bahamut - giant, immortal, all-knowing fish that lives in the waters surrounding Qaf.

Bial'dabaye - were-hyena created from human children

Drakonte - giant snake with feathery wings. Used as a battle mount by the Shihalan military. Originally from Fyre.

Namur - giant cat used for riding

Tset aldhayle - six-tailed foxes, children of the stars. These swift and intelligent creatures are used to deliver mail in many parts of Qaf.

The Five Winds (Qafian Directions):

Bahamut, Janu'ub, Sharq, Gharb, Shamaal

ARABIC:

Alba, Abi - father (dad)

Alḥamdu lillāhi rabbil ᶜālamīna - Praise be to God, Lord of the universe

Alhamdulillah - Praise Allah

Alqatil Alkhalid - The Immortal Killer

Amira - princess

Ana muhtaj - I am in need

As-salam Alaikum - peace be with you

Ayah - verse, from the Quran

Ayuni - my eyes (term of endearment)

Aziziti - sweetie (term of endearment)

Bismallah - In the name of Allah

Fatat ghayr muhtarama - disrespectful girl

Fatati - my girl

Fi Amanillah - go with god (lit. I leave you in the custody of Allah)

Ghula - ghoul

Hal tafham? - Do you understand?

Hammam – bath, bathhouse

Huba hayati - love of my life

jazirat aljamila - beautiful island

Jida - grandmother

Khazina - treasury

La samah allah - God forbid

Malaka - my queen

Malakiun - my king

Qafiz - traditional Arab unit of measure

Sabah alkhayr - good morning

Saghirati - my little one (term of endearment)

Sayida -miss

Shaqiq - brother (respectful title between men)

Shukraan jazilaan lak - thank you very much

Taealaa li - come to me

Taeazi - condolences

Tahadath bialearabia - speak Arabic

Umma, Umi - mother (mom)

Wa 'alaikum-as-salam - and peace be with you (hello)

Wahash bahriun 'usturiun - kraken

Waliu aleahd - crown prince, heir apparent

Ya 'ilahi - oh my god

SPANISH:

Así es la vida - such is life

Buenos noches, señorita - good night, miss

Dulces sueños - sweet dreams

El árbol se la llevó - the tree took her

Fuera de aquí ahora! ¡Vayate! - get out of here now. Get!

La muerte es todo lo que es seguro en la vida - death is all that is certain in life

Lárgate - get away

Niña - girl (child)

Pequeña - small

Perdóneme - excuse me?

Pollo asado y verduras con crema de azafrán - roast chicken with vegetables and saffron cream

Por qué estás en mi casa? - why are you in my house?

Puaf - oof, yuck

Qué estás haciendo? - what are you doing?

Que linda - how beautiful

Sacerdotisa Aldonza la Indomable - High priestess Aldonza, the Indomitable

Ven aquí - come here

TURKISH:

Affedersiniz - excuse me

Aman tanrım - for crying out loud

Amca - uncle

Anne - mother

Ben - I am, my name is

Cadı - witch

Edirneli - somebody from Edirne

Hala - aunt (paternal)

İyi geceler - good night

Nazar - charm against the Evil Eye

Nu yere koy - put that down

Oha! - Hey! Wow!

Peshtemal - cotton towels

Sadiqa - my friend

Sen Türkçe biliyor musun? - do you speak Turkish?

Seni seviyorum - I love you

Efendim - sir, madam, my friend (also Arb.)

CURSE WORDS:

Al'ama - blindness (damn it)

Alqarf

Allaena

Sakhif

Sharmouta - whore/prostitute

Mierda (Esp)

Hijo de puta – son of a whore (Esp)

Alrataq – darn

Eahira – whore

OTHER:

Batoude, cerceau, casse-cou - acrobatic terms (French)

Modus Vivendi - way of living, animal nature (Latin)

GUIDE TO DJINN EYE COLORS

Humans read facial expressions; djinn read emotions in one another's eyes. In moments of high emotion, djinn's eyes flash with regular and predictable colors.

Black: Fear. Mist swirling in the eyes

Blue: Hope, Anticipation

Green: Jealousy, Envy

Purple: Sadness, Grief, Despair

Gold: Happiness, Jo

Pink: Anxiety, Nervousness

Red: Lust. Glows in pupils

Silver: Compassion, Commiseration

White: Shock, Surprise. Lines like lightning

Yellow: Disgust, Disdain, Loathing

Orange: Embarrassment, Humiliation

Copper: Confidence, Bravery, Pride

Brown: Malice

Gray: Awe, Amazement

Eyes are Clear: Honesty, Forthrightness

Eyes flash with bright light: Anger

Colors do not match what is being said: Deceit

THE EIGHT MOONS OF QAF

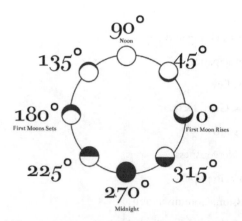

Time is measured in degrees based on the orbit of the First Moon. One degree is equal to roughly four minutes. And 15 degrees is equally to roughly one hour.

The First Moon:

A rough, rusty sphere of copper. The First Moon is the largest and brightest of the eight, taking up a full eighth of the sky when it is full. The path of the First Moon is the Qafian equivalent of 'daylight' and it is their main means of telling time. It comes up in the sharq and sets over the Bahamut Sea.

The Second Moon:

Quick-moving silver moon that passes through the sky about ten and a half times every 360 degrees. This moon follows the first moon, rising sharq and setting bahamut.

The Third Moon:

Pale pink, this moon crosses the sky perpendicular to the first moon, bouncing back and forth as it chases the swish of the Bahamut's tail. It rises janu'ub/gharb to shamaal. It is common lore that the Bahamut's former lover lives on this celestial body, pulling and yearning for its true love and creating the Qafian tides. The position of the third moon is preferred for telling time because it is always visible except for when it dips behind each horizon.

The Fourth Moon (The Lover's Moon):

A dim yellow, this moon is nearly impossible to see when the First Moon is out and is sometimes called the "night moon". It only shines brightly during Qaf's *night*. It is often referred to when saying people are up to no good because only criminals, ne'er do wells, and lovers stay up late enough to see the Fourth Moon.

This moon passes twice for every single pass of the First Moon, once during Qaf's day unseen, then once through Qaf's night when visible. This moon rises sharq/shamaal to bahamut/shamaal.

The Fifth Moon (The Witch's Moon):

The witch's moon of soft green that passes through the sky five times, following the Five Winds and crossing the sky 45 degrees (or 3 hours in Ard equivalence) at a time (with another 45 degrees to pass over to the other side beneath Qaf). It starts sharq and crosses to bahamut, then rises in janu'ub and sets shamaal, then rises gharb and sets sharq, then inverts and rises bahamut and sets janu'ub, then rises shamaal and sets gharb, then rises sharq and sets bahamut, like it started. This follows a 405 degree (or 27 hour)/27 day pentagon cycle and is difficult to track. It is the fortune teller's moon as they track its erratic behavior through the heavens and is often associated with Saqueia and the 5 Winds.

The Sixth Moon:

A soft-white moon that crosses the sky three times, 30 degrees after the rise of the First Moon, 60 degrees after midday, and at midnight. It travels from janu'ub to shamaal on each pass. It is the easiest moon to tell time by, has a medium heat, and most resembles Ard's moon.

The Seventh Moon (The Shadow Moon):

This moon appears in odd years as a black circle in the sky that blots out the stars but does not give off any of its own light or heat. It takes an entire year to pass over the sky, and then is gone for an entire year. The measurement of Qaf's year and the seasons are determined by the movements of this moon.

It rises sharq/shamaal and sets gharb, dividing the upper and lower continents. It separates them but also forces them to look toward each other whenever they look at it and reminds them they share Qaf. Wars take place more often in the year this moon is hidden. It is also believed by some that it gives off no heat or light because it is the servant of a celestial that is dead or away or because the celestial they serve is.

The Eighth Moon:

A rare bright blue moon that only rises once every thirteen years—The Festival of the Eighth Moon. It rises janu'ub and sets bahamut/shamaal, rising directly behind Fyre. Every 130 years the appearance of the eighth moon will coincide with every other moon being visible in the sky. This is the "Festival of the Eight Moons," Qaf's most important holiday as it only comes once in most djinn's lifetimes.

It is the warmest moon, and Fyrans believe it serves the Origin, gaining its power from beneath Qaf like lava and only appearing rarely as a reminder to Qaf that the Origin is equal in power to the Bahamut, Celestials, and other minor deities.

The Moonless Night:

Every fourteen cycles of the First Moon in a shadow year of the Seventh Moon comes The Moonless Night, when all of the Eight Moons of Qaf are hidden beyond the horizon. During this time, all heat is sucked from the land and the stars shine their brightest. It does not last the whole night.

ABOUT THE AUTHORS

Kyro Dean has written over 20 novels, including The Baron's Ghost, which can be found on Kindle Vella.

In addition to her works for Eight Moons Publishing, she owns and edits for the blog, Vanilla Grass Writing Resources.

She loves to speak and present and has shared her knowledge at many conferences. When not writing, she loves spending time with her delightfully curious children and talking with her plants, though they often give terrible advice.

Check out her website www.kyrodean.com. Or check her out on social media (Twitter and Insta): @kyro_dean

Laya V Smith's debut novel "The Lumbermill", published by Black Rose Writing, won the 2021 Maxy Award for Best Thriller and was a finalist for 2021 IAN Award for Best Debut Novel. She is the co-founder and co-editor of Eight Moons Publishing, a new boutique press specializing in upmarket romantic fantasy. When she isn't writing or reading, you can usually find her daydreaming, cooking, laughing at stand-up comedy, or playing with her children.

Made in United States
Troutdale, OR
02/04/2024

17395679R00226